THE BOOKSHOP SECRET

THE BOOKSHOP SECRET

BROOKWOOD MYSTERIES
BOOK 1

JORDAN JACE

EPub ISBN: 978-1-967657-45-2

Print ISBN: 978-1-967657-46-9

*To Alice—my partner in love, words, and wonder.
Thank you for believing in every story, and for sharing this
beautiful journey of writing together.*

CONTENTS

Foreword   ix
Prologue – The First Whisper   xiii

1. The Fog Rolls In   1
2. The Bookshop Key   15
3. Coffee and Old Wounds   33
4. The Locked Room   43
5. The Recipe Book   54
6. Tea Leaves and Ghost Whispers   64
7. Covered in Time   74
8. A Light in the Lighthouse   84
9. The Founding Map   93
10. The Jazz Festival Planning Meeting   104
11. The Healer's Symbol   113
12. Bakery Secrets   123
13. Candle of Memory   132
14. Coffee Beans and Founders' Tales   141
15. The Covered Bridge Encounter   150
16. The Necklace in the Wall   158
17. Ship's Log and the Sea Captain's Tale   165
18. The Music Box Melody   173
19. Rainstorm and Revelation   181
20. The Festival Begins   194
21. The Lighthouse Signal   203
22. Bookshop Confession   213
23. The Founder's Letter   222
24. The Apothecary Ledger   240
25. Memory Shared, Vision Revealed   249
26. Truth at the Covered Bridge   260
27. A Light Left Burning   271
28. Town Hall Confrontation   281

29. The Book of Brookwood 291
30. A New Chapter 301

Epilogue: The Circle Holds 313
The Bridge of Echoes 323
Afterword 345
About the Author 349

FOREWORD

When Marley Taylor returns to Brookwood, she expects a simple duty: settle her late aunt's estate, close the door on an old seaside bookshop, and retreat to the life she's carefully built elsewhere. What she doesn't expect is for the foggy coastal town of her childhood to greet her with suspicion— and secrets.

The bookshop itself seems to breathe. An odd draft curls through the shelves, and behind its walls Marley finds things that shouldn't exist: a brass key etched with strange initials, a sealed room no blueprint admits, and journals whispering of a healer named Aurelia whose legend the town has quietly erased. Each discovery pulls Marley deeper into Brookwood's forgotten past, where history has been deliberately buried—and where memory itself seems to have a voice.

The townspeople know more than they let on. The café owner hints her aunt was "into strange things." An elderly historian warns Marley not to "stir the roots." And as the town prepares for its annual jazz festival, whispers spread that she's digging too deeply, chasing shadows better left alone.

But Marley is not entirely alone. Damien Hawthorne—widowed historian, guarded father, and a man wrestling with grief of his own—appears first as an obstacle, then as a reluctant ally. Drawn together by overlapping losses and an undeniable pull, Marley and Damien find themselves caught between caution and desire. Their conversations crackle with tension, their silences ache with what might be, and slowly, trust begins to take root.

As Marley unravels the mystery of the bookshop, the Green Healer legend sharpens into startling clarity. Hidden recipe books, coded ledgers, and protective herbal blends reveal that Aurelia was never just a story told to children—she was part of a clandestine circle of women who safeguarded knowledge the town's founders wanted forgotten. Brookwood was built on more than industry and salt air. Its true foundation is a legacy of women who healed, remembered, and resisted.

And now that legacy is pressing on Marley.

Visions haunt her dreams. Whispers curl around her when she touches the artifacts her aunt left behind. The lighthouse flickers strange signals, the covered bridge carries echoes of children's voices, and the more Marley digs, the more Brookwood itself seems to respond. The past is not finished. The Circle of Seven demands to be remembered.

But memory has its cost. The deeper Marley goes, the more the town closes ranks. Old powers bristle. New dangers stir. And as the line between past and present begins to blur, Marley must decide: will she retreat into safety, or will she claim the inheritance her aunt left—a bookshop full of secrets, a legacy bound in whispers, and perhaps even the possibility of love?

In The Bookshop Secret, the first installment of the Brookwood Mysteries, readers will step into a world where fog curls through the streets, history hides in plain sight, and every object may carry a story. At once a slow-burn romance and a haunting mystery, this novel invites you to rediscover home, reclaim legacy, and believe that love—and truth—can survive even the silence of centuries. This book delivers equal measures of intrigue, romance, and community.

Brookwood is waiting. Its lighthouse has been flickering. Its covered bridge has been whispering. And its bookshop holds the key to secrets that will change everything.

Open the door. The story begins here.

PROLOGUE – THE FIRST WHISPER

The fog never truly left Brookwood. It clung to the coastline in layers, soft as wool in some places, heavy as stone in others, and always—always—it crept inland as if it had a mind of its own.

On the night everything began, before Marley Taylor had even thought of returning, Brookwood's lighthouse cut its beam through that fog in steady rotations, the old glass lens groaning faintly as it turned. The rhythm was meant to guide sailors into safe harbor, but to those who had lived here long enough, there were nights when the beam felt like a signal of another kind—warning, waiting, whispering.

Clara, Marley's aunt, had always believed that the light carried memory. She said the lighthouse remembered every shipwreck, every storm, every life lost or saved along Brookwood's jagged shoals. To her, the fog was more than weather. It was presence.

On that final night, Clara was alone in her bookshop, her hands brushing dust from the edge of the oak writing desk she had claimed as her own since the seventies. Outside, the streets were still, shutters drawn, the tide rising with a hush of insistence against the pilings. Inside, candles burned low, leaving pockets of shadow that seemed to breathe between the shelves.

She was writing—not letters to family, not the inventory of sales, but something stranger. She had the leather-bound recipe journal open in front of her, its pages layered with ink and pressed herbs, and beside it a sheaf of loose paper where she copied certain phrases in her tight, slanted hand. The words were old ones: *circle whole, memory in matter, the grove remembers.*

Her candle sputtered.

Clara glanced up, listening. The foghorn moaned from the water's edge, long and low, as if echoing her own unease. She returned to her notes, but her hand shook when she wrote the next line. She could feel the weight of the walls pressing inward.

There was a draft again—she knew that draft too well. It came from nowhere and everywhere at once, raising goose-flesh on her arms, curling the candle flame sideways though the windows were shut tight. The draft carried scent: rosemary, sage, the faint bite of wormwood. She whispered into the shadows, "I know. I hear you."

For a moment, there was silence. Then, softly, as if from the other side of the sealed wall, came the answering whisper. It was not words, not exactly, but it raised the hairs at her nape all the same. She pressed her palm flat on the journal, steadying herself. "I will keep it safe. Until she's ready."

Her eyes shifted to the shelf against the far wall—the one that had never fit the floor plan, the one no carpenter could explain. Behind it lay the small sealed room, and within it, the objects no one in Brookwood had spoken of for over a century. Clara had kept its key hidden in plain sight, brass and heavy, marked only with the initials L.S. She had told no one. Not even Marley.

Another draft shivered through the shop, colder this time, and the candle guttered to a final spark before it died. In the darkness, Clara closed her eyes. She could almost see the circle again—the seven women, their hands outstretched, placing stones in a spiral beneath the full moon. She could almost hear Aurelia's voice, steady and calm: *We are not gone. We wait.*

Clara whispered back, "She'll come. I promise."

The lighthouse beam swept once more across the fog, catching for a brief instant on the bookshop window. To anyone walking the cobbled street, it might have looked like nothing more than old glass reflecting light. But Clara saw it as a vow.

When the light turned away again, she set her pen down, folded the unfinished page, and tucked it inside the hollow spine of an atlas that no customer ever pulled from the shelf. The page bore no date, no signature—only a single phrase, underlined twice: *The circle must remain whole.*

Outside, the tide surged. Inside, the bookshop breathed. Clara rose, her joints stiff, her voice breaking as she whispered a final plea: "Let her find what I could not."

The whisper that came back was faint, but it carried through the dark like a thread of certainty: *She will.*

The bookshop did not sleep.

When Clara's final candle went out, the shadows did not disperse. They seemed instead to expand, stretching into the corners, seeping between the shelves, pressing into the seams of the floorboards. The air remained weighted, fragrant with the faint bite of sage and the ghost of rosemary long since dried. And though the desk was closed, though the journal lay still, the room itself seemed to remember her.

Nights in Brookwood had their rhythm—gulls fell silent, the tide rolled in with its hushed insistence, shutters clattered once or twice before resigning to the damp wind. But within the bookshop, the rhythm shifted. It became irregular, marked by drafts that had no source, by creaks of wood that did not belong to settling beams, by a sense that the air itself was breathing.

The shelves groaned lightly in the hours after Clara's hand left their surfaces. Books that had sat untouched for decades seemed suddenly restless. A thin atlas with its hollowed spine held its secret too tightly, the page folded within it almost trembling in anticipation. The recipe journal—so thick with pressed sprigs and scribbled margins—seemed to carry a pulse of its own, faint but insistent, as if it too waited for another hand.

The sealed wall behind the bookcase did not give itself away to sight. To any customer who might have come wandering in—though none would at this hour—it was just another piece of architecture in an old building long accustomed to drafts and quirks. But the wall was not silent.

It breathed.

Sometimes it sighed in the cold hours of the morning. Other times it whispered in tones that were not quite voices, carrying syllables too old to translate. And always, always, it exhaled herbs—wormwood, thyme, basil that had long since turned to powder in the locked room but somehow lingered as fresh as harvest. The smell clung to the shelves. It seeped into the papers. It would find its way into Marley's skin soon enough, though she had not yet returned.

The lighthouse across the harbor threw its beam, steady as ever, cutting through the fog. Each sweep caught on the shop windows, glimmering faintly against the imperfect glass. With each pass, something in the shadows stirred. The draft quickened. The floorboard in front of the desk creaked without weight pressing it. It was as if the light was keeping vigil with the shop, watching the relics within the sealed room.

Clara's final whisper still hung in the air: *She'll come. I promise.*

The building seemed to echo it in silence, its timbers accepting the vow, holding it like marrow.

Days passed, and the shop remained locked, the blinds drawn. But the presence did not fade. The desk still carried warmth though no hands touched it. The faint smell of rosemary sharpened in the hours before dawn. The journal's pages occasionally fluttered, though no window was open. And in the quiet hours of the night, the whispers pressed closer—voices murmuring names, fragments of oaths, syllables of the spiral.

The circle was waiting.

1

THE FOG ROLLS IN

The fog rolled into Brookwood like a tide that refused to recede—thick, lingering, and strangely purposeful, as though it had business with the town. Marley Taylor felt it before she saw it. The SUV's headlights cut no further than a dozen feet ahead as she turned onto the winding coastal road, the beams scattering against a wall of white that clung to the cliffs and swallowed the sea.

It had been years since she'd driven this way. Ten, to be exact. Ten years since she had left Brookwood in a hurry, swearing she'd never look back, convinced the town and its whispers had nothing left to give her. Yet here she was, key in hand, a small leather satchel riding shotgun beside her, summoned not by choice but by obligation—the sudden passing of her Aunt Clara.

Marley shifted in her seat, one hand tightening around the steering wheel. The hum of the engine filled the silence. She tried the radio, but the static felt too hollow, so she let the sound of tires on gravel and the muffled crash of unseen waves be her company.

When she reached the crest overlooking the town, she slowed. Brookwood lay beneath her, a patchwork of small streets and Victorian rooftops, its lamps flickering like watchful eyes through the haze. The lighthouse, steadfast on its rocky perch, sent out a muted pulse every thirty seconds, a rhythm Marley remembered as the heartbeat of her childhood.

Her throat tightened. Nostalgia always had teeth.

THE BOOKSHOP APPEARED on the corner of Willow and Main, just as crooked and stubborn as she remembered. Clara's Nest of Books, the hand-painted sign declared in faded teal letters. The door leaned slightly inward, the green paint peeling like bark on an old cedar. Marley parked, killed the engine, and sat staring at it for a long moment.

"This is it," she whispered to herself, the words both anchor and burden.

She gathered her satchel, stepped out into the damp air, and nearly stumbled on the uneven stone path leading up to the porch. Everything smelled of salt, moss, and rain-soaked timber. Wind chimes above the door tinkled, as if welcoming her home—or warning her away.

The key Clara had left her was brass, heavy, worn smooth from decades of use. Marley slid it into the lock, expecting resistance, and wasn't surprised when it caught halfway. She jiggled it, muttering a soft curse, before the mechanism gave with a sigh and the door creaked inward.

The scent struck her immediately. Old paper. Dust. And something sharper, almost herbal—rosemary, perhaps, or sage. It was as though Clara's presence lingered in the air itself, as if she'd only just stepped out and might return at any moment.

Marley stepped across the threshold, the wooden floor groaning beneath her boots. Shadows stretched long between the shelves, broken only by thin shafts of light filtering through the tall front windows. Rows of spines lined the walls, some leather-bound and brittle, others bright paperbacks whose colors had dulled with time. Stacks of unsorted boxes leaned precariously in the corners, labeled in Clara's hurried scrawl: "Botany," "Ship Logs," "Recipes," and one ominously marked "Not This One."

Her chest tightened again, but this time it wasn't nostalgia—it was weight. Responsibility. The shop wasn't just an inheritance. It was legacy.

MARLEY SET her satchel on the counter, brushing a hand over the worn oak surface. The wood bore grooves and nicks from years of use, and she could almost see her aunt's hands arranging books, sliding coins into the old register, offering that knowing smile to each customer who walked through the door.

She closed her eyes, letting the memory form, when a sudden draft brushed against her skin.

Her eyes snapped open.

The door was shut. The windows were latched. Yet the air stirred around her, cool and insistent, carrying with it the faint rustle of pages turning in the back of the shop.

Marley's pulse quickened. She forced herself to move toward the source, down the narrow aisle between the shelves. Each step creaked louder than the last.

The draft grew stronger near the far corner, where a crooked bookcase leaned against the wall. Several titles lay scattered across the floor as though someone had passed in haste. She crouched to gather them—volumes on botany, folklore, and one peculiar journal with no title at all—before noticing the faint line of dust along the floorboards beneath the case.

The wood shifted ever so slightly, as though the shelf wasn't as permanent as it appeared.

Marley reached out, pressing her palm flat against the frame. To her surprise, it yielded. A low click echoed, the kind that raised the hairs on the back of her neck.

She jerked her hand back. The draft intensified, cool air whispering from somewhere unseen, carrying with it the scent of lavender and something older—earthier.

Her heart pounded.

Aunt Clara had kept secrets. Marley had always known that. But standing there, fingers trembling just inches from a hidden seam in the wall, she realized the truth was deeper than she had imagined.

The shop wasn't just dusty shelves and paperbacks. It was waiting.

And she wasn't sure she was ready for what it had to show her.

THAT NIGHT, Marley stayed upstairs in the apartment above the shop. She'd forgotten how small it was—two rooms, a kitchenette barely large enough for one, a window that overlooked Main Street. The mattress sagged, the radiator clanked, but exhaustion pressed heavier than discomfort.

Sleep, however, didn't come easily. The fog outside pressed against the glass, so thick it seemed alive. Somewhere in the distance, the lighthouse beam swept its rhythm across the town, though even that glow felt muted, restrained.

She dreamed—or thought she dreamed—of footsteps moving through the shop below. A woman's voice hummed a lullaby she almost recognized. When Marley stirred awake, the air smelled faintly of smoke, though no fire burned.

She pressed her palms to her eyes, whispering, "You're imagining things."

But deep down, a memory stirred—of being a child, hiding beneath those same shelves, listening to Clara murmur stories of the Green Healer, the woman who once saved Brookwood with her remedies and her secrets. Legends, Clara had called them. But Marley had believed.

And now, with the draft in the wall and the strange journal clutched tight beneath her pillow, belief returned like fog: thick, unsettling, and impossible to ignore.

Morning light broke over Brookwood reluctantly, as though the sun itself struggled to pierce the thick curtain of fog. Marley descended the narrow staircase from the apartment, her boots knocking softly against the worn steps. The air below was heavy with the scent of paper and cedar, the stillness of a place long closed, waiting.

She flipped the sign in the window. **Closed** became **Open**.

The gesture felt monumental—like turning a page she hadn't realized she was ready to read.

At first, nothing happened. A gull screeched outside. The fog drifted past the window. Then, slowly, as though word had already traveled through invisible channels, the town began to take notice.

The first to appear was Mrs. Ruth Bennett from the bakery across the street. She carried herself like someone who had lived here forever, her apron still dusted with flour, her arms folded as she watched Marley through the glass. Ruth didn't step inside. She only tilted her head slightly, a mix of curiosity and caution etched in her face, before moving along.

Next came Elias, Ruth's husband, lugging a crate of bread loaves to the café two doors down. He paused, his eyes meeting Marley's for a brief moment. A nod, curt and unreadable, then he moved on.

It went on like that all morning. Locals drifted by—some slowing, some peering through the window, a few entering just far enough to glance around and mumble polite greetings. No one lingered. No one welcomed her back.

Brookwood had always been like this: quiet, watchful, a place where secrets stuck as firmly as sea mist to glass.

Marley forced herself to move through the motions, dusting shelves, unpacking boxes Clara had never gotten to, arranging small displays near the front counter. Each book she touched carried history—not just the history of its content, but of her aunt's hand placing it there, of the customers who once thumbed its pages.

Yet beneath the motions ran a hum of tension she couldn't ignore. It wasn't hostility, not exactly. But neither was it warmth.

She stepped outside briefly to sweep the porch. Across the street, Ruth stood at her bakery's doorway again, whispering something to a woman Marley didn't recognize. Both women turned to look at her in unison.

The broom stilled in Marley's hand.

She had expected nostalgia, perhaps even sympathy in the wake of Clara's passing. But the eyes that followed her were different—measured, uncertain, almost guarded.

· · ·

By noon, she had only a handful of customers. A teenage boy bought a used novel for school. An older man in a fisherman's cap asked after a maritime atlas Clara once stocked but left empty-handed when Marley couldn't find it.

It wasn't until Hazel Merrow arrived that anyone actually stayed long enough to talk.

Hazel, owner of the metaphysical shop down the street, moved with the certainty of someone who belonged to the very bones of the town. Her hair was pinned back in a neat twist, her hands scented faintly of lavender. She stepped through the doorway with an expression that hovered between sympathy and expectation.

"Marley Taylor," she said softly, voice carrying the weight of recognition. "I wondered how long it would take you."

Marley managed a smile. "Only ten years and a tragedy later."

Hazel's eyes softened. She laid a hand on Marley's arm. "Clara thought the world of you, dear. She wanted you to have this place for a reason."

The words stirred something Marley didn't want to name. She busied herself with rearranging a stack of books on the counter. "The town doesn't seem too thrilled to see the doors open again."

"They're curious," Hazel corrected gently. "And cautious. Brookwood doesn't forget easily. Nor does it welcome change without question." She tilted her head, studying Marley as though she were a puzzle. "You'll have to earn their trust."

"I'm not here to upset anyone," Marley said, more defensively than she meant. "I just... this shop was Clara's life. It feels wrong to leave it locked and gathering dust."

Hazel smiled faintly, as if Marley had just said something that confirmed what she already knew. "Then you're already doing what she hoped."

Before Marley could press for meaning, Hazel slipped a small candle from her bag, setting it on the counter. Rosemary and sage, blended with beeswax. "For protection," Hazel said simply. "Light it tonight."

Marley picked it up, inhaling its scent. The same aroma that had lingered faintly when she first entered the shop. A chill brushed her skin.

Hazel gave a knowing nod, then left without another word.

THE REST of the day unfolded in fragments. The café owner, Evelyn Grant, stopped by with a thermos of chai, her kindness a small reprieve. A few tourists wandered in, oblivious to the undercurrents, thumbing through paperbacks and postcards.

But whenever Marley caught sight of a local, their reactions mirrored the same guarded curiosity—measured words, quick glances, whispers that faded when she turned her head.

By late afternoon, as the fog began to thicken once more, Marley sat behind the counter, weary. She opened Clara's ledger, skimming through the neat columns of names and dates. So many familiar surnames. Families who had bought books here for decades. Yet she couldn't shake the feeling that her name—Taylor—didn't belong among them.

The bell above the door chimed. Marley looked up.

A man stood silhouetted in the doorway, tall, broad-shouldered, his coat damp from the mist. His eyes swept the shop, settling on her with a flicker of recognition—or was it surprise?

For a moment, neither spoke. The hush of the shop, the muffled cry of gulls outside, the slow drip of fog-melt from the eaves—all of it pressed in.

Then he stepped inside, his voice low but steady.

"I didn't think anyone would ever open this place again."

Marley rose slowly, her hand resting on the counter for balance. "Well," she said, mustering composure, "I guess someone had to."

THE MAN EXTENDED A HAND. "Damien Hawthorne. Historical Society."

His grip was firm, his gaze thoughtful, though shadowed. Marley remembered the name—his family had tended the lighthouse for generations. Widower, if she recalled the town gossip correctly.

"Marley Taylor," she said, though he likely already knew.

His eyes lingered on her just long enough to stir unease, then drifted to the shelves, the ledger, the candle Hazel had left on the counter. Something unreadable crossed his face.

"You'll find Brookwood remembers things differently than outsiders," he said finally. "Even if you were born here."

The words stung, though his tone wasn't unkind—just matter-of-fact, like a lighthouse beam cutting through fog, whether you liked it or not.

Marley straightened, her voice firm. "Then maybe it's time some memories were dusted off."

Damien's mouth curved—not quite a smile, but the suggestion of one. "We'll see."

The bell chimed again as he left, swallowed once more by the fog.

Marley stood in the quiet shop, heart beating faster than she'd admit.

The town had spoken. Not with open arms, but with wary eyes, whispered words, and a lighthouse historian who looked at her as though she'd stepped into a story he already half-knew.

And beneath it all, the draft still whispered from the hidden seam in the wall.

Waiting.

BY THE TIME twilight bled across Brookwood, Marley was exhausted. The weight of reopening the shop, the stares from the townspeople, the encounter with Damien Hawthorne—all of it pressed heavily on her shoulders. She brewed tea upstairs in the apartment and carried it down into the shop, deciding she would tidy for another hour before turning in.

The fog outside had grown denser, smothering the streetlamps until they glowed like distant embers through smoke. Shadows stretched differently at night in Brookwood, bending in ways that unsettled her. The bell over the door jingled faintly though no one entered, and she had to steady her breath before realizing it was the wind slipping through unseen cracks.

She lit Hazel's rosemary-and-sage candle, placing it on the counter. Its flame wavered, casting long fingers of light across the walls. The scent was calming, but beneath it lay something sharper—like iron, or old stone.

Marley gathered a stack of journals Clara had left behind the counter. Most were ledgers, recording sales and shipments, but one bore no title, its leather worn and unmarked. She set it aside, intending to inspect it later. The act of sorting steadied her, gave her hands purpose even as her mind drifted to questions she couldn't answer: Why had Clara never told her about the candle Hazel left? Why had the town looked at her with such caution?

A creak sounded in the far corner.

She froze.

The draft returned, stronger now, curling cold around her ankles before rising up her spine. It carried the scent of lavender and earth again, that same unsettling fragrance she had noticed when she first pressed against the crooked bookshelf earlier in the day.

The candle's flame flickered violently though no window was open.

Marley set down the ledger, her pulse quickening. She crossed the shop slowly, each step groaning beneath her weight. The draft thickened as she neared the far corner, the one with the leaning bookcase. She knelt, running her hand along the floorboards. Dust clung to her fingertips, but beneath it she felt something else—a faint vibration, as though air moved beneath the wood.

"Clara?" The word slipped out before she could stop herself, ridiculous and trembling, but she couldn't shake the thought. The air felt intentional, as though summoned, not random.

No answer came, only the sound of her own breathing and the faint rattle of the wind chimes outside.

Still, the draft persisted, curling around her like a presence.

Marley reached for the shelf again, pressing against its frame. The faint click she had heard earlier echoed once more, deeper this time, almost like a sigh. The draft rushed outward, chilling her skin despite the warmth of the room.

She stumbled back, hand clutching the edge of a nearby table.

Something—or someone—was waiting.

She blew out the candle. The room fell into darkness except for the pale glow of the streetlamp beyond the window. For a moment she stood frozen, breath ragged, pulse hammering. Logic told her it was nothing more than faulty construction, an old shop with drafts seeping through gaps in the foundation. But instinct whispered otherwise.

Memories stirred—childhood afternoons spent crouched in the shop's aisles while Clara told her stories of Brookwood's legends: the Green Healer, the woman who brewed remedies from herbs and whispered blessings over the sick. Clara had called them folklore, half-truths meant to entertain a young girl. But Marley remembered the conviction in her aunt's voice, the way her eyes had gleamed as if she believed more than she let on.

Now, with the draft rising from a hidden seam in the wall, Marley couldn't help but wonder if those stories were less legend and more warning.

She relit the candle and placed it near the corner, watching its flame dance wildly. The light illuminated faint etchings on the wood she hadn't noticed before—tiny scratches, almost symbols, worn down by time. She traced them with her fingertip, feeling grooves that didn't belong to simple wear and tear.

Her throat tightened.

The draft grew colder, sharper, as though urging her closer, daring her to press again and see what lay beyond.

But she wasn't ready—not tonight. She wasn't sure she'd ever be ready.

She backed away, forcing herself to return to the counter. The ledger sat open where she had left it, the unmarked journal resting atop the pile. She pulled it closer, flipping it open.

Inside were handwritten notes—recipes, sketches of plants, small fragments of phrases. One line caught her breath:

"The bridge sings again. A circle once broken must be mended in green."

Her hand trembled as she closed the book.

Outside, the lighthouse beam swept across the fog, casting its muted glow through the shop window. Each rotation felt like a watchful eye, a steady rhythm reminding her she wasn't alone—not in the shop, not in Brookwood, not in whatever legacy Clara had left her.

Marley placed the journal beneath the counter, snuffed the candle, and locked the shop for the night. But as she climbed the stairs to the apartment above, the draft whispered once more from the corner, cool and insistent, like breath on the back of her neck.

Something waited in Brookwood.

And it had been waiting for her.

By the time Marley pulled the quilt over herself that night, she knew two things with certainty:

The town hadn't welcomed her home with open arms—it had greeted her with silence, whispers, and a wary watchfulness that felt almost protective. The bookshop wasn't just a building. It was a keeper of secrets, and it wasn't done with her.

In her dreams, she stood on the covered bridge in the fog. A woman's voice whispered her name, and a hand reached for hers through the mist.

When Marley woke, heart pounding, she knew the story wasn't beginning in the present. It had begun long ago. And she was now a part of it, whether she wanted to be or not.

2

THE BOOKSHOP KEY

Marley woke to the sound of gulls. Their cries cut through the fog, sharp and plaintive, echoing off the cliffs before settling in the narrow streets below. She lingered under the quilt for a few moments, listening, before pulling herself upright. Sleep had come reluctantly, fractured by dreams of voices on bridges and candlelight flickering against unseen walls.

By mid-morning she had brewed coffee in the kitchenette upstairs and carried a mug down into the shop. The space looked different in daylight, though not friendlier. The sun, veiled by fog, filtered through the windows in muted silver bands, revealing just how much work needed to be done. Dust lay thick on certain shelves, boxes were stacked haphazardly against walls, and piles of old receipts littered the counter.

Marley set the mug aside and tied her hair back, rolling up her sleeves. If she was to make the shop presentable—if she was to even consider reopening it fully—she would have to start somewhere.

She began with the boxes. Clara had left them everywhere: beneath tables, behind the register, stacked three high in the back hallway. Some were labeled— "Winter Recipes," "Children's Classics," "Ship Logs, 1920–1940"— while others bore only Clara's rushed handwriting scrawled in shorthand Marley couldn't decipher.

She chose one near the corner, its top caved slightly inward, the cardboard soft with age. Inside she found a jumble of items: receipts tucked into old envelopes, newspaper clippings, a chipped teacup, even a photograph of Clara standing in front of the shop thirty years earlier, smiling despite the wind tugging at her hair.

Marley paused over the photo, tracing the outline of her aunt's face with her thumb. Clara had always seemed larger than life—equal parts eccentric and wise, as comfortable quoting poetry as she was fixing a leaking pipe in the shop's basement. She had been a woman of contradictions, and now, with her gone, Marley felt the absence like a hollow space she wasn't sure how to fill.

At the bottom of the box, beneath a stack of old ledgers, Marley's hand brushed something cool and metallic. She drew it out, surprised at its weight.

A key.

Heavy brass, tarnished with age. Its bow was ornate, shaped like an elongated oval with a swirling pattern etched into its surface. The teeth were broad, uneven, designed for a lock older than anything she'd seen in recent years. Attached to it was a small tag, its edges curled, the ink faded but still legible.

Two letters: **L.S.**

Marley turned it over in her palm, heart quickening. L.S. What did it mean? "Library Storage"? "Locked Safe"? "Living Space"?

Or something else entirely.

The key carried a weight that was more than physical. She felt it as soon as she closed her fingers around it—a quiet gravity, as if Clara herself had meant for Marley to find it, had tucked it away for this very moment.

SHE SET the key on the counter, staring at it as she returned to unpacking. But her focus frayed, pulled back again and again to the brass glint beneath the muted light.

By afternoon, she decided she needed a break from boxes. She pulled out the old floor plans Clara had left in a folder near the register. The papers were yellowed, edges fraying, but the inked lines remained clear. The layout of the shop had always seemed straightforward: front entrance, wide central room lined with shelves, a back hallway leading to a storage closet, then the narrow staircase to the apartment above.

Yet as Marley traced the lines with her finger, something didn't add up.

The exterior walls on the plan didn't match what she knew of the building's outside dimensions. The east wall, the one where the crooked bookshelf leaned, seemed thinner than it should have been. A gap existed between what the plan showed inside and what she recalled outside.

She frowned, pulling her notebook closer and sketching the outline from memory. Outside, the wall extended at least four feet farther than the plan suggested. Inside, that space didn't exist. Unless—it was concealed.

Her pulse quickened again.

She thought of the draft that had curled around her ankles the night before, the faint click when she pressed against the bookcase, the symbols etched faintly into the wood.

The key, heavy and waiting.

"L.S."

Her fingers hovered over the plan, tracing the empty space.

Clara had left her more than a shop. She had left her a puzzle.

THE BELL over the door jingled. Marley startled, slamming the folder shut.

It was only a tourist couple, raincoats dripping, looking for something to pass the foggy afternoon. They browsed a few paperbacks, bought a map of the coast, and left with polite nods. But Marley's nerves buzzed, and she locked the folder in the drawer after they left.

She couldn't shake the feeling that whatever Clara had concealed wasn't meant for casual eyes.

BY LATE AFTERNOON, Marley decided she needed fresh air. She pocketed the key, grabbed her coat, and stepped into the fog-laden streets. The air smelled of brine and woodsmoke, the kind of scent that clung to Brookwood perpetually. She walked without purpose, letting her feet lead her past the bakery, the Moon & Morrow metaphysical shop, the covered bridge looming faintly through mist.

Her path ended, almost unconsciously, at the library.

The Brookwood Library was a grander structure than most of the town's buildings, its Victorian facade weathered but dignified. Stone columns flanked the entrance, and ivy crawled up the walls as though trying to reclaim it. Marley pushed through the heavy oak doors, the scent of paper and polish greeting her like an embrace.

She hadn't stepped foot in this building since high school. Nostalgia collided with disorientation as she moved between the shelves, running her fingers along the spines. Here too lay history, layered and waiting.

A voice broke her reverie.

"Didn't expect to see you here."

She turned.

Damien Hawthorne stood near the reference desk, a stack of books in his arms. He wore a dark sweater beneath his coat, his hair still damp from fog, and his expression was equal parts curiosity and reserve.

Marley straightened. "I could say the same."

He set the books down, adjusting his stance. "Research. The Historical Society asked me to catalog a series of documents on Brookwood's early years."

Her eyes flicked to the spines of his books: *Women of the Pacific Northwest*, *Herbal Traditions in Settlement Communities*, *Lineages of Early Brookwood*.

"Early Brookwood women?" she asked before she could stop herself.

His gaze sharpened, the faintest flicker of surprise crossing his features. "That's right."

"Why?"

Damien hesitated, then shrugged, his voice even. "Because history forgets them too easily. And because I think their stories matter more than we realize."

Something in his tone lingered, an undercurrent Marley couldn't quite name. He studied her a moment longer, then added, "Clara used to check out half the herbal archives we have. She believed in preserving what others dismissed as folklore. Maybe you'll do the same."

Marley opened her mouth, then closed it again. She thought of the key burning in her pocket, of the odd gap in the floor plan, of Hazel's candle flame flickering wildly in the draft.

Maybe Clara had believed in more than folklore.

And maybe she wanted Marley to believe, too.

THE FOG HAD THICKENED AGAIN by the time Marley returned to the shop from the library. Evening pressed close against the windows, the glass slick with condensation, the world beyond little more than blurred lamps and shadowed outlines. Inside, the shop was hushed, as if waiting.

Marley set her coat aside and laid the heavy brass key on the counter once more. She hadn't mentioned it to Damien —not yet. Some instinct told her it wasn't time. Instead, she carried Clara's folder of floor plans to the back table, spreading the sheets carefully beneath the lamplight.

The more she studied them, the less they made sense.

The east wall of the shop, according to the drawings, should have been flush with the outer structure. But Marley remembered clearly—when she'd walked past the exterior that morning—that the wall extended several feet farther. Outside, the bricks stretched into the alley at a distance that didn't exist inside.

She traced the line again with her fingertip, then lifted her gaze toward the very wall in question. Bookshelves stood there now, tall and crooked, their edges casting long shadows against plaster. Dust motes drifted lazily in the lamplight, and for a moment she swore she saw them swirl, caught in a faint current of air.

The draft.

Her skin prickled.

She pushed back from the table, crossing the room to press

her palm flat against the wall. It was cool, the plaster uneven beneath her hand. She ran her fingers downward, over cracks and faint impressions, until she reached the seam of the floor. A subtle vibration pulsed there—like hollow space behind stone.

Marley drew in a breath and forced herself to step back. She grabbed a tape measure from Clara's desk drawer and stretched it across the room. Twelve feet. She noted the number, then strode out into the fog-thick alley with her coat thrown back over her shoulders.

There, in the dim yellow glow of a streetlamp, she measured again. Sixteen feet.

Her heart thudded.

Four feet of space unaccounted for.

A room—hidden, sealed, forgotten.

The discovery sent a jolt of adrenaline through her, yet also a tremor of fear. Why would Clara conceal such a thing? And what could possibly be inside?

Marley returned to the shop and shut the door firmly against the fog. She leaned back against it, exhaling. She thought of Hazel's words—*Clara wanted you to have this place for a reason.* Perhaps this was what she had meant.

Still, reason or not, Marley felt the weight of a secret pressing in from every angle.

SHE RETURNED TO THE TABLE, her notebook open. She sketched the floor plan anew, marking the measurements she had taken. The discrepancy loomed large on the page, a box of empty space demanding explanation.

The key sat beside her, gleaming faintly in the lamplight. She picked it up again, holding it between thumb and forefinger. Heavy. Cold. The letters *L.S.* etched into the tag seemed to shimmer, though she knew it was only her tired eyes.

"L.S.," she whispered aloud, as though the walls might answer.

Library Storage? She had been at the library only an hour ago—Damien, standing with his arms full of books on Brookwood women, his eyes shadowed and unreadable. Could the key belong to something there? Or was the library too obvious?

Locked Space. Lost Secrets. Living Sanctuary. She turned the letters over and over, until the words blurred and dissolved into meaninglessness.

At last, she set the key down and rubbed her temples. She hadn't expected this—any of it. She had come to Brookwood to settle an estate, to sell off books if she must, to tidy the pieces of Clara's life. Not to uncover hidden walls and brass keys with cryptic initials.

But now, with the fog pressing harder against the windows and the draft curling cold beneath her chair, Marley knew she couldn't ignore it. Clara had left her the shop, yes—but she had also left her something more.

A responsibility.

THE FLOOR CREAKED SOFTLY above her—the apartment settling, perhaps, or something more. Marley stilled, listening. The silence thickened until she could hear her own pulse. She rose and walked back to the corner where the bookcase leaned.

It looked so ordinary. Shelves sagging under the weight of mismatched spines. A cracked globe perched on the top. A thin veil of dust over the edges.

And yet.

Marley reached out, pressing her hand against the side. Once again she felt it—the faint give, the subtle click, the rush of cold air seeping through seams that shouldn't exist.

Her breath caught.

She pressed harder. The shelf resisted, then shifted almost imperceptibly, like a door that had been locked too long. She pulled back quickly, nerves jolting.

The key burned in her pocket.

Not tonight, she told herself, retreating toward the counter. The thought of forcing the shelf open, of stepping into whatever darkness lay beyond, was more than she could bear alone. Not yet.

Still, her curiosity gnawed at her like a restless tide.

She lit Hazel's candle again, setting it near the register. The rosemary-sage scent filled the air, pushing back the draft but not erasing it. The flame wavered violently, casting wild shadows that made the walls look thinner, the shelves taller, the room stranger.

"Clara," Marley whispered, voice breaking against the silence. "What did you leave me?"

No answer came, only the echo of her own voice bouncing faintly off walls that hid more than they revealed.

SHE RETURNED TO THE TABLE, notebook open, sketch of the floor plan before her. She circled the empty space, wrote the letters *L.S.* in the margin, and drew an arrow toward the hidden wall.

A key, a room, initials that refused to reveal themselves.

And one man who might know more than he admitted.

Damien Hawthorne.

The thought of him unsettled her—his quiet gaze, the way he had studied her in the library when she mentioned early Brookwood women. He knew things, perhaps too many, about the town's history. But could she trust him with this? With Clara's secrets? With her own growing sense that the shop itself was alive with waiting?

Marley closed the notebook, her decision made for now. She would not share what she'd found—not yet. This belonged to Clara, to her, to the walls of the bookshop that whispered when the fog pressed close.

Tomorrow, perhaps, she would dig deeper.

Tonight, she would try to sleep.

But as she climbed the narrow staircase, candle extinguished, key clutched tightly in her hand, the draft followed her like breath at her heels.

And she knew—whatever lay hidden in that missing space—wasn't going to let her rest.

MORNING THINNED the fog only slightly, turning Brookwood into a grayscale sketch—pale light, darker lines, everything softened around the edges. Marley locked the shop behind her and crossed Main with her collar up, the brass key tucked in her pocket where it seemed to acquire its own pulse. She didn't plan to tell anyone about it, not yet. But the part of her that had always loved maps and margins wanted something factual to push back against the strangeness in the walls: lines, measurements, ink that didn't argue.

The library's oak doors breathed out that old, familiar scent—paper, polish, dust that had settled into peace. Inside, the hush felt earned rather than imposed, the way silence sometimes does after a storm. Marley nodded to Mrs. Delaney at the front desk, who eyed her with polite curiosity and a librarian's protective suspicion of people who might reshelve things badly.

"I'm looking for property records," Marley said. "Fire insurance maps, if you have them. Late nineteenth century."

Mrs. Delaney lifted a brow at the specificity, then softened. "Sanborn maps are in the local room. Street indexes in the top drawer. Holler if the lamp flickers—it does that when the fog's thick."

The local room sat like a chapel at the library's heart—long table, handled drawers full of brittle paper, magnifier lamps with heavy brass arms. The floorboard at the threshold sighed under Marley's weight the way Clara's shop floor did, and that tiny kinship steadied her more than she expected. She tugged open the SANBORN drawer, flipped through labeled envelopes—1889, 1892, 1901—and slid the 1892 set onto the table.

She found Brookwood faster than she thought she would, the town etched in square, colored blocks—brick in pink, frame buildings in yellow, special hazards shaded in blue. Sheet 3 held Main Street. There: a tidy rectangle where Clara's Nest of Books now stood, but not labeled "bookstore." In neat hand: **Books / Apothecary**. A dotted line split the rectangle in two, a partition wall that didn't exist anymore. A notation in the margin had faded to a shadow of graphite, but under the magnifier lamp she made out the letters: **L.S.** scrawled beside a tiny square in the back corner.

Marley's breath left her in a thin line. She pressed the cold rim of the magnifier to the paper until the glass fogged, then forced herself to ease back, to take it in like a rational person. The shop was once divided. A small, square something—closet, vault, cabinet—sat in the back corner where the crooked bookshelf leaned now. And a set of initials that matched the tag on her key clung to the page like a footprint no weather had managed to wash away.

"Find something?"

She flinched. Damien Hawthorne stood in the doorway, jacket open over a dark sweater, the damp in his hair not yet surrendered to the library's warmth. He wasn't looming; he simply filled a space the way some people do without trying.

Marley steadied the map with her palms. "Sanborns. 1892." She made her tone light. "Romantic reading."

"Don't knock it," he said, coming closer. "Cartographers were the poets of municipal fear."

She looked up at him, caught off guard by the line, and found he wasn't smiling exactly, but the corner of his mouth had conceded a fraction. On the table in front of him he set a stack of titles. *Women of the Pacific Northwest. Midwives and Memory. Herbal Traditions of Settler Communities.* A slim ledger with Minutes—Ladies Benevolent Society, 1890–1897 written in hand that had learned penmanship from a stern teacher and a straightedge.

"You're in deep," she said.

"Deeper than I expected." He slid the ledger a touch nearer the lamp. "I'm cataloging the early women who did work the charters never recorded. Midwives, teachers, apothecaries." He tipped the ledger open to a page where the minutes circled a charity drive for a family on the north bluff. Names trailed down the margin—Mrs. Hannah Gearhart, Joan Nye, Eliza Merrick, a handful of initials and surnames. Halfway down, a secretary's addendum noted a payment for "glass vials, rosemary oil, and willow bark—L. Sparrow."

"L. S.," Marley said before she could throttle the words. She felt the key in her pocket like a skipped heartbeat.

Damien's gaze flicked to her, sharpened. "You know the name?"

"I—" She forced herself to breathe. The fog might have been in the room with them, the way it softened the outline of things you swore you knew. "My aunt used to tell stories," she said carefully. "About a healer. Folk tales. They blur."

"Most folk tales are city records with the names rubbed off." He turned the ledger, scanning a few lines with that focus of his that felt like a lighthouse beam—steady, not prying, but you knew when it passed over you. "Lydia Sparrow shows up in the benevolent minutes for six years. Sometimes as L. Sparrow. Sometimes as 'the woman at the back counter.' The apothecary was attached to the book-shop then."

Marley traced the dotted line on the Sanborn map. "A partition," she said. "Back room."

"And sometimes," Damien added, tapping a note squeezed in the ledger's margin, "as simply— 'the green woman.'"

She looked up. The phrase went through her like cold water. He noticed—of course he did—but he didn't press it, just let the words sit between them like a specimen cured in glass.

"What are you hoping to find?" she asked, but what she meant was what are you hoping to prove.

"That they were there." He closed the ledger gently, like a hand placed on a shoulder. "That the town's story wasn't built by one kind of hand. That legacies don't disappear because someone didn't like the handwriting."

"And the lighthouse?" she asked, because he carried that history the way she carried Clara's shop—inside the bones somewhere. "You're the one who said outsiders remember wrong."

"I said Brookwood remembers differently." He glanced to the window. On fog days, the light filtered through like a secret kept by the glass. "I grew up with men who thought the beam belonged to them. But men didn't keep the lamps trimmed alone. They didn't deliver babies in the keeper's quarters or grind bark into tea for fever. We use 'he' for the lighthouse out of habit. That doesn't make it true."

Mrs. Delaney coughed discreetly at the doorway as if to remind them that libraries were for whispers, not confessions. Damien stepped back a fraction. Marley felt the small absence as if someone had taken a weight off a shelf and the wood groaned in relief.

He nodded toward the map. "Sanborns mark hazards. Fire, explosives. Places with flammable spirits, like apothecaries, get special notation. If you're trying to understand the architecture of an old building, those maps tell you where the town thought the danger lived."

"And where did Brookwood think the danger lived?" Marley asked.

"In the corners where women stored knowledge nobody could tax," he said softly. "In rooms without windows."

Her hand found her pocket. The key sat there, heavy and unarguable. She thought of the initials on the tag—**L.S.** —and the little square sketched beside the back wall of her shop, and the breath of cold that slipped under the shelf when she pressed. Lydia Sparrow, maybe. Ladies' Society, possibly. Or something functional and prosaic: **Lamplight Storage. Locked Safe.** It was both enormous and small, the way a single unlabeled drawer can hold a life.

He must have read something in her face, because his voice gentled. "You don't have to tell me what brought you in here."

"I'm not sure I could, even if I wanted to," she said truthfully. "I used to think grief was a clean line. Now it's like... a room I can't see yet."

Damien's mouth tugged again at that almost-smile. "Brookwood does love a room you can't see yet."

They stood with it—the moment, the maps, the ledger with the lives of women recorded in the margins—until Mrs. Delaney's desk clock made the careful little sound of a quarter hour.

"I have to pick up Sophie," he said, glancing toward the door. He didn't explain who Sophie was. He didn't have to. The name fit in the way some names do when you already see the outline. "If you want copies, Delaney can run them. And—" He hesitated, then slid a card from his wallet, edges softened by use. **Brookwood Historical—D. Hawthorne.** A phone number. In the corner, in pen, he'd written: **Sanborn 1892 Sheet 3 / Benevolent Minutes: 1890–97.** "If you find anything that looks like it wants a second pair of eyes."

Marley took the card, the pads of her fingers brushing his just long enough to be aware of the contact. It was almost nothing, almost accidental. It landed like a promise anyway.

"I'm not sure what I'm finding," she said, pocketing the card with the key.

"That's how you know you're close," he said. Then he nodded toward the map. "Sheet Seven sometimes lists substructures. Check it for cisterns, coal chutes, safes. People call a room hidden when all they mean is *inconvenient to men with keys.*"

The corner of her mouth lifted despite herself. He saw it, startled faintly, as if he hadn't expected the expression to cross her face today. Then he stepped back into the library's larger hush, lifted a hand in a near-wave, and went.

Marley exhaled when he was gone, the way you do after holding yourself still for too long. She went back to the drawers, found Sheet Seven, and pulled it under the lamp. The ink had bled more here, but the annotations were crisp enough to read if you leaned close and accepted that your spine would complain later. The building footprint appeared again—a tidy rectangle—with a sharply penciled **S** in a square in the back corner. The legend at the bottom coded **S** as **Safe**. Another margin hand, different from the first, added a notation barely there: **L.S.—keeper**.

Keeper. The word tugged at something that had nothing to do with safes and everything to do with lighthouses and the people who kept lights lit. Lydia Sparrow, perhaps, had been appointed to keep something that needed keeping. Or **L.S.** wasn't a person at all but a designation—lamp safe, lamp storage. Every possibility was an opening.

She asked Mrs. Delaney for copies of Sheets Three and Seven and the two ledger pages that mentioned Lydia Sparrow. The copier groaned like a retired sailor, then did its duty. While she waited, Marley watched the fog move past the high windows—how it could be motion and stillness at once. When the pages were warm in her hands, she tucked them flat into a folder, thanked the librarian, and stepped out into the careful gray.

Back at the shop she didn't turn on the front lights right away. The afternoon had gone to that hour when the town couldn't quite decide if it would commit to day or yield to evening. In that in-between, the shop's interior shadows looked less like shadows and more like doorways in training.

She laid the copies on the counter and pressed the magnifier lamp close, over the Sanborn square that indicated **Safe**. The exact corner. The crooked shelf. The draft that came like a suggestion rather than a warning.

The key warmed against her palm when she took it out. She wasn't being fanciful; metal does that with skin. But there was feeling layered on feeling—Clara's absence, Damien's ledger, the shape of a hidden room pressed against the shape of her life until she couldn't tell which outline belonged to which.

"Okay," she said to the air. The shop creaked once, politely. "Okay."

She moved the cracked globe from the top of the crooked shelf and set it on the floor. She lifted the bottom row of books carefully, stacking them in three neat piles. Her fingers found the wood behind them and, lower, the base molding. The seam she'd felt before answered her touch like a puzzle piece worn soft at the edges. She pressed where the map suggested space might begin—and felt the faintest metallic kiss against her knuckle.

Marley froze. Slowly, she traced the inside of the molding until her nail found a burr—no, not a burr. A pinhole. A keyhole hidden in the trim, painted over and then nicked enough by time to betray its position.

She sat back on her heels. The room seemed to inhale.

The key in her hand wasn't the delicate variety meant for jewelry boxes. It was meant to turn something that wanted not to be turned. She lifted it, brought the bow to her lips without thinking, tasting brass and the past, and then lowered it toward the tiny, stubborn hole that had waited long enough.

She stopped a breath away.

Not fear—no, not quite. A sense of right timing. A sense that once turned, some doors don't just open; they rearrange the house.

Marley lowered the key, set it in the dish beside the ledger, and closed her hand until her knuckles protested. She wasn't alone in this, not entirely. If Damien's work was about restoring names to their rightful lines in the ledger of the town, then hers might be about restoring rooms to their rightful light. But not in the last light of this fog-dulled day, not when the town's eyes felt close even through glass. Tomorrow, she told herself. Not a promise she would be able to sleep on, but a promise with a spine.

She replaced the books carefully, set the globe back on top, and turned the **Open** sign to **Closed**, the old chain clinking against so much painted wood. In the window's reflection she caught her own outline, the shelves behind her, the faint waver of something where the wall should be still. She let the sight pass, like a boat you choose not to name until the tide comes in.

Upstairs, she set the copies beside the kettle, and as water took its time reaching the boil she ran a fingertip over the penciled: **L.S.—keeper**. She liked the word on her tongue. Keeper. A person who tends a thing so it doesn't go out. A person who knows which drawers stick and which doors need coaxing instead of force.

Tonight, tea. Tomorrow, the key.

And in the quiet just before the kettle clicked, Brookwood breathed back at her—through floorboards, through walls, through the inch of space in which a secret had lived comfortably for more than a century—as if to say that keeping, too, is a kind of love.

3

COFFEE AND OLD WOUNDS

The café door jingled with the kind of bell that had marked time in Brookwood long before cell phones told people when to breathe. Marley stepped inside, shaking off the damp. The fog had followed her as if reluctant to let her go, pressing close even here, blurring the windows until the town looked like a half-finished watercolor beyond the glass.

The warmth hit her instantly—roasted beans, baked bread, the faint sweetness of cardamom and vanilla. It was the smell of mornings she hadn't thought about in years. Clara used to bring her here on Saturdays after errands, a cinnamon roll between them, the newspaper spread across the table, stories about fog advisories and fishing hauls folded into their own rhythms.

Behind the counter stood Evelyn Grant, her hair in a neat braid, her eyes bright with the kind of warmth that could either welcome you or burn straight through your armor depending on her mood. She paused mid-pour when she saw Marley.

"Well," Evelyn said, voice neither sharp nor soft—just weighted. "Look who the fog dragged back."

Marley forced a small smile. "Hi, Evelyn. It's been a while."

"A decade's worth of whiles." Evelyn set the pitcher down with precision. "Coffee still your language?"

"It's the only one I speak fluently."

That earned her the barest flicker of a grin, gone as quickly as it came. Evelyn poured a mug, slid it across the counter with practiced ease. "On the house. First time's nostalgia."

Marley wrapped her hands around the ceramic, grateful for its heat. She scanned the room, taking in the familiar mismatched tables, the chalkboard menu written in Evelyn's careful script, the paintings of coastal scenes done by local artists. It hadn't changed. Or maybe it had and the fog simply blurred the differences.

At the far corner, a figure sat by the window, posture unmistakably composed: Damien Hawthorne. His coat draped over the chair beside him, his coffee untouched, a notebook open with lines of neat handwriting she couldn't quite read from here. His gaze flicked up just once, catching hers, before dropping back to the page. No greeting. No wave. Just awareness.

The air tightened.

Evelyn leaned on the counter, following her line of sight. "Be careful with that one."

Marley looked back. "Damien?"

"He's been carrying more ghosts than coffee these days," Evelyn said simply, wiping down the counter with a cloth. Then her tone shifted, sharper around the edges. "But I suppose you'd know something about ghosts, wouldn't you?"

Marley blinked. "Meaning?"

Evelyn straightened, eyes narrowing just enough to make the question sting. "Your aunt. Clara. People say she was into... strange things. Candles, herbs, whispers about the bridge. Half the town came here after dark at one point or another, saying she had answers no doctor could provide."

Marley's stomach tightened. She thought of Hazel's rosemary-and-sage candle, the hidden draft behind the bookcase, the initials *L.S.* etched on that brass key. "Clara was a reader," she said carefully. "She collected stories."

Evelyn's mouth curved, but it wasn't a smile. "Stories are one word for it. Secrets are another."

The words hung there, bitter as unsweetened espresso.

Marley carried her coffee to a table near the center, deliberately not choosing one too close to Damien, though she could feel his presence like a tide pulling against her footing. She set her notebook down, intending to sketch floor plan discrepancies, but the pen hovered uselessly above the page.

The bell chimed again. A man entered, tall and lean, with a tweed jacket that looked as though it had survived decades of academic debates. His hair was white but thick, his eyes sharp behind rimless glasses. He moved with the kind of certainty that comes from knowing you belong everywhere you go—or believing it hard enough that no one dares contest it.

"Professor Ashcroft," Evelyn greeted from behind the counter, her tone polite but distant.

"Coffee, black," the man said. Then his gaze swept the

room, landing on Marley. It stayed there, appraising, the way a historian might study a fragment of pottery.

He approached her table without waiting for invitation. "You must be Clara's niece."

Marley rose slightly in her chair, coffee mug a small anchor in her hands. "Marley Taylor. Yes."

"Edmund Ashcroft. History Professor." He adjusted his glasses, his eyes never leaving hers. "I heard you've reopened the shop."

"I'm sorting through things. It seemed wrong to leave it closed."

"Wrong," he repeated, the word tasting odd on his tongue. "Or dangerous?"

Marley frowned. "Excuse me?"

Ashcroft leaned forward just enough that she could smell the faint scent of old paper clinging to him. "Your aunt was a respected woman, but she... entertained certain eccentricities. Herbal journals, coded notes, whisperings of healers and circles long since buried. The shop kept its balance because Clara knew the difference between story and fact. I hope you do too."

Her spine stiffened. "I'm just trying to honor her legacy."

His eyes glinted, sharp as a blade polished thin. "Then take my advice, Ms. Taylor. Do not stir the roots. Brookwood is built on delicate soil, and some things are better left where they lie."

The silence that followed was heavy enough to draw glances from other tables.

Damien had lifted his head now, his expression unreadable, though Marley thought she caught the faintest flicker of disapproval—not at her, but at Ashcroft.

Marley steadied her voice. "Thank you for the advice, Professor. I'll keep it in mind."

He studied her a moment longer, then gave a curt nod and retreated with his coffee to a table at the back.

HER PEN still hovered over the notebook, but now the page seemed heavier with implication. Clara's name. Secrets. The warning not to stir the roots. She thought of the brass key pressing against the lining of her pocket, the faint draft curling from a hidden seam in the bookshop wall. Roots were already stirring—whether she wanted them to or not.

And across the room, Damien Hawthorne finally closed his notebook and lifted his coffee, his gaze finding hers again. This time, he didn't look away.

The weight of Professor Ashcroft's warning still hung in the air, like the lingering scent of burnt coffee grounds. Marley tried to shake it off, but her hand tightened unconsciously around her mug. She took a slow sip, mostly to buy herself time, then let her gaze drift to the window where fog pressed like a living thing against the glass.

When she lowered her eyes again, Damien was watching her.

Not openly, not rudely—just that steady, measured kind of awareness that made it impossible to pretend he wasn't. His coffee sat untouched, steam long since vanished, while his notebook rested closed beneath his hand. He didn't look away this time. And that, Marley realized, was somehow worse.

Their eyes caught. A breath passed between them, silent but charged, before Damien rose with deliberate calm and crossed the room toward her table.

"May I?" His voice was quiet, but it carried, and Evelyn, behind the counter, glanced over as though to mark the moment.

Marley gestured to the chair opposite hers. "It's a free town," she said lightly, though her tone cracked under the weight of nerves.

He pulled the chair out and sat, every movement composed, as though he'd had practice keeping emotions tucked into precise lines. For a long beat, neither spoke. Only the hum of conversation around them filled the silence —laughter from a table of teenagers near the back, the hiss of milk frothing, the clink of porcelain.

"You didn't deserve that," Damien said finally.

Marley blinked. "What?"

"Ashcroft. He's spent too long digging through bones and calling it gardening. Don't mistake his warnings for wisdom. They're fear. Nothing more."

Marley studied him. His jaw was set, but not unkindly. It was the steadiness of someone who'd endured enough storms to know when one was bluffing. Still, the remark didn't ease the knot in her chest. "He seemed pretty certain," she murmured.

Damien's mouth twitched, not quite a smile. "Certainty is easy when you don't risk anything by being wrong."

The words sat between them, heavy, and Marley felt the truth of them hum in her own bones. Clara had risked something—she didn't know what yet, but she could feel it in every corner of the shop, in the brass key tucked deep in her pocket, in the uneven floor plans. Risk left residue. It clung.

"You grew up here," she said, her tone more guarded than she meant. "You'd know better than I would if there's truth to what he said. About... stirring roots."

Damien's gaze flicked to the window, where fog swirled like ink. "I know that Brookwood remembers what it chooses to. And forgets with just as much intention." He leaned forward slightly, his eyes catching hers again. "But roots? They grow whether you stir them or not."

For a moment, she thought he might say more. But then he leaned back, distancing himself, folding his arms in that way people do when they've already said more than they meant.

Marley traced the rim of her mug with her fingertip. She hadn't expected their conversation to feel like this—measured, yes, but also threaded with something deeper. Not hostility, not exactly, but a wariness layered with recognition. As if each of them carried scars that the other couldn't see but somehow understood.

"I'm not here to cause trouble," she said finally.

Damien's expression softened, almost imperceptibly. "Neither was Clara."

The name hung between them, tender and raw. Marley swallowed hard. "You knew her."

"I knew of her," he corrected. "Everyone did. But I also... spoke with her, here and there. At the lighthouse mostly. She cared about the things most people dismissed. Patterns. Names. The way stories repeat themselves if you let them."

A flicker of grief crossed his face, so quick she might have missed it if she hadn't been watching him closely. His voice dropped, lower, carrying a weight she recognized because she carried it too. "She reminded me of someone."

Marley's chest tightened. She didn't press. Some silences belonged to the living, and some belonged to the dead. She knew enough of the difference to respect it.

Still, the charge between them deepened, an unspoken acknowledgment: they both knew loss, and loss recognized its own.

Across the café, Professor Ashcroft lifted his head from his book just long enough to glance their way. His eyes lingered, sharp as glass, before he lowered them again. The warning still clung to the room, no matter how much Marley wished it gone.

Damien noticed, too. His voice hardened a fraction. "Don't let him decide what you see. Brookwood has enough ghosts without borrowing his."

Marley wanted to believe him. She wanted to take that calm conviction and let it anchor her against the fog creeping into every corner of her life. But she also knew conviction was easier to hold when you weren't the one inheriting the secrets.

"Maybe I don't get a choice," she whispered.

For the first time, Damien's composure faltered. Just slightly, but enough. His eyes searched hers, quiet, almost startled by her honesty. Then he stood, slow, deliberate, his chair scraping softly against the wood floor.

"You always get a choice," he said, and left his coffee untouched as he walked back toward the fog-smeared window, leaving Marley with her mug gone cold, her heart unsteady, and the sense that the ground beneath her had shifted.

MARLEY SAT LONGER than she meant to, her coffee cold, her thoughts restless. Damien's words—*You always get a choice*—still hummed under her skin, though his absence had left the café feeling hollow in ways she didn't want to name.

The bell above the door jingled again. Professor Ashcroft had only stepped out briefly, it seemed; now he returned, his presence immediately reshaping the atmosphere. He carried no books this time, only his sharp-eyed suspicion, as if he'd decided their earlier exchange had left too much unsaid.

He claimed a table near hers, not close enough for conversation, but close enough to remind her of his presence. The deliberate act of it unsettled her more than words could. Evelyn shot Marley a glance from behind the counter, as though silently weighing whether to intervene. But Evelyn had always been pragmatic—she'd let Marley fight her own battles.

Ashcroft stirred his coffee slowly, methodically. Then, in a voice pitched to carry just far enough, he said, "The thing about roots, Ms. Taylor, is that once disturbed, they rot. They loosen the soil until everything around them collapses."

The café stilled. The teenagers in the corner hushed. Even Evelyn's cloth paused mid-swipe on the counter.

Marley's heart thudded. She turned to face him, her chin lifted. "And the thing about roots," she replied evenly, "is that sometimes they outgrow the soil that cages them."

The silence afterward was thick as fog, pressing into every corner of the room.

Ashcroft's eyes narrowed. He gave a faint, humorless smile and returned to his coffee as if she'd passed some test —or failed one. Marley couldn't tell.

She gathered her things. Her notebook felt heavier than paper had a right to be. Sliding it into her satchel, she nodded once to Evelyn, who returned the gesture with the briefest flicker of solidarity.

The café bell jingled as Marley stepped back into the street. The fog swallowed her instantly, muting the sounds of cups clinking and voices behind her. The air was damp, cold enough to seep through her coat, and thick enough that even the glow of the streetlamps looked like lanterns suspended in clouds.

She pulled her satchel closer, the brass key pressing

against her side through the lining. Damien's business card, tucked into the same pocket, seemed to warm under her touch as though reminding her she wasn't entirely alone in this.

Still, the professor's warning echoed, and the sense of eyes on her refused to fade. She turned down Main, footsteps muffled on the wet stone. Once—twice—she glanced back, certain she'd catch someone trailing her. Each time, the street stretched empty behind her, only fog rolling in slow currents like the breath of something vast and unseen.

Yet the unease didn't leave.

By the time she reached the bookshop, her pulse was quick, her breath clouding in the lamplight. She fumbled the lock, slipped inside, and shut the door with more force than she intended. The chime above the door rang out, sharp and jarring, before the silence closed in again.

The shop smelled of paper and rosemary, faint traces of Hazel's candle lingering like a benediction. But tonight, even that scent felt weighted. Protective, yes—but also warning.

Marley pressed her back against the door and closed her eyes. She hadn't stirred the roots yet, not really. But the town already seemed to know she was thinking of it.

And somewhere in the fog outside, she was certain the roots were stirring back.

4

—————

THE LOCKED ROOM

The key felt heavier than it should as Marley turned it in her hand. Brass, tarnished, etched with the initials *L.S.*—a puzzle her aunt Clara had left tucked away among ledgers and dust. She had thought about it for days, felt its weight in her pocket while she swept, unpacked boxes, even while sipping coffee under Professor Ashcroft's watchful eyes. Every time she reached for it, her breath caught with the same mixture of dread and anticipation.

That evening, she could no longer resist.

The bookshop was closed, the streetlamps outside swallowed by fog so dense it pressed against the windows like damp cloth. Marley lit Hazel's rosemary-and-sage candle and placed it on the counter, the flame a fragile tether to steadiness. Then she crossed to the crooked bookshelf.

Her fingers traced the uneven molding at its base until they found the faint, hidden seam. She crouched, heart racing, and slid the brass key into the pinhole she'd discovered days earlier. For a moment, nothing happened. The key resisted, stiff from years of disuse. Then, with a reluctant turn, the mechanism gave way, releasing a click that echoed like a secret finally exhaled.

The shelf shuddered, then shifted outward an inch. Dust trickled down in lazy spirals. Marley pushed, her palms flat against the wood. Slowly, groaning as though protesting its own betrayal, the bookshelf swung open on unseen hinges.

Beyond lay darkness.

Marley lit a second candle from the first, shielding the flame with her hand as she stepped inside. The air was cooler, denser, carrying a scent that unsettled her—a mingling of earth, dried herbs, and the faint tang of iron. It clung to her clothes, her hair, as if she had stepped not into a room but into someone else's memory.

The chamber was small, barely larger than a pantry. Its walls were brick, the mortar dark with age. Wooden shelves lined two sides, sagging under the weight of boxes and jour-nals. The single window had been bricked over from the outside, its outline still visible in the uneven stone. No light had touched this room in decades.

Marley's candle cast trembling shadows as she stepped farther in. She set the flame on a low shelf and began to look.

The boxes bore names written in Clara's hand: *Eliza Merrick, Hannah Gearhart, Lydia Sparrow, Joan Nye.* All women's names. All unfamiliar, save Sparrow, which echoed the ledger Damien had shown her in the library.

Marley crouched, brushing her fingers over the spidery ink. She lifted a lid. Inside lay a bundle of dried herbs wrapped in linen, brittle but still fragrant—laven-der, willow bark, rosemary. Beneath them, a journal bound in worn leather, its pages filled with precise hand-writing.

Her throat tightened as she read the first line:

"We keep the circle, unseen but unbroken. May the town never know what it owes."

She turned the page. Dates stretched back to 1891. Recipes for tinctures, notes about illnesses cured, whispers of rituals performed on nights of heavy fog.

This was no simple storage closet. It was an archive. A sanctuary.

And someone—Clara, or perhaps the women before her—had bricked it away deliberately.

Marley stepped back, the candlelight wavering. The room pressed close, both protective and oppressive. Why had it been sealed? What had Clara been trying to preserve—or protect her from?

Her eyes lingered on the bricked window, the mortar thick and uneven. From outside, no one would suspect a room lay hidden here. The sealing had been purposeful, careful. And recent enough that the herbs still held their scent.

She whispered aloud, though no one was there to hear. "What were you hiding, Aunt Clara?"

The silence that answered wasn't empty. It carried weight, the way silence sometimes does when it belongs to a place rather than the absence of sound.

Marley pressed her hand against the nearest box, steadying herself. She would need to look deeper, read every journal, follow every name. But not tonight. Tonight, the discovery itself was enough to rattle her to the core.

She backed out of the chamber, pulled the shelf closed until it clicked back into place, and leaned against it, her breath coming in shallow waves.

The key glinted in her palm. The candle guttered, flame struggling against a draft that curled from behind the hidden wall, as if the room were still breathing, still waiting.

Marley knew now that Clara's legacy wasn't the shop alone. It was this—an inheritance bricked away, sealed from light, entrusted only to those willing to risk stirring the roots.

And she was no longer sure if she wanted to be one of them.

MARLEY RETURNED to the hidden chamber the next night, candle in one hand, notebook in the other. The memory of that first discovery had pressed at her all day, her thoughts restless even as she tried to sort through the mundane tasks of opening and closing the shop. No matter what she touched—dusty spines, receipts, the kettle handle upstairs—her mind returned to the sealed room. To the boxes. To the bricked window.

Tonight, she would not stop at discovery. Tonight, she would read.

The air inside was thick and unmoved, a place where time seemed reluctant to pass. Her candle's flame quivered, lighting the brickwork in fits of gold. The shelves sagged with their burden of forgotten things.

She slid the nearest box forward—its lid creaking, its label faded but still legible. Eliza Merrick.

Inside, another journal rested beneath a neat bundle of pressed flowers tied with twine. Their colors had long since drained to pale browns, but the faint scent of chamomile lingered. Marley lifted the journal carefully. The leather was soft with age, the pages edged with dust. She opened to the first entry, written in a steady hand.

"April 3rd, 1891. The boy's fever broke after the tincture. His mother insisted on payment, but we agreed no coin was necessary. Only her word to join us on the solstice."

Marley frowned. Solstice. The word clung to the page. She turned it, reading more.

"We gathered at dusk. Lydia brought willow bark, Joan the rosemary, and I the oil. Together we repeated the circle's vow. What we do, we do unseen, and what is unseen, the town may never name."

Her breath caught.

The circle.

Marley set the journal aside and reached for the next box. Hannah Gearhart. Inside: sprigs of dried rosemary, a strip of cloth embroidered with a symbol—a spiral, carefully stitched. Another journal, this one more worn, the ink fading, but legible.

"November 12th, 1893. The bridge cracked again. The men speak of carpenters, but we know better. The fog took what it wished, and the roots below shift when stirred. Lydia warns against binding them too tightly. Still, we cannot let the town forget the price. We meet again under the lighthouse."

Marley's pulse quickened. The bridge. Roots. The lighthouse. All names and places that threaded through Brookwood's present like whispers, and now here they were written plainly, decades old.

She pulled the third box down. Lydia Sparrow. The name made her throat tighten, echoing from the ledger Damien had shown her. Inside, the contents were heavier— bundles of dried bark, vials sealed with wax, a rosary whose beads smelled faintly of cedar. Beneath them, a thicker journal.

She opened it, her hand trembling.

"August 6th, 1895. They call me the Green Woman now. I do not mind it, though the name is spoken in fear as often as gratitude. We saved the Merrick child. We eased the labor for Hannah's cousin. But when Joan spoke too openly, she was met

with stares. The men in the Society say we meddle. They do not see that we keep them alive. We agreed to seal our notes if the time came. A safe was chosen, the window bricked. One day, another woman will find it, and she must decide whether to keep or to scatter."

Marley closed the journal quickly, her heart pounding. The words struck with eerie precision. It was as if Lydia had written across a century, her hand reaching directly toward Marley now.

She set the candle on the shelf, light trembling across the brickwork. The room suddenly felt less like a chamber and more like a vault—a place intentionally hidden, not only to preserve what was stored but to protect it from prying eyes.

Every box bore a woman's name. Each journal, another piece of a circle that had lived quietly beneath Brookwood's history. They were midwives, apothecaries, healers. Women who had tended the sick and guided the living when official records barely gave them space. And Clara—her aunt—had inherited their trust. She must have been the last to guard this secret, until now.

Marley touched the bricked window. The mortar was cold, rough beneath her palm. Why seal it? To keep the room hidden from the outside world, yes—but perhaps also to prevent escape. The thought unsettled her more than she wanted to admit.

She pressed her forehead against the cool brick, whispering, "What were you protecting me from, Clara?"

The silence answered with weight. Not absence, but presence—the way old places sometimes carry their own pulse.

She turned back to the journals, gathering them into her arms. Their weight surprised her, heavier than paper should be, as though every story inside had gained mass with time.

When she stepped back into the bookshop, closing the shelf behind her, Marley felt the shift instantly. The shop's air seemed lighter, freer. But she carried the heaviness now.

At the counter, she spread the journals out. Their spines cracked faintly as they settled. She ran her fingers over each name, whispering them aloud. Eliza Merrick. Hannah Gearhart. Lydia Sparrow. Joan Nye.

Names the town had forgotten. Names the town had perhaps chosen to forget.

Marley lit Hazel's candle again, the rosemary-sage scent curling through the air, mingling with the faint trace of herbs from the sealed room. She opened her notebook and began copying passages carefully, her pen moving with urgency.

If Brookwood's roots had been stirred, then so be it. Someone had to remember.

And someone had to ask why they had been buried in the first place.

MARLEY LINGERED in the shop long after the last streetlight outside blurred into a faint amber halo swallowed by fog. The journals lay open across the counter, their pages whispering in the lamplight as if the women who had written them breathed still. The names stared up at her—Eliza Merrick, Hannah Gearhart, Lydia Sparrow, Joan Nye—like a roll call across time, each one waiting to be spoken back into existence.

But it was the bricked window that haunted her.

When she closed her eyes, she could feel its cold surface beneath her palm, rough mortar against skin. Why brick over a window? A window was meant for light, for air, for witness. Blocking it seemed purposeful, almost violent, like silencing a voice that threatened to speak too loudly.

She imagined the act: men stacking bricks under the cover of night, sealing away a room while the women whose journals she now read stood by, powerless to stop them. Or perhaps it was the women themselves who bricked it—choosing concealment over exposure, knowing their circle's survival depended on shadows. Which version was true? Which was more dangerous?

The candle on the counter guttered, pulling her back into the present. She leaned over the journals, scanning the entries again, searching for anything that explained the window. Lydia Sparrow's voice came closest, her words written in bold strokes that spoke of defiance. *"We agreed to seal our notes if the time came. A safe was chosen, the window bricked."*

Marley mouthed the words slowly. The time came. What time? What threat had pressed so heavily on these women that they locked their history away in darkness?

Her mind spun with possibilities—fear of persecution, fear of exposure, or perhaps fear of something more intangible, something that lived in the very fog that cloaked Brookwood.

She pressed her hands flat against the counter, grounding herself. The shop creaked around her in the familiar way of old wood, but tonight each sound seemed sharper, more deliberate, as if the place itself were listening.

"Clara," Marley whispered, her voice thin. "What did you expect me to do with this?"

There was no answer, only the faint echo of her words folding back into the silence. But the weight of responsibility settled heavier on her shoulders. Clara had chosen not to destroy these journals. She had kept them safe, bricked behind a wall, left for someone to find. Left for Marley.

That thought alone made her chest tighten. Clara had trusted her—or trapped her.

SHE TURNED another page in Lydia's journal and paused.

"Joan warns that to read too much is to carry too much. Memory is a burden if not shared. To keep the circle unbroken, another must know. Alone is a dangerous word."

Marley's fingers trembled as she traced the line. Alone is a dangerous word.

She thought of Damien in the café, his words circling in her head: *Roots grow whether you stir them or not.* He had been right, though she hated to admit it. Already the roots were winding through her days, binding her nights. And alone, they threatened to strangle.

Could she trust him with this? Could she trust anyone?

Professor Ashcroft's face rose in her memory, sharp-eyed, lips curved in warning: *Do not stir the roots.* His suspicion had been real, his gaze heavy with the kind of knowledge that wanted to keep itself locked in shadows. He would not be an ally.

But Damien? His presence carried its own weight, his grief something she recognized, even if unspoken. He had seen Clara, spoken with her, remembered the way she looked at patterns others dismissed. And he was already digging into the past—into the very women whose names now filled Marley's shop.

The choice pressed against her: to remain silent, clutching the journals like contraband, or to share the burden before it consumed her.

Alone is a dangerous word.

. . .

THE FLAME DIPPED LOWER, shadows stretching across the shelves. Marley rubbed her temples, exhaustion pulling at her bones, yet she couldn't let go of the thought of that bricked window. It was more than an architectural oddity; it was a message.

Windows were meant to open. To illuminate. To reveal.

To brick one was to declare that what lay inside should never be seen again.

But Clara hadn't destroyed the room. She had left it intact.

Which meant she wanted Marley to decide whether the window stayed sealed—or whether light was allowed back in.

Marley pushed away from the counter, pacing the length of the shop. Her footsteps echoed faintly. She imagined the voices of the women layered in the walls, urging her forward, warning her back. Each name she had read felt like a presence now, following her in the silence.

Eliza. Hannah. Lydia. Joan.

She whispered them aloud as if reciting a litany. The air seemed to thicken, the candle's flame flaring briefly as though in answer.

"God," she muttered, dragging a hand through her hair. "I'm talking to shadows."

Yet the weight remained. The journals had called her. The sealed window had judged her. And the fog outside pressed closer against the glass as though waiting for her decision.

. . .

S HE BLEW OUT THE CANDLE. The darkness settled heavy, relieved only by the faint glow of the streetlamps outside. For a long moment, she stood there in the stillness, letting the silence close around her.

Her aunt's voice, in memory, seemed to echo faintly: *You'll know when it's time, Marley.*

The bricked window was a wall. But it was also a choice.

Tomorrow, she would decide. Tomorrow, she would choose whether to remain a keeper of shadows—or a breaker of them.

Tonight, she gathered the journals back into the sealed room, careful with each, as if she were laying bones back to rest. She locked the shelf again, the click sharp in the silence, the key cool and heavy in her hand.

Upstairs, she lay awake beneath the quilt, fog pressing against the glass, the women's voices stirring at the edges of her dreams.

Brookwood's roots were moving. And Marley knew she could not keep them buried forever.

5

THE RECIPE BOOK

The journal was thicker than the others, its leather binding cracked and mottled with age. Marley had noticed it before, tucked beneath Lydia Sparrow's box in the locked room, but she hadn't dared to lift it until now. It looked less like a ledger and more like something that had been meant to last—a book created to endure handling, weather, and time itself.

She carried it upstairs to the apartment above the shop, the candlelight bouncing across its scarred surface. The leather felt soft beneath her fingertips, but there was a density to it, a weight that seemed disproportionate to the size. She laid it gently on the kitchen table, poured herself tea, and only then dared to untie the fraying ribbon that kept it shut.

The first page held a single word in bold, elegant script:

Recipes.

But this was no cookbook. The first entry was not about bread or stews but tinctures, teas, and salves. *Chamomile infusion for sleep,* written in a precise hand, followed by notes in the margin: *dosage matters; too much and the dreams are no longer gentle.*

Marley turned the page. Each one contained a similar mixture of practical instructions and cryptic commentary.

Rosemary oil for memory—burn on fog nights. Strengthens recall. Beware of lingering voices.

Comfrey poultice for broken bones—apply with prayer. Bones heal, but they remember.

The notes unsettled her more than she wanted to admit. These were not household tips; they were incantations hidden within recipes. The language threaded between botany and ritual, straddling the line between science and something older.

She leaned back in her chair, sipping her tea, and let the pages flutter beneath her hand. Doodles of leaves and stems curled into the margins, sometimes labeled with Latin names, sometimes with phrases she didn't recognize. And then, written with striking frequency, one name appeared.

Aurelia.

It surfaced in the margins like a refrain: *Aurelia says the bark must steep longer. Aurelia warns not to harvest under waning moon. Aurelia teaches that memory binds itself to scent.*

The repetition made Marley's breath catch. Aurelia wasn't mentioned in the other journals, at least not yet. Was she the Green Healer Clara had told her about in childhood? The woman of legend who had saved Brookwood with her remedies, her presence lingering in the town's whispers?

The thought stirred something in Marley, both wonder and unease.

She returned to the first recipe and read carefully: a calming salve made of lavender, chamomile, beeswax, and a few drops of rosemary oil. The notes were precise: *Best for restless children. Rub gently into the temples. Works even when memories crowd too close.*

Marley glanced toward the shelves in her aunt's kitchen. Clara had left jars of dried herbs, beeswax blocks, small bottles of oil. She could almost hear her aunt's voice—steady, certain, urging her to try.

Her pulse quickened. It was reckless. Foolish, even. But the urge to test it pressed against her like the fog pressing at the window.

She gathered the ingredients one by one. The chamomile still smelled faintly sweet; the lavender had grown brittle but strong. She melted the beeswax, stirred in the herbs and oil, and poured the mixture into a small tin she found in the cupboard.

When it cooled, she dipped her fingers into the salve. Its texture was smooth, its scent calming yet sharp.

She rubbed a little onto her temples, closing her eyes.

At first, nothing happened. Only the familiar smell of lavender and chamomile, the comfort of warmth. She almost laughed at herself. But then—

The room shifted.

The air thickened, her chest tightening as though she'd stepped into water. A memory surged, sudden and vivid, not just remembered but relived.

She was six years old again, sitting on Clara's lap in the bookshop, her head tucked beneath her aunt's chin. The fog outside was so dense she couldn't see the street, and she had cried, frightened of the way the world disappeared. Clara had taken a small tin from the counter, rubbed salve gently into her temples, and whispered, *"Breathe, Marley. The fog can't take you if you remember who you are."*

Marley gasped, opening her eyes. The apartment blurred, the candle flame trembling, her heart pounding against her ribs. The memory receded, leaving her breathless, trembling, both comforted and unsettled.

The salve had unlocked something. Not just memory—presence. It was as if Clara had reached across years to touch her again.

And beneath that presence, a whisper lingered. One word:

Aurelia.

THE MEMORY LINGERED LIKE AN AFTERTASTE, bittersweet and impossible to shake. Marley pressed her palms flat against the kitchen table, trying to steady her breath. The calming salve sat in its small tin beside her, ordinary in appearance yet heavy with what it had just revealed.

Clara had always told stories about the Green Healer, about women who carried knowledge the town chose to forget. But now Marley felt that the stories weren't just tales meant to comfort a child. They were echoes of something real. Something passed down.

She turned the pages of the recipe book with newfound urgency. The candlelight caught the strokes of ink, illuminating entries that grew stranger as she read.

"Ash of yew bark, ground fine, placed beneath the pillow of the grieving. Dreams soften; voices return with gentleness. Do not attempt on new moon."

"Sea fennel tea for fever. Effective only if gathered at the tide's highest reach. Aurelia warns against cutting roots, for the plant resents its severing."

"Juniper smoke to clear the air. Three turns of the sprig, east to west, to keep sickness at bay. Without the words, the smoke is only smoke."

Marley's pulse quickened. Each entry balanced uneasily

between instruction and invocation, medicine and magic. She could not tell where one ended and the other began.

In the margins, Aurelia's name appeared again and again. Sometimes instructive—*Aurelia warns, Aurelia insists, Aurelia corrects.* Sometimes reverent—*Aurelia remembers what the others forget.* At times, almost cryptic: *Aurelia carries the green flame. She alone hears what the fog conceals.*

Marley sat back, the words blurring. Who had written these entries? Was Aurelia the author, or the teacher behind the pen? And why did her name feel both familiar and foreign, as though Marley had whispered it once long ago and forgotten until now?

Her hand hovered over another recipe, curiosity battling unease.

"Infusion of lemon balm and mint, steeped beneath starlight. For clarity when decisions weigh heavy. To be taken with stillness, never haste."

Marley traced the line with her fingertip. Clarity. God knew she needed it. The locked room, the bricked window, the journals that revealed a secret history—all of it pressed on her, demanding choice.

She set water to boil, her movements deliberate, her breath shallow with anticipation. She gathered what she could find in Clara's cupboards: a jar of lemon balm leaves, their edges curled but still fragrant; dried mint that released a sharp, cool scent when crushed. She placed them in a ceramic cup, poured the water, and carried it to the window where the fog pressed thick as wool against the glass.

She waited until the steam curled upward, breathing in the herbal scent. Then she drank.

The taste was sharp, earthy with a bitter edge. She set the cup down, pressing her palms into her thighs as she waited. At first, nothing. Then—

A shift.

The room seemed to fall away, replaced by a sweep of coastline she hadn't seen since childhood. She stood on the cliffs above Brookwood, the sea roaring below, fog swirling like living smoke. A woman's figure emerged in the mist, tall, cloaked in green, her hair a pale shimmer that caught what little light filtered through the fog.

Marley tried to speak, but her voice failed. The woman lifted a hand, palm outward in both greeting and warning.

A single word drifted through the fog, carried on wind, distinct though no lips moved.

Aurelia.

The vision cracked, as sudden as it had come. Marley stumbled backward, her chair scraping across the floor, her chest heaving. The cup toppled, tea spilling across the table, seeping into the recipe book's leather cover before she could grab it. She cursed softly, blotting the page with her sleeve, her fingers trembling.

The image burned in her mind: the woman in green, the fog alive around her, the word Aurelia resonant as though it had been spoken into her very bones.

She sank into the chair again, her pulse racing.

Aurelia wasn't just a name scrawled in the margins. She wasn't a distant myth Clara had dressed up for bedtime stories. She was real—or had been. The Green Healer. The woman who had once walked Brookwood's fog-drenched streets, carrying knowledge others feared, recording her teachings in journals that the town later buried.

And somehow, through recipe and ritual, she was reaching across time.

Marley shivered. The calming salve had given her a memory. The infusion had given her a vision. If she tested another recipe, what might happen next?

She stared at the book, the ink glistening faintly where the tea had spilled, as though the pages themselves were alive. Every instinct told her to close it, to lock it back in the sealed room and walk away. But another voice, quieter yet insistent, pressed against her ribs.

The circle unbroken. The window bricked. Another must know.

Marley pressed her hands to her face, fighting the urge to weep. She had not asked for this inheritance. Yet it was hers. Clara had made sure of it.

When she lowered her hands, her eyes fell once more on Aurelia's name.

And for the first time, Marley wondered if the Green Healer's story had never ended at all.

MARLEY SAT at the table long after the tea had cooled and the candle had burned low, her mind circling the vision of the woman in the fog. Aurelia. The name still pulsed in her ears like a bell struck long after its sound should have faded.

She rubbed her temples, the calming salve's faint scent still clinging to her skin. Two recipes—two responses. A memory, then a vision. Both too vivid to dismiss as coincidence, both carrying the weight of intent. These weren't harmless household remedies. They were doorways.

And each doorway opened into something that didn't want to stay in the past.

Marley turned the thick leather-bound recipe book again, staring at the page that had soaked in the tea. The ink had bled slightly, darkening into a blot that obscured one of the botanical drawings. She brushed her fingers across it, half afraid of what might emerge. Nothing moved, but the sense of danger settled deeper into her bones.

What if every recipe in this book wasn't simply medicinal but a kind of key? Each mixture, each infusion, capable of unlocking not just memories but presences—echoes, voices, fragments of a history Brookwood had tried to bury?

Her rational mind fought to regain ground. It could be suggestion, she told herself. The power of belief. She was grieving, raw, vulnerable. Clara's death had left her more open to imagination. That was all.

Yet the memory of being six years old in Clara's lap was sharper than any dream she had ever had. And the vision of the green-cloaked woman on the cliffs was unlike anything grief alone could conjure.

The truth pressed against her, undeniable: she was stirring things that had been sealed for a reason.

Marley closed the book firmly, her hands trembling. She paced the apartment, trying to walk off the energy buzzing through her body. Her reflection in the window startled her —the fog pressed so close to the glass that her outline looked ghostly, her face pale and blurred. For a moment, she almost thought she saw another figure standing beside her, a faint silhouette that vanished when she blinked.

Her stomach turned. She gripped the edge of the counter until her knuckles whitened.

She couldn't keep testing recipes. Not like this. The book wasn't just an heirloom; it was a responsibility, maybe even a warning. Clara had kept it hidden, after all. She hadn't left it on a shelf for anyone to find. She'd locked it in a bricked room, sealed away from curious hands.

And now Marley had cracked it open, just as Professor Ashcroft had warned against. *Do not stir the roots.* His voice, sharp and clinical, echoed in her mind. She hated the man's suspicion, but for the first time she understood his fear.

Still, she couldn't unlearn what she had seen. The

recipes held truths—about Clara, about Brookwood, about Aurelia. If she closed the book forever, she'd be complicit in burying those truths again. And that thought was unbearable.

The candle sputtered, sending shadows leaping across the walls. Marley sank back into her chair, pulling the book toward her once more. She didn't open it, not yet. Instead she rested her hand on its cover, as though steadying herself on a living creature.

"What do you want from me?" she whispered, though whether she meant Clara, Aurelia, or the book itself, she couldn't say.

The silence that followed was not empty. It was thick, waiting.

A knock echoed faintly from below.

Marley froze. The shop was closed, the lights extinguished. The knock came again—three firm raps against the front door. Her breath caught in her throat. She blew out the candle instinctively, plunging the room into darkness.

The knock didn't come a third time.

She stood in the silence, listening hard, heart hammering. No footsteps retreated down Main Street. No creak of carriage wheels, no hum of voices. Only the fog, pressing close, as if it too listened.

Marley sank back into her chair, her skin crawling. She tried to steady her breath, but the unease lingered. Whoever had knocked knew she was here—or had simply wanted to remind her that the shop, and everything inside it, wasn't as private as she wished.

She lit the candle again, her hand shaking as the flame caught. Its glow spilled across the recipe book, and in that fragile light she saw it—the faintest impression on the cover, one she hadn't noticed before. Not words, but a symbol pressed into the leather: a spiral of leaves curling inward, nearly worn smooth with time.

Her pulse quickened. She had seen this symbol before, embroidered on the cloth in Hannah Gearhart's box in the locked room. It was the mark of the circle.

Her aunt had left her more than a shop. She had left her the circle's legacy—and maybe its unfinished work.

Marley touched the symbol, her breath unsteady.

And then, faint as fog, she heard it. A whisper, low but distinct, curling through the room like smoke.

Aurelia.

The candle flickered violently. Marley jerked back, heart racing. The voice hadn't been memory or vision this time. It had been here, in the room, alive in the present.

Her hands clenched into fists.

Aurelia's presence wasn't confined to the past.

She was here.

6

TEA LEAVES AND GHOST WHISPERS

The fog had thinned into a soft drizzle by morning, dampening Brookwood's streets and leaving the salt smell of the ocean sharp in the air. Marley stepped carefully along the sidewalk, her satchel pressing against her hip, the recipe book tucked inside. Every step carried both anticipation and unease. She wasn't sure if what she was about to do was reckless or necessary.

Hazel Merrow's metaphysical shop sat three doors down from the bakery, its painted sign—*Moon & Morrow*—swinging faintly in the mist. The shop had always been a place of comfort for Marley as a child: the scent of beeswax and herbs, the warm glow spilling through its windows. Now, though, she approached it with the gravity of someone carrying a secret she wasn't certain she should share.

The bell above the door chimed as she stepped inside. The warmth hit her immediately—spice, citrus peel, dried lavender, and something deeper, resinous, that spoke of hidden earth. Shelves lined the walls, crowded with candles in glass jars, bundles of dried herbs, and tins of loose-leaf teas labeled in Hazel's careful handwriting. A kettle hissed quietly from behind the counter.

Hazel herself appeared from the back room, her hair pinned neatly, her apron smudged with wax. She smiled when she saw Marley, though her eyes held the same watchfulness they had in the bookshop days before.

"Marley Taylor," she said, her voice warm but grounded. "Twice in one week. Either Brookwood's fog has turned you restless, or you've come looking for something you can't name."

Marley managed a faint smile, though her hands tightened on the strap of her satchel. "Maybe both."

Hazel studied her for a moment, then gestured to a small round table near the window. "Sit. The kettle's almost ready. You can tell me what's on your mind."

Marley lowered herself into the chair, the satchel heavy in her lap. She hesitated, then pulled the recipe book free and set it gently on the table. Hazel's eyes flicked to it immediately, her expression sharpening.

"That belonged to Clara," Hazel said softly, not a question.

"Yes." Marley's throat tightened. "I've been reading it. Some of the recipes—they don't feel like recipes. They feel... older. Like they were written for more than healing a cough or soothing a fever."

Hazel's brows arched slightly, though she said nothing. Marley opened the book, flipping to a page where a blend of herbs was listed in a neat hand: *bay leaf, mugwort, fennel, rosemary*. In the margin, Aurelia's name appeared again: *Aurelia warns this blend should not be burned lightly. It calls what lingers.*

Marley slid the book toward Hazel. "What do you make of this?"

Hazel leaned closer, adjusting her spectacles. She traced the ink with a fingertip, not touching the page but hovering just above it, as if reverence demanded distance. Her lips moved silently as she read, her expression unreadable.

Finally, she looked up. "This isn't a recipe for tea, though some of the ingredients can be steeped. It's protective. Very old. Older than Clara. Likely passed down hand to hand, quietly, outside the records the men kept."

Marley's chest tightened. "Protective? Against what?"

Hazel's gaze lingered on her, heavy with meaning. "Against what you can't see. Against what presses close when the fog grows too thick. Brookwood has always been a place where the veil thins, Marley. Your aunt knew that. And whoever wrote this—Aurelia, perhaps—knew it too."

The name Aurelia on Hazel's lips sent a shiver down Marley's spine. "You know that name?"

Hazel hesitated. "I've heard it. A whisper here, a scrap there. Clara never spoke of her directly, but she circled around her. She believed some women carried gifts that others wanted forgotten. Aurelia was one of them."

Marley's fingers tightened on the edge of the book. The truth pressed closer, heavier, but so did the fear. She leaned back in her chair, the drizzle outside streaking the windowpane, the air inside thick with the scent of dried herbs.

Hazel closed the book gently, resting her palm atop it. "Whatever you've begun, Marley, you need to be careful. Knowledge like this isn't meant to be handled casually. It binds. It remembers who opens it."

Marley swallowed hard. "I already know that," she whispered.

Hazel studied her, then nodded slowly, as though Marley had confirmed something she had suspected all along. She rose, poured steaming water over a handful of chamomile blossoms, and set the cup before Marley.

"Drink," Hazel said. "And decide what you're willing to carry."

Marley wrapped her hands around the mug, the heat seeping into her skin. She knew Hazel was right. The recipes weren't just words on paper. They were threads, and once pulled, the whole fabric shifted.

And now she had no choice but to follow where it led.

Hazel didn't touch the recipe book again, not at first. She let it sit between them, its leather binding absorbing the lamplight like something alive. Marley could feel the weight of it even from her side of the table, as if the book itself waited for Hazel's judgment.

Hazel's hands moved instead to the mug of tea she had poured herself. She sipped once, her eyes distant, as though she were tasting not the chamomile but the silence that lay behind Marley's question. When she finally spoke, her voice was quieter, layered with something older than conversation.

"Bay leaf, mugwort, fennel, rosemary," Hazel repeated. "Each of them has a story. Each of them carries more than a taste or a smell." She glanced toward Marley, gauging her reaction. "Bay is for warding. It keeps unwanted eyes from crossing thresholds. Mugwort opens dreams—and closes them when they're too sharp. Fennel cleanses. Rosemary binds memory."

She leaned back, her braid slipping over her shoulder, her gaze steady. "This isn't a blend meant for comfort. It's meant for keeping something at bay. Not sickness, not fever, but what walks when it shouldn't."

Marley's stomach tightened. "You mean... ghosts?"

Hazel didn't answer immediately. She folded her hands, her thumb brushing across her knuckles in a slow rhythm. "Call them ghosts if you like. Others would call them whispers, shadows, the residue of memory too heavy to pass on. Brookwood has always had them. Especially in the fog."

The word *fog* seemed to thicken in the air between them. Marley's hand tightened around her cup. She thought of the salve that had brought her Clara's voice, of the tea that had conjured Aurelia on the cliffs. She thought of the bricked window in the sealed room, the journals heavy with names.

Hazel watched her closely, as if she could see the thoughts rising and falling in Marley's eyes. "This recipe is old. Very old. Older than Clara. Older than me. It was passed quietly, never written in the ledgers the town keeps. Women shared it when they trusted someone enough to bear the weight. That you've found it means Clara believed you were ready. Or at least, that she had no choice but to let you be ready."

Marley exhaled shakily. "Why me?"

Hazel smiled faintly, but it wasn't unkind. "That's the question every woman who came before you asked. Lydia Sparrow. Hannah Gearhart. Eliza Merrick. Joan Nye. None of them wanted the burden, not at first. But they carried it because someone had to. Because Brookwood has a way of demanding keepers."

The names struck Marley like stones, echoing from the boxes she had touched in the locked room. "You know about them," she said, her voice low.

Hazel inclined her head. "Pieces. Whispers. Stories my grandmother told me when she thought I was asleep. Women who were healers, midwives, watchers. The town dismissed them as eccentrics, but they knew things no one else dared to know. And when the men sealed the records, the women sealed their knowledge in other ways. In recipes. In rooms bricked shut. In journals hidden behind shelves."

Marley's pulse raced. "Aurelia," she whispered.

Hazel's eyes sharpened. "So you've seen her name."

"More than a name." Marley hesitated, then pressed on. "I think she was the Green Healer. The one Clara used to tell me about."

Hazel's expression shifted, shadowed by something Marley couldn't name. "That name— 'Green Healer'—was never meant as praise. It was meant as fear. But Aurelia... yes. I believe she was real. A teacher. A guardian. Maybe more. Every story I've ever heard places her at the edge of things—bridges, cliffs, fog. Always where the veil thins. Always watching."

The words curled through Marley, at once chilling and strangely comforting. She thought of the vision in the tea, the woman's hand raised in both greeting and warning. She thought of the whisper that had slipped into her room after the knock at the shop door.

Hazel leaned closer, her voice dropping. "What did the recipe give you, Marley?"

Marley swallowed. Her instinct was to protect the truth, to lock it away the way Clara had locked the journals. But Hazel's eyes, steady and unflinching, pressed for honesty.

"A memory," Marley admitted. "And... a vision. Not just imagination. Something sharper. I saw her. I saw Aurelia."

Hazel closed her eyes briefly, as if confirming something to herself. When she opened them, her gaze was heavier. "Then the book has chosen to answer you. That means its protections are no longer passive. They've recognized you."

Marley shivered. "Recognized me?"

Hazel nodded slowly. "The recipes aren't just instructions. They're bindings. When you use them, they open the door in both directions. They let you see—and they let what lingers see you."

The words rooted in Marley's chest, cold and undeniable. She pushed her chair back slightly, needing distance, needing air. "So I'm not imagining it. The whisper I heard last night—it wasn't just me."

"No." Hazel's voice was steady. "It was her. Or something that carries her echo."

Marley pressed her hands to her face, dread and awe tangling in her chest until she couldn't tell one from the other. "I don't know if I can do this."

"You don't get to decide that anymore," Hazel said softly, but firmly. "Clara left you the book. The room answered you. The recipes called you. The circle doesn't choose lightly, and it doesn't choose twice. Whether you want it or not, you are its keeper now."

Marley's throat ached, but she managed a whisper. "And if I fail?"

Hazel reached across the table, her hand resting briefly atop Marley's. "Then Brookwood remembers in its own way. But if you succeed—if you listen, if you learn—then the circle is unbroken. And Aurelia's voice will not go to silence."

Marley stared at the book, its cover scarred and waiting, Aurelia's name pulsing like a heartbeat across its pages. She felt both the weight of burden and the strange pull of belonging, two currents dragging her in opposite directions.

Her tea had gone cold. She lifted it anyway, sipping once, the taste bitter now, heavy with mugwort's shadow.

Hazel's words echoed: *They let you see—and they let what lingers see you.*

The thought made her shiver, but she didn't close the

book. She couldn't. The roots had been stirred, and the soil of Brookwood was shifting.

And Aurelia was no longer just a name.

MARLEY RETURNED to the bookshop with the drizzle clinging to her coat and Hazel's words echoing in her ears. *It binds. It remembers who opens it.* The protective blend still lingered in her senses, a sharp memory of herbs on her tongue and Hazel's steady gaze warning her not to mistake curiosity for safety.

The shop was quiet, the fog pressing hard against the windows. Marley moved through the front room on instinct, her hand brushing against the spines of books as if they might anchor her. She carried the recipe book upstairs to her aunt's old writing desk—a piece of furniture Clara had always treated like an altar. Its surface bore candle wax stains and scratches from years of use, the grain worn smooth where Clara's hands had rested countless times.

Marley set the book down gently, almost ceremonially. The leather cover caught the lamplight, the faint spiral symbol embossed on it barely visible but impossible to ignore. She traced the spiral with her fingertip, the motion steadying her, grounding her in something both foreign and familiar.

The desk creaked faintly beneath the weight of the book. Marley eased into Clara's chair, the old wood sighing under her. She remembered sitting here as a child while Clara wrote letters or tallied accounts, the smell of ink and wax lingering in the air. It felt strange now, as though Clara might step in at any moment and scold her for snooping.

She opened the recipe book to the page Hazel had studied, the protective blend scrawled in the center. The ink seemed darker than she remembered, the letters standing proud from the page. She leaned closer, brushing her hair from her face.

That was when she heard it.

A whisper.

Soft, like breath barely moving through the room. It carried no words at first—just the sound of someone present where no one should be. Marley froze, every muscle taut, her heart hammering in her chest.

"Who's there?" she whispered, her voice shaky.

The silence thickened, and for a moment she thought she'd imagined it. Then it came again, clearer this time, curling around her like fog through an open window.

Aurelia.

The name unfurled in the air, soft but insistent. Marley's breath caught. She whipped her head around, scanning the room. Nothing. Only the faint flicker of the lamp and the fog smearing the window.

She pressed her palms against the desk, steadying herself. "What do you want from me?"

The whisper shifted, almost like a sigh, and she thought —though she couldn't be sure—that she heard words layered beneath the name. Fragments. *Keep the circle. Do not let it break.*

Her skin prickled. The journals. The bricked window. Hazel's warnings. It all converged here, at this desk, in this moment. She wasn't only reading history—she was inside of it now.

Marley closed the book quickly, her hands shaking. The whisper faded with the motion, leaving only the heavy silence of the room. She sat there in the dim light, her pulse loud in her ears, waiting for it to return. It didn't.

Still, the weight of presence remained.

She stared at the leather cover, her reflection faint in its sheen. This was no longer a question of curiosity or folklore. Aurelia was here. Not just in the pages, not just in the fog of memory, but here, in this room, calling to her.

And Marley realized with a shiver that whether she wanted it or not, she had answered.

7

COVERED IN TIME

The fog thinned by afternoon, revealing slivers of blue sky, though the air still smelled of rain-soaked wood and brine. Marley was shelving books in the shop when the bell above the door jingled. She looked up expecting Hazel, but it was Damien Hawthorne.

He stood in the doorway with that stillness he carried like a cloak, a quiet command of space. His hair was damp, his coat unbuttoned, and there was something in his eyes—intent, though not unkind.

"You're free?" he asked, his voice even but low.

Marley hesitated, setting down the volume in her hands. "Free enough. Why?"

"I want to show you something."

Her pulse quickened. A week ago she would have declined, too wary of him, of herself, of the way the town seemed to shift under her feet. But after Hazel's warnings and the whisper at Clara's desk, she felt that strange tether tugging her again—toward the fog, toward the circle of names, toward whatever Damien was about to reveal.

"Where?" she asked.

"The covered bridge," he said simply.

THE WALK TOOK them through the edge of town, where the pavement became cobblestones and finally gave way to dirt softened by rain. The bridge loomed ahead, a dark silhouette against the pale sky. Marley remembered it from childhood: weathered timbers, a roof that sagged slightly at the center, the sound of water rushing beneath. Clara had once told her the bridge was older than the town itself, rebuilt but never replaced, its foundations sunk deep into soil that remembered more than people ever could.

Up close, the bridge felt alive. The timbers creaked with each shift of wind, and the scent of damp wood and moss filled the air. Damien led her inside, his footsteps echoing on the planks. The light dimmed beneath the roof, filtered through slats and cracks, casting long beams that striped the floor.

Marley trailed a hand along the railing, her palm brushing grooves worn by generations of travelers. "I haven't been here in years," she murmured.

"Most people avoid it now," Damien said. "They say it's unsafe. Too old. But that's not the reason."

He stopped near the center, where the planks creaked louder under their weight. He crouched, brushing aside a layer of moss on one of the beams. His fingers traced something etched into the wood.

Marley leaned closer. It wasn't a name or an initial carved by bored teenagers. It was a symbol. A spiral of leaves curling inward.

Her breath caught. She had seen it before—on the recipe book's cover, faint but undeniable. And on the cloth in Hannah Gearhart's box.

Damien glanced up at her, reading her expression. "You recognize it."

She nodded slowly. "It's in Clara's things. In... other places too."

He studied her, then returned his gaze to the carving. "I found this months ago while researching the bridge's history. Officially, there's nothing unusual—just dates of repairs, records of tolls. But the wood tells another story. The engravings are too deliberate to be idle marks. Someone wanted this remembered."

Marley traced the spiral with her fingertip. The grooves were shallow but precise, softened by time yet still clear. She felt a faint hum in her skin as she touched it, like the vibration of a plucked string.

"The circle," she whispered.

Damien raised an eyebrow. "So you know of it."

Marley hesitated. She wasn't ready to spill everything—the sealed room, the journals, Aurelia's name whispered in her ear. But she couldn't lie, not when the evidence stood carved into the bridge itself.

"I know... pieces," she said carefully. "Enough to know it matters."

He leaned back, his expression unreadable. "Brookwood's history isn't in the archives. It's here. In what people tried to erase but couldn't. The bridge remembers. The lighthouse remembers. And now"—his eyes flicked to her—"so do you."

Marley swallowed hard. The wind whistled through a crack in the roof, sending a shiver through her. She wanted to ask him what he knew of Aurelia, what he suspected of Clara, but the words tangled on her tongue.

Instead, she whispered, almost to herself, "What if remembering is dangerous?"

Damien's gaze didn't waver. "Then it's exactly what we need."

As they left the bridge, the water below roared louder, swollen from the recent rains. The fog had begun to gather again, curling over the surface like smoke. Marley lingered at the edge, her hand resting on the damp railing, the spiral etched into her mind.

They walked back in silence until the path split— Damien toward the lighthouse road, Marley toward the bookshop. He paused, nodding once. "Keep looking," he said. "The past doesn't hide without reason."

She watched him walk away, his figure fading into the mist.

That was when she heard it.

Her name.

Soft, drawn out, carried on the water's breath.

"Marley..."

She spun, scanning the fog. No one stood near the bridge. The path behind her was empty. The sound had risen from below, from the rushing water itself.

Her heart pounded. She stepped back, clutching her satchel, the fog curling closer.

There was no second call. Only the roar of the river, relentless and unbending, as though it had swallowed the voice whole.

Marley turned and walked quickly back toward town, the symbol carved into the bridge burning in her memory, the whisper of her name clinging to the air like a promise— or a warning.

· · ·

THE SPIRAL CARVED into the beam held Marley's attention like a hook buried deep. She could not stop tracing it, her fingertip circling its grooves, though each touch made her skin prickle as if the wood itself remembered her aunt—or someone older still.

Damien crouched nearby, silent, his gaze fixed not just on the symbol but on her. He seemed to study her reaction as carefully as the engraving itself.

"You've seen it before," he said finally. It wasn't a question.

Marley kept her hand on the wood a moment longer before pulling it back, rubbing her fingers against her palm to chase off the tremor. "In passing," she said, too quickly.

Damien tilted his head slightly, as if weighing her words. "Most people dismiss it as graffiti. They think it's some teenager's idle carving from fifty years ago. But it isn't. The spiral shows up across Brookwood—in places people don't think to look."

He reached into his coat pocket and pulled out a folded sheet of paper. He opened it carefully, the creases deep, the ink faint but legible. It was a rubbing—black charcoal pressed against thin paper, the spiral emerging bold and dark.

"This one's from the lighthouse doorframe," he explained. "Buried under layers of paint. I found it last winter."

Marley felt her chest tighten. The lighthouse. The journals had mentioned gatherings there. *We meet again under the lighthouse.* The memory of Lydia Sparrow's words stirred like an echo.

Damien tucked the paper back into his coat. "The same symbols on the old foundation stones at the north end of town. And in the cemetery, though worn so thin you'd miss it unless you knew where to look. It isn't random. It meant something. Still does."

Marley swallowed, torn between fear and the urge to spill everything she knew. She could almost hear Hazel's voice in her ear: *Knowledge like this isn't meant to be handled casually. It binds.* If she told Damien about the sealed room, about Aurelia's name whispering from her aunt's desk, would that make the binding stronger—or would it help her share the weight?

She forced her voice steady. "You've been looking for it."

"Yes." His gaze drifted back to the carving. "For years. Ever since I realized the official records didn't add up. Brookwood's history is full of gaps—whole chapters cut away, women's names disappearing overnight. But the spiral keeps surfacing. Like a thread someone tried to snip but couldn't."

His voice carried a quiet conviction, not boastful but driven. "I think the symbol belonged to a circle. A group who kept knowledge the town didn't want recorded. Remedies. Rituals. Maybe more."

Marley felt her stomach clench. The circle. He was naming it aloud, though without the certainty of someone who had held their journals in her hands.

"And you think Clara knew?" she asked carefully.

Damien's eyes flicked to hers. "Everyone knew Clara saw more than she said. But I think she protected something. Maybe the last piece of the circle. Maybe its memory. That shop of hers wasn't just a place for books."

The truth of it pressed against Marley with unbearable clarity. He was close—so close—yet still circling around the edges. She could end his guessing in an instant. Tell him about the key, the bricked window, the recipe book that whispered her name. He would believe her; she knew it. He had already chosen to believe in the spiral.

But a part of her recoiled. Hazel's warning echoed: *The recipes aren't just instructions. They let you see—and they let what lingers see you.* If she spoke the words, would she be inviting Aurelia closer? Or binding Damien to the same whisper that had found her?

She turned back to the symbol, buying herself time. The wood smelled of damp and moss. She leaned closer, almost whispering. "It feels old."

Damien nodded. "The first bridge was built in 1842. This beam survived the fire that took half the town thirty years later. When they rebuilt, they used what they could salvage. Which means this carving predates the fire."

Marley's fingers hovered above the spiral again, her pulse quickening. Pre-1890s. The same decade stamped into the journals. The same years Aurelia's name appeared again and again.

Damien's voice softened, more thoughtful now. "You know, most people think history is written in books, in records. But it isn't. It's carved in beams, hidden in ledgers, sealed in walls. The past survives where it's least expected. Brookwood is covered in time, Marley. Layer upon layer. And sometimes the older layers bleed through."

The words struck her with uncanny force. Covered in time. That was exactly how she felt—like she was walking through layers of someone else's life, their voices seeping into hers.

Her throat felt dry, but she managed to say, "And if some layers weren't meant to resurface?"

Damien's gaze lingered on her, his expression unreadable. "Then maybe they're the very ones we need most."

The silence between them deepened. Marley's pulse

thundered, her secret pressing against her ribs like a stone she could neither carry nor drop.

Finally, she looked away. "You think this symbol is a key."

"I think it's a map," Damien corrected. "Not to a place, but to memory. To a story Brookwood hasn't finished telling."

Marley drew in a slow breath, the damp air thick with river scent. She wanted to trust him. She wanted to unburden herself. But something held her back—an instinct, a whisper of Aurelia's name threading through her mind.

Not yet.

"Maybe," she said instead, forcing her voice light. "Or maybe it's just a spiral someone thought looked nice."

Damien's mouth tugged faintly, though not in amusement. "You don't believe that."

She didn't answer.

The water roared beneath the bridge, steady, relentless. The spiral lay between them, silent but insistent, carved into wood that had endured fire and storm. Marley turned away first, her gaze fixed on the fog curling through the beams.

And though she kept her silence, she knew Damien was right. The spiral was a thread. And she was already holding it.

THE FOG WAS thickening by the time Damien and Marley left the bridge. The mist rolled off the water in shifting veils, coiling through the timbers like smoke escaping from an unseen fire. Damien walked a few paces ahead, his stride sure despite the uneven planks, while Marley lingered, her eyes still drawn to the spiral etched into the beam.

At the far end of the bridge, the path split in two directions—toward the lighthouse and the headland, or back into town. Damien paused at the crossroads, his coat brushing damp against his frame. For a long moment, he looked as though he wanted to say more, but the words stayed caught somewhere between them.

"You should go back," he said finally. His voice carried the edge of caution, though his eyes softened when they met hers. "The fog's turning heavier. It's not a night to walk alone."

Marley managed a small nod, though her heart beat faster at the quiet gravity in his tone. "And you?"

"I'll take the lighthouse road." He gave a faint, almost weary smile. "Old habits."

There was nothing left to say. He inclined his head, then turned away, his figure swallowed quickly by the fog as if it had been waiting for him. Marley stood still, her hand brushing the strap of her satchel, unwilling to move just yet.

The river below thundered with restless water, swollen from the rain. She stepped closer to the railing, peering down. The surface frothed and swirled, the current carrying fragments of branches and leaves downstream. The sound should have been enough to drown all else, but it wasn't.

Because she heard it.

Her name.

"Marley..."

The voice was soft, almost tender, but it came from nowhere she could place. Not from the path, not from behind her. It rose from the river itself, as though the water carried it.

She jerked back from the railing, her breath catching. "Who's there?" Her voice sounded thin against the roar of the current.

Silence answered her. Then, just as she steadied herself, it came again—clearer this time, unmistakable.

"Marley."

She spun, scanning the fog. The bridge behind her was empty. Damien was gone, too far now to have spoken. The path into town stretched desolate. Only the fog breathed, curling thick around her ankles, climbing higher as though trying to pull her into its folds.

Her hands shook. She pressed them hard against the railing to ground herself, to remind her of the wood beneath her palms, the tangible world still here.

But the whisper clung, curling through her mind. It wasn't Clara's voice—too unfamiliar, too old. Yet it carried a strange resonance, like the voices she had heard when the recipes stirred. A voice shaped not by distance, but by time.

Her pulse hammered in her ears. She forced her feet forward, stumbling across the last few planks of the bridge until she reached solid ground again. The whisper faded with each step, but her name still seemed to hang in the fog behind her, as if the river itself had spoken and would do so again.

By the time she reached Main Street, her coat damp and her heart racing, she knew two things with aching clarity.

The spiral carved into the bridge wasn't decoration. It was a marker. A reminder.

And whatever called her name from the water knew her now.

8

A LIGHT IN THE LIGHTHOUSE

The sea wind was sharper on the headland, carrying with it the salt of the tide and the cry of gulls circling above. Marley followed Damien along the narrow trail, her coat tugged by gusts that seemed determined to push her back toward town. Ahead, the lighthouse rose against the gray sky—a weathered tower of whitewashed stone, its beacon glass clouded by salt and time.

Damien walked with the steady pace of someone who knew the way blindfolded. He carried no umbrella, no hesitation. Marley had the sense he belonged here, though not because of the town's acceptance—Brookwood still looked at him with the same wary suspicion it gave her. His belonging came from something deeper, as though the wind itself leaned around him rather than through him.

When they reached the base of the lighthouse, Damien slowed, his hand brushing the iron railing as though greeting an old companion. "I come here when the rest of the town is too much," he said quietly, his gaze lifting toward the beacon above. "The sea drowns out the noise."

Marley tilted her head, studying him. He rarely spoke unguarded. "You mean the gossip?"

His mouth curved faintly, though not with humor. "That. And memory." He leaned against the railing, his eyes on the waves. "I wasn't always here. I came after..." His voice trailed, caught on the edge of something.

She waited.

After a long pause, he drew a slow breath. "My wife. Jackie. She died three years ago. Car accident. We were supposed to be leaving the city for a new start—she wanted quieter streets, a slower life. She didn't get to see it. I came here anyway, though at first I didn't know why. Brookwood was supposed to be temporary. It still feels temporary some days. But the lighthouse—" He gestured toward the tower. "It makes sense of things. Maybe not the way I want. But enough."

The rawness of his voice surprised her, quiet though it was. Damien carried himself with such restraint, but here, at the edge of sea and sky, the mask cracked. Marley felt the pang of recognition—the hollow ache of loss, familiar in its weight.

"I'm sorry," she said softly.

His eyes flicked to hers, searching, then nodding once. "You lost someone too. I can see it."

Marley hesitated, then nodded. "My aunt. Clara. She raised me more than my parents did. Losing her feels like losing a piece of the ground under my feet."

Damien's gaze held hers. "Then maybe that's why we're here. The lighthouse doesn't stand because it avoids storms. It stands because it was built to endure them."

The words lingered between them, carried by the wind. Marley felt both comforted and unsettled.

He pushed the door open and gestured for her to follow.

The hinges groaned, the smell of salt and oil rushing out to greet them. Inside, the spiral staircase wound upward, narrow and steep, its iron steps slick with damp. Marley followed, her hand gripping the railing, the sound of their footsteps echoing up the stone walls.

At the top, the lantern room spread wide, the glass panes mottled with salt spray. The great lamp stood silent for now, its mechanism resting until night. Marley moved toward the outer ledge, the sea stretching vast and restless in every direction.

That was when she noticed it—something wedged between two bricks near the base of the window. A glint of glass, half-hidden.

"Damien," she called softly.

He turned, watching as she knelt. Her fingers dug carefully around the edges, pulling free a small glass bottle, dusted with salt. Inside, curled tight, was a folded scrap of paper.

Marley's heart raced. She uncorked the bottle, sliding the paper out with delicate care. The fold was brittle, the ink faint, but a map revealed itself—sketched lines of Brookwood's coast, the river, the bridge. And marked in the margin, that same spiral symbol.

Her breath caught.

Damien crouched beside her, his brow furrowing. "You've seen that before."

She nodded slowly, unable to find words.

The spiral stared back at her from the map like a key, waiting to be turned.

THE MAP WAS NO LARGER than a handbill, its edges brittle, its ink faded to a sepia brown that spoke of decades—if not centuries—spent hidden away. Marley smoothed it on the floorboards of the lantern room, the great lamp looming above her like an unblinking eye. The sea thundered far below, muffled by the thick stone walls.

Damien crouched beside her, his brow furrowed in thought. "Look here," he murmured, tracing one finger along the jagged coastline sketched in careful lines. "It's Brookwood, but it's not the Brookwood we know. The headland's drawn longer, the river wider. The bridge isn't marked at all."

Marley leaned closer, her breath catching at the spiral symbol inked near the cliffs, exactly where the lighthouse now stood. Another spiral, smaller, hovered by the river bend just north of town.

Her skin prickled. "It's the same mark," she whispered.

Damien's eyes flicked to hers. "The spiral." His tone carried both certainty and weight. "Whoever drew this wanted us to see it."

Marley's hands trembled as she traced the line of the river. The placement wasn't random; it mirrored the locations whispered in the journals—places where the women gathered, where the circle had met. The lighthouse. The river. The bridge. Each marked, each tied by the spiral.

She swallowed hard, the urge to tell him surging. To confess the truth of the sealed room, the recipe book that whispered, the journal pages heavy with Aurelia's name. He would understand. He was already piecing it together, his research circling the same truths. Together, maybe they could unlock it.

But Hazel's warning pressed sharp against her ribs: *They let you see—and they let what lingers see you.* Sharing the burden might not lessen it. It might widen it.

Damien studied her, his gaze narrowing slightly. "You know something."

The words struck like an accusation, though his voice was calm. Marley forced herself to keep her expression neutral, though she felt the blood rise in her cheeks.

"I've... seen the symbol before," she admitted cautiously. "In Clara's things."

His brow furrowed deeper. "What things?"

Marley hesitated, choosing each word with care. "Papers. Notes. She kept records most people would have thrown away. Old stories, fragments. She... she believed the past mattered more than the town liked to admit."

Damien's eyes didn't leave hers, but his shoulders eased, just slightly. "That sounds like Clara." He leaned back on his heels, looking again at the map. "If she had pieces, and this —" He tapped the spiral at the lighthouse with his finger. "—then she was keeping the same watch the women before her did."

Marley's pulse jumped. "The women before her?"

He glanced at her, then nodded toward the spiral. "You've read the plaques in town. The history's all men—founders, fishermen, builders. But there were women too, ones who don't make it into the records. Midwives, herbalists, healers. I've found their names buried in footnotes, in letters. Always circling at the edges, never at the center. I think the spirals are theirs. Their map, their mark."

Her chest tightened. *Eliza Merrick. Hannah Gearhart. Lydia Sparrow. Joan Nye.* The names echoed in her mind. He was closer to the truth than he knew.

Marley pressed her hand against the map, feeling the rough texture of the paper beneath her palm. "So what does it mean?" she asked softly.

Damien's voice dropped, almost reverent. "It means Brookwood was never just a fishing town. It was something more. Something built on layers the council and the historians chose to bury. And someone—maybe Aurelia, maybe another—left this as proof."

The name struck her like a bell, though she hadn't spoken it aloud. She looked up sharply, but Damien's gaze was fixed on the spiral, unaware of the shiver that rippled through her.

Aurelia. The whisper at Clara's desk. The figure on the cliffs. The voice from the river. Always there, waiting.

Marley curled her fingers into a fist against the map. She wanted to tell him, to let the truth spill out, to share the terror and awe that pressed against her ribs. But something inside held her still. Once spoken, the truth would bind them both, and she wasn't sure she had the right to drag him into Aurelia's shadow.

Instead, she forced a breath and said, "It doesn't explain why it was hidden."

Damien's mouth tightened. "Secrets always outlive the reasons they were born. Maybe the spiral meant protection. Maybe defiance. Maybe warning. But it was hidden because someone feared what it could reveal."

Marley looked down at the spiral again, her hand hovering over the ink. She thought of the whisper from the river, her name carried on water. Feared, or invited? The line between the two felt thinner each day.

She folded the map carefully, sliding it back into the bottle. "Then the question isn't what it meant back then," she said quietly. "It's what it wants from us now."

Damien met her gaze, and for the first time, she saw uncertainty flicker in his steady composure.

The great lamp above them groaned as though stirred by unseen weight. The sea wind howled against the glass. And Marley knew the spiral was no longer just a mark in the past.

It was alive in the present, waiting for them to follow.

THE BOTTLE with its brittle map stayed in Marley's satchel, heavier than glass and paper had a right to be. She had walked back from the lighthouse with Damien, but when they reached the fork in the road, she chose silence. He had shared his grief with her, opened a door she hadn't expected him to open, yet she couldn't bring herself to reveal the full truth about the symbol, the journals, or Aurelia. Not yet.

Back in the bookshop, the evening settled heavy around her. The fog pressed against the windows, muting the lamps along Main Street until they looked like smudges of flame behind frosted glass. She made tea but left it untouched, sitting at Clara's old desk with the map unfolded beside the recipe book. The spiral inked at the lighthouse burned in her thoughts. It wasn't just a mark. It was a tether—pulling her somewhere she didn't fully want to go but could no longer avoid.

As night deepened, the urge to return to the headland grew unbearable. Something in her chest whispered insistently, urging her back. At last she wrapped herself in her coat, slid the map into her pocket, and stepped into the fog.

THE TRAIL WAS slick with mist, the cliffs breathing salt into the air. The lighthouse loomed ahead, its whitewashed sides catching what little moonlight slipped through the clouds.

The beacon above turned slowly, a solemn rhythm Marley had known all her life—steady, reassuring, the light that kept ships from wrecking against Brookwood's rocks.

She paused at the base of the tower, her hand resting on the cold iron of the railing. The sea below was restless, waves striking the cliffs in relentless bursts. She might have turned back then, but the light above shifted, catching her eye.

It flickered.

At first she thought it was the fog. But then it came again—deliberate, distinct. Three short flashes. A pause. Two long.

Marley's breath hitched. It repeated: three short, two long. Not random. A pattern. A signal.

Her fingers dug into the railing. She tried to steady her thoughts, but her pulse was quick, her breath shallow. The spiral on the map, the carving on the bridge, the voices in the recipes—each had spoken in its own way. Now the lighthouse itself was speaking.

She whispered aloud, her voice almost swallowed by the sea. "What are you trying to tell me?"

The light answered in rhythm, unwavering. Three short, two long.

She thought of Clara, of the journals bricked away, of Hazel's warning that the recipes bound those who opened them. She thought of Aurelia, the woman in the fog, her hand lifted in both warning and welcome. And she realized with a shiver that whatever message the light carried, it wasn't just for sailors. It was for her.

The beacon swept across the sea again, cutting through the fog. The rhythm repeated once more, steady and sure. Three short. Two long.

Marley pressed her hand against the map in her pocket, the spiral burning against her palm. She wasn't imagining it. She couldn't be.

Something in Brookwood was calling her name. Not in whispers this time, but in light.

And the circle was no longer history. It was alive.

9

———

THE FOUNDING MAP

The morning in Brookwood had the brittle clarity of glass—sun trying to pierce through thin clouds, air sharpened by the salt rolling off the sea. Marley sat at Clara's old desk with the fragile map spread wide across its scarred surface. The brittle edges threatened to crumble with each touch, but she couldn't look away.

The spirals inked onto the hand-drawn coast commanded her attention. The first, bold and unmistakable, sat where the lighthouse now rose. Another curled along the bend of the river north of town. And then there was the third, faint but deliberate, marking a small rise inland. Whoever had sketched this hadn't intended cartography for sailors. This was something else entirely—a chart of memory, a ledger carved in ink.

When Marley lifted the corner of the page, she noticed something strange: a thickness along one fold, as though a second layer clung beneath. Carefully, she teased it open. A thin sheet of onion-skin paper slid free, translucent and nearly weightless, but ink bloomed across it in a circle of names.

Seven names.

Eliza Merrick. Hannah Gearhart. Lydia Sparrow. Joan Nye. Mirabel Colvin. Ruth Averill. And the last, pressed darker than the rest, as if written with conviction or defiance: Aurelia.

Beneath the ring of names was a single line of text: The Circle must remain whole.

Marley let the words settle. They weren't decorative. They weren't idle. They were instruction. Commandment. Warning.

Her breath quickened as she placed the onion-skin against the map, aligning its center with the lighthouse spiral. The ring of names sat almost perfectly over the faint inland spiral. *Witch's Rise*, the margin note whispered, in Clara's hand. Marley mouthed the words, and the air seemed to shift around her, as if the town itself listened.

The rise had been renamed in her lifetime—Seaberry Terrace, with its neat rows of houses and small gardens. Clara had once told her, half offhand, that every name in Brookwood was borrowed, rewritten, or painted over. Yet seeing the phrase *Witch's Rise* scrawled in Clara's script gave the truth a sharper edge.

She folded the onion-skin back into the map and slipped both into her satchel. She needed to see the place.

THE WALK CARRIED HER UPHILL, through side streets that still held frost in their shadows, until she reached Seaberry Terrace. The garden sat just as she remembered—a cheerful little square enclosed by iron fencing, its gate painted green. A sign announced it proudly: **SEABERRY TERRACE COMMUNITY GARDEN.** Below, a placard offered rules in neat script: *No pesticides. Share the harvest. Leave the gate latched.*

Inside, cedar boxes lined in rings held sturdy kale, rosemary hedges, winter pansies still in bloom despite the cold. At the very center, a sundial cast a short wedge of shadow across its stone base.

Marley unlatched the gate and stepped in. The geometry of the garden struck her immediately. It wasn't random. It wasn't convenience. Seven beds in the inner circle. She counted again, just to be sure. Seven.

Her steps carried her to the sundial. The stone beneath it was older than the garden, older than the cedar, older than the plaque on the gate. It had the softened edges of something pulled from a river or quarried generations ago. She crouched and brushed a scatter of leaves away. There, shallow but deliberate, was the spiral.

The same spiral etched into the covered bridge beam. The same she had traced on Clara's recipe book. The same she had carried from the lighthouse map.

Her chest tightened.

A voice behind her said, "If you're looking for a plot, the waitlist is eight months."

Marley startled, straightening too fast. An older woman stood at the gate, gloves tucked into her pocket, gray hair tucked under a cap. Her stance was firm, rooted, the way only someone who had lived in a place long enough to know where the soil hid its secrets could stand.

"I'm just visiting," Marley managed. "It's beautiful."

"It's tidy," the woman replied. "Mags Ortega. I keep the list, keep the peace, and stop the rabbits when the fence fails." She stepped closer, eyeing Marley with frank curiosity. "You're Clara's girl. The bookshop."

"Yes," Marley said, her throat tightening on the word.

"Clara knew the old names for this hill. Liked to remind people of them, even when they didn't want reminding." Mags's eyes flicked toward the sundial. "She used to say Witch's Rise. My grandmother called it that too. My mother preferred to let the name die. Easier that way."

Marley lowered her voice. "Why 'witch'?"

Mags tilted her head. "Because the men writing the ledgers didn't have a better word for women who gathered without them. Because women with herbs in their pockets and circles in their gardens frightened them. Call it what you like—it's soil that remembers."

Her words sat heavy. Marley looked down at the sundial stone, the spiral etched there. She wanted to press her hand against it, to feel if the earth itself would answer. Seven names. A circle that must remain whole.

Mags watched her steadily. "Be careful where you step here, Marley Taylor. Some corners stir back."

Marley nodded faintly, the phrase echoing like Hazel's warning days before. She lingered another moment, hand hovering above the sundial stone, before slipping back through the gate.

As she walked downhill toward the library, the onion-skin page pressed warm against her ribs, and the phrase etched itself deeper into her mind:

The Circle must remain whole.

THE LIBRARY'S local history room smelled faintly of old paper and lemon polish, as if Mrs. Delaney had spent the morning preserving not just the shelves but the ghosts of every volume inside them. Marley slipped the key into the brass lock and entered, her satchel pressing heavy against her hip. Inside, Damien was already bent over the microfilm reader, his face lit by the ghostly glow of magnified type.

He looked up when the door shut behind her. His eyes registered her expression before she said a word. "You found something," he said.

Marley pulled the map and the onion-skin page from her satchel and spread them carefully across the table. The fragile paper seemed to absorb the light from the overhead lamp, its circle of names almost luminous. "It was hidden in the folds," she said softly. "Seven women. And this line—'The Circle must remain whole.'"

Damien leaned forward, his elbows on the table, and read the names aloud. "Eliza Merrick. Hannah Gearhart. Lydia Sparrow. Joan Nye. Mirabel Colvin. Ruth Averill." His voice lingered on the last name. "Aurelia."

Marley's throat tightened at the sound of it. "The way it's written—it's darker, as if the writer pressed harder. Like Aurelia mattered more than the others."

Damien didn't answer right away. He shifted his gaze to the map. "And here," he murmured, tracing the spirals with a gloved finger. "The lighthouse. The river bend. And the rise."

"It's the community garden now," Marley said. "But Mags Ortega called it by its old name. Witch's Rise. She knew."

He sat back, exhaling. "Of course she did." He tapped the onion-skin circle again. "These aren't just names. They're signatures. An oath." He glanced at her. "And the phrase— 'The Circle must remain whole'—it's not metaphor. It's instruction. Maybe warning."

Marley's pulse quickened. "You've seen the spiral before. You said it's in other places."

"Yes," Damien said, rising and moving to the cabinet

along the wall. He pulled open a drawer labeled **BROOK-WOOD—FOLKWAYS** and removed a thin stack of index cards, each written in his careful script. He spread them across the table in front of her.

The first read: **Spiral—bridge beam (1938 survey). Noted by town surveyor, dismissed as 'youth carving.' Filed under Graffiti Complaints.**

The second: **Spiral—Keeper's House doorframe. Three layers of paint over carving. Earliest dated to 1890s. Filed under Decorative Motif.**

The third: **Spiral—north row cemetery stone. Half-erased. Notes dismiss as 'wind damage.' Filed under Folklore.**

Marley scanned the cards, her chest tightening. Each discovery was real, undeniable, and yet every official note had nudged it out of history. Graffiti. Decoration. Folklore. Nothing to see here.

Damien placed one more card on the table, this one in darker ink, his handwriting firmer. **Seaberry Terrace—community garden sundial. Spiral etched on stone. 20th-century records omit mention. Folk tale reference only.**

"You wrote this," Marley said.

"I added it after I saw the stone for myself last winter," Damien replied. "But officially? It doesn't exist. The record books call the garden a civic beautification project. Any mention of Witch's Rise is buried in appendices or letters from the nineteenth century. And even then—filed under folklore."

Marley lowered her hand to the onion-skin page. The circle of names looked back at her like eyes. "So every time the spiral surfaces—"

Damien finished for her. "—it gets erased by labeling it story. Folklore is the town's convenient way of saying *not fact, not dangerous, not ours to answer for.* But the symbols don't care what file you put them in. They keep showing up."

Marley felt a shiver climb her spine. "And the women's names? They're not in any records?"

Damien shook his head. "Not in the official ledgers. Not as a group. Individually, you'll find hints. Hannah Gearhart listed once in a midwifery note from 1892. Joan Nye mentioned in a ledger about sewing blankets during a winter outbreak. Lydia Sparrow in a teacher's payroll. All scraps. No recognition of connection. No mention of a circle."

"But they were there," Marley said, her voice low.

"They were there," Damien agreed. "The spiral is proof. And now this." He touched the onion-skin page with reverence, not pressure. "This is the first time I've seen their names together."

Marley sat down heavily, the weight of it pressing against her chest. Clara had hidden the journals for a reason. Hazel had warned her about knowledge that bound. And now the circle of names stared back at her, asking her to carry what others had tried to bury.

"The Circle must remain whole," she whispered, as if testing the phrase on her tongue.

Damien's eyes met hers. "Which means they feared it could be broken. That's what the town never wrote down. Not just who they were, but what they were holding together."

The words sank into Marley's bones. Broken circles. Bricked windows. Whispers carried on water. And now, here, the proof that the women of Brookwood had made something whole—something the town had worked hard to fracture.

She folded the onion-skin page carefully, her fingers

trembling. For the first time, she felt not just like a seeker stumbling across fragments but like a participant, someone the spiral had chosen to see.

And that realization terrified her more than anything.

THE SILENCE in the library after Damien's words stretched taut, like the pause before a storm breaks. Marley stared at the onion-skin page lying between them. The ring of names seemed to glow under the lamplight, and the phrase—*The Circle must remain whole*—echoed in her mind with the weight of an oath, not a note.

Damien leaned back in his chair, folding his arms. "Folklore," he said, almost spitting the word. "It's how they bury truth in plain sight. File it under story, and no one has to reckon with what it really means."

Marley pressed her fingertips lightly against the paper, careful not to tear it. "But this isn't story."

"No," he agreed, his voice low, steady. "It's record."

Marley wanted to argue, or maybe to run. Because if this wasn't just folklore, if it was record, then she wasn't just a curious bookseller poking through her aunt's boxes. She was part of something deliberately hidden, something that didn't want to stay silent.

"The Circle must remain whole," she whispered again, the words catching in her throat. "What if it isn't? What if it's already broken?"

Damien's gaze flicked to her, searching, weighing her silence the way he weighed archival evidence. "Then someone has to put it back together. Maybe that's why the pieces keep surfacing—maps, engravings, names. The past doesn't like being erased."

Marley's breath caught. She thought of the bricked window in the hidden room, the journals sealed away, the recipes that called to her in whispers. They hadn't survived by accident. Clara hadn't kept them out of sentimentality. She had been safeguarding a lineage, one that insisted on being remembered.

But *why her?*

She closed her eyes, trying to quiet the rising tide of her thoughts. The map in her satchel. The onion-skin page. The recipes she had tested. Hazel's warning. The voice at her desk. The light in the lighthouse flickering like code. The whisper of her name from the river. All of it pressed against her at once, not random, not scattered, but forming something like a pattern.

The circle.

Whole.

She opened her eyes and found Damien watching her, the intensity of his gaze tempered by something gentler— patience, maybe, or recognition. He didn't press her for what she wasn't saying, though she could feel the questions stacked behind his eyes. He was letting her choose whether to let him in.

"I don't know if I can carry this," she admitted, her voice barely more than a breath.

"You already are," Damien said.

The words settled over her with terrible simplicity. He was right. Every step she had taken since reopening the shop had pulled her deeper into the circle, whether she wanted it or not. Every choice to follow a draft, to turn a key, to test a recipe—each one had bound her further.

Marley lifted the onion-skin page and slid it back into the map. The paper crackled faintly, like a whisper she couldn't quite catch. She folded it carefully and tucked it into her satchel, then pressed her hand flat against the leather flap.

"If the circle must remain whole," she said slowly, "then it's not just history. It's demand. And demand implies consequence."

Damien nodded once. "That's what frightens me most. Not what they did, but what they feared losing."

The room felt smaller then, crowded not with books but with presence. The names on the page. The women in the journals. Aurelia's whisper in the dark. The circle pressed close, reminding her that secrecy had always been less about hiding from others and more about surviving long enough to be found by the right eyes.

She thought again of Clara, of her quiet laugh and her stubborn kindness, and wondered if her aunt had known that Marley would be those eyes. The thought both steadied her and broke her heart.

The bell at the front desk rang faintly—Mrs. Delaney's signal that closing time drew near. Damien gathered his cards with the same deliberate care he'd shown before, sliding them back into their drawer as if tucking them into bed.

Marley lingered, her fingers grazing the table's edge. She didn't want to leave. Not the map, not the weight of discovery, not the sense that she stood on the threshold of something larger than her grief. But the lamps dimmed slightly, and the world insisted on moving forward.

She and Damien stepped out into the evening together. The fog was rolling in again, shrouding the streetlamps, softening the town into blurred outlines. The lighthouse beam swept through the haze in the distance, its rhythm steady. Marley caught herself counting without meaning to: one, two, three—pause—one, two.

Three short. Two long.

She stopped in the street, her breath sharp in her chest. Damien glanced at her.

"What is it?"

"Nothing," she said quickly, but her voice betrayed her.

He didn't press, but his eyes lingered.

As they parted ways—Damien toward the headland, Marley toward the bookshop—she couldn't shake the certainty that the circle wasn't content to rest as ink on a page. It wanted wholeness. It wanted action. It wanted her.

Back inside the bookshop, she climbed the stairs to Clara's desk. She laid the map out once more, the onion-skin page trembling faintly in the lamplight. She whispered the names in a ring, barely audible, as though repeating them might re-knit something torn.

Eliza. Hannah. Lydia. Joan. Mirabel. Ruth. Aurelia.

The room seemed to shift at the edges, a draft moving without doors open. Marley pressed her hand flat against the desk. "I hear you," she said.

For the first time, she wasn't entirely sure she spoke into silence.

10

___

THE JAZZ FESTIVAL PLANNING
MEETING

Brookwood's Town Hall smelled faintly of lemon oil and dust, a combination Marley associated with both ceremony and neglect. The wide meeting room—arched windows, wood-paneled walls that had darkened with age—was already filling with townspeople when she arrived. The folding chairs were arranged in a circle rather than rows, an intimacy designed to look inviting but which, Marley suspected, made it easier to see who was speaking and who wasn't.

She had not volunteered for this. Hazel had appeared at the shop that morning, waving a clipboard and wearing her slyest smile. "The committee needs fresh blood," she said, sliding the clipboard onto Marley's counter. "And since you're Clara's niece, you're practically *heritage stock*. They'll want you."

Marley had protested—she knew nothing about organizing festivals, let alone Brookwood's biggest annual event —but Hazel had waved her off with a tone that brooked no refusal. "You'll learn. Besides, you could use the company."

So now she sat two seats down from Hazel, across from

Mr. Barlow, who had run the Brookwood Hardware store since before Marley was born. He wore suspenders and a permanent squint, his pen scratching furiously at a yellow notepad even before the meeting began. Next to him was Mags Ortega, who raised a skeptical eyebrow when she spotted Marley, as if wondering how long she'd last.

The mayor, a barrel-chested man named Richard Connelly, clapped his hands for attention. "All right, folks, let's settle. This year's jazz festival will mark our sixty-second annual gathering. We want to make it memorable. Suggestions for headliners, logistics, fundraising—we'll cover it all."

A murmur rippled through the circle. The jazz festival was Brookwood's crown jewel, drawing tourists from across the county to hear music spill through the town square and down to the waterfront. Marley remembered coming with Clara as a child—spending the day perched on folding chairs, her aunt tapping her foot in time, the notes blending with the smell of fried dough and salt air.

Connelly launched into the agenda, assigning committees for ticketing, vendor coordination, and music programming. Hazel raised her hand to suggest adding a "heritage spotlight" on Brookwood musicians. Barlow insisted the fireworks should be larger than last year's. Mags wanted to budget for better lighting along Seaberry Terrace, arguing it would keep the festival safe after dark.

When Hazel nominated Marley to help coordinate marketing and signage, Marley blinked. "I—" she began, but Hazel's grin was victorious.

"You've got a bookshop, dear," Hazel said. "You know your fonts."

The room chuckled lightly. Marley felt her cheeks warm

but forced a nod. "All right," she said, trying to sound capable.

The meeting pressed on, but as ideas flew—food vendors, local sponsorships, stage setup—Marley began to notice sidelong glances slipping her way. At first she thought she was imagining it, but then she caught a murmur ripple between two of the town's older men seated near the back. She heard her name, then Clara's, then the word "digging."

"Digging too deep," one of them whispered, low but pointed.

Marley stiffened. Her gaze slid to Hazel, but Hazel was focused on the mayor's notes. She tried to return her attention to the agenda, but her pulse beat hot at her temples. *Digging too deep into what? Clara's past? The journals? The map?* She hadn't spoken of it outside Damien and Hazel, yet somehow the whispers were spreading.

After the meeting adjourned, chairs scraping, Marley slipped toward the side door, hoping to escape before anyone cornered her. But a familiar figure lingered at the edge of the crowd.

Damien.

He caught her eye and gave the barest tilt of his head. She hesitated, then followed him out into the cool evening.

The town hall steps opened onto Main Street, where the lamps glowed yellow against the encroaching fog. The air tasted of damp wood and the faint promise of rain. Damien walked beside her without speaking at first, his stride unhurried.

Finally, he said, "You heard them."

Marley's throat tightened. "So it wasn't just in my head."

"No." His voice was quiet but firm. "They're talking."

"About Clara?"

"About you." He stopped and turned to her, his gaze steady. "They say you're digging too deep."

Marley swallowed hard. The phrase struck like a warning bell. She wanted to deny it, laugh it off as small-town gossip, but Damien's eyes searched hers, and she couldn't summon the lie.

She looked away, her fingers curling around the strap of her satchel. "Maybe they're right."

THE FOG HAD THICKENED by the time they left the town hall behind, wrapping Main Street in its low, shifting veil. Lamps along the street glowed as blurred orbs, their halos cut by the damp. The town itself seemed to retreat under the mist, as though Brookwood preferred to watch rather than be seen. Marley tugged her coat closer and walked in step with Damien, their footsteps soft against the brickwork.

"They're whispering because they're afraid," Damien said finally, his voice steady against the hush of the fog.

"Afraid of what?" Marley asked, though she already suspected.

He glanced at her, his jaw tight. "Of what you might uncover. Of what it means if the stories are more than stories."

Marley pressed her lips together. For days she had danced around this very thought, treating the visions and whispers as fragments, echoes—hauntings she could keep compartmentalized. But the garden, the map, the lighthouse, the whisper at Clara's desk—they were not fragments anymore. They were converging.

She slowed her pace, her eyes tracing the line of the fog curling down an alley. "What if they're right? What if I am digging too deep?"

Damien stopped, his breath visible in the damp air. He turned to her fully, his expression searching. "That's not the real question, Marley. The real question is whether you believe what you're seeing."

Her stomach tightened. She opened her mouth to deflect, to say she wasn't sure, to pretend she was still weighing it all. But something in his tone—steady, patient, unyielding—unraveled the last of her hesitation.

She looked away, past his shoulder, where the lighthouse beam pushed its rhythm faintly through the fog: sweep, pause, sweep. She thought of the whisper of her name carried on the water. Of Aurelia's voice pressing against her ears at the desk. Of the recipes that worked in ways science could not explain.

"Yes," she said, her voice low but clear. "I believe they're real."

The admission startled her as much as it steadied her. It felt like stepping onto ice and finding it didn't crack.

Damien didn't flinch. If anything, the faintest relief flickered across his features, as if he had been waiting for her to say it. "Good," he said simply. "Because pretending otherwise won't protect you. It'll only make you easier to break."

Marley exhaled, her breath shaking out of her. "You say that like you know."

"I do." His eyes held hers, the grief in them like a tide that never receded. "When Jackie died, people told me I was imagining things. That the way I kept seeing her in the corner of rooms, the way I'd hear her voice when no one else did—that it was grief talking. But grief doesn't carve spirals into stone. Grief doesn't whisper your name in patterns that repeat themselves across centuries."

Marley's heart ached at the rawness in his voice. He wasn't just speaking about Jackie. He was speaking about belief, about the cost of denying what pressed itself against you.

She nodded slowly. "Then what do we do with it? With all of this?"

He resumed walking, more slowly now, as if giving her time to breathe. "First, you accept that it's not just the past. It's the present. And if the circle was meant to remain whole, then someone has to hold the pieces together. Whether that means uncovering, protecting, or both—we'll find out."

The fog swirled around them as they walked. Marley felt the weight of the map in her satchel, the onion-skin page folded carefully inside. The names pulsed in her memory, one by one: Eliza, Hannah, Lydia, Joan, Mirabel, Ruth, Aurelia. A circle not finished, not broken, but waiting.

For the first time since returning to Brookwood, she allowed herself to stop resisting. The visions weren't just echoes of Clara or shadows of her grief. They were real. And by speaking it aloud, she had stepped into the circle, not as an observer but as part of it.

And though fear still pressed at her ribs, so too did a strange sense of belonging—dangerous, heavy, undeniable.

THE BOOKSHOP'S front windows glowed faintly in the fog as Marley approached, the kind of warmth that seemed to promise sanctuary. But tonight, even the glow felt unsettled. She unlocked the door, the bell chiming with its usual bright note, though the sound fell flat in the heavy silence that followed.

She set her satchel on the counter and didn't light the lamps yet. For a moment she stood in the dimness, listening to the creaks of the old building settling into the night. Normally those sounds felt companionable—Clara's shop breathing, stretching, alive. Tonight, they felt like eyes watching.

Her ears still rang with the whispers from the meeting. "Digging too deep." She had heard them as clearly as if the words had been spoken into her ear. And Damien had confirmed it—she wasn't imagining it. The town was watching her. Not just curious, not just wary, but afraid.

She moved upstairs, her hand trailing the banister, and sat at Clara's desk. The onion-skin page lay waiting where she had left it. She unfolded it and smoothed it flat, her fingers brushing the names in the circle.

Eliza. Hannah. Lydia. Joan. Mirabel. Ruth. Aurelia.

Their presence pressed against her, silent but insistent. She could almost hear the murmur of voices layered one over the other, carried forward across time. The phrase at the bottom—*The Circle must remain whole*—burned sharper than before.

Marley leaned back in the chair, her hand over her mouth. *Whole.* That meant more than remembrance. It meant responsibility. She was no longer allowed to simply study or witness. If the circle demanded wholeness, then someone had to act to keep it intact. And by finding the map, by hearing the whispers, by admitting the visions were real, she had been pulled into that role.

The thought made her stomach churn. She hadn't chosen this. She had only come to Brookwood to settle Clara's estate, to reopen the shop, to breathe. She hadn't asked for a circle of names, a map of spirals, a lighthouse beacon flashing messages across the fog. And yet, here it was—demanding, waiting, watching.

She closed the onion-skin page carefully and tucked it back into her journal, as though containing it might quiet its pull. But the silence in the shop shifted. She could feel it.

Whispers—too faint to catch words—seemed to seep through the walls, threads of voices curling around her ears. She spun in the chair, heart pounding. The shop was empty, of course. Only shadows and shelves. Yet the sound persisted—not in volume, but in presence.

She rose and crossed to the window. The street outside was blurred by fog, but she could see figures moving at its edges—neighbors, maybe, passing on their way home. And yet the fog warped them, their shapes stretching, faces obscured. For a moment it felt like all of Brookwood lingered there, watching, whispering.

Marley pressed her hand to the glass. "What do you want from me?" she whispered.

The glass was cool under her palm, but the question pulsed back at her in her own chest. She knew the answer. Not remembrance. Not curiosity. Action.

The circle did not want to be studied in notebooks or filed away as folklore. It wanted to be whole. And that meant her.

She drew the curtains sharply, shutting out the view, but the sense of being watched lingered. She moved back to the desk, her pulse uneven. For a moment she considered locking the onion-skin page back in the hidden room with the others. To put the weight back where it belonged. But something inside her rebelled. That wasn't what the circle wanted. Clara hadn't saved the page for it to be hidden again.

Marley sat heavily, her hands clasped. For the first time she let herself say the truth aloud, in the empty room, into the silence that wasn't silence at all.

"I believe you're real. And I believe you want me to do something about it."

The whisper of sound in the shop stilled then, as if the walls themselves held their breath.

Marley closed her eyes, the weight of the words pressing against her chest. She felt both terrified and steady in equal measure, as if the ground beneath her had shifted but she knew, at last, what direction she was meant to walk.

The circle wasn't just history. It wasn't just Clara's past.

It was hers now.

11

THE HEALER'S SYMBOL

The bookshop was quiet, but not the kind of quiet that came from stillness. It was layered—like the hush of a forest where every rustle is its own voice. Marley had come to recognize the difference. Tonight, she worked alone, sorting through Clara's desk, the weight of recent weeks hanging in her shoulders.

The desk had always seemed ordinary—oak polished by decades of use, drawers that stuck slightly in the damp. But Clara had left her too many breadcrumbs for Marley to dismiss the feeling that it held more than receipts and ledgers. Hazel's words, Mags's warnings, Damien's certainty —all of it pushed Marley to look deeper.

She pulled the bottom drawer out entirely, setting it aside. Behind it, the wood paneling looked unremarkable— until her thumb traced the seam at the corner. The grain didn't quite match, and when she pressed, the wood gave a little, like a latch waiting to be sprung.

Heart quickening, Marley fetched the brass key she had worn around her neck since discovering it in Clara's belongings. It had opened more than one door already, literal and otherwise. She tested the panel again. No lock, but the key slid against the groove and caught. She pressed harder.

The panel creaked and released, swinging inward with a dry sigh. Inside, a shallow compartment yawned—dust thick on the bottom, but the air carried that faint, herbal tang she had come to recognize from the hidden room.

And there it was, carved into the panel's interior: the spiral.

Not painted, not scrawled, but etched deep into the oak with patient strokes. Its curves were the same as the bridge beam, the sundial stone, the lighthouse map. But here, in Clara's desk, the lines felt personal—less like a warning to outsiders and more like a mark of belonging.

Marley brushed her fingers over it. The ridges were smooth with age, as if touched countless times before. A keyhole for no key. A door that led inward, not outward.

She whispered into the silence, "What were you trying to tell me, Clara?"

The spiral didn't answer, but something in her chest steadied. She took out her journal and copied the symbol again, sketching it carefully. Her hands trembled—not from fear but from the weight of recognition. This wasn't coincidence. The spiral wasn't a single person's sign or a family quirk. It was everywhere, across wood and stone, across time.

When she stepped back from the desk, she nearly tripped over her satchel. The map still lay folded inside, the onion-skin names pressing like a heartbeat against the leather. The desk spiral, the map spirals, the journals—they were all pointing to the same truth.

But what truth?

The knock on the shop's door startled her. She froze,

breath held. The bell didn't chime, so it hadn't been opened. Another knock came—steady, not urgent.

Damien.

She crossed the room quickly and let him in. His coat was damp with fog, his hair tousled. He looked as though he had walked with purpose.

"I think I found something," she said before he could speak.

"I did too," he replied, his voice carrying that low intensity she had come to recognize as discovery.

They stood for a beat, both caught between urgency and the comfort of not being alone with what they'd found.

"Show me," he said at last.

Marley led him upstairs to Clara's desk. She pulled the drawer free again and revealed the hidden panel, the carved spiral glowing faintly in lamplight. Damien crouched, his expression sharpening.

"So it's here too," he murmured.

"Not just here," she said. "It feels like everywhere I turn, the spiral is waiting. But this—" She touched the lines. "This feels deliberate. Like Clara wanted me to find it."

He nodded, then straightened. "I brought something from the historical society." He reached into his satchel and pulled out a thick ledger, its leather cracked with age. "Town records. Not official minutes, but side documents—occupational notes, tax ledgers. Look."

He laid the book on the desk and opened to a marked page. Columns of names ran down the paper, some fully written, others reduced to initials. But beside a series of names, a symbol had been penciled in the margins—small spirals, faint, but unmistakable.

"Here," Damien said, pointing. "1864. Occupations listed. Blacksmiths, merchants, shipwrights. But the women—look how they're recorded. Not names. Initials. And each one tied to a title like 'midwife,' 'herb-woman,' 'tender.' Always the spiral beside them."

Marley bent closer. Her chest tightened as her eyes traced the ink.

"H.G.—herbs. L.S.—tender. R.A.—midwife. And there —A.W."

Her throat caught. "Aurelia W."

Damien nodded gravely. "They weren't erasing them. Not entirely. They were reducing them, compressing them into code. The spiral marked them. The initials preserved them."

Marley sat back, the weight of it rushing through her. For weeks, she had wondered if the Green Healer was a singular woman, a figure cast in myth and shadow. But here, in black ink on ledger paper, was something larger.

"What if the Green Healer wasn't just one woman?" she said slowly. "What if it was all of them? A collective? A circle, exactly as the onion-skin page said. Seven names, initials in the ledger, marked by the spiral. They weren't alone. They were never alone."

The words rang in the room, sharp and clear. For the first time, the story of Brookwood's past felt less like fragments scattered across time and more like a deliberate pattern—the circle echoing itself, whole across generations.

Damien's gaze met hers. "And if they were a collective, then the question isn't *who* the Green Healer was. It's *what* the Green Healer was."

The spiral at the desk seemed to pulse in agreement, a silent witness to their revelation.

Marley whispered, "A circle that must remain whole."

And she knew, with a certainty that both steadied and terrified her, that she was standing inside it.

. . .

THE LEDGER'S pages crackled like thin fire as Damien turned them. The ink had browned with age, but the meticulous hand of the recorder gave it a kind of permanence—as though the town itself wanted to be remembered even when the names it wrote down were made deliberately small.

Marley leaned over his shoulder, the lamplight casting a circle on the open page. The initials glared back at her.

"H.G.," Damien read aloud. "Herbs." He tapped the notation beside it. "L.S.—Tender."

"R.A.—Midwife," Marley whispered, tracing the faint spiral drawn beside it. "They're not just names. They're roles."

"Professions," Damien said. "But not formal. These were never considered trades the way blacksmithing or shipwrighting were. This was the other ledger—the shadow column of work that mattered but wasn't recognized."

Marley scanned the page. More initials, more spirals. "Look at the pattern," she said, her pulse quickening. "It isn't random. Every spiral falls beside a woman's initials. And every initial connects to a profession of healing—midwife, herb-woman, caretaker. Not one beside a male name. Not one beside a merchant or craftsman."

Damien nodded slowly. "The spiral was their mark. They couldn't be named outright, but they could be recorded like this. Protected by initials, but preserved by symbol."

Marley sat back, letting the thought unfurl. For weeks she had tried to reconcile the scattered pieces—the recipe book, the hidden journals, the spiral carved into wood and stone. She had thought the Green Healer was a singular woman, a figure whose name had been smeared into legend. But here, in ink and spiral, was a collective.

"They weren't one person," she murmured. "They were many. The Green Healer wasn't a woman—it was a circle of women."

Damien looked up at her, and she saw in his eyes the spark of a historian connecting threads he had suspected but never proven. "Yes," he said quietly. "A collective hidden inside the town itself. And Brookwood buried them by filing everything under folklore."

Marley's gaze returned to the ledger. The initials swam together, not anonymous now but luminous, each one a cipher waiting to be spoken aloud. *H.G., L.S., R.A., A.W.* She mouthed the letters slowly, tasting them, giving them back some of the weight they had been denied.

Her throat tightened when she reached A.W.—Aurelia W. The darker name on the onion-skin page. The one Clara had underlined, almost reverent.

"Look at the dates," Damien said, flipping forward a few pages. "Every decade has a cluster. Always initials. Always the spiral."

Marley leaned closer. The pattern repeated: women marked by initials, roles coded as herbs, tending, midwifery, nursing. The spiral in the margins, sometimes faint, sometimes bold.

"This isn't accident," she said. "This was deliberate recordkeeping. Not the town clerk, maybe. Someone else. Someone who knew the circle was there and wanted it remembered."

Damien tapped the margin with his finger. "The hand that drew the spirals—it's not the same as the ledger hand. Look at the stroke. The ledger is precise, formal. The spirals are more fluid, less rigid. Someone added these later. Someone guarding the record."

Marley's breath caught. "A secret within a secret."

They sat in silence for a moment, the weight of it pressing on them. The desk spiral. The garden beds. The lighthouse light. All of it converged here, in this brittle ledger, as if the past itself were conspiring to be remembered.

Marley traced the initials again, her heart heavy. "These women... they weren't myths. They weren't just stories. They were real. And they worked together. The Green Healer wasn't singular. It was a name the town gave to what they couldn't understand—a network, a collective of women keeping Brookwood alive."

Damien's eyes softened, but his voice carried steel. "And the town feared them enough to reduce them to folklore. They didn't erase them, Marley—they diminished them. It's worse than erasure. They preserved the labor but stripped the names."

Marley thought of Clara, of the journals sealed in brick, of Hazel's warnings. She thought of the whisper at her desk, Aurelia's voice calling across time. A legacy passed in fragments, carried by women who knew the cost of being remembered.

"What if this is what Clara was trying to tell me?" she asked softly. "That the Green Healer wasn't just one story, but many? That it wasn't hers alone to carry, but mine now too?"

Damien shut the ledger gently, the sound final. He looked at her, his eyes dark and certain. "Then the question isn't whether you'll believe it. It's what you'll do with it."

The spiral on the desk seemed to pulse faintly in the lamplight, an echo of the ledger's margins, the garden's stone, the lighthouse's beam. A circle whispering, not for memory but for wholeness.

Marley pressed her hand flat against the closed ledger. The paper was warm under her palm, or maybe it was just her pulse echoing against it. Either way, she knew the truth she had been circling since the day she reopened the shop.

The Green Healer had never been a myth.

It had been a circle all along.

And the circle was still waiting.

THE SHOP WAS silent after Damien left, but it wasn't the kind of silence Marley could settle into. It pressed around her, thick with presence, the kind of quiet that asks questions instead of giving rest. She sat at Clara's desk, the ledger still open before her, the initials staring back like unfinished prayers.

Her hand drifted across the page. *H.G., L.S., R.A., A.W.* She whispered them aloud, tasting them in sequence. They weren't just letters. They were women. Hands that mixed herbs, that held fevered children, that stitched wounds and whispered comforts into the night. Women who had been compressed into initials, hidden inside a ledger that recorded the men of Brookwood in full.

Every time she read the spirals in the margins, her heart beat harder. They weren't decorative. They were signatures. Someone—maybe Clara, maybe someone before her—had risked their name and hand to draw them. To mark what the town had tried to reduce.

She leaned back, staring at the ceiling, but the names followed her. They pressed against her ribs like weights, demanding to be carried. Clara's journals had whispered. The recipes had murmured. The lighthouse had pulsed its rhythm. Now the ledger spoke in its own way—quiet, insistent, undeniable.

Marley closed her eyes, and the circle unfolded behind them. Not one woman in green, but many. A gathering. A network. A collective that had moved unseen through Brookwood's past, binding themselves together with spirals and secrecy.

Her breath caught at the thought: *The Green Healer was never one person.* The town's myth had simplified it—one woman, cast out, remembered in whispers. But the truth was broader, deeper, more dangerous. The Green Healer was a mantle, carried across hands, initials, lifetimes. A circle that defied erasure by multiplying.

Her pulse raced. If the Green Healer had always been many, then the circle wasn't finished with Aurelia. It wasn't finished with Clara. It wasn't finished with her.

The realization landed heavy, like a stone dropped into deep water. She pressed her hands against her knees, grounding herself. She hadn't come to Brookwood to become part of anything. She had come to clean up, to mourn, to begin again. But the circle had found her anyway.

She rose, pacing the shop floor in the dim lamplight. The shelves loomed tall and shadowed, the books like silent witnesses. She half-expected Clara's voice to emerge from the stillness, but only her own breath filled the room.

At the back wall, her hand brushed the crooked bookshelf hiding the sealed room. She lingered there, her palm flat against the wood, the memory of Aurelia's whisper curling in her ear. She knew, with sudden clarity, that every step she took brought her deeper inside the circle—not as an observer, but as someone expected to act.

She whispered, "What do you want from me?"

No sound answered. But she felt it—the same steadiness

she had touched at the sundial stone, the same pulse she had sensed at the bridge, the same rhythm from the light-house beacon. The circle was whole only if someone kept it that way.

And Clara, Hazel, even Damien—it wasn't just about them. It was about her.

She returned to the desk, shut the ledger with careful hands, and placed it beside the onion-skin page. Two different records. Two different centuries. Both pointing toward the same truth: the circle endured, but only because someone carried it forward.

Marley pressed her palms flat against the desk, her head bowed. She felt the weight of the names settle over her—not crushing, but anchoring. As if they were leaning on her, not to bury her, but to steady her.

She exhaled, and with the breath came an admission she hadn't wanted to face.

"I'm part of this now."

The words rang soft in the shop, but their echo filled her chest. She had stepped into the circle. And there was no stepping back out.

12

—————

BAKERY SECRETS

The bell over the bakery door jingled with a sound that was too cheerful for Marley's mood. She paused just inside, blinking against the warmth and brightness. The bakery smelled of butter and sugar, but also rosemary and lemon zest, the kind of scent that tugged at memory even before she could place it.

Behind the counter stood Mrs. Ruth Bennett, tall and stooped from years of early mornings, was pulling trays of golden scones from the oven—cheeks flushed pink, flour dusted over her hair—looked up with a broad smile.

"Marley Taylor," Ruth said, wiping her hands on her apron. "It's about time you came in. Hazel said you've been living on coffee, tea, and nerves."

Marley managed a laugh, though it sounded thin to her own ears. "She exaggerates."

"Hazel never exaggerates," Ruth said dryly, setting down the tray with a solid thunk. "She multiplies."

Marley smiled faintly, then stepped closer to the counter. "I actually came because... I think something you have might connect to my aunt. And to the bookshop."

Mrs. Bennett exchanged a quick glance—one of those wordless communications that came from a lifetime of shared work, leaned her elbows on the counter. "Go on."

Marley pulled her satchel around and drew out Clara's recipe book, carefully wrapped in cloth. She opened it to a page marked with sprigs of dried lavender tucked between the sheets. The entry was written in her aunt's looping hand: *Calming Scone Blend.* The ingredients read almost like a joke: butter, flour, cream, sugar, lavender buds, lemon balm, rosemary. But tucked in the margins were notations—measurements in odd fractions, small drawings of spirals and leaves.

"I found this in her journals," Marley said, sliding the book forward. "It looks like a recipe, but it's not like any scone recipe I've seen."

Ruth peered down, then snorted softly. "That's because it's not mine. Mine has been in the family since before I was born. Lavender, lemon balm, rosemary—my family has made it the same way for decades. People say it tastes like memory itself. Your aunt came here often, you know. Bought flour from us when she didn't need to. Asked questions about the recipe. I suppose she was copying it down."

"Not copying," Marley said quietly. "Recording."

Mrs. Bennett tilted her head. "Recording what?"

Marley hesitated, but the warmth of the bakery—the yeasty air, the hum of ovens—made her feel braver. "Connections. The same herbs in this recipe appear in others. Salves, teas, tinctures. And the spiral symbol..." She tapped the margin where her aunt had drawn it. "...it shows up everywhere. On bridges. On sundials. Even carved into wood."

Mrs. Bennett exchanged another look, sharper this time. Ruth wiped her hands on her apron, then disappeared into the back room. She returned with an old baking tin, battered and blackened with decades of use. She set it gently on the counter and lifted the lid.

Inside, embossed faintly on the base, was a pattern Marley recognized immediately: a spiral within a circle, surrounded by small leaves.

Her breath caught. "That's it."

Ruth smiled faintly, though her eyes carried weight. "This tin belonged to my grandmother. She said it came from her grandmother before her. I never paid much attention, except to keep it. But your aunt did. She asked about it once. Said the pattern meant something. I never asked what."

Marley reached out, brushing her fingertips over the spiral. It wasn't just decoration. It was deliberate. A sigil. A mark of belonging.

Behind her, the bell jingled again. Damien stepped in, shaking fog from his coat. He spotted them at the counter and came over, his eyes falling immediately on the open recipe book and the tin.

"What did you find?" he asked, his voice low with interest.

Marley gestured to the book and the tin. "The same recipe. The same herbs. The same symbol. It's everywhere, Damien. Even in the food."

He picked up the tin, studying the spiral with reverence. "Of course. Recipes." He set it down and turned to Marley, his eyes sharp with thought. "You know what this means, don't you? The recipes weren't just cooking instructions. They were codes. Ways to preserve oral traditions under the guise of domesticity. No one would question a woman writing down a recipe. But a ritual? That could get her cast out."

The words settled heavily in the warm bakery air. Marley felt a shiver trace her spine. The scones cooling on the counter no longer smelled simply of butter and herbs. They smelled like history disguised as comfort.

She looked back at Mrs. Bennett, whose face betrayed nothing but a quiet, measured watchfulness. And for the first time, Marley wondered if they too carried more than flour and sugar in their family legacy.

DAMIEN SET the battered tin on the counter again, his fingers resting lightly on its rim as though afraid too much pressure might erase what was embossed there. The spiral, faint but undeniable, gleamed in the lamplight, softened by flour that had long ago seeped into its grooves.

"Think about it," he said, turning toward Marley. "Recipes are the safest kind of writing. Men wouldn't scrutinize them. A woman could keep a ledger of herbs and blends right in plain sight, and everyone would assume it was for the kitchen."

Marley glanced down at Clara's journal still open on the counter. The familiar looping script, the herbs, the odd measures, the spirals in the margins. "So this wasn't about food," she said slowly. "It was about survival. Passing down knowledge under the guise of recipes."

Damien nodded. "Exactly. Oral traditions pressed into flour and butter. Herbs disguised as seasoning, when they were really medicines. Sigils disguised as decoration, when they were really instructions."

Marley turned back to Mrs. Bennett who were listening quietly. Ruth crossed her arms, her eyes narrowing slightly. "You're saying my grandmother's scones were spells?"

"Not spells," Damien said carefully. "Preservations.

Remedies. Warnings. Think of it like language. Each recipe was a way of encoding wisdom—sometimes for the body, sometimes for the spirit. Your family's tin carried the spiral because it marked you as part of the chain."

Marley's heart thudded at his words. The bakery, the garden, the bookshop—they weren't random corners of Brookwood. They were sanctuaries. Places where the circle had hidden its knowledge in plain sight, knowing no one would think to look there.

She turned the tin in her hands, running her thumb over the spiral. "This isn't just about scones. This is about identity. About belonging."

Damien drew one of Clara's journals closer, flipping to a page thick with notes in the margins. He tapped the sketches her aunt had drawn. "See here? The spiral is matched with clusters of leaves—lavender, rosemary, balm. The same blend in the scone recipe. Your aunt wasn't just recording herbs—she was preserving a lineage. She knew what she was doing."

Marley bent over the page, the smell of parchment and flour mingling oddly in her senses. The faint ink spirals now looked less like doodles and more like instructions, a cipher layered into everyday life. She imagined generations of women kneading dough, measuring herbs, etching spirals into tins or margins—not for superstition, but because it was the only way to preserve what could not be spoken aloud.

Ruth Bennett broke the silence first. "Grandmother always said baking was a way of remembering. I thought she meant family. Now I wonder if she meant something larger."

Marley looked up. "Maybe she did."

Damien leaned back, his expression tight with thought. "If this is true, then Brookwood itself is built on a network of codes. Recipes, tools, carvings, whispered instructions. The spiral is just the connective tissue. The kitchen wasn't just domestic space. It was a sanctuary. A classroom. A ledger of memory written in flour."

The words made Marley's skin prickle. She thought of her aunt late at night, stirring herbs into teas, writing in her journals. She thought of Hazel's quiet strength, Mags's sharpness, the Bennetts' watchful eyes. None of them were random. They were echoes of a circle that had never truly gone away.

She picked up the tin again, heavier now in her hands than its metal warranted. It wasn't just cookware. It was testimony. Proof that what her aunt had guarded was not fantasy, not superstition, but a coded inheritance stretching back generations.

And Marley knew, deep in her chest, that the circle wasn't just asking her to remember it.

It was asking her to continue it.

THE BAKERY HAD GONE quiet after Damien's theory. The ovens ticked as they cooled, and the faint scent of lavender hung in the air, mingled with butter and flour. Ruth busied herself behind the counter, brushing crumbs into her palm, though Marley sensed it was less about tidiness and more about giving herself something to do. Ruth Bennett leaned her elbows on the wood, chin resting in her flour-dusted hands, studying Marley with a look that was part curiosity, part something older, heavier.

Marley traced the spiral on the tin again, her fingertip catching in its shallow grooves. Each time she touched it, her chest tightened with the same recognition she had felt at Clara's desk, at the sundial stone, at the covered bridge.

The spiral wasn't just symbol—it was thread. And here, in the warmth of the bakery, she felt the thread tug harder than ever.

Her mind leapt unbidden to her aunt. Clara had always seemed most alive in the kitchen—measuring, stirring, humming softly as she worked. Marley had thought it was her aunt's way of soothing grief or filling silence. But now she saw it differently. The kitchen had been her aunt's sanctuary, the same way this bakery was for Mrs. Bennett. A place where knowledge could be stored, exchanged, and passed forward without suspicion.

Marley let her hand fall to her lap, but the weight of the tin stayed with her. She looked at Damien, who was still bent over the journal, flipping pages with deliberate care. His brows were furrowed in thought, his lips moving faintly as if he were muttering connections to himself. When he finally glanced up, his expression was not just curiosity—it was resolve.

"You see it now," he said quietly.

Marley nodded. "The kitchen wasn't just where they cooked. It was where they remembered. Where they taught."

"Exactly," Damien said. He tapped the margin of the recipe page, where Clara's looping spiral nestled beside measurements. "And every time they baked, they reinforced memory. Not just for themselves—for their daughters, their neighbors, anyone they fed. The act itself became part of the record."

Mrs. Bennett shifted, her flour-dusted apron rustling softly. "So every time we rolled scones, every time Grandmother told us to add just a pinch of lavender... we were keeping something alive, and we didn't even know it?"

Marley met her gaze. "Yes."

The words hung in the air, and the sisters let them settle. Ruth finally set down her cloth, her voice low. "Then it's not just family tradition. It's responsibility."

The word hit Marley harder than she expected. Responsibility. That was what the circle demanded. Not passive memory. Not idle curiosity. Responsibility. The weight of the onion-skin page, the ledger initials, the journals, the recipes —they weren't just fragments to be studied. They were instructions waiting for someone to carry them forward.

She rose slowly, feeling the air shift as if even the bakery walls were listening. "It's been waiting," she said softly. "All of it. The recipes, the spirals, the stories. They've been waiting for someone to recognize them. To act."

Ruth crossed her arms. "And you think that's you?"

Marley hesitated. The easy answer would have been to shake her head, to retreat. But she thought of Clara, of Hazel, of the whisper at her desk, of Aurelia's name pressed darker than the rest. She thought of Damien, who had asked her point-blank if she believed the visions were real. She thought of herself, whispering in the silence: *I'm part of this now.*

Her voice trembled, but the words came anyway. "Yes. I think it has to be."

For a long moment, no one spoke. Then Mrs. Bennett pushed the tin across the counter toward Marley. "Then take it," she said simply. "If it means something more than scones, it belongs with you now."

Marley's throat tightened. She wanted to refuse, to insist it stay where it had always been. But she also knew the weight in her chest wouldn't let her. She lifted the tin, holding it close. It was heavier now, as though the spiral itself had sunk into her bones.

She thanked them quietly, and with Damien beside her, stepped back into the night.

The fog had thickened again, curling around the street-lamps, muting the clatter of the harbor. Marley clutched the tin against her chest, the spiral pressing faintly into her palm through the metal. She felt the ledger initials whispering in her memory, the onion-skin page glowing like a lantern, the recipes unfolding like coded prayers.

This wasn't just about uncovering the past anymore. It was about stepping into it, carrying it forward. The circle had hidden itself in kitchens, in gardens, in bakeries, in bookshelves—for centuries waiting for someone to hear it.

Now Marley had.

And as she walked back toward the bookshop, the weight of the tin and everything it represented steady against her, she understood something with a certainty that silenced her fear:

The traditions hadn't survived by chance. They had been waiting. For her.

13

CANDLE OF MEMORY

The metaphysical shop sat tucked at the far end of Brookwood's main street, its narrow windows glowing like lanterns against the fog. Marley had passed it a hundred times as a child, trailing beside Clara on their way to the post office or the grocer. The sign above the door— *Moon & Morrow* —still swung gently on its iron hook, the paint faded but intact.

She stepped inside, and the scent hit her immediately—beeswax, sage, rose, and something deeper, a resinous undertone that clung to the back of the throat. The walls were lined with shelves crowded with jars and votives, tall tapers bundled with twine, and wax molds pressed with floral patterns. Light flickered from dozens of flames, throwing the whole place into a shimmering, shifting glow.

Hazel was there, as always—her scarf tied loosely at her neck, her hands busy dipping fresh wicks into a pot of molten wax. She looked up as the bell over the door chimed, her sharp eyes softening at the sight of Marley.

"Clara!" she said, her voice low and certain. "How are you?"

Marley hesitated, her fingers brushing the edge of her satchel. "I'm not sure what I'm looking for."

Hazel's smile was knowing. "That's never the point. It's what finds you." She wiped her hands and moved to a shelf at the back, selecting a jar wrapped in parchment and bound with twine. She set it on the counter between them.

Marley untied the twine and lifted the lid. The scent rose in a wave—familiar, though she couldn't place it. Sweet but grounding, floral but edged with something sharp. Beeswax laced with lavender, rosemary, lemon balm.

Her pulse skipped. "These are the same herbs," she whispered. "The ones from Clara's book."

Hazel nodded. "The blend is older than either of us. My mother made it. Her mother before her. Not for fragrance— for clarity. For remembering what must not be forgotten."

Marley glanced up sharply. "You know?"

Hazel's eyes glinted in the candlelight. "I know enough. The women in this town were not fools. They preserved what mattered in ways no one would question. Candles, bread, scones, teas—simple, ordinary things. Ordinary enough to outlast suspicion."

Marley closed the jar, her throat tightening. She had heard this pattern before—from Damien, from the Bennetts, from her own discoveries. The circle had written itself into everything mundane, leaving behind codes no one would think to erase.

Hazel leaned in slightly, her voice dropping. "Burn it tonight. On Clara's desk. You'll see."

Marley's fingers trembled as she took the jar. "See what?"

"Not what," Hazel said softly. "Who."

The words sent a shiver crawling up Marley's spine.

· · ·

THAT NIGHT, the bookshop was silent save for the faint creak of wood as the fog pressed against the windows. Marley placed the jar on Clara's desk, her heart hammering as though she were about to perform something illicit. She struck a match, the sulfur sharp in her nose, and touched the flame to the wick.

The beeswax melted quickly, releasing the blend of herbs into the air. The scent was rich, thick, filling the room like memory incarnate. She closed her eyes, her breath catching.

For a moment, nothing. Then the silence shifted.

The air thickened, and the room tilted—not physically, but as though she had stepped through a veil. When she opened her eyes, the desk was gone. She stood beneath the full moon, its light pooling silver across the garden at Seaberry Terrace.

And Clara was there.

Her aunt stood in a circle of stones, her hands lifted, her face luminous in moonlight. Around her feet, herbs burned in a shallow dish, their smoke curling upward. She murmured words Marley couldn't quite catch, but the cadence was steady, ritualistic. Not prayer, not spell, but something in between—a binding of memory to presence.

The spiral shimmered faintly in the earth around her, traced in chalk or ash. Clara bent, pressing her palm against its center, her lips moving faster now, urgent, insistent. The smoke from the herbs rose higher, twisting into the night air like a thread of light.

Marley stepped forward, but the vision shifted as if pushed by a tide. Clara turned, her eyes meeting Marley's for the briefest moment—clear, unwavering. Then the vision fractured, the smoke collapsing, the moon fading into darkness.

Marley gasped and stumbled back into her chair, the candle still burning steadily on the desk, its flame dancing as though nothing had changed.

Her chest heaved. She pressed her hands to her face, but the image of Clara beneath the moon burned behind her eyelids. Not memory. Not imagination. Presence.

The circle had not only written itself into recipes and ledgers. It had written itself into ritual, carried forward even in secret.

And Clara had been part of it.

MARLEY BARELY SLEPT. The dream—or vision, she wasn't sure what to call it—haunted her long after the candle burned low. Each time she closed her eyes, she saw Clara's face bathed in moonlight, her lips moving in that urgent, unbroken chant. The spiral traced at her feet. The rising smoke that seemed to carry memory itself upward.

When dawn finally broke, pale and weak through the fog, Marley still sat at the desk, the candle a stub beside her. She tried to convince herself it was grief's trick or her subconscious stitching together fragments of stories she'd been chasing. But grief didn't smell of rosemary and beeswax. Grief didn't carry the weight of command in Clara's eyes.

She wrapped herself in her coat and walked the fog-heavy streets until she reached the library. Damien was already there, leaning against the steps with a cup of coffee. His posture was rigid, his gaze distant. When he saw her, he straightened quickly, almost too quickly, as if he'd been waiting.

"You look like you didn't sleep," he said.

"I didn't," she admitted. "I... something happened."

He gestured toward the benches at the edge of the square, where the fog thinned enough to see the fountain. They sat, the stone damp beneath them. Marley clasped her hands tight, forcing herself to speak.

"I lit the candle Hazel gave me. The beeswax blend. The same herbs from Clara's book. And I saw her."

Damien turned sharply. "Clara?"

"Yes. Not just as memory. Not just as a dream. She was there, Damien. At Seaberry Terrace, under the full moon. She was performing some kind of ritual. There was a circle of stones, herbs burning, the spiral traced in ash. She looked at me. She saw me."

Her voice cracked on the last word, but Damien's expression didn't waver. He didn't look surprised. If anything, he looked grim.

"You're not alone," he said softly.

Marley blinked. "What do you mean?"

He leaned forward, his elbows on his knees, his hands clasped. "Last night, I dreamed too. But it wasn't Seaberry Terrace. It was the lighthouse. I saw a woman standing at the edge of the rocks, holding a lantern. The light pulsed like the beacon—three short, two long. She wasn't Clara. She was... older, somehow. Or maybe not older, but from another time."

Marley's breath caught. "You saw her the same night I saw Clara."

"Yes." He looked at her, his eyes sharp, steady. "That's not coincidence. That's not grief. That's connection."

The words settled between them, heavy and undeniable. Marley shivered. She wanted to argue, to retreat into skepticism, but the memory of Clara's eyes—clear, unyielding—wouldn't let her.

"I thought maybe I was imagining it," she whispered.

"That the candle triggered something in my head. But if you saw her too—"

"Then it's real," Damien finished. "It has to be."

Marley pressed her hands to her face, then lowered them slowly. "Why us? Why now?"

"Because we're listening," Damien said simply. "Clara listened. Aurelia listened. The others before them did too. But the circle doesn't survive on memory alone. It survives when someone answers."

Marley shook her head. "It feels like too much. The ledger, the recipes, the spirals—it's all pressing in. And now dreams. How am I supposed to carry all of this?"

Damien's gaze softened. "You already are."

The same words he had spoken before, when she admitted believing the visions were real. They struck her again, steadying her and terrifying her in equal measure. She had already stepped inside the circle. And now the circle was answering back.

Marley looked at him, searching his face. "Do you believe it, Damien? Truly? That these aren't just echoes but something alive, something waiting?"

He nodded slowly, with the kind of weight that came from resisting too long and finally giving in. "I didn't want to. I told myself it was grief, or history, or the way obsession twists the mind. But when I saw her last night—the woman with the lantern—I knew. This is not past. It's present. It's here."

The fog swirled around them, muffling the town's morning stirrings. Marley felt the air thicken again, the same way it had in Clara's room when the whisper first brushed her ear. The circle was not content to stay hidden. It was pressing forward, closer, insistent.

She whispered, almost to herself, "Then what do we do with it?"

Damien's reply was quiet, certain. "We follow it. Wherever it leads."

Marley drew a shuddering breath. For the first time, she didn't argue.

THE FOG DEEPENED AGAIN that evening, curling through Brookwood's narrow streets and pressing against the bookshop windows. Marley sat at Clara's desk with the candle jar still close, its wick blackened from the night before. She hadn't dared to light it again, not after what she'd seen, but its presence filled the room anyway. The beeswax scent clung faintly to the air, weaving itself into the wood and paper as though it belonged there.

She told herself she would sleep early, that she would give her mind rest after the relentless days of discovery. Yet when she climbed into bed, the ledger initials, the embossed spiral on the tin, the dream of Clara beneath the full moon—all of it burned behind her eyes. Every time she closed them, fragments of the circle pushed forward. Smoke curling upward. A lantern swaying in fog. The phrase etched into her chest: *The Circle must remain whole.*

She turned on her side, pulling the quilt up around her shoulders, but the stillness of the room only sharpened the sound of her own breath. Somewhere outside, the lighthouse beacon swept its rhythm through the fog: one, two, three—pause—one, two. She counted without meaning to, as though her body recognized the pattern more than her mind.

Sleep came in fragments, jagged and insistent.

At first, the dream was soft. She stood in the bookshop,

its shelves towering higher than they ever did in waking life. A faint golden glow spread from the spiral carved into Clara's desk, illuminating the journals stacked around her. She reached for one, but as soon as her fingers brushed the cover, the shelves shifted, melting into a circle of standing stones.

The air outside was damp and heavy, the sky spilling silver light from a full moon. She stood not alone but surrounded—shadows of women in cloaks, their faces blurred but their presence undeniable. They held herbs in their hands, pressed to their hearts. At the center of the circle, a spiral glowed faintly in the earth.

Marley wanted to step forward, to ask them what they wanted, who they were, but her voice caught in her throat. One of the shadows raised her head, and Marley saw her clearly for the first time. Not Clara, not Aurelia, but someone older, eyes green as sea glass, her lantern lifted high. The light from it wasn't steady. It pulsed. Three short, two long.

The same rhythm as the lighthouse.

The same rhythm she had counted in her chest.

The woman's gaze fixed on her, sharp and demanding. Then her lips moved. Marley strained to hear, but the words blurred into a low chant, threads of sound braided together. She caught only fragments: *whole... keep... remember...*

The dream fractured with sudden force, the circle dissolving into smoke. Marley jolted awake, her breath ragged, her heart hammering against her ribs. The room was dark, the candle unlit on the desk, but the air still smelled of rosemary and beeswax, stronger now than before.

She pressed her palms to her face, her body trembling. It hadn't been just Clara this time. It hadn't been grief or memory. The circle itself had pressed closer, showing her not fragments of history but something unfinished, something waiting.

Marley swung her legs over the side of the bed and walked barefoot to the desk. She touched the candle jar, her fingers lingering on its glass.

"Why me?" she whispered into the dark.

The silence didn't answer, but it felt alive—like breath against her neck, like a heartbeat echoing her own. She closed her eyes and saw the spiral again, glowing beneath the moon, the lantern light pulsing, demanding.

It wasn't memory. It wasn't history.

It was summons.

She sat heavily, her hands shaking against the wood, and finally admitted the truth she had been circling for days.

The circle wasn't showing her the past.

It was pulling her toward what remained unfinished.

And whether she wanted it or not, she had already begun to answer.

14

COFFEE BEANS AND FOUNDERS' TALES

The bell above the café door chimed softly as Marley stepped inside. Warmth enveloped her immediately, carrying the aromas of dark roast coffee and freshly baked pastries. Brookwood's café had always been a gathering place—wooden tables scuffed from decades of use, walls lined with mismatched photographs, and a fireplace that always seemed to hold a gentle ember glow.

She remembered coming here with Clara on Saturday mornings, the clink of mugs, the hush of voices carried on steam and laughter. Today, though, she entered with a different purpose. The weight of the candle dream still pressed against her ribs, but she needed answers that only the living might hold.

"Morning, Marley," called Evelyn Grant, the café owner. Her hair was tied back in a neat bun, her hands moved with a youthfulness as she wiped down the counter. Evelyn had inherited the café from her mother, who had inherited it from hers. Like most of Brookwood's businesses, it was rooted not just in commerce but in continuity.

"Morning," Marley replied, sliding onto a stool. "Hazel said you might have... stories."

Evelyn smiled knowingly, as if the word carried more weight than casual conversation. She set a steaming mug of coffee in front of Marley, its surface swirling with curls of cream.

"You mean the tales my grandmother used to tell," Evelyn said, lowering her voice. "Not the kind folks put in books. The kind spoken when the lights were low and the children were supposed to be asleep."

Marley leaned in, her palms cupping the warmth of the mug. "Yes. Those."

Evelyn glanced around to make sure the café was empty. Only one man sat by the window, reading his newspaper. Satisfied, she pulled up a stool behind the counter and rested her elbows on the worn wood.

"My grandmother told me about the green-eyed healer," she began, her voice taking on the cadence of memory. "Said she was one of the first women to walk Brookwood's shores. She knew herbs better than anyone, knew which leaves cured fever and which roots soothed pain. But knowledge frightens people, especially when it rests in the hands of a woman. They called her dangerous. Said her eyes weren't natural. Said she consorted with forces not meant to be touched."

Marley's pulse quickened. Green eyes. The same description Damien had given of the woman with the lantern. The same color Marley had glimpsed in her dream.

"What happened to her?" Marley asked, her voice hushed.

Evelyn's lips pressed thin. "They cast her out. Unjustly. That was the word my grandmother always used—*unjustly*. The town took her knowledge, her remedies, her healing, but when the winds turned against her, they cut her loose. Drove her into the hills. Some say she died alone. Some say she didn't die at all."

The last words hung in the air, sharp as a struck bell. Marley thought of the spirals carved in wood and stone, the coded recipes, the ledger initials. Not death. Not erasure. Continuity.

Evelyn leaned closer, her eyes narrowing. "Your aunt believed in her. Clara came here often, asking about herbs we didn't even stock. Rare things—valerian root, wild mugwort, blue vervain. I told her those hadn't grown here for decades. She just nodded, like she already knew. Said she'd find them another way."

Marley's throat tightened. Clara had been gathering, preserving, preparing. Not just running a bookshop. She had been part of something larger, older.

The bell over the door chimed again, and Marley turned. Damien stepped in, the fog still clinging to his coat. He scanned the room quickly, then joined them at the counter. Evelyn gave him a nod, poured him a mug without asking.

"You're in the middle of something," he said, sliding onto the stool beside Marley.

"She was telling me about the green-eyed healer," Marley said softly.

Damien's eyes flickered. "Aurelia."

Evelyn frowned. "That wasn't the name my grandmother used. But names change. Stories bend."

Marley felt the pieces pressing closer together, like stones clicking into place. Clara's journals. The embossed tin. The candle dream. Now Evelyn's oral tale of the green-eyed healer. It wasn't just myth. It was memory preserved in fragments, hidden in kitchens and whispered in back rooms.

Damien took a slow sip of his coffee, his gaze fixed on Marley. "There's something else you should know. In the archives, I came across references to an estate. A hillside property on the far edge of town, abandoned since the late 1800s. Some of the founders lived there. Some say the healer lived there after she was cast out."

Marley's breath caught. "The hillside estate?"

He nodded. "If the stories are true, it may hold what she left behind. Or what the town tried to bury."

The café felt suddenly smaller, the air heavier with steam and story. Marley's heart pounded, not with fear this time but with certainty. Every path was pointing toward the same truth.

The circle was leading her somewhere.

And the hillside estate might be the next step.

THE CAFÉ HAD QUIETED after Evelyn drifted toward the kitchen, leaving Marley and Damien alone at the counter. The steam from Marley's coffee curled upward, vanishing into the low light, while Damien's gaze remained fixed on the grain of the wooden bar, as though the story he was about to tell carried more weight than the room could comfortably hold.

"The hillside estate," he began, his voice low, "wasn't just a home. It was a seat of power. The Sanborn family owned it —early settlers who claimed land when Brookwood was still little more than scattered cottages and fishing boats. They had money, influence, and, more importantly, reach. People deferred to them." He looked at Marley, his expression sharp. "If a healer was driven out of town, it would make sense she ended up there—close enough to keep watch, far enough to stay unobserved."

Marley's stomach tightened. "You think they sheltered her?"

"Maybe." Damien sipped his coffee, his fingers tapping lightly on the mug. "Or maybe she sheltered herself there. The estate was large, filled with cellars and outbuildings. Easy to vanish in plain sight. The records I found don't mention her directly, of course—just the initials. A.W. But the timing matches. The ledger entries stop abruptly the same year the Sanborn estate went quiet."

Marley pressed her palms against the warm ceramic of her mug, grounding herself. It was one thing to hear stories whispered by Evelyn, to see symbols carved into wood, but to imagine the healer living just beyond town, watching, waiting—it felt too close, too present.

"Clara ordered herbs," she said suddenly, the memory flashing like a blade. "Hazel mentioned it. Evelyn too. Things no one grows here anymore. Valerian. Blue vervain. Mugwort. I found invoices tucked in her papers—shipments arriving from out of state, sometimes overseas. She wasn't just curious. She was trying to replicate something."

Damien leaned forward. "Or continue something."

Marley's chest tightened. "You think she was connected to the estate?"

"Clara was a scholar," Damien said gently. "But she wasn't chasing history for history's sake. She was preserving. That's what you've been finding, isn't it? Recipes disguised as scones. Sigils hidden in tins. Journals written in half-code. Clara wasn't building a puzzle for you to solve. She was safeguarding a tradition. And those herbs—those were the ingredients she couldn't find here anymore. Which means once, they were here. Cultivated. Used."

Marley thought of the candle dream, of Clara's hands pressing against the spiral, smoke rising in a ritual that was neither prayer nor spell. She imagined her aunt unpacking crates of herbs at this very desk, laying them out like a continuation of something older, something deliberately carried forward.

She shook her head. "It feels impossible. How could all of this—candles, scones, spirals—be more than fragments? How could it have lasted this long without being exposed?"

"Because it hid in plain sight," Damien replied. "Think about it. A healer's knowledge preserved in kitchens, written into ledgers as initials, whispered in bedtime stories. The estate might have been the root. The town, the branches. And Clara—" His voice caught briefly. "Clara was one of the last to tend it."

Marley's eyes stung. She hadn't let herself cry since she arrived in Brookwood, but grief welled at the edges now—not just for Clara's death but for the magnitude of what her aunt had carried, alone, without telling her.

Damien's hand rested lightly against the counter near hers, not touching, but close enough she felt the warmth. "You don't have to carry it the same way she did," he said. "But you also can't ignore it. Not now."

Marley looked down at her hands. They trembled faintly, though whether from fear or the weight of realization, she couldn't tell. She thought again of Evelyn's story— the green-eyed healer, unjustly cast out, blamed for her knowledge. And she thought of Clara, who had died with secrets stitched into her notebooks, leaving Marley to stumble into them piece by piece.

"What if the estate still holds something?" she asked, her voice barely more than breath. "Records. Journals. Herbs. Anything."

Damien's gaze was steady, unwavering. "Then we'll find it. And if it does, we'll know Clara wasn't working alone. That she was part of a chain stretching back to the beginning."

Marley swallowed hard. The words felt both terrifying and necessary. A chain. A circle. A collective bound by spirals and secrecy.

The realization pressed in as sharp as the candle vision had: the healer's knowledge hadn't been scattered. It had been preserved—intentionally, deliberately, waiting for someone willing to look.

And somehow, that someone had become her.

THE CAFÉ HAD BEGUN to hum again as more patrons drifted in—fishermen finishing their morning rounds, a pair of tourists speaking in low tones by the window. The world of Brookwood continued as if Evelyn's story and Damien's history lesson hadn't cracked the air open. But for Marley, the atmosphere was different now. Every scrape of a chair, every ring of the cash register, felt muted, as though the real conversation was happening beneath the surface of things.

She finished the last swallow of coffee, though the taste was bitter, her throat tight with thoughts she couldn't yet shape into words. Damien remained beside her, quiet, letting her turn it all over in her mind. That was something she was learning about him: he pressed when he needed to, but he also knew when silence had more weight.

When they finally rose, Evelyn offered Marley a small smile from behind the counter. "Remember, child," she said softly, "stories last because someone decides they matter."

Marley nodded, though her chest felt heavy. She

followed Damien outside, the bell above the door giving a faint chime that dissolved into the fog.

The street was quiet, the kind of stillness that felt half like sanctuary and half like conspiracy. Marley drew her coat tighter, the cold damp sinking into her skin. She and Damien walked side by side without speaking at first, their footsteps muffled against the cobblestones.

It was Damien who broke the silence. "You're thinking about the estate."

Marley let out a low breath. "I can't stop. If Aurelia—if the green-eyed healer—was driven there, if the Sanborn's sheltered her, then that place is more than abandoned stone. It's part of the circle. Maybe the heart of it."

Damien glanced at her, his expression unreadable in the fog. "Places carry memory. Just like recipes, ledgers, candles. You've seen that. The estate might hold traces Clara couldn't keep in the shop. Or couldn't risk leaving here."

Marley slowed her steps, staring down the narrow street ahead of them, where the fog thickened and the outlines of rooftops blurred. Clara had been gathering herbs from far away, marking spirals in her journals, pressing fragments into recipes and maps. It hadn't been random. It had been purposeful.

"She wasn't chasing ghosts," Marley said finally, her voice trembling but certain. "She was preparing. All this time, I thought Clara was just eccentric, too steeped in the past. But she knew. She was trying to keep it alive long enough for me to find it."

The admission settled in her bones, heavy and liberating at once. Clara's journals, the locked room, the recipes— every fragment had been chosen. Not just for Clara's sake, but for Marley's. Clara hadn't left her an inheritance; she'd left her a responsibility.

Damien stopped walking, turning to face her. His eyes searched hers, the fog curling between them like a veil. "And you believe that now? Not just the visions, not just the stories—but that Clara meant for you to continue this?"

Marley swallowed hard. "Yes. I believe it."

For a moment, the fog swallowed their silence, thick and complete. Then Damien gave a single, steady nod. "Then the estate is where we go next."

They resumed walking, though Marley's thoughts were no longer on the streets of Brookwood. They were on a hill beyond the town, where stone walls crumbled under ivy, where the wind carried echoes of voices that had been silenced but not erased. She could feel it already, pulling at her the way the spiral had, the way the candle flame had.

The circle wasn't finished. Clara hadn't been studying for herself. She had been preparing Marley to step into it. And now, with each revelation, Marley knew there was no turning back.

When they reached the bookshop, Damien lingered at the door. "Get some rest," he said. "Tomorrow, we'll see what the hill has been hiding."

Marley nodded, but she knew rest would not come. As she stepped into the shop, the door closing behind her with its familiar chime, she pressed her hand against the brass key at her neck, against the weight of everything Clara had left.

For the first time, she didn't feel like she was stumbling into her aunt's secrets.

She felt like she was walking a path Clara had set before her all along.

15

———

THE COVERED BRIDGE ENCOUNTER

The fog over Brookwood thickened toward evening, spilling low across the water and winding into the trees. Marley found herself drawn once again to the covered bridge—a place that had unsettled her from the start, but also whispered with a kind of insistence she could no longer ignore.

The bridge stood like a relic, its wooden beams dark with age, the roof sagging slightly but still steady. Lanterns no longer hung along its posts, but in the twilight, the place felt lit from within, as if memory itself gave it glow. Marley hesitated at the edge, her boots crunching against gravel, before stepping inside.

The air was different beneath the roof—colder, carrying the scent of damp timber and moss. Her footsteps echoed softly as she crossed, the sound reminding her of childhood games she and Clara had played here, racing from one end to the other, their laughter swallowed by wood and wind.

But tonight, the laughter was gone. Tonight, something else lingered.

Halfway across, Marley stopped. The silence pressed

close, broken only by the faint creak of the beams shifting under her weight. She let her hand rest against one of the supports, the grooves of carved initials long faded by time. Lovers had left their marks here, generations of names entwined in hearts, scratched by penknives. But the spiral she had seen before still lingered faintly on one beam, almost erased but not gone.

And then, like before, she heard it.

"Marley."

A child's voice. Soft. Near.

Her breath caught. She spun, but the bridge was empty —only fog pressed at its edges, curling inside like breath. The voice had been close, so close it brushed her ear.

Her heart hammered. She whispered into the silence, "Who are you?"

No answer. Only the creak of wood.

A gust of wind surged suddenly through the bridge, rushing from one end to the other. Marley shivered, bracing herself against the side. The wind caught at her coat, tugging until she stumbled back a step. And then she heard it—the clatter of wood beneath her boots.

One of the planks had shifted.

She crouched quickly, her hand brushing across the seam where the board sat loose. Another gust rattled it, and she saw it lift just enough to glimpse something glinting beneath. Her pulse quickened. She wedged her fingers beneath the edge and pulled. The plank groaned, but it gave, revealing a shallow hollow beneath.

Inside, nestled against the damp wood, was a small metal locket. Tarnished with age, its chain knotted around itself, but still intact. Marley reached in with trembling hands and lifted it free. The chill of the metal seeped into her palm, and for a moment she thought she heard the faintest echo of a girl's laugh, like wind slipping through reeds.

She held the locket up, brushing away grime with her thumb. When she pressed the clasp, it clicked open, stiff with rust. Inside, the faint engraving of two initials gleamed against the dim light.

A.W.

Marley's breath shuddered out.

She closed the locket carefully, holding it tight in her fist. The bridge groaned again as though acknowledging her discovery. She glanced around once more, her heart still pounding, but the voice did not return. Only the fog, only the silence.

She slipped the locket into her pocket and stood. She needed to show Damien. She needed to know if what she feared—and what she hoped—was true.

Because if A.W. was who she thought it was, the circle had just placed Aurelia W. into her hands.

And nothing in Brookwood would remain the same.

Damien's office at the library was cluttered, as always, with books stacked in uneven towers, loose papers scattered like fallen leaves, and the faint smell of dust and ink clinging to the air. A single lamp cast a golden circle across his desk, and Marley placed the locket carefully in the center of it.

He leaned forward immediately, pushing aside his notes to get a better look. "Where did you find this?"

"The covered bridge," Marley said, her voice still carrying the tremor of discovery. "I heard the voice again. A girl's voice. It led me to a loose plank. This was hidden underneath."

Damien picked up the locket with careful hands,

turning it so the lamplight caught the engraving. He worked the clasp, and the hinges groaned faintly as it opened. The initials gleamed back: A.W.

Damien's jaw tightened. "A.W." He set it down again and opened the ledger he had left on the side of his desk. Flipping quickly through the pages, his finger traced down the list of initials, pausing halfway. He turned the book so Marley could see.

There it was. A.W. Written in the same steady hand as the rest, marked with the spiral in the margin.

Marley's breath hitched. "So it's her."

"Yes." Damien's voice was low, weighted. "Aurelia W. The one your aunt underlined. The one Hazel whispered about. The one Evelyn's grandmother called the green-eyed healer. This isn't just story anymore. This is proof."

Marley pressed her hands against the edge of the desk, grounding herself against the rush of it. Proof. After weeks of fragments—spirals carved into wood, recipes coded with herbs, whispers in dreams—here was something undeniable. A name pressed into both wood and metal. A.W.

"Do you realize what this means?" Damien asked, his eyes sharp with intensity. "The bridge wasn't just a crossing. It was a hiding place. Someone—maybe Aurelia herself— tucked this locket away where only someone listening, truly listening, would ever find it. And now it's resurfaced. With you."

Marley shook her head slightly, overwhelmed. "Why me?"

"Because Clara prepared you for it," Damien said firmly. "She didn't just leave journals or recipes. She left threads that would draw you here. The bridge. The spiral. The candle. All of it was leading to this."

Marley's throat tightened. She remembered Clara's

handwriting in the journals, the way she underlined Aurelia's name with such care. She remembered Hazel's voice urging her to burn the candle, Evelyn's story of the healer unjustly cast out. And now Damien, showing her the ledger entry that matched the locket she held in her hands.

The circle was no longer a theory. It was no longer half-whispered folklore. It was flesh and bone, initials and metal, voices and dreams.

Damien leaned back slightly, his eyes never leaving the locket. "Do you see? They left markers. Not enough to be condemned, not enough to be erased—but enough to be found. A collective can't survive in the open. But it can survive in secrets, in symbols, in hidden objects like this."

Marley touched the locket again, her fingers brushing the cool metal. A strange calm washed over her, a sense of connection so strong it nearly felt like touch. She imagined Aurelia clasping it around her neck, pressing it into her palm during rituals, whispering over it in the moonlight. She imagined Clara knowing it was still out there, trusting that Marley would one day find it.

The weight of it was enormous. But it wasn't crushing. It was steadying, as though Aurelia herself was leaning across centuries to say: *You are not alone.*

She looked up at Damien, her voice steadier now. "This isn't just about remembering. This is about preserving. Continuing."

"Yes." His eyes softened, though his voice held conviction. "The circle wasn't made to be legend. It was made to be whole. And you've just recovered one of its missing pieces."

Marley closed the locket carefully, slipping it back into her palm. It was small, no larger than a coin, but it carried more weight than anything she had ever held.

For the first time, she no longer doubted. Aurelia was real. The circle was real.

And the bridge had given her its secret.

THE LOCKET'S weight stayed with Marley long after she left the library. Damien had offered to walk her back to the bookshop, but she'd refused gently, saying she needed air. In truth, she needed silence—the kind of silence where whispers could be heard.

The fog clung to the streets, muting the lamplight into faint halos. Each step back toward Seaberry Terrace echoed in her ears, not because of the cobblestones, but because of the voice from the bridge. *Marley.* The sound had been unmistakable—childlike, intimate, insistent.

She pulled the locket from her pocket and let it rest in her palm. A.W. Aurelia W. She whispered the name under her breath, testing it in the fog, letting it join the night. For a moment she thought she heard something stir in return—the faint creak of rope, the soft thrum of air moving through wood. The bridge's breath, carried all the way to her.

Her steps slowed. What did the voice want? The locket had been hidden there for more than a century, buried under a plank no one would think to pry loose. Yet she had been drawn to it—not by chance, not by curiosity, but by summons. The voice of a girl. Aurelia as a child? Or someone else bound to her name?

Marley pressed the locket against her chest, the chill seeping through her coat. She realized with a shiver that the circle wasn't content with her simply uncovering these relics. It was pushing her. First the candle and the dream. Now the bridge and the locket. The circle wasn't whispering of remembrance; it was demanding continuation.

When she reached the shop, she didn't light the lamps immediately. She stood in the dark, letting her eyes adjust, listening to the creak of the old floorboards and the faint hum of the sea beyond the glass. The bookshop had never felt more alive—every shelf pressing close, every spine whispering like mouths half-open in the dark.

She sat at Clara's desk, the candle stub still resting beside the journals. She placed the locket next to it, the two objects casting shadows across each other in the dim glow. Ledger, locket, recipes, tin, map—threads weaving themselves tighter, no longer scattered, no longer passive. They were pieces of a living design.

Her mind replayed Damien's words: *The circle wasn't made to be legend. It was made to be whole.*

Whole. The phrase from the onion-skin page rose in her memory, as if underlined by unseen hands: *The Circle must remain whole.*

She pressed her forehead into her palms, a tremor running through her. Clara had known. Clara had trusted that Marley would piece this together. Not as history, not as comfort, but as instruction.

The bridge's voice echoed again inside her mind, not as sound this time but as presence. A reminder that discovery was never the end. Discovery was the beginning.

Marley lifted her head, staring at the candle stub. "What do you want from me?" she whispered into the shadows.

The silence pulsed in return, heavy, alive. She didn't need the flame or the fog to understand the truth. The circle wanted her to step forward—not as observer, not as collector, but as participant.

Her fingers closed around the locket, its metal cold and solid. She felt the initials press into her palm, as though Aurelia herself was reaching through the years. And with that pressure came the undeniable certainty: the circle wasn't asking for remembrance.

It was demanding action.

Marley sat back in the chair, her heart pounding. Whatever waited at the hillside estate, whatever lay hidden in Brookwood's roots, she could no longer delay. She was in the circle now—not by accident, but by inheritance.

And the circle had begun to close around her.

16

THE NECKLACE IN THE WALL

The bookshop had grown so familiar to Marley in the past weeks that she thought she knew every groan of its floorboards, every knot in its wood. Yet the building still found ways to surprise her.

It began with a draft. A thin whisper of cold air in the upstairs hallway, brushing against her arm even though the windows were closed. She followed it with the stubbornness that Clara herself would have admired. Her fingers trailed along the wall, feeling for seams in the plaster. And then, near the back corner, she noticed it—a panel that didn't quite sit flush.

She crouched, her heart pounding with a mixture of anticipation and unease. Clara had already led her to the locked room, the journals, the recipes. What could possibly still be hidden?

Her fingers found the lip of the panel, and with a little force it gave way, revealing a narrow cavity in the wall. Inside, wrapped tightly in oilcloth, was a small bundle. Marley pulled it free, her breath catching at the weight of it.

She unwrapped it slowly, the cloth brittle and faintly

stained with age. Inside lay a necklace. The chain was delicate, the kind of handiwork that spoke of centuries rather than decades, its metal darkened with tarnish. At its center hung a pendant—an oval of green stone, faintly marbled, set in a filigree of silver.

The moment Marley's fingers brushed the stone, the air shifted.

The bookshop fell away.

She was standing in another time, another room, its walls lit only by candlelight. A young woman stood before her—dark hair braided, her hands clutching the very same necklace. Her breath came fast, her face taut with fear. Men's voices shouted outside the door, the sound of boots striking earth.

"Hide," another woman hissed from the shadows. "Now, before they see."

The young woman pressed the necklace against her chest, eyes wide. She looked directly at Marley—though Marley knew she couldn't possibly be seen—and for a moment Marley thought she recognized her. The same shape of the jaw as the portrait Clara once kept hidden, the same fierce green eyes Evelyn had described.

Aurelia.

The door shook with pounding fists. The young woman gasped, shoving the necklace into the wall before anyone could stop her. She pressed the panel closed with trembling hands just as the door burst open and the men stormed inside.

Marley felt the terror crackle in the air—the sense of being hunted for knowledge too dangerous to name. She tried to reach forward, to call out, but the vision collapsed like shattered glass, and she was back in the bookshop, on her knees, the necklace trembling in her palm.

Her breath came ragged, her body slick with sweat despite the chill of the draft. The pendant seemed to hum faintly, as though the vision still lingered inside it.

She cradled it carefully, whispering into the silence: "You were forced to hide. And now... you want to be found."

The words echoed in her ears, and she realized she wasn't only speaking of Aurelia. She was speaking of Clara too.

The necklace lay heavy in her hands—not just as relic, but as testimony.

MARLEY DIDN'T WAIT until morning. The vision had left her shaken, the echo of Aurelia's fear lodged in her chest like a splinter. She wrapped the necklace back in its brittle oilcloth and hurried through the fog-choked streets toward the library.

Damien was still there, a solitary figure in the yellow light of his office. He looked up as she entered, his eyes widening when he saw her pale face and trembling hands.

"What happened?" he asked, standing quickly.

Marley set the bundle on his desk, unwrapping it with careful hands. The green pendant gleamed faintly in the lamplight. "I found it in the bookshop wall. And when I touched it..." Her throat tightened, but she forced the words out. "I saw her, Damien. I saw Aurelia. She was hiding it— this necklace—just before men burst into her room. She knew they were coming for her."

Damien stared at the pendant, then back at Marley, his expression torn between fascination and alarm. "You're saying the vision came when you touched it? Not a dream this time, not the candle. Touch."

"Yes." Marley's voice was raw. "It wasn't memory. It was

happening around me. I felt her fear. I felt the pounding on the door. I saw her hands place this necklace into the wall before they dragged her away."

Damien exhaled, running a hand through his hair. He circled the desk, coming closer, but not reaching for the necklace. "Marley, listen to me. This is dangerous."

Her head snapped up. "Dangerous? It's proof. It's Aurelia's story preserved in more than ink or code. It's her voice, her life."

"And it's tearing through you." His tone sharpened, though his eyes were filled with worry. "Look at yourself. You're shaking. You're pale. Your body isn't meant to carry centuries of memory like this. Clara prepared you, yes—but that doesn't mean you can bear everything at once."

Marley pressed the necklace into her palms, the stone cool against her skin. "I can't stop now. Every piece is pulling me forward. The locket at the bridge, the candle, the ledger. And now this. It's all connected. Don't you see? Aurelia isn't gone. She's been waiting."

Damien leaned against the desk, crossing his arms, his jaw tight. "Waiting for what? For you to relive her terror? For you to burn yourself out on fragments you can't control?"

His words struck deep, not because they were cruel, but because they carried truth. Marley's body ached with exhaustion, her mind fogged by too many nights without rest. And yet...

"You don't understand," she said, her voice trembling but firm. "This isn't just about remembering Aurelia. It's about continuing what she started. The circle isn't history— it's present. It wants me to act."

Damien's eyes softened then, though his worry didn't fade. "And if acting destroys you? Clara may have trusted you, but maybe she didn't mean for you to throw yourself into the fire."

Marley shook her head, clutching the necklace tighter. "She meant for me to find this. She meant for me to feel it. Why else would she leave so many threads for me to follow? She knew. She trusted I could bear it."

Damien's hand hovered as though he might reach for hers, but he stopped short, his restraint palpable. "Marley, I don't doubt what you saw. I don't doubt what you feel. But I've watched you change these past weeks. Each vision takes more from you. If you keep pushing without rest, without balance, you could lose yourself."

She met his gaze, the green stone glinting faintly in her palm. "And if I stop, I'll lose the circle. I'll lose Aurelia. I'll lose Clara."

Silence stretched between them, heavy with truth neither wanted to name. Damien's concern pressed against Marley's certainty, each side weighted by love—for the past, for the present, for each other.

Finally, Damien lowered his voice. "Then promise me one thing. If you're going to continue, you won't do it alone."

Marley closed her eyes briefly, then nodded. "I promise."

But as the pendant hummed faintly in her hand, she knew some parts of the journey would always be hers alone.

THE LIBRARY LAMPS had long since gone out by the time Marley returned to the shop. Damien had urged her to rest —his eyes clouded with worry, his voice softer than usual— but his caution felt impossible to obey. She needed solitude, the kind of silence where memory pressed in and the circle's voice could be heard clearly.

The bookshop was dark except for the pale spill of

moonlight through the front windows. Marley moved slowly upstairs, the pendant still wrapped in oilcloth but thrumming faintly, as if it carried its own pulse. Each step seemed to draw her deeper into an unspoken pact, one Clara had entered before her, one Aurelia had endured before Clara.

She set the bundle on the desk, unwrapped it again, and let the necklace rest in her palm. Even without touching the stone, she felt the weight of the vision clinging to it—the pounding fists on Aurelia's door, the fear that had hardened into ritual, the desperate act of hiding.

Damien's warning echoed in her ears: *If you keep pushing without rest, you could lose yourself.*

Her hands trembled, but she closed her fingers around the necklace all the same. The chill seeped into her bones. She could almost hear voices in the walls—the hushed urgency of women whispering, *hide it, now, before they see.*

She sank into Clara's chair, her body heavy with exhaustion but her mind alive, pulled taut between terror and belonging. Clara had meant for her to find this. Of that, she was certain. Every hidden object, every coded recipe, every whispered fragment—it was never about idle remembrance. It was a trail, an inheritance.

The necklace wasn't just a relic. It was Aurelia's testimony, smuggled forward through time, demanding to be carried.

Marley pressed it against her heart, her breath shaking. "I hear you," she whispered, her voice breaking. "I won't let you be forgotten. I won't let the circle break."

The silence in the room shifted. It thickened, alive, as though the walls themselves bent closer to listen. A draft rustled a loose page from Clara's journal, lifting it into the air before letting it fall again, faceup on the desk. Marley's eyes caught the underlined phrase: *The Circle must remain whole.*

She felt tears sting her eyes. Damien had been right—this path was dangerous. But the danger was no longer reason enough to turn away. The circle's call had passed through recipes, spirals, maps, candles, and now relics of metal and stone. Each piece had pressed tighter around her, until she could no longer pretend choice was possible.

Marley sat there until the moon shifted in the sky; her body weary but her spirit pulled taut with certainty. She knew then, with a clarity that made her tremble:

The circle wasn't finished.

It didn't want her to remember.

It wanted her to act.

No matter the cost.

17

SHIP'S LOG AND THE SEA CAPTAIN'S TALE

Damien's knock came early the next morning, sharp against the glass door of the bookshop. Marley had barely slept—her dreams had been restless but unformed, weighed down by the lingering pulse of the necklace—but she pulled her cardigan close and let him in.

He carried a leather satchel under one arm, and his expression was taut with excitement. "I was at the historical society until past midnight," he said without preamble. "I found something."

Marley gestured him to the desk, her pulse quickening at his urgency. Damien pulled a bound volume from the satchel, its spine cracked, the pages yellowed and fraying at the edges. "A sea captain's log," he explained, setting it down gently. "Dated 1861. Captain Elias Morton, who sailed the *Windward Star* along the coast. There's an entry I need you to see."

Marley leaned in as he flipped through the pages, his fingers careful despite his urgency. The ink had faded but remained legible, scrawled in a neat, firm hand. Damien turned to a page marked with his own slip of paper and tapped it.

"Here," he said.

Marley read aloud: '*A woman aboard—name withheld by her request—proved herself more vital than any compass. She saw into storms before they struck, calming the men with herbs and whispered prayers. Never have I known such skill, nor such certainty. She disembarked near Brookwood before the wreck of the White Shoal.*'

Her breath caught. "A healer."

Damien nodded. "Not just any healer. She left the ship near Brookwood. And the timing matches perfectly with when Aurelia disappears from the town ledger."

Marley touched the page lightly, her fingertips tingling against the faded ink. *She saw into storms before they struck.* The phrasing sent a shiver down her spine, not only because of its poetry but because it sounded like the circle itself—vision, foresight, the ability to weave survival from what others could not see.

"And then the wreck," Damien said quietly. "The White Shoal went down days later, killing most of its crew. If she hadn't disembarked, she might have been lost. Instead, she was here."

Marley closed her eyes, imagining it: the healer standing on the deck, the sea raging around her, herbs crushed in her hands, words carried into the wind. She imagined her stepping off the ship into the fog of Brookwood, carrying not only her life but her knowledge, her presence, her belonging to the circle.

"It's her," Marley whispered. "It has to be Aurelia."

Damien's eyes softened, though his voice remained measured. "I can't prove that, not yet. But it fits. And it tells us the circle's reach extended beyond this town. It wasn't just Brookwood preserving fragments—it was traveling, protecting, warning. That woman wasn't merely a healer. She was a navigator of storms."

Marley opened her eyes and looked at him, her chest tight with certainty. "And she's still navigating us."

The words slipped out before she could stop them. But Damien didn't dismiss them. He only held her gaze, the silence between them heavy with agreement.

The log lay open on the desk, its ink shimmering faintly in the morning light. Marley traced the line again—*herbs and whispered prayers*—and knew the night ahead would bring her closer. She could already feel it stirring, the pull of dreams not her own.

And when she finally fell into sleep, she knew the healer would be waiting.

THAT NIGHT, Marley lay awake long after she closed the shop. The captain's words from the log circled her mind: *she saw into storms before they struck.* It was more than metaphor —it was invocation, a recognition of something beyond ordinary skill. She set the pendant necklace on the night-stand, the locket tucked close beneath it, as though the arti-facts themselves might keep vigil while she slept.

Sleep came reluctantly, but when it arrived, it seized her fully.

The dream began with salt. The sting of it filled her lungs, sharp and raw, and the roar of the ocean surrounded her. She was standing on the deck of a great ship, its masts towering overhead, the sails straining against a furious wind. The year felt different—older—but the urgency was unmistakable.

Men scrambled across the planks, their faces pale, their

voices broken with terror. Lightning split the sky, illuminating the vast curl of waves rushing toward them. Marley gripped the slick railing, her body trembling though she knew she was more witness than participant.

Then she saw her.

A woman stood at the center of the chaos, her dark cloak whipping in the wind, her hands cupping herbs crushed into paste. Aurelia—though not as the frightened girl Marley had seen hiding the necklace. This was Aurelia grown, fierce and commanding, her green eyes burning with clarity.

She knelt and spread the herbs across the deck, pressing them into the wood, whispering words that threaded through the storm's roar. Her voice was steady, a rhythm that matched the lightning's flash, a counterpoint to the thunder. The men who had moments before been wild with fear stilled as her voice carried over them.

One sailor fell to his knees, pressing his forehead against the herbs she scattered, as though the scent itself calmed his pulse. Another clutched a pendant at his throat and began echoing her words, broken but earnest. Soon the air thickened with prayer and smoke, as if the ritual itself had bent the storm's edge.

Marley felt her chest tighten with awe. This was no passive healer, no woman tucked away in kitchens or hidden rooms. This was Aurelia commanding the sea, not as owner but as partner—reading its tempers, answering its violence with calm and clarity.

A wave crashed hard against the hull, drenching the deck, but instead of panic, the crew shouted together, their voices braided with hers. Aurelia raised her hands, and the storm's force bent just enough for the ship to crest the wave rather than capsize beneath it.

Marley staggered, drenched though untouched, her heart pounding. She wanted to call out, to ask Aurelia what she was seeing, what she knew, but the healer's eyes were fixed forward, beyond storm and fear, into something Marley could not name.

Then Aurelia turned suddenly. For an instant, her gaze met Marley's across time. The shock of recognition pierced through Marley's chest like a flare. The woman's lips moved, forming words Marley couldn't hear over the storm, but she knew, with the certainty dreams sometimes bring, that they were meant for her.

The deck shuddered. A blast of lightning tore the sky open, and when Marley blinked, Aurelia was gone. The ship's planks dissolved beneath her feet. The sea fell silent.

Marley woke with a cry, her body slick with sweat, the smell of salt and herbs still thick in the air. The pendant and locket on her nightstand gleamed faintly in the moonlight, as if they too had been part of the storm.

She pressed her hand against her racing heart. The dream hadn't been story. It had been testimony, carried forward through the log, through the relics, through the circle itself.

Aurelia had not only survived the storm. She had commanded it.

And now Marley felt the same demand echoing inside her: to steady herself in the midst of chaos, to answer the storm not with fear, but with presence.

The circle's call was not soft history. It was living instruction.

MARLEY JOLTED upright in her bed, her breath ragged, heart hammering as though she'd run a mile uphill. The remnants of the dream clung to her like seawater, heavy and brine-stung. She pressed a hand to her chest, but the thundering of her pulse would not still.

The room was quiet—too quiet. No storm outside, no lightning striking the horizon. Only the soft fog pressing at the windowpanes, the lighthouse beacon turning its slow, steady sweep across the town. Yet the smell of salt lingered in her nose, and she swore her skin was damp as if the sea itself had clung to her.

Her eyes shifted to the nightstand. The necklace lay there, the pendant catching what little moonlight seeped into the room. Beside it, the locket gleamed faintly, almost as though they breathed together. She drew the quilt tighter around her shoulders and stared, waiting for the trembling in her body to quiet.

But it did not.

The dream had not been like the others. The candle's vision had been soft, smoke-bound, carrying Clara's face in ritual light. The necklace had pressed Aurelia's terror into her skin. But this—this was different. The ship's log had served as door, opening into a storm so vivid Marley could still hear the roar of the sea and the steady chant of Aurelia's prayer.

And more than that—the healer had seen her.

The memory burned into Marley's mind. Aurelia's eyes had cut through storm and centuries, locking on hers as though the distance between them did not exist. Her lips had moved, words swallowed by wind, but Marley felt them still inside her, a weight in her chest.

"What are you asking of me?" Marley whispered into the room. Her voice cracked, brittle in the stillness.

The silence that followed was no comfort. It pressed close, heavy, alive.

Marley rose from bed, her legs unsteady, and moved to the desk where Clara's journals lay stacked. She opened one at random, her hands shaking, and saw the spiral drawn again and again in the margins. Beneath it, Clara's looping script: *The storm is not destruction—it is revelation.*

Marley traced the words with her finger, her throat tightening. The storm in her dream had not destroyed the ship. Aurelia's presence had bent it, guided it, reshaped its violence into survival. The storm had revealed the healer's power, her necessity, her role.

Marley sank into the chair, her hands pressed to her face. She wanted to believe Damien's cautions, to honor his fear that she was burning too fast, taking on too much. But the dream had left no space for hesitation.

Brookwood's storms were not just weather.

They were memory unraveling, demanding to be named. They were the circle testing her resolve, pressing her to stand where others had stood, to hold the line between terror and trust.

She lifted her head, tears stinging her eyes, and looked again at the necklace. The stone seemed to pulse faintly in the dim light, a heartbeat of green fire.

Clara had known. Clara had left her these relics not to comfort her, but to prepare her. Every hidden object, every whispered vision was a storm pulling her deeper into its eye.

And now she understood: storms came not to be fled, but to be endured. To be read. To be calmed.

Her body trembled, exhaustion pulling at her bones, but her spirit—God help her—felt electrified, awake in a way she had never known before.

She whispered into the stillness, her voice steadier this time. "I'll see it through. Whatever it asks. Whatever it costs."

The fog outside thickened against the windows, the lighthouse beam sweeping slow and silent. And for the first time, Marley didn't feel like the storm was something outside her.

It was already inside, unraveling memory, rewriting her resolve.

18

———

THE MUSIC BOX MELODY

The afternoon sunlight stretched thin through the bookshop windows, casting slanted lines across the hardwood floor. Marley had meant to busy herself with the day's small tasks—sorting through Clara's old invoices, sweeping the steps, polishing the brass bell above the door—but her mind refused to settle. The storm-dream still lived in her, thrumming beneath her skin like an undercurrent she could neither silence nor outrun.

When the sun dipped lower, she found herself wandering upstairs, toward Clara's bedroom. She hadn't yet spent much time there. Even weeks after her aunt's passing, the room felt too personal, too weighted with the imprint of its former inhabitant. Clara's shawl still hung across the bedpost. A faint trace of lavender clung to the linens. Marley stood at the threshold for a long moment before crossing it.

She told herself she was searching for answers. But it felt more like Clara had been waiting for her.

The closet door creaked when she opened it. Inside, the shelves were stacked with boxes of folded sweaters, a hatbox, and a row of dresses shrouded in garment bags. She crouched to look at the floor, her hand brushing against something small wedged in the back corner. Dust coated the wood, and beneath it, the shape of a box emerged.

Marley pulled it free and carried it to the bed. The box was wooden, no larger than a loaf of bread, its surface carved with delicate floral patterns. Tarnished brass hinges held it shut. She brushed dust away, her fingertips lingering on the fine craftsmanship, before lifting the lid.

Inside, nestled in velvet, was a music box.

Her breath caught. The sight of it stirred something deep, a familiarity that made her throat ache. She wound the small brass key on its side with trembling fingers. A moment later, the tune began—soft, lilting, rising and falling in notes that curved like memory.

Marley froze.

It was the same melody from her dreams. The one that had played beneath the candlelight, that had threaded through the storm, that had haunted her since the moment she stepped back into Brookwood.

Her eyes blurred with tears. She let the melody carry her, each note tugging her deeper into a place both foreign and intimate. She saw the circle of women in her mind's eye, their hands clasped, their voices woven together with the music. She saw Clara, smiling softly, her head bowed as though listening for a harmony just beyond reach.

When the last note faded, Marley drew a shaky breath. Her fingers brushed the inside of the box again—and caught on something tucked in the lining. She pulled it free.

A folded slip of paper, yellowed with age, written in Clara's familiar hand.

She smoothed it open and read aloud: *"Only when the melody plays under moonlight will the truth reveal itself."*

Her heart pounded. Clara had left her riddles before,

but this one was different. This wasn't a fragment hidden in recipes or initials coded in ledgers. This was instruction. A directive.

Marley stared at the words until her vision blurred. She imagined the music box set on a windowsill, the moonlight spilling across it, the melody carrying into the night air. What truth would it reveal? Another vision? A memory not her own? Or something more tangible—something hidden in Brookwood itself?

A knock at the door startled her. She jumped, clutching the note.

"Marley?" Damien's voice. "It's me."

She opened the door and let him in, the music box still in her hands. His eyes went immediately to it, then to her pale face. "What did you find?"

She set it on the desk and wound the key again. The melody filled the room, fragile yet commanding. Damien stilled as he listened, his brow furrowed.

"I've heard that before," he said slowly. "Where—" He broke off, shaking his head. "It doesn't matter. What matters is that you've been hearing it too, haven't you? In the dreams."

Marley nodded, her voice caught in her throat. She handed him the slip of paper. He read it, his frown deepening.

"Moonlight," he murmured. "That's not metaphor. That's instruction."

Marley sank onto the edge of the bed, her hands trembling. "But what truth? What am I supposed to see?"

Damien looked at her, his gaze steady. "Whatever it is, Clara wanted you to find it. And she left you the key. The note says under moonlight—so that's when we test it. And the next full moon isn't far."

Marley closed her eyes, the melody still playing behind her eyelids. The circle wasn't done with her—not by a long stretch. The storms had demanded her resolve. The music would demand something more.

She opened her eyes again and whispered, "Then we wait for the moon."

DAMIEN TURNED the slip of paper over in his hand, his thumb tracing the faded ink. "Your aunt's handwriting," he said quietly, though it sounded less like a statement and more like an invocation. "Clara never left anything by accident."

Marley nodded, still staring at the music box. The melody had finished, but its echo seemed to hum faintly in the room, as if the wood itself remembered. She could not shake the feeling that if she wound it again, Aurelia's presence would fill the air beside her.

Damien sat, drawing the music box closer beneath the lamplight. He studied the brass key, the hinges, the carving along its sides. "Look here," he said, pointing to one of the floral motifs etched into the wood.

Marley leaned closer. Her breath caught.

The design wasn't merely floral. The petals curved into a spiral, the same symbol she had seen carved into the bridge, drawn in Clara's journals, marked beside initials in the ledger. Here it was again, hidden in plain sight, worked into decoration so subtle she might never have noticed.

"The circle marked even this," Damien murmured. "Not just journals or recipes. Objects. Everyday things transformed into carriers of memory." He looked up at her, his expression sharp with certainty. "Your aunt didn't just keep this as a keepsake. She knew what it was. She meant for you to use it."

Marley touched the spiral with her fingertip, the grooves rough beneath her skin. "And the note... 'Only when the melody plays under moonlight will the truth reveal itself.' Do you think it's literal?"

Damien sat back, crossing his arms. "I've spent years chasing Brookwood's half-myths. Most of them are metaphor dressed as fact. But this—this feels different. It doesn't read like parable. It reads like direction. Play the melody. In moonlight. Something will happen. Not maybe —will."

Marley swallowed hard. The thought of it unsettled her, but it also drew her forward, the way every fragment had since she'd reopened the shop. "The full moon is in three nights," she whispered.

Damien's gaze lingered on her, steady but filled with concern. "Then that's when we'll test it."

Marley opened her mouth to argue, but he lifted a hand gently. "Not you alone. Not this time. Whatever Clara intended, she left enough of a trail that you were never meant to carry it by yourself. You've been walking into visions that leave you trembling, pulling relics out of walls, listening to whispers no one else can hear. If the circle wants you to act, then let me stand with you when you do."

She looked away, her throat tightening. His words reminded her of the ship's dream, Aurelia standing firm on the deck while the men steadied themselves in her presence. Marley wanted to believe she could stand like that. But the truth was, Damien was right. Each step into Clara's world left her more drained. Each vision took more than it gave.

She brushed her hand along the box's edge, the wood

smooth but humming faintly beneath her palm. "You really believe it too, don't you? That this isn't coincidence. That it isn't madness."

Damien's mouth quirked with something between a smile and a grimace. "I stopped believing in coincidence the day I walked into this town and found every record of its history edited to look ordinary. I've seen enough of your aunt's papers, enough of these objects, to know something was being preserved. And now you're the one unearthing it. Not because you stumbled into it—because it chose you."

Marley felt the words settle into her chest, heavy but certain. She wanted to protest, to claim that she had been dragged into this, that she had never asked for it. But even as the thought formed, she knew it wasn't true. Clara had left her more than keys and journals. She had left her trust.

Damien closed the music box gently, the melody silenced for now. "Three nights from now, the full moon will rise over Brookwood. We'll bring the box outside, set it under the light, and play the song. If Clara was right—and she usually was—something will reveal itself. The truth, as she called it."

Marley drew a shaky breath. "And if it's something we can't handle?"

"Then we handle it anyway," Damien said softly, his eyes steady on hers.

The room fell quiet, the weight of their pact unspoken but undeniable. Marley felt the fatigue of the day in her bones, but beneath it pulsed something sharper, something alive. The melody had called to her across dreams, threaded through storms and visions, until finally it found its way into her hands in wood and brass.

And now it waited, as patient as moonlight.

Marley rested her hand atop the box, her voice low but firm. "Then we wait for the moon."

THE NIGHT before the full moon, Marley could not sleep. She had tried—curled beneath Clara's quilt, the sea air drifting through the open window, the rhythm of the tide meant to calm her. But the melody refused to leave her. It pressed at the edges of her mind, soft but insistent, like a song hummed by someone standing just beyond the door.

She turned over, her eyes drawn yet again to the nightstand. The music box sat there, closed, its brass key glinting faintly in the moonlight. Even in silence, it seemed to hum with anticipation. Marley pulled herself upright, pushing the quilt aside, and sat staring at it for a long time.

Clara's note burned in her thoughts: *Only when the melody plays under moonlight will the truth reveal itself.* The words carried the same weight as the ledger entries, the onion-skin page, the spirals carved into wood. Instruction, not metaphor. A key disguised as poetry.

But what kind of truth could a melody reveal?

She stood and carried the box to the desk, placing it beside the locket and the necklace. Together, the objects looked less like heirlooms and more like parts of a ritual— anchors meant to call something into being. Marley touched each in turn, her fingertips lingering on the cold green stone of the pendant before returning to the box.

She did not dare wind it again, not yet. Damien was right—they would wait for the full moon. But her body ached with the need to hear the song. To feel its pull. To know what it wanted.

She sank into the chair, her hands clasped in her lap, and closed her eyes. The melody rose in her memory, weaving through her mind with the same certainty as breath. She could see Aurelia in the storm, herbs crushed in her hands. She could see Clara beneath the candle's glow, bowing her head as the tune threaded through ritual. And she could see herself—standing at the edge of something vast, holding the music box as the moon painted everything silver.

Marley shivered. The circle had led her step by step, relic by relic, vision by vision. Now it was drawing her to a threshold. She felt it pressing, urging her forward. Not simply to remember, but to stand where Aurelia had stood. To carry what Clara had carried. To act.

She rose and crossed to the window. Outside, the night was thick with fog, the lighthouse beam sweeping slow arcs across the water. Tomorrow night the full moon would rise, clear and heavy, and she would place the box beneath its light. The thought filled her with both dread and exhilaration.

She pressed her forehead to the glass, whispering into the dark. "Clara... Aurelia... whoever's listening. I'm ready."

The fog stirred faintly, brushing against the panes like a hand. Marley stepped back, her chest tight, her pulse racing. For a moment she thought she heard the first faint notes of the melody carried on the wind. She gripped the windowsill, holding her breath until the sound faded.

When she finally returned to bed, the music still played in her head, each note a promise. She knew then, with certainty, that whatever waited tomorrow would change more than her understanding of Clara's secrets.

It would change Brookwood itself.

19

RAINSTORM AND REVELATION

The weather had promised calm. The late morning sky had been clear, the sea a steady roll of gray-green, the air still. Marley and Damien had chosen the lighthouse for its vantage, hoping to inspect the structure more closely, to search for anything Clara or the circle might have hidden in stone or iron.

The climb was long but familiar now. Marley felt each step of the winding staircase vibrate beneath her boots. Damien carried a lantern, though it was unnecessary at first —the narrow windows admitted strips of daylight. The higher they climbed, the more the sea spread wide beneath them, until the small town of Brookwood was a cluster of roofs wrapped in fog.

At the landing, they paused, breathing hard. The interior of the lighthouse smelled of salt and rust. Marley trailed her fingers along the curved wall, feeling the rough stone, the iron bolts that held everything together. She had expected stillness, but there was something alive about the place, as if the lighthouse itself remembered every storm it had endured.

Damien raised the lantern higher, his brow furrowed. "Look here," he said, pointing to a section where the stone joined with the floor. A faint mark, nearly erased by time, curved across the seam.

Marley bent low. Her heart tightened. The spiral again.

It was faint, so worn she might have mistaken it for a crack, but once seen it could not be unseen. The same symbol carved into wood and pressed into journals was etched here in stone, as if to remind her that no place in Brookwood stood untouched by the circle.

Before she could speak, thunder rolled overhead. The sound startled them both, deep and immediate, shaking the glass panes in the lantern. Damien crossed quickly to one of the narrow windows and peered out.

"Storm," he said, his tone edged with disbelief. "That wasn't in the forecast."

Marley joined him, pressing close. The sea that had been calm was now thrashing, waves cresting white against the rocks. The sky had darkened, clouds folding over one another like bruises. Sheets of rain struck the glass.

Lightning split the horizon, illuminating the coastline. Thunder followed almost instantly, so loud it rattled the walls. Marley flinched, grabbing the stone for balance.

"We're not getting back to town in this," Damien said, his voice low but firm. "We'll have to wait it out here."

Marley nodded, her pulse racing. The spiral at her back seemed to hum, as though the storm itself had awakened it. She thought of Aurelia aboard the ship, her prayer rising above crashing waves, and shivered.

The rain thickened, pounding the lighthouse roof in relentless rhythm. Damien set the lantern down and leaned against the wall, water dripping from his hair. For a long moment neither of them spoke. The storm pressed so close it felt as though they were inside its chest, their own breathing synced to its ragged pulse.

Finally, Damien broke the silence. "I used to scoff at this," he admitted, his eyes fixed on the storm beyond the glass. "Stories of women who whispered to storms, recipes that doubled as codes, journals written in riddles. I thought it was just small-town folklore, the kind of thing people cling to when history feels too ordinary. But now—"

He looked at Marley then, his expression raw. "Now I'm standing inside it. And part of me still can't believe what I've seen. That you've seen. And the worst of it is, I feel guilty. Guilty that I didn't believe sooner. That I doubted Clara, doubted the town, doubted…"

He trailed off, but the weight of the words hung between them.

Marley's chest tightened. She wanted to tell him he wasn't alone, that she too had doubted, that she had resisted every pull until the circle pressed too hard to ignore. But before she could find the words, another crack of lightning tore the sky, flooding the lighthouse with blinding white.

The spiral at her back seemed to pulse in the light, alive for just an instant.

The storm was no longer outside. It was here, inside them, demanding revelation.

THE THUNDER TOOK up residence inside the lighthouse, settling into the spiral of stone like a low, unbroken growl. Wind hurled itself along the glass panes and rattled the iron casements; rain spooled sideways, needling the narrow windows until each drop sounded like the tap of a fingernail. The world had shrunk to this column of stairs, this round of stone, the small gold lake of the lantern on the floor between them.

Damien didn't try to hide the way his hands shook when the next peal rolled over them. He braced his palms on the sill and watched the sea convulse. The skin beneath his eyes looked bruise-dark in the blown light.

"I told Jackie once that storms were only weather," he said at last, voice rough. "She'd stand at our old apartment window and swear she could hear something in them— like a change of key you feel in your bones before you hear it in your ears. I said she was being romantic." He huffed a breath that wasn't a laugh. "It felt like the practical thing to say. Like I was keeping us tethered to the ground."

Marley said nothing, letting the storm fill the spaces between his words. It was the first time he'd brought Jackie into a room with lightning this close.

"I've been thinking about that a lot," he continued. "How sure I was that staying rational was the same as keeping her safe. And then she got sick, and I kept telling both of us that medicine is a straight road. You take it and it takes you where you're meant to go." He swallowed. "Except sometimes it doesn't. And the thing I can't forgive in myself is how much I didn't listen. To her. To myself. To anything that wasn't measurable."

He turned from the window. Even in the lantern's small circle, Marley could see he was shaking less from cold than confession.

"I came to Brookwood telling myself it was for quiet," he said. "But it was also penance. I thought if I could name every fact, catalogue every ledger, restore order to a worn-out archive, I could reduce the ache to a problem with a solution." His mouth tightened. "And then you unlocked a room in a bookshop wall and the facts started speaking in a language I don't know."

"The facts were always speaking," Marley said softly. "We just weren't listening."

Another flash. The room bleached white and then slammed back to gray. The spiral at the base of the wall seemed to shiver in the light, a ripple caught in stone.

He followed her gaze. "That mark... I've spent a career learning to ignore what doesn't fit. Here it is. In a lighthouse foundation." He lowered his head, the admission catching on his breath. "I'm sorry I asked you to be the reasonable one when you said you believed. I had no right to put that on you."

"You didn't," Marley answered, and surprised herself with how easily truth came. "I put it on myself. Calling everything a coincidence was how I pretended I still had a choice."

"What about now?"

She looked toward the window. Rain swept across the glass in bands, the sea heaving under its own breath. "Now I think the only choice is whether I stand in it or let it knock me under." She rubbed her arms, suddenly cold. "But I don't know how to stand without turning into someone I don't recognize."

"Maybe that's the point," he said.

She met his eyes and found them steady, not soothing but honest. The honesty warmed her more than any blanket would have.

Another shudder of thunder. Somewhere above them the beacon groaned and turned, the old mechanism shouldering its ancient duty. The lantern at their feet flickered.

Damien stooped to adjust the wick. "There's something else."

Marley waited.

He set the lantern back down and remained crouched, elbows on his knees. "When I told you I felt guilty, I meant more than not believing. I meant wanting two opposing things at once." His lips shaped a grim smile. "To follow every sign this town gives us, deeper and darker if we must, and at the same time to keep you two steps back from it all. To keep you safe." He shook his head. "I know how that sounds. Controlling. Patronizing. I don't mean it that way. I just—" He stopped, searching for a word that wouldn't diminish either part of him. "I don't want to lose someone because I couldn't translate a warning fast enough."

"You won't," Marley said, and heard the steadiness in herself as if it belonged to someone older. "Not because you didn't translate. If the circle wants a price, I don't think it will be paid in cleverness."

His eyes lifted to hers. "Then what does it want?"

"Presence," she said, surprising them both. "Someone willing to stand in the middle of a thing and not run."

He rose slowly. Close like this, with the storm pressing the world smaller, she could smell the salt in his coat, the iron tang of wet stone on his skin. The lantern's light frayed around his shoulders. The narrow room turned them, inch by inch, toward each other.

"Presence," he repeated, as if testing the contour of the word. "That I can do."

A gust shouldered the lighthouse and the old tower answered with a groan from its spine. Instinct kicked them a step closer together. His hand found the curve of the wall behind her—the only place to put it—and hers landed, without thinking, against the fabric at his chest. Even that small pressure grounded him; she felt the exhale leave him and realized her own breath had synced to his.

"You asked me once what I believed," he said. "I was careful with the answer because carefulness felt like fidelity. To who I was. To who I lost." He looked at her the way someone studies a horizon for the first sliver of land. "I believe you. I believe the spiral is not ornament. I believe the melody is a key. I believe your aunt laid an arrow-straight path and that you've been brave enough to walk it. And I believe I want to stand where you stand."

Her fingers tightened a fraction. It startled her, how much it mattered to hear want that wasn't couched as duty. Outside, the rain raked the glass in long fingers; inside, the warmth between them pooled and gathered, something like a held note resolving.

"Damien—" she began, meaning to thank him or warn him or both, but language thinned under the storm's pressure. He dipped his head without quite meaning to, and she felt the small charge when their foreheads nearly touched. Not a rush, not heat—something steadier, like a knot cinching instead of unraveling.

"I don't know how to do this," he admitted, voice almost lost to the wind. "Any of it. Belief. Or... this."

"We'll learn," she said. "We already are."

For a suspended heartbeat neither of them moved. The sea lifted somewhere beyond stone; lightning lifted with it, breathing. He looked at her mouth, then back to her eyes as if asking a question he wasn't sure he should voice. She answered by not looking away.

He inclined the last inch. So did she.

Lightning cracked open the world.

The flare was instantaneous and entire. The lantern's small gold died, swallowed in a sheet of white that made their shadows vanish. The blast shook the glass, the air, the old bones of the tower. Marley's hand flew against his chest in reflex; his arm came around her shoulders the way a body protects what it has only just admitted it wants.

They didn't kiss. They couldn't. The sound scraped the room clean and left it ringing. Rain hammered harder, as if roused by its own brilliance.

"The beacon!" Damien shouted over the thunder, half-turning toward the narrow window. The light had faltered—one, two staggered beats—then steadied with a hard, mechanical sigh.

"You okay?" he asked, breathless, his arm still around her.

She nodded; neither of them moved away right away. The flare had left an outline in her eyes, a negative of the world. Shapes ghosted in the afterimage: the ladder, the window, the curve of masonry.

He drew back first, clearing his throat, embarrassment warring with the relief of simply finding her unshaken. "That... was close."

"The lightning," she said, though both of them knew what else she meant.

He let out a thin, startled laugh that wasn't quite a laugh. "Yes. The lightning."

They stood listening while the storm rearranged its furniture. Then Damien angled toward the window again, squinting through the rain. "Hold on," he said. "When it flashed—did you see—"

Another tremor rattled the panes. He pressed closer to the glass, trying to find the line of the outer platform through water and glare.

"See what?" Marley moved beside him, shoulder to shoulder. The sea lurched and threw back its own light.

He kept his eyes fixed on some point just beyond the curve of the stairs that ringed the tower's skin. "I don't know.

For a second it looked like—" He broke off, as if naming it might make it less true. "Nothing. Or I'm seeing what I want to see."

"Say it," she said.

"A mark," he answered. "On the exterior stone. Like the spiral, but... longer. Lines. An inscription."

Another flash tried to birth itself and failed; only a pale smear showed through the clouds. The rain retreated half a degree, enough to make the platform's rail shiver into view.

"We can't go out there now," Marley said, reading the same calculation in his face that the storm etched in hers. The wind would peel them off the steps. The spray would make the iron teeth-slick. "When it breaks."

"When it breaks," he echoed.

They stood very still, watching the window for the next white blade of light that might carve meaning into the stone. The space between flashes stretched long enough for their breathing to slow, for the physical nearness they'd been thrown into to soften into something chosen.

He looked at her then—not away from the storm, but through it, as if whatever the lightning had almost showed had to be answered first in here. "This doesn't cancel the things I said," he told her. "The wanting—both kinds."

"It doesn't cancel mine either," Marley said.

The lighthouse exhaled another enormous breath; the beacon turned with its ancient patience. Outside, the sky massed itself for one more strike. Damien reached past her to steady the lantern and his sleeve brushed her wrist. It felt like a promise too small to name and too solid to ignore.

The next flash, when it came, cracked somewhere farther out, the white quick and angled. The window brightened and went dark again, leaving only the echo and their held breath.

"Did you—?" he started.

"I think so," she said. "I think there's something there."

They didn't rush the moment. The storm would tell them when to move. For now, the nearness and the almost, the confession and the restraint, lived together in the small room with the spiral breathing in the stone at their backs.

Outside, the rain changed its sound, a fraction less furious, as if the sky had said what it came to say and was deciding whether to repeat itself.

They waited, the not-quite-kiss still sparking between them like a remembered chord, the promise of reading the exterior stone coiling tight as the next bolt gathered itself beyond the horizon.

THE STORM GATHERED itself into a single colossal breath, the kind that seemed to draw the whole sea into its chest. Inside the lighthouse, the walls shivered with its strength. Damien and Marley stood side by side at the narrow window, their shoulders almost touching, their reflections flickering pale against the glass.

Neither had spoken for several long moments. The nearness between them carried its own language. Their earlier words—of guilt, of belief, of wanting—still hung in the air, not erased but sharpened by the storm's insistence.

Damien turned, his face half-lit by the lantern's wavering glow. His hand brushed hers on the sill, not deliberately, but not by accident either. Marley didn't move away. If anything, she leaned a fraction closer, drawn into the quiet gravity that pressed between them.

Lightning rolled far out across the water, its flash throwing their shadows against the curved wall. Damien's voice was low, nearly lost to the thunder.

"Marley," he said, the syllables rough, as if her name itself carried more weight than he knew how to manage.

She looked up, meeting his eyes. The world shrank in that instant—not to the lighthouse, not to the storm, but to the distance between them. His expression was open in a way she hadn't seen before, stripped of careful restraint. She felt the pull, steady and undeniable, a tether tightening around them.

Her breath caught. "Yes?"

He shook his head slightly, as though chastising himself for what he was about to say—or not say. Then, with a half step forward, he closed the space between them. Their foreheads nearly touched, and she could feel the heat of his breath.

Everything slowed. The thunder dimmed. The rain softened to a background hum. For a heartbeat, Marley thought the storm itself had paused to watch.

And then it came.

The lightning strike hit with the violence of revelation. It split the sky open above them, pouring blinding white into the window, flooding the room so completely that their nearness shattered into brilliance. The thunder followed instantly, shaking the glass, rattling the iron beams. Marley flinched, her hand flying instinctively to Damien's chest. His arm went around her shoulders, steadying her as the lighthouse itself seemed to convulse.

When her eyes adjusted, the afterimage of the flash lingered, white-green against the glass. Damien still held her, but his gaze was fixed beyond her shoulder.

"Look," he said, his voice hoarse.

Marley turned.

The lightning had done more than blind them. In that instant of raw illumination, the storm had revealed something outside—on the outer wall of the lighthouse, just below the platform that circled it. A set of carved lines, faint but unmistakable, had glowed in the flash: spirals unfurling into script, a pattern so deliberate it could not have been erosion.

Marley pressed closer to the window, her breath fogging the glass. "It's an inscription," she whispered.

Damien nodded slowly, his arm still lingering against her shoulder though neither of them seemed to notice. "I thought I saw it before. But now—" His voice caught. "The lightning made it undeniable."

The storm battered the lighthouse again, as though angered by its own revelation. Rain coursed down the glass, momentarily obscuring the view. But Marley had seen enough to feel her pulse thunder louder than the storm.

The circle had marked the lighthouse not only within its walls but without. And the storm itself had chosen the moment to reveal it.

Marley's hand slipped from Damien's chest, but her fingers lingered on the fabric of his coat for a heartbeat longer. Their almost-kiss still hung between them, not lost but transformed, folded now into the greater urgency of the inscription outside.

She drew a sharp breath. "When the storm passes, we'll have to go out there. We need to see what it says."

Damien finally released her, though his eyes remained on the rain-smeared glass. "We will. But not tonight. The storm would kill us before we made it down the steps."

She nodded, though the urgency in her chest clawed for more. The storm had shown them a glimpse, then sealed it away again. It felt like being handed a truth only to have it snatched back.

They stood in silence, shoulder to shoulder, watching as

the waves hurled themselves against the rocks and the beacon turned its patient circle. The moment between them —confession, closeness, almost—remained unspoken but alive, humming beneath the storm's roar.

Marley placed her hand against the cold glass, tracing the space where the inscription had glowed in the lightning. She whispered, almost to herself, "The circle isn't finished."

Damien's voice answered, low but steady. "No. It's only beginning."

The storm howled on, but Marley felt the shift inside her—the same shift she had seen in Aurelia standing on the ship's deck. Fear and certainty braided together, demanding she remain present. Tomorrow they would read the stone. Tomorrow they would know more.

For tonight, the storm had done its work. It had revealed.

And it had reminded them both that storms, like truths, never came to be ignored.

20

THE FESTIVAL BEGINS

The streets of Brookwood thrummed with sound and color as the annual jazz festival unfurled across the town square. Banners stretched between lampposts, their fabric snapping lightly in the breeze. Vendors lined the sidewalks with stands offering everything from crab cakes and clam chowder to candied nuts and cinnamon-sweet pastries. Children darted through the press of bodies, their laughter weaving between the bright brassy notes of a horn section warming up on the main stage.

Marley threaded through the crowd slowly, a paper cup of coffee clasped in her hand, though she had already forgotten it had gone lukewarm. The aroma of roasting beans mixed with fried batter and salt air, grounding the senses, but her mind hovered elsewhere. Every sound, every flicker of movement seemed faint compared to the storm that had burned itself into her only nights ago.

She kept her smile polite when townsfolk greeted her, though she noticed the hushes that followed, the sidelong glances she couldn't quite name. "Digging too deep," they whispered. "Chasing what shouldn't be stirred." She wondered if Clara had felt the same faint resistance pressing against her whenever she walked into public life—the weight of being seen as both one of them and apart from them.

The main stage erupted with applause as the festival officially opened. The first band launched into a rollicking number, a parade of brass and drums filling the square with jubilant clamor. Marley felt it in her chest, the rhythm demanding she sway, demanding she give herself over to delight. But beneath the bright notes, another melody tugged.

She drifted toward the edge of the square where Damien stood near a line of wooden benches. He was dressed more casually than she'd ever seen him, his shirt collar open, his hair mussed slightly by the breeze. He offered her a faint smile, and though the soundscape was bright, she felt the hush of something private pass between them.

"You're not hearing it either, are you?" he asked softly, as though already knowing her answer.

She shook her head. "I'm trying. I want to. But it's... like I'm in another rhythm entirely."

His gaze softened. "You're carrying too much. Let the music carry you for a while instead."

She tried. She let herself listen more deeply to the notes spilling out across the crowd, but instead of happiness, she felt a prickle of unease. The horn section faded for a moment, the band easing into a slower tune. And then—

Her body stilled.

A violin began to play.

It wasn't part of the band on stage. The sound came from a smaller ensemble tucked off to the side, a group of younger musicians playing in the round near the fountain.

Their bows moved in unison, lifting a tune that curled like a thread of smoke into the air.

The melody.

The same melody that had haunted her dreams, that had played from Clara's music box, that had whispered through every vision. It rose pure and unbroken, as if it had always belonged to the air itself, waiting only to be played.

Marley's breath left her in a rush. Her cup of coffee tilted precariously in her hand, forgotten. She took a step forward, the crowd blurring, her ears straining to catch every note.

Damien moved beside her, his expression taut with recognition. "You hear it too."

She nodded, unable to speak.

The violinist was a young woman she didn't recognize, her eyes closed as though the music carried her somewhere else. She played with the surety of someone who had known the melody all her life, though Marley knew that was impossible. She had asked Clara about it once, years ago, when she was still a girl—Clara had only smiled cryptically. The music box had been hidden until recently.

"How?" Marley whispered. "How can she be playing this? She's never heard it."

Damien's face was pale in the glow of the lanterns strung overhead. "Because it isn't just a song. It's a memory. A call. And memory doesn't stay buried forever."

The final notes lingered like smoke before dissolving into the square's chatter. The young violinist bowed quickly, shyly, before turning to another sheet of music. No one else seemed unsettled, not in the least. The crowd clapped, chatted, went back to their food. For them, it was simply a pleasant tune in the air.

For Marley, it was everything.

Her hands shook. She clutched the coffee cup

tighter, grounding herself in its warmth, though she hadn't taken a sip in minutes. She felt Damien's hand brush hers briefly, a steadying touch, before slipping away again.

The band on the main stage launched into another jubilant number, trumpets blaring, drums pounding. But Marley barely heard it. Her pulse thundered with a different rhythm—the music box melody played by someone who should not have known it, someone who had brought the circle's secret into the open square of Brookwood, whether she realized it or not.

Marley scanned the edges of the crowd, her chest tightening with an old instinct. Clara's note had been clear: the truth would reveal itself under moonlight. But the circle was not waiting for the moon. It was moving here, now, in the midst of firelight and brass.

She caught a flicker at the far edge of the festival grounds, just beyond the glow of lanterns strung over the booths. A ripple of green in the shadows.

Her breath hitched.

But when she blinked, it was gone.

THE MUSIC from the stage rose like smoke, curling and shifting, wrapping the crowd in its jubilant spell. Laughter and brass tangled together, cymbals clashing like fireworks before their time. But Marley felt none of it. The melody from the violin still pressed against her, sharp as a blade held close to the skin.

She moved through the crowd with the strange sense that she was walking against a current. Families swayed to the music, friends clinked glasses of beer and cider, couples laughed in bright relief. But Marley's eyes skimmed past them all, searching for that flicker of green she had seen at the edge of the square.

Everywhere she looked, the festival distracted her. Lantern light bounced across faces, cotton candy spun high on paper cones, the flash of a saxophone's bell caught her eyes at every turn. But beneath it all pulsed the melody. Even though the violinist had stopped playing, Marley still heard it, soft and insistent, as though it had slipped into the rhythm of her blood.

She threaded past the fountain, where the young musicians now played a lively reel. The violinist who had carried the melody bowed her instrument with quick, effortless strokes, smiling as her companions kept pace. To them, it was just another tune, another chance to fill the air with their practice and their youth.

But Marley knew better. She could almost taste the truth of it on her tongue—the circle had found a way to bleed its secrets into the open, to pass them like shared breath.

Damien caught up with her near the edge of the crowd. He laid a steady hand on her arm. "Slow down. You'll draw attention."

She turned to him, her eyes sharp with urgency. "She was playing it, Damien. Exactly. Note for note. How could she know it?"

He scanned the fountain, his face unreadable. "Maybe she doesn't. Maybe she picked it up from someone who picked it up from someone else. A tune that was never written down, only remembered. Oral history becomes music, music becomes memory."

"Or maybe," Marley whispered, "the circle isn't finished. Maybe it's still weaving through the people here."

Before Damien could answer, she felt it again—the prickle at the back of her neck, the air shifting as if someone had stepped close though no one had touched her. She turned sharply.

There, just beyond the glow of lanterns strung across the food stalls, a figure lingered. Tall, cloaked in something that shimmered faintly like green silk in the dark. The crowd moved around it without notice, children running past without turning their heads. But Marley saw it, clear as breath, the figure's edges wavering as though stitched from fog.

Her heart thundered. She stepped forward, but a man carrying a tray of drinks passed between them. When the way cleared again, the figure was gone.

Marley pressed her hand to her chest, trying to calm the tremor in her breath. "She was there. Right there."

Damien studied her face, and for once, he did not doubt. He only said quietly, "Aurelia?"

Marley could not answer. The music from the stage swelled again, horns announcing the next act, drums pounding in bright cadence. The crowd cheered. But Marley barely heard it. The melody—the circle's melody—threaded through her veins, refusing to let her go.

The festival spun on around her, bright and ordinary. But she knew now that beneath its bustle, something unseen was moving, watching, choosing its moment.

And the circle, long dormant, had decided its song would not stay hidden any longer.

THE NIGHT WORE ON, the square pulsing with music and laughter until the hours blurred. Lanterns swayed gently above the booths, their golden light mingling with the harsher glow of stage lamps. Families gathered with paper baskets of fried fish, lovers leaned close on the benches near the fountain, and the brass band played as if it could hold off the darkness itself.

But for Marley, each note seemed threaded through with that other melody—the one no one else noticed. It curled at the edge of every song, surfacing between drumbeats, whispering between trumpet blasts. She felt it as a vibration more than a sound, humming against her skin as if the circle itself had slipped into the bloodstream of the festival.

By the time the announcer stepped onto the stage to declare the fireworks would begin, Marley felt wrung out, her nerves drawn tight. She tried to listen to the applause, to let the moment feel like celebration, but her chest ached with anticipation. She knew—without knowing how—that the night had not yet finished what it came to do.

The crowd thickened as people pressed toward the open space near the harbor where the fireworks would be launched. Children clambered onto parents' shoulders, their small hands sticky with sugar. Vendors shouted last calls for roasted nuts and cider. The air grew thick with warmth, with breath, with expectation.

Marley and Damien stood near the far edge, where the square met the slope that fell toward the water. From here the lighthouse was a pale shadow on the horizon, its beam slicing slow arcs through the fog. Damien's hand brushed hers again—not grasping, not demanding, only steadying— and for once she didn't pull away.

The first firework rose with a shriek and burst above them in gold. The crowd roared approval. Another followed, red spilling into white. Children gasped. Musicians struck a chord to match the rhythm of the display.

Marley tilted her head back, the colors painting her face, but she felt only the tightening in her chest. The fireworks burst like signals in the sky, but beneath the explosions she heard it again: the melody, as clear as though it had been written into the air itself.

And then she saw her.

At the edge of the crowd, just beyond the last circle of lantern-light, stood the figure in green.

Marley's breath caught. This time, there was no mistaking her.

The woman's form was clearer now, less mist than presence. A gown of deep green shimmered faintly, like fabric woven from seawater and leaves. Her hair fell in dark waves, her eyes luminous even in the half-light. She stood utterly still, as though the festival's chaos moved around her without touching her.

Marley knew her name before she dared speak it, her lips shaping the word soundlessly: *Aurelia.*

The ghostly figure lifted her gaze, and for a fleeting second Marley swore those luminous eyes met hers across the distance. Recognition shivered through her like lightning. Not menace, not malice—only knowing. As though Aurelia had been waiting for her to see, to acknowledge, to accept.

"Marley?" Damien's voice was low at her side, urgent. "What is it? What do you see?"

But Marley couldn't answer. She stepped forward, her body moving before her mind could catch up. The crowd shifted, parting for her only slightly, the press of shoulders and laughter blurring around her. She kept her eyes fixed on the figure at the edge of the square.

Aurelia did not move. She did not speak. But her presence filled the space between heartbeats.

Another firework screamed into the sky and exploded in silver, showering sparks that fell like a veil across the crowd. For an instant the light illuminated Aurelia fully, her gown glittering, her hands clasped at her waist. Marley's throat tightened with awe. She could almost believe the figure would step forward, cross the last distance, and place something tangible into her hands.

But the silver sparks fell, the smoke drifted—and Aurelia was gone.

Marley stumbled forward, her breath tearing in her chest, the space where the figure had stood now only shadow and fog. She searched desperately, her eyes straining, but the green had vanished as though it had never been.

Damien's hand found her arm, steadying her. "Marley. Talk to me."

She shook her head, unable to find words. Her heart pounded in her ears, louder than the next volley of fireworks. She knew what she had seen. She knew the circle had chosen this night, this festival, this moment to show her Aurelia not as memory, not as dream, but as presence.

The crowd cheered as gold and red bloomed overhead, but Marley heard none of it. Her entire being pulsed with the certainty that she had glimpsed the heart of the circle itself—and that Aurelia's vanishing was not an ending. It was a summons.

As the final firework cracked open the sky, scattering white light across the harbor, Marley whispered into the night, "I see you."

And though the figure was gone, the certainty remained.

The circle was not finished with her. Not with Brookwood.

Not yet.

21

THE LIGHTHOUSE SIGNAL

The sea was restless again. Marley could hear it long before she reached the lighthouse—waves smacking against the jagged rocks, the undertow rumbling deep, like a creature shifting in its sleep. The fog had not yet rolled in, so the tower stood tall and stark against the horizon, its lantern eye sweeping across the coastline in steady arcs.

She had not planned to come back here so soon. After the festival, she had told herself she needed rest, a night without questions or visions, but the rhythm had been waiting. Three short, two long. The memory of the flicker gnawed at her, until sleep became impossible. So she walked, her coat buttoned against the salty wind, her boots striking the path with the certainty of someone called rather than someone choosing.

The beacon flared once as she reached the base of the tower, its light spilling across her face. She tilted her head back, squinting against the brightness. Then she waited. One. Two. Three quick pulses. A pause. Two long.

Her breath caught. It was no accident.

The lighthouse's machinery might be old, its rhythm sometimes uneven, but this was deliberate—like a hand tapping against her shoulder, again and again, until she turned to listen.

She pushed through the heavy door, the smell of rust and oil enveloping her. The spiral staircase loomed above, and she climbed quickly, her hands grazing the cold iron rail. Each step creaked, echoing her heartbeat. By the time she reached the lantern room, her chest was tight, though whether from the climb or anticipation she couldn't tell.

Damien was already there. He turned as she entered, his face shadowed, a thick book under one arm.

"I knew you'd come," he said simply.

Marley stopped, catching her breath. "You've seen it again, haven't you?"

He nodded. "Three short. Two long." He tapped the book. "I brought something from the maritime archive."

The lantern's massive lens rotated slowly, the mechanism groaning. For a moment, Marley felt they stood inside the belly of a great, breathing thing. Damien set the book on the narrow table and flipped it open. The pages were thin, filled with columns of tiny script—an old codebook, its spine worn by years of use.

"It's Morse code" he said, running his finger down a column. "Three short, two long. It could be interpreted a couple of ways."

Marley leaned over, scanning the page. The code leapt at her, black marks translating the flicker into letters.

"A.W.," Damien murmured. "Or..." He paused, then tapped another line. "Trust."

The words hung in the air between them.

Aurelia Ward. Trust.

Marley swallowed hard. The circle wasn't just history—

it was speaking. From lighthouse beams, from melodies, from visions pressed into necklaces. Memory lived in matter, yes, but memory was also restless. It wanted to be remembered.

She pressed her palm against the glass, watching the light sweep across the water. "It's calling."

Damien's expression tightened, his voice low. "The question is—to whom? You? Me? The town? Or..." He trailed off, but the silence completed his thought. Or the circle itself, reaching forward through time.

Before Marley could respond, the light shifted again. Three short, two long. She felt it inside her chest this time, like a pulse syncing with her heart.

And then—without warning—her vision blurred.

The glass before her darkened, the sea beyond receding until it was only shadow. She clutched the table, gasping. Damien's voice called her name, distant, muffled, but she could not answer. The world folded in on itself, pulling her somewhere else entirely.

She stood at the edge of a forest clearing. The air was thick with the scent of pine and damp earth. The moon hung high, silver and watchful. Before her, seven women worked in silence, their figures cloaked in green, their hands moving with solemn care.

They carried stones—smooth, rounded, some marked with faint sigils—and placed them carefully in a spiral pattern on the ground. One by one, they stepped back, their breath misting in the cold night air.

Marley recognized one of them immediately. The tilt of her chin, the steadiness in her gaze. Aurelia.

The women joined hands around the spiral, their voices rising in a low hum that resonated in Marley's bones. The sound was not melody so much as vibration, a frequency that seemed to stir the very earth beneath their feet.

The spiral glowed faintly, the stones catching moonlight as though lit from within.

Marley felt her knees weaken. The spiral wasn't just symbol. It was practice. It was invocation.

She tried to step closer, to hear the words, but the vision trembled, the edges of the clearing dissolving. The hum deepened, reverberating through her chest, until it shook her awake.

The lantern room snapped back into focus. Damien was gripping her shoulders, his eyes sharp with concern.

"You went somewhere," he said, his voice taut. "Didn't you?"

Marley's lips trembled. "The forest. A spiral. Stones. And Aurelia was there."

The beacon flared again behind them—three short, two long—washing their faces in light.

And Marley knew with bone-deep certainty: the circle was not finished with her. It was leading her to the forest's edge.

THE LANTERN SWUNG its slow rotation, flooding the glass with arcs of light that seemed to breathe as much as burn. The steady pulse filled the chamber with an eerie rhythm: three short, two long. Three short, two long. As if the lighthouse itself had become a metronome set to memory.

Damien kept his hands braced against the codebook, knuckles pale under the strain. Marley, still trembling from the aftershock of the vision, pressed her back against the curved stone wall, trying to root herself. She pulled in lungfuls of salt-heavy air, but even that couldn't dislodge the echo of the women's chant or the glow of the spiral burning in her mind.

Finally, Damien broke the silence. His voice was measured, but beneath it she caught the thread of awe. "Tell me everything you saw."

Marley swallowed, then spoke, her words faltering at first but growing steadier as she recalled the vision. "It was the forest. A clearing I didn't recognize. Seven women. They were... building something. A spiral of stones. Not carved like monuments, but chosen, placed deliberately. Aurelia was with them." Her hands gestured unconsciously, tracing the coil of the spiral in the air. "And they weren't just arranging rocks. They were—invoking. It felt alive, Damien. As if the earth itself answered them."

The lantern beam swept across their faces, and for a heartbeat neither of them moved. Damien closed the codebook, the heavy thud startling against the relentless groan of the machinery.

"Three short, two long," he said again, as if needing to ground himself. "It could be 'A.W.' Aurelia Ward. That alone is enough to chill me." He rubbed the back of his neck, his voice tightening. "But it could also be 'Trust.' And that..." He shook his head. "That carries weight. If it is a message—and I think it is—it could mean more than just a name. It could be instruction. A warning. A request."

Marley pressed her palms together, feeling the heat of her own skin. "But if it's both...?"

"Then it's both," Damien finished, his eyes narrowing. "Aurelia Ward. And trust."

The words seemed to hang in the chamber like a chord left unresolved.

Marley's chest tightened. The memory of Aurelia's eyes in the vision lingered—steadfast, unyielding, lit with purpose. She could almost believe the lighthouse was not only repeating her initials but demanding faith in her.

"Objects carry memory," Marley murmured, recalling Clara's notes. "But maybe places do too. The lighthouse. The bridge. Now the forest. They're not just landmarks. They're messages waiting to be read."

Damien leaned back against the table, his jaw working. "And the spiral?"

Marley hesitated, then forced herself to speak the truth aloud. "I think it's real. Not metaphor, not dream. I think the circle built it somewhere in the woods."

He considered this with the weight of someone who had spent a lifetime sorting fact from folklore. The lantern beam glided past again, etching light into his profile, and she saw the struggle there—his instinct to dismiss wrestling against his dawning conviction.

"If it exists," he said slowly, "it would have to be close. Something the women of Brookwood could reach on foot, gather without drawing too much attention. Hidden, but not unreachable. Which means—"

"The forest," Marley interrupted, her pulse quickening. "Not far from town. A clearing that could stay untouched for over a century."

Damien gave a small, grim smile. "Brookwood has plenty of those. Enough that we'd need more than guesses to narrow it down." He opened the codebook again, flipping back to the page. His finger tapped the column. "Three short, two long. Aurelia. Trust. Maybe it's both message and map. Maybe it's telling us not only who but how."

Marley frowned. "How what?"

"How to find it," he said. "How to enter the spiral. How to carry forward what they began."

Her skin prickled. The vision's echo seemed to stir inside

her, the hum of the women's chant vibrating again in her chest. She rubbed her arms to steady herself.

"But Damien," she whispered, "what if finding it isn't the problem? What if standing in it is?"

The words landed between them like stones in still water. Damien didn't dismiss them. Instead, he closed the codebook again and looked at her with something steadier than logic: concern.

"You're already carrying too much of this," he said quietly. "Visions. Objects that burn you with memory. Now a spiral that might not want to stay buried. If we find it—if it finds us—you can't stand there alone."

Marley met his eyes, and for the first time since Clara's death, she felt the faintest shift of weight—not an easing, not yet, but a sharing.

Still, she pressed. "But you saw what the town did at the café. At the Historical Society meetings. They don't want this uncovered. What if it's not just folklore they're protecting? What if the spiral itself is why?"

Damien didn't flinch. "Then we'll find out. Together."

Another pulse of light swept through the chamber: three short, two long. The word in her chest was clear now, not ambiguous at all.

Trust.

Marley exhaled. Her vision had not been warning her away. It had been drawing her nearer.

And the forest was waiting.

The lantern beam swept the chamber again—three short, two long—and Marley felt its rhythm pulse inside her chest as though the lighthouse itself had become her second heartbeat. She stood frozen, hand pressed to the glass, watching the light fade out over the water, only to return again, relentless and certain.

Every time it came, she felt Aurelia there. Not just a memory, not just a name in ledgers or a ghostly figure glimpsed in smoke and dream, but a presence as real as Damien beside her. Aurelia stood in the rhythm, in the flicker, in the weight that pressed against Marley's ribs until her breath came shallow.

This is mine now, she thought. *No—ours. But it chose me first.*

She shivered and drew back from the glass, wrapping her arms around herself.

Damien watched her closely, the codebook still under his palm on the table. "You feel her, don't you?" he asked quietly. It wasn't mockery this time, or even skepticism. It was something closer to fear—and respect.

Marley hesitated, then nodded. "Every flicker. She's there."

"Or the circle," he said.

Marley closed her eyes. The vision had shown seven women, not one. Their hands linked, voices humming until the air vibrated like a plucked string. Aurelia had led them, yes, but the spiral had not belonged to her alone.

"She's part of it," Marley murmured. "But she isn't all of it. The spiral isn't hers. It's theirs." She opened her eyes again, meeting his. "And now it's ours to find."

Damien looked at her for a long moment, and she saw the argument form on his lips. He wanted to warn her again, to tell her that chasing visions through the woods would only bring more danger. But he didn't. He only said, "If we go looking, Marley, we can't pretend it's just history anymore. It won't stay in books or journals or code. It will demand something of us."

The words landed like stones in her gut. She turned away, staring at the rotating lens, the huge mechanism that caught and bent the flame until it became a beacon. The light was steady, tireless, never choosing when to shine or when to rest. And yet here it was, flickering in a pattern that defied accident, spelling out initials, spelling out faith.

Trust.

The word pressed at her, insistent.

She thought of Clara, who had kept the recipe book hidden but not destroyed, who had wrapped the necklace in oilcloth and sealed it behind wood, who had left bread-crumbs through the locked room, the locket, the ledger. Clara had not wanted Marley to inherit just property or debt. She had wanted her to inherit memory. To pick up what others had carried.

Marley's throat tightened. "Clara knew this would come for me. That's why she left everything. Not just to remember. To act."

She pressed her fists against her chest, as though she could hold herself together. "But what if I'm not strong enough? What if I can't carry what they carried?"

Damien stepped forward then, closing the distance, his voice low but firm. "You're already carrying it. You've been carrying it since the moment you set foot back in Brook-wood. And every step since, it's gotten heavier. But you're still standing."

Marley's breath caught. She turned her head, searching his face, finding no mockery there now, only a steadiness that felt like an anchor.

Still, the fear pressed sharp in her chest. The spiral in her vision had glowed with a power she couldn't explain. What if stepping into it meant losing herself? What if it demanded more than she could give?

The lantern beam swept again, three short, two long, and her body answered. Her heart thudded in rhythm. Aurelia's presence pressed close, not crushing but urging.

"Trust."

The word rose not from the light but from inside her, as though her bones themselves spoke it.

Marley let her breath go slowly. "I can't stay away from it. The spiral. I have to find it."

Damien's jaw tightened, but he nodded once. "Then we'll find it. Together."

She turned back to the glass, watching the beam sweep the sea, carving light into darkness. Each pulse felt less like instruction and more like covenant: Aurelia was leading her. The circle was waiting. The forest held the next chapter.

And when the lantern flared again, flooding the chamber in its strange rhythm, Marley no longer flinched. She pressed her hand flat against the glass and whispered, so quietly she wasn't sure Damien even heard, "I'll come."

The signal faded. The fog thickened over the water. The spiral waited.

And Marley, heart pounding, knew she would walk into the woods until she found it—no matter the cost.

22

BOOKSHOP CONFESSION

The bell above the shop door chimed faintly as Marley pushed it open, but the sound seemed swallowed by the silence inside. Evening had already settled over Brookwood, the streetlamps glowing against the damp mist creeping in from the harbor. The bookshop, with its shelves of mismatched wood and its lingering smell of paper and dust, felt both sanctuary and burden. Every time she stepped inside, she carried more with her than she had before.

Damien followed her in, his coat damp from the drizzle. He shook it off lightly before hanging it on the hook near the door. His eyes scanned the shop with the same curiosity he always carried here, but there was tension at the corners of his mouth, as though he sensed that tonight's conversation would carve them deeper into dangerous territory.

Marley walked past the front desk, brushing her hand against the scarred surface as she went. She hadn't planned to share this, not yet. But after the lighthouse—after seeing the signal flare again and the vision it had pulled her into—

she couldn't keep it back. The necklace's weight in her pocket burned like a truth demanding to be spoken.

She stopped near the writing desk where Clara used to sit, the one that had already revealed hidden panels and strange inscriptions. Damien came to stand beside her, his gaze steady, waiting.

"There's something I haven't told you," Marley said softly, her voice almost lost in the shadows of the shop.

Damien folded his arms, not impatient, but bracing himself. "Go on."

Marley reached into her pocket and drew out the oilcloth bundle. Slowly, she unwrapped it, revealing the antique necklace with its dull silver chain and green-stoned pendant. The light from the desk lamp caught its surface, making it gleam faintly, as if it still carried moonlight inside.

"This was in the wall," she said. "Hidden, wrapped, sealed away."

Damien's brows knit. "And you didn't tell me before?"

Her throat tightened. "Because I didn't just find it. It... showed me things."

She lifted the necklace, letting it dangle from her fingers. The chain swayed, and for a moment, she thought she heard the faintest whisper of breath. She pressed on, forcing the words out before fear silenced her.

"When I touched it, Damien, I saw her. A young woman —hiding, running, terrified. And then another time, I saw her forced into silence, pressed down by something bigger than herself. It wasn't just imagination. It was memory. And it's getting stronger."

Damien stared at the necklace, his jaw tightening. "You mean visions. Again."

"Yes. And more than before." Her voice cracked. "The lighthouse, the spiral, all of it—it's not separate. The objects, the places, they're conduits. Clara knew it. She wrote it down once, in her notes: *memory lives in matter.* She believed objects can carry emotion, memory, truth. Not just as keepsakes, but as vessels. This necklace isn't just jewelry. It's a witness."

Damien dragged a hand through his hair, exhaling sharply. His voice, when it came, was low and measured, as if he were trying to balance on a wire strung between disbelief and fear. "Marley... you realize what you're saying. That Brookwood itself has been seeded with... artifacts. Objects carrying visions? History you can feel instead of reading?"

Marley's grip on the necklace tightened. "Yes. And Clara left them here for a reason. She trusted me to find them. To remember."

Damien paced a short line across the narrow floor, then turned back to her. His expression was fierce, but not unkind. "You need to understand what this means. Every step deeper you go, the more resistance you'll meet. Not just whispers in cafés or suspicious glances at the library. The people who have protected this version of Brookwood's story—they won't let it go quietly. They never have."

Marley met his gaze. "And you think they'll come for me."

He didn't flinch. "I know they will."

The necklace pulsed cold in her palm, the green stone catching her reflection in its surface. She thought of Aurelia, of the women in the forest, of Clara's careful secrecy. None of it had been preserved by accident.

Marley lifted her chin, steadying herself. "Then let them come. Because silence has already cost too much."

The bell from the lighthouse echoed in her memory, three short, two long. Aurelia Ward. Trust.

Marley set the necklace gently on the desk between

them, the weight of her confession settling into the air like a stone dropped into water. Whatever came next would ripple out from here.

Damien studied her for a long moment, his face unreadable. Then, slowly, he nodded.

"Then we'd better be ready."

DAMIEN PULLED the desk chair back and sat down heavily, his elbows braced on his knees. The light from the lamp threw sharp lines across his face, deepening the furrow in his brow. He gestured toward the necklace that Marley had laid between them.

"Clara wrote *memory lives in matter*," he said slowly, as if testing the phrase on his tongue. "Do you believe she meant that literally? That these objects—this necklace, the music box, the journals—are repositories of memory that can... transmit visions?"

Marley remained standing, her arms crossed tightly. "I don't just believe it. I've felt it. When I touch the necklace, I'm not inventing these images. I'm pulled into them. I can smell the damp of the hiding place. I can hear the breath of the girl, how quickly she was breathing. I can feel her fear, Damien. It's not imagination. It's residue."

Damien ran a hand over his jaw, his eyes fixed on the stone's faint glimmer. "Residue." He said the word carefully, almost academically. "As if emotions could soak into matter the way salt soaks into the sea air, staying long after the storm has passed."

"Yes," Marley said quickly, grateful he was reaching for her meaning instead of discarding it. "That's why Clara hid these things instead of destroying them. She knew they carried the weight of what happened. They are... witnesses."

He leaned back in the chair, exhaling slowly. "That's a beautiful idea, Marley. Poetic. But it's also dangerous. If memory lives in matter, it can also be twisted. Misread. You're trusting that what you see is truth, not distortion."

Her throat tightened, but she held her ground. "Then why does it keep matching? The ledger, the locket, the music box—all separate pieces, and yet they echo the same story. Aurelia. The circle. The spiral. If I were inventing this, wouldn't it unravel instead of weaving tighter?"

Damien didn't answer immediately. He reached for the codebook, still open on the table from the lighthouse. He thumbed its fragile pages, not reading, just grounding himself in something physical. Finally, he looked back at her.

"I don't doubt that you believe what you're seeing. And I'm not blind—I've seen enough with you to know there's more happening here than I can explain. But if you're right —if these objects are truly conduits of memory—then others must know too. Others who've kept it hidden. And if they've worked this hard to bury the truth for over a century, they won't smile politely while you dig it up."

The words were quiet, but sharp. Marley felt them cut. She had sensed the whispers around town, the caution in people's eyes, but hearing Damien lay it out so plainly forced her to confront the danger head-on.

"You think they'll come after me," she said.

He gave a humorless laugh. "I think they already are. You've noticed it too, haven't you? The way people pause when your name comes up. The way they lower their voices. What you call whispers are warnings, Marley. They're testing how far you'll go before they act. And if you keep going—and I know you will—those whispers will harden into something more."

Marley's chest tightened, but she refused to shrink back. "Then let them harden. Silence is worse. What they did to Aurelia—what they did to all of them—it deserves to be remembered. Clara didn't leave me this so I could hide."

Damien studied her for a long moment, his expression torn between admiration and dread. "You sound like her," he said finally.

"Like Clara?"

"No." His eyes softened, almost reluctantly. "Like Aurelia."

The silence that followed pressed heavy, punctuated only by the faint tick of the clock above the shelves. Marley looked down at the necklace, its green stone catching the lamplight. She thought of the spiral in her vision, the glow of stones in moonlight, the hands of seven women linked together.

"Then maybe that's the point," she whispered. "That their voices don't die. They find someone to carry them forward."

Damien shook his head, but it wasn't dismissal. It was a slow, reluctant acknowledgment of a truth he didn't want but couldn't deny. "Then you need to be prepared, Marley. Because the more you carry, the more visible you'll become. And the more visible you become, the more dangerous this will get."

Marley raised her chin, the fire in her chest refusing to dim. "I'd rather carry danger than bury truth."

The words hung in the lamplight between them, and Damien leaned back at last, conceding—for now.

The necklace lay still on the desk, but Marley swore she could feel it humming faintly, as if the matter itself approved.

.   .   .

THE SILENCE in the bookshop stretched long after Damien's words faded. Outside, the drizzle had hardened into rain, tapping against the windowpanes in a rhythm almost like the lighthouse signal: steady, insistent, impossible to ignore. Marley stood by the desk with the necklace between them, the weight of his warning pressing against her chest.

She could feel it—the collision of two truths inside her. One was the burden of what Damien had said: the more she uncovered, the more the town would resist. She had seen enough in their eyes to know he wasn't exaggerating. The protectors of Brookwood's official story would not welcome her work; they would tighten their hold on silence until it cut like wire.

But the other truth was stronger, and it lived not in Damien's warning but in Clara's whisper, in Aurelia's steady gaze, in the hum of the spiral. She couldn't turn back. Even if she wanted to.

Damien shifted in the chair, studying her with an intensity that made her throat dry. "I'm not saying stop. I know you too well to waste the breath. But you need to understand, Marley: carrying memory like this—it changes you. You'll become a lightning rod. And not just for visions. For people. For their fear."

Marley's hand drifted to the necklace. Her fingers traced the cold stone, and she felt again the shiver of the vision, the young woman's ragged breath, the way terror had clung to her like a second skin. She thought of the ledger, the locket, the music box—each object not just an artifact but a vessel. Clara had been right. *Memory lives in matter.*

But it lived in people, too. In blood, in bone, in the marrow of those who carried the line forward. She felt it now pressing through her, not as possession but as inheritance.

"You're right," Marley said finally, her voice low but steady. "It will change me. It already has. I don't sleep the same. I don't think the same. Sometimes I feel like I'm standing in two centuries at once. But if Clara trusted me with this—if Aurelia is reaching through these visions—it isn't to leave it buried. It's to let it breathe again."

Damien leaned back, his jaw tight. "And what if letting it breathe means the town suffocates you for it?"

Marley turned to him, meeting his gaze without wavering. "Then I'll still breathe first."

The words surprised even her, but once spoken, they rang true.

Damien didn't answer right away. He studied her as though weighing something heavier than doubt—responsibility, perhaps, or fear for what his own loyalty might cost. Finally, he exhaled, and his eyes softened, though the tension didn't leave his frame. "Then I suppose I'll just have to make sure they don't get the chance."

The rain outside thickened, the rhythm building like drums in the distance. Marley glanced at the window, then back at the desk where the necklace lay. In the lamplight, the green stone glowed faintly, no longer dull but alive, as if responding to her words.

For the first time, Marley didn't shrink from its weight. She reached down and clasped it in her palm, the coolness grounding her.

"This isn't just their story anymore," she whispered. "It's mine now. And I won't stop."

The confession lingered in the air, heavier than the rain, louder than the ticking clock. Damien nodded once, the kind of nod that carried more promise than words.

The shop felt different then—not just a place of books and dust, but a sanctuary of truth, waiting to be claimed.

Clara had known. Aurelia had known. The circle had always been waiting for someone to listen.

And Marley, with the necklace burning steady in her hand, vowed she would not turn away.

No matter the resistance. No matter the cost.

23

THE FOUNDER'S LETTER

The locked room always carried a weight with it, as if its walls remembered being bricked up and pressed into silence. Marley had begun to think of it as both vault and confessional: a place that yielded only what it chose, when it chose. That evening, she entered with a lantern balanced in one hand, her other hand trailing against the uneven plaster as if the room might whisper something new into her skin.

The shelves along the far wall sagged under the burden of boxes and forgotten volumes. She had combed through them before, careful, methodical, but tonight she felt something different—a pull, the same way she had felt at the lighthouse when the beam stuttered its pattern across the sea. It wasn't sound this time, nor light, but a gravity tugging her toward the bottom shelf where old ledgers leaned against one another like tired men in a tavern.

She crouched and ran her fingers along the spines. One book, bound in cracked leather, seemed oddly light. When she pulled it free, a faint rattle inside caught her attention. Frowning, she set the lantern down, spread the book across her lap, and opened it. The pages inside were glued together, hollowed out with crude but careful hands.

Her heart hammered.

Inside, folded and pressed flat, was a letter. Its edges were torn, the paper thin as onion skin, but the ink still clung stubbornly to the fibers. Marley lifted it with trembling fingers, aware that she was holding not only a relic but a testimony deliberately hidden.

The date leapt at her first: *October 12, 1883.*

Then the signature—though faint, smudged, and incomplete—curved at the bottom. Her breath caught as she scanned the body of the letter.

To whom it may concern—

This letter I set down with both fear and conviction, for the truth must live even when men seek to kill it. There is among us a woman, Aurelia, who has healed what men feared to name. She has eased fevers, tended wounds, comforted mothers and children where no doctor would go. Yet for this, she is maligned. They say she meddles with nature, that she whispers to what should be silent. But I say she has preserved what our town might otherwise have lost.

I beg you, if these words survive me, to remember Aurelia not as outcast but as healer. She carries within her a gift I cannot explain, only witness. She has bound us not by fear, but by care. She is the memory of what compassion looks like when men turn their eyes away.

The lines fractured there, the bottom corner of the letter missing, as if it had been torn away deliberately. But the final fragment remained, smudged and urgent:

Protect her, if you can. For the circle cannot hold if one is broken.

Marley sat frozen, the words trembling in her hands.

Her breath came shallow, and the lantern flame flickered as though it too felt the tremor.

The founder's wife. This had to be her hand, her plea. The letter dated just a few decades after the town's founding, carrying not just acknowledgment but protection—an appeal for Aurelia against the very forces that sought to erase her.

Marley whispered the words aloud, her voice shaking: *"Healed what men feared to name."*

Clara's phrase—*memory lives in matter*—pressed against her thoughts. This letter wasn't only memory. It was proof.

She felt Aurelia's presence again, faint but insistent, as though the words themselves had carried her across a century. This was not legend. This was not mere dream. This was the founder's wife pleading that history be preserved.

And it had been hidden—buried in a hollowed-out book, locked in a bricked-up room. Protected, yes, but also silenced.

Marley's hands shook as she refolded the letter, unable to stop her tears. For the first time, she did not only feel Aurelia's story pressing into her as vision or whisper. She held it as ink, as paper, as fact.

The circle could not hold if one was broken.

The words clung to her chest as she rose to her feet, lantern swinging shadows across the narrow room. Clara had left this for her, waiting like a seed beneath soil, ready to bloom only when someone dared look closely enough.

And Marley—shaking, breathless, alive with certainty— knew she would take it straight to Damien.

Marley didn't bother with the bell. She shouldered through the library's side entrance, the one Damien had shown her weeks ago that bypassed the squeaky front doors and the watchful eye of whoever happened to be at the desk. The rain had followed her from the bookshop; it jeweled the shoulders of her coat and tapped down her hairline as if the sky couldn't stop signing its name to the evening.

Damien was at the long worktable in the archives room, jacket off, sleeves pushed to the elbow. A green-shaded lamp cast a soft circle of light over a scatter of index cards, a spool of cotton gloves, and a magnifying loupe. He looked up at the sound of her steps and read the urgency before she spoke.

"What did you find?" he asked.

Marley placed the cracked-leather volume on the felted mat in front of him and opened it to show the hollowed center. She laid the folded sheet inside that negative space as reverently as if she were returning a bone to its socket. "A letter," she said, breathless. "Hidden in a book from the locked room. October 12, 1883. From the founder's wife."

The expression that crossed his face was that rare mixture she had come to recognize in him—scholar's thrill braided with human dread. He put on the gloves, lifted the paper, and held it to the light. The onion-thin sheet went pale and luminous; the tear at the bottom corner looked fresh even after a century, as if the hand that ripped it had only just lifted away.

"Read," he said softly.

Marley did, keeping her voice even, though it wanted to shake. The phrases cinched in the air as if the room itself were a listening instrument: *There is among us a woman, Aurelia, who has healed what men feared to name... Remember her not as outcast but as healer... The circle cannot hold if one is broken.*

Damien didn't speak for a long breath. He lowered the paper, set it flat, and bent so close his breath made the fibers tremble. "Ink composition looks right," he murmured, almost to himself. "Iron gall—see the brown-black shift where it's oxidized along the ascenders? And the hand..." He angled the loupe over the signature fragment and the lines above it. "Late-nineteenth-century round hand taught from copybooks. But there's personality here—look at the capital A's, that open-bellied form. And the crossbar on her lowercase t—high and long, almost arrogant."

"You can match it?" Marley asked, keeping her palms pressed to the table to ground herself.

"If we get lucky." He straightened, already moving. "Come on."

He led her through the narrow door into the back stacks, where the library's public quiet gave way to the deeper hush of paper in long sleep. The smell of paste and dust and linen thread was almost sweet. He unlocked a gray metal cabinet that she had never seen open and slid out a flat archival box labeled in his neat hand: *BROOKWOOD HISTORICAL SOCIETY: ACCESSIONS, GIFTS & BEQUESTS, 1875–1902.*

"The Society made a habit of clipping donor letters and pasting them into scrapbooks," he said, carrying the box back to the table. "Parade of gratitude. Also, an indexer's nightmare. But sometimes they left the original notes inside the volumes they donated. Lazy, lucky, or both."

He set two albums on the felt and opened the first. Inside, glued by their corners or pinned with rusted tacks, were calling cards and notes, stilted thanks, and the occasional lavish flourish from someone who wanted their name to land harder than their gift. He turned pages with the care of someone touching skin.

"There," Marley said, breath clicking in her throat.

Halfway down a page of clipped ribbons and embossed seals was a short note on cream rag paper. The signature had been snipped off, but the hand—its light pressure, its confident looped y's—felt like a cousin to the one on the letter from the hollow book. At the top, a printed letterhead read: *Whitcomb House.*

Damien grunted, pleased. "The Whitcombs were money from sawmills and shipping—Jonas Whitcomb sat the first council. His wife was Eleanor." He flipped to the next page, then the next, faster now, hunting. "Come on, Eleanor, give me something with the full flourish."

Another box. Another album. Rain made a hush of the roof. The lamp's green halo looked like a pond they were fishing. On the third album's first leaf, Damien's finger stopped. "There," he said again, but this time the word came out like a breath let go after too long.

A dedication on the flyleaf of a donated Bible. *For the reading room at the People's Library, that all may have light, 1884—Eleanor A. Whitcomb.* The hand matched the earlier clipped note. The open-bellied A. The swaggering t-cross. The lowercase r that hooked back slightly, like a woman glancing over her shoulder.

"Gloves," Damien reminded gently, and Marley tugged them on before easing the Bible closer. He slid the loupe toward her. "Go on. See what you see."

Up close, the ink bled into the paper's weave like a tide —darker along the downstrokes, feathering where the pen paused. The capital E in Eleanor. The capital W in Whitcomb. Marley found herself tracing the shapes in air with her free hand, matching motion to stroke: the lift, the press, the tremor where a breath caught. She laid the torn letter fragment beside it, aligning nothing and everything.

"It's her," she said, the certainty ringing in her chest. "The same hand. Look at the A in *all,* look at the y in *may—* the tail runs long, almost to the margin. And this—" She pointed to the phrase in the letter: *healed what men feared to name.* "That crossbar. You called it arrogant. I'd call it deliberate."

Damien smiled without humor. "We can split the difference and say it's a woman used to being ignored who learned how to underline." He leaned in again, eyes narrowed. "The pressure profile's consistent. The width of the nib is the same. And see how she dots her i's? Not circles, not slashes. Square dots—little nails. She's pinning the word to the page."

A thrill ran through Marley that was half relief, half grief. Proof made happiness and sorrow kiss. "Eleanor Whitcomb wrote this letter," she said, touching the hollow-book page as if it might feel the naming. "The founder's wife begged someone—anyone—to protect Aurelia."

"And someone hid that plea in a wall of books," Damien said softly. "Preserved it and smothered it in the same gesture."

He carried the Bible and the letter to the light box, switched it on, and the table became a small winter noon. Side by side, the documents glowed from within. He set a transparent grid over them, aligning baselines, marking angles with a wax pencil: the lean of the hand, the tilt of the crossbars, the height of ascenders. He wasn't rushing. He was building a bridge plank by plank.

"Eleanor's a known donor to the Society," he said, almost absently as he worked. "Her name sits on half the early accession cards. Children's readers, medicine chests for the poor, a sewing machine for the widow's room. She funded the lighthouse repairs after the White Shoal wreck." He paused and looked up, his expression shifting as two lines touched in his mind. "That's the year the captain's log mentions the healer disembarking near Brookwood."

"Aurelia," Marley said.

"Aurelia," he echoed. "Eleanor sees a wrecked coast and repairs the light. Eleanor sees a hunted woman and tries to brighten the history around her. It doesn't erase guilt. But it's a ledger entry the town forgot to balance."

He recorded photographs on the overhead rig—front lit, raking light, backlit on the box—each click a small generosity. Evidence layered upon evidence. When he was done, he let the lamp's halo fall back to a single pool and rubbed the bridge of his nose.

"There's still the tear," Marley said, eyes on the letter's missing corner. "What do you think was there?"

He didn't give her a comfortable evasion. "Names," he said. "Places. A directive too sharp to survive." He tapped the final line with a gloved fingertip: *The circle cannot hold if one is broken.* "Whoever hid this kept the plea and clipped the map."

A soft sound came from the hall—the building settling, or the rain changing its handwriting. Both of them turned reflexively. No one stood in the doorway. The library breathed its slow, old breath.

Damien packed the Bible back into its cradle and slid the album into the box. "We log this under controlled access," he said, brisk now, the professional tone returned but thinner over the nerves. "We make high-resolution scans and keep the originals off any public register until we know who we can trust. If the Society's board gets wind of Eleanor's letter before we're ready, they'll bury it in a loving cup and tell you you're hysterical for thinking the cup has a double bottom."

"You're saying hide it," Marley said, surprised at the heat in her own voice.

"I'm saying sequence it," he countered, steady. "Truth

without a frame is a target. We need to set the context, build the chain—Aurelia in ledgers, Aurelia in the captain's log, Aurelia in music and light—and then Eleanor's letter goes like a keystone. If we sling it now, they'll claim it's a forgery or a misreading."

Marley looked down at the page. *Healed what men feared to name.* The words had weight in her palm even when she wasn't touching the paper. "Eleanor tried to keep the circle whole," she said. "She asked for protection in the only language she could write."

"And now the language is ours," Damien said. He capped the wax pencil and set it aside. "We match the hand. We link the donor. We prepare for the fight."

He moved to the card catalog—one of the tall, honey-colored cabinets that the town wanted to replace with a database until Damien had argued the cards themselves were history. He slid open a drawer labeled *WHIT–WIL* and began to flip. The thrum of search filled the room: the tap of card against card, the whisper of a thousand names. He stopped at *Whitcomb, Eleanor A.* and drew the card free.

"Look," he said, handing it to Marley. In old, neat script: *Major donor. Chair, Ladies' Committee. Benefactress: lighthouse fund (1881). Gift: volumes for People's Library (1884). Notation: Private bequest—papers retained at Whitcomb House.*

"Papers," Marley breathed. "Retained."

"Which means there's a box somewhere in a parlor or an attic that the Society smiled at and let be. Or there was, until a house sale scattered it." He slid the card back and shut the drawer with a gentle push. "But we have what we need for the match. Eleanor's hand on a public dedication. Eleanor's hand in a private plea. The founder's wife isn't a rumor on a bronze plaque—she's a voice, and she's taking your side."

The relief that rose in Marley felt suspiciously like grief.

She folded her arms across her ribs as if to hold herself together while the past came to stand beside her. "Thank you," she said, because the words were small but right.

Damien shook his head. "Don't thank me. Thank the habit of women who write what men will not record." His mouth softened. "And thank whoever hollowed a book instead of a grave."

They worked another hour—cataloging photographs, writing a neutral entry for an internal register, slipping the letter into a Mylar sleeve so light it seemed like a second skin. When they were finished, Damien locked the flat box back into the gray cabinet. The click sounded both protective and ominous, like the last turn of a key in a story they were still living.

On their way out, the rain had gentled. The library's fluorescent corridors hummed. At the door, Marley paused. "Eleanor Whitcomb," she said, tasting the name as a promise. "A donor to the Society. The founder's wife. And she begged them to protect Aurelia."

Damien met her eyes. "Now we can prove it."

"And once we can prove it," Marley said, "we can ask the town why they pretended not to know."

He didn't smile, but something like it lived at the corner of his mouth. "That," he said, "is the question they've been training themselves not to hear for a hundred and forty years."

They stepped out into the night, the air rinsed clean by rain. Somewhere beyond the roofs, the lighthouse turned its patient eye to sea. Marley lifted her face to the damp and felt the words on the page become weather in her lungs. Eleanor's hand. Aurelia's name. The circle closing a little tighter around the truth.

Tomorrow, they would decide who to tell. Tonight, they

had matched a signature to a plea, a donor to a defiance. The founder's house had been built on records; its wife had built a record on courage.

And the town would have to learn the difference.

They left the library together, carrying nothing that could be seen and everything that mattered. Rain misted the streetlights into halos, and the town's after-hours hush made each footstep sound like a choice. Down at the harbor, rigging chimed in a thin wind; somewhere beyond, the lighthouse turned its slow, patient eye.

At the shop door, Marley paused, key in the lock, the hollow ache of adrenaline ebbing. "Say it once more," she asked, half to steady herself, half to tie the present to the past. "So I can hear it in your voice. Not just mine."

Damien didn't make her beg. "The hand on the letter is Eleanor A. Whitcomb," he said. "Founder's wife. Known donor to the Brookwood Historical Society." He met her eyes, letting the words plant. "And in 1883 she wrote that Aurelia 'healed what men feared to name.'"

The lock turned; the bell gave its small, private chime. Inside, the bookshop's dark greeted them with a familiar grain: wood, paper, dust, the faint shadow of lavender that still clung to Clara's things. Marley set the lantern on the front desk and lit it, turning the wick until the flame cupped the room in gold. She didn't bring the letter—Damien had sealed it in Mylar and left it under lock—but the words came with them anyway, as if they'd soaked into her skin.

She crossed to the writing desk, ran a hand over the scar along its surface, and felt the old ache—that her aunt had sat here knowing what the town pretended it did not, that she had hidden because honesty would have stripped the books from the shelves and the roof from above her head. "If Eleanor wrote that," Marley said, voice careful, "then at least one of the founders' houses knew, believed, and tried to protect her. It wasn't just kitchen talk or rumor. It was recorded compassion."

"Recorded and then tucked away," Damien said, shrugging off his damp coat. "The town didn't have to burn the truth if it could file it where no one would think to look."

He moved to the desk with her, the two of them taking their old places on either side of a line no one else could see. The music box still sat near the ink blotter; the necklace's chain pooled like a green-tinged creek beside it. Marley touched the pendant with one fingertip. The stone felt cool, as if it had been standing outside in the mist.

"Do you think Eleanor knew the circle?" Marley asked.

"Enough to write as she did," Damien said. "Enough to risk her reputation so they wouldn't break Aurelia entirely." He gave a small, grim smile that didn't reach his eyes. "It's a funny thing about benefactors: they're either posting plaques or paying ransoms. The letter reads more like the latter."

They fell quiet. The lantern flame licked the glass, throwing a tremulous ring of light across Clara's blotter, across the little divots where a pen had tapped while someone thought too hard. Marley could feel the next step forming in them like tide under moon. Part of her wanted to race to Whitcomb House tonight, to knock, to pry up floorboards and insist the world deliver her the rest of the torn page. Another part knew that moving without care now would prod the town's nerves and make enemies reach for their gloves.

Damien saved her from the swinging needle. "We sequence," he said, as he had in the archives. "Eleanor's hand. Captain Morton's log. The ledger initials. The carving in the lighthouse. The melody in public air." He glanced at her, making sure she was with him. "Then we add the letter —proof that the founders' circle, whatever you call it, had allies in high rooms."

"Had," Marley repeated softly. "Past tense."

The pendant warmed under her touch. A picture rose unbidden: a parlor with closed curtains, a woman at an escritoire, pausing between sentences to listen for the sound of boots. Marley's throat tightened. "We need to find the rest," she said. "If there is a rest. And the donor card—"

"—said 'private bequest—papers retained at Whitcomb House,'" Damien finished. "Which means either they're in an attic trunk or they were sold with a box of candlesticks three houses ago." His mouth bent wryly. "I've found a county's history stuffed under Christmas ornaments before."

He pulled a notebook from his coat and wrote in his compact hand: **Eleanor A. Whitcomb — private papers — contact descendants — deed chain for Whitcomb House — probate filings.** He tore out the page and slid it to Marley. "Tomorrow I'll pull the deeds at the clerk's office. With any luck, the house stayed in family or the papers were inventoried during a sale."

"With any luck," Marley echoed. The phrase sat poorly in her mouth. Luck had carried too much weight lately. She was tired of leaning on it.

She moved behind the desk and opened the narrow drawer where she kept Clara's commonplace book—the one with aphorisms copied as if they were recipes. She paged through careful hands until a line leaped up with a sting: *A town that forgets owes interest to the truth.* Under it, in Clara's smaller script: *The debt will be collected in full.*

Marley read it aloud. Damien listened, then nodded once. "Your aunt understood accounting."

"She understood more than that," Marley said. "She understood how a body carries what a ledger refuses."

Her fingers drifted to the necklace again. She hadn't told Damien everything—about how the visions were getting stronger, about how Aurelia's presence sometimes came with a weight so precise it felt like a palm pressed to her sternum. She opened her mouth to confess and heard in her head his warning from the night before: **You'll become a lightning rod.** She didn't fear the lightning. She feared the men who built roofs low enough to keep the sparks inside.

"Damien," she began, and he lifted his head, attentive. She faltered—not out of caution, but out of wanting to get it right. "Matching Eleanor... it's more than evidence to me. It's... permission. Not to slow down. To continue."

"I know," he said quietly. "I felt it in the archive. When the hand matched, I felt the hinge give. That letter wants to swing the door."

"Then we go through."

"We go through," he said.

They worked in a hush that felt almost ceremonial—Marley copying the letter's text into a fresh notebook so she could hold the words without risking the original; Damien sketching the distinctive features of the hand, the open-bellied A, the long, sure t-cross, penciling arrows like a teacher annotating a map. When she finished, Marley dated the page and underlined the phrase that would not let her go: **healed what men feared to name.** The ink blotted, a small dark comet she decided to keep—proof of her own unsteady hand in the record.

The bell over the door rattled once, very softly, although no one entered. Both of them looked up. Only drafts, Marley told herself, the old building settling while the harbor exhaled. And yet in the lantern's small firelight, the shop felt watched. Not by malice—by expectation.

"Someone will know we have this," Damien said, as if plucking the thought from the shelf over her shoulder. "Maybe not tonight. But the people who keep the story tidy have a sixth sense for what threatens the starch in their collars."

Marley hugged her elbows. "Then let them feel threatened."

He smiled, small and sad. "They already do."

They went over next steps with the tacticians' care they'd learned fast: he would scan the photographs first thing and file neutral descriptions in a private index; she would search Clara's locked room again with fresh eyes—if a letter hid in a hollow book, what else had learned to hide in plain sight? They would avoid the Historical Society's board for now, and the mayor's office, and anyone who used the phrase "for the good of the town" as a drop cloth. They would ask quiet questions about the Whitcomb descendants and pretend, if anybody asked, that they were only cataloging donations for the bookshop's anniversary.

"And the spiral," Marley added, the word arriving like a seabird to the rail. "The forest. I saw the stones when the light drew me under. We have to look for it."

"We will," Damien said. He didn't hedge. "But not by blundering in with shovels. We'll start with maps—old surveyors' plats, notes on commons and woodlots that fell out of use. If the women met on land no one claimed loudly, it'll be there in the negative space. A clearing that shows up in 1880 and stubbornly stays empty in 1905."

"Ordinary absence," Marley said.

"The kind no one thinks to fence because it already belongs to something older," he answered. "Or someone."

He helped her draw the curtains. The shop narrowed to its warmest parts: the lantern circle, the desk, the two of them. Somewhere outside, fog nosed up the street; the night smelled of kelp and rain-wet brick. Marley tightened her cardigan and turned the music box key once, not to make it sing, only to feel the resistance—the small, precise wound of it, the promise stored.

"This started as grief," she said, surprising herself with the clarity. "Clara was gone and I didn't know what to do with the house she left in my blood. But it isn't just grief anymore. It's... stewardship."

Damien's eyes softened. "Stewardship," he repeated, as if the word might seat itself more firmly if he tried it on his tongue. "You know that's how lighthouse keepers talk about their lights."

He stepped closer then—not to collapse the last inches between them but to make a constellation: desk, lamp, the two of them, the necklace's green, the unplayed melody, the promise of paper. "Eleanor wrote like a keeper, too," he said. "So did Clara. When a storm comes, you don't turn down the wick and hope the coast learns its lesson. You keep the glass clean and the fire fed, and you trust that somebody out there is reading your code."

Three short. Two long. The idea carried across the room without sound.

Marley lifted the necklace, the chain slipping cold and smooth over her knuckles. She didn't put it on. She pressed the pendant into her palm until the edges made a small constellation in her skin. Eleanor's hand on the page, Aurelia's name in the mouth of the town's oldest house, the circle that would not hold if one was broken—each fact braided tight enough now to bear weight.

"I'll go where it leads," she said, finally giving voice to

the vow that had been ripening in her since the letter slid free of its paper coffin. "Even if they shut doors. Even if they call it a lie. I'll go."

Damien didn't argue with the danger. He nodded once, as if sealing something between them. "Then I'll be there. With the codebooks and the maps and the awkward apologies when I get it wrong. With the kettle when the visions leave you empty. With the key when a door needs opening."

The lantern hissed softly, wick needing a turn; Marley obliged, and the flame steadied, fuller, sure. In the thicker light she could see how tired he looked, and how resolved, and how both states could live in the same face without canceling each other.

They blew out the lamp and stood for a breath in the gathered dark. Out on the point, the lighthouse shook a sleeve of light over the water—their private rhythm hidden inside the public beam. In the near black, Marley felt the shop breathe around them like a creature settling for sleep.

"Tomorrow," she said into the dark, "Eleanor's name goes in the ledger I'm making. The one that belongs to us."

Damien's voice came back low, almost a murmur. "The Book of Brookwood."

"Not yet," she said, a whisper of a smile. "But soon."

She locked the door behind him and leaned her forehead against the cool glass, listening to his steps fade. The fog pressed around her. The pendant cooled in her palm. Eleanor's italic hand moved beneath her skin like a tide chart. Memory in matter. Memory in light. Memory in names that would not stay obediently quiet.

"Protect her, if you can," the torn letter had begged. Marley closed her fist around the stone and answered the woman who wrote it and the woman it named.

"I will," she said. "I am."

She turned back into the dim and let the room hold her. Outside, the town slept with its better history tucked under a pillow. Inside, she kept vigil—keeper of a small flame, reader of a stubborn code, custodian of the proof that a founder's house had once told the truth.

In the morning, they would begin to find the spiral in the forest and the papers in the attic and the line between donor and conspirator. Tonight, the vow was enough— heavy, luminous, alive.

And the circle, unbroken, pressed closer.

24

THE APOTHECARY LEDGER

The cellar of the bookshop had always unnerved Marley. It wasn't the cold, nor the scent of damp wood and iron—it was the sense that the air beneath the floorboards had been breathing long before she came, and would go on breathing long after. Clara had rarely spoken of it, and Marley's childhood memories of being sent down for preserves or kindling always came with a sense of being watched by something more patient than human eyes.

But that evening, lantern in hand, Marley pushed through the heavy door and descended the narrow wooden steps. The storm from earlier in the day had left the air thick with salt and mildew. The stairs creaked beneath her, each step a conversation with age. She reached the stone floor and set her lantern on a crate, the shadows leaping into corners where cobwebs draped like forgotten veils.

She had been combing through Clara's papers upstairs when one reference caught her eye—a brief note, scribbled in the margin of a recipe: *Cellar ledgers, under the old crates.* It wasn't the first time Clara had left her riddles, but Marley felt her pulse quicken. Clara had been meticulous. If she noted something, it was because she wanted Marley to find it.

The crates were stacked along the far wall, wood swollen by decades of damp. Marley dragged one forward, then another, coughing as dust broke loose and filled the air. Beneath the third, she saw it: a sliver of leather, cracked and stiff but unmistakably a book's spine.

Her hands shook as she lifted it free. The ledger was heavier than she expected, its cover mottled with mold but intact. When she brushed away grime, the embossed letters became visible, pressed deep into the worn leather: *A. Ward, Apothecary.*

The sight froze her.

She knew the initials already. Knew the whisper of Aurelia Ward from the ledger of initials in Damien's archive, from the locket with A.W., from Eleanor Whitcomb's plea. But here, in her hands, was no rumor, no coded line. Here was Aurelia's full name, written without disguise.

Marley sank to the cellar floor, lantern at her side, and opened the ledger.

The first page greeted her with a flourish of script: *Aurelia Ward, Brookwood Apothecary, 1861.* The ink had browned with age, but the lines carried a steady hand. No initials. No fear. Just ownership.

She turned the pages with careful fingers. Each leaf was filled with neat rows—lists of herbs, tinctures, and balms, some familiar, some strange. Yarrow. Willow bark. Pennyroyal. Then others she had only seen in Clara's book: moonwort, widow's bane, sea-lavender resin. Alongside each recipe, names appeared—sometimes full, sometimes initialed—men, women, children of Brookwood. Patients.

Marley leaned closer. She read entries aloud under her

breath: "For E. Cartwright, fever of unknown cause. For J. Nolan, poultice of comfrey and sage." The notes were precise, clinical, and compassionate. Aurelia had kept a physician's record, though the town's physicians had denied her.

But interspersed among the treatments were stranger lines, written in the same calm hand but carrying a resonance that unsettled Marley. *When the bell forgets to ring, remember the Grove. Seven names to bind the circle, but the spiral must remain open. If fire takes the bridge, seek the river's second bend.*

These were not medicinal notations. They were codes, warnings, instructions passed through the only ledger Aurelia could keep safe.

Marley's breath quickened. She pressed her hand to the page as though to still its pulse. Clara must have known this ledger existed—she must have left the note as a compass. Marley realized that she was not the first in her family to follow Aurelia's trail. She was only the next.

The lantern hissed as its oil sank lower. Shadows stretched against the walls like listening figures. Marley traced the letters again: *Aurelia Ward.* The name lived here, in matter and memory, exactly as Clara had promised.

And Marley knew, with the same certainty she had felt upon opening Eleanor's letter, that this discovery could not stay buried.

She closed the ledger gently, holding it to her chest. The cellar seemed to vibrate faintly, as if the stones themselves acknowledged the return of a keeper to the book.

Her next thought was immediate: she had to show Damien.

The man who had spent nights cataloging her aunt's papers, matching Eleanor Whitcomb's hand, carrying his grief into their shared discoveries—he had to see this. Because if Aurelia's ledger was real, then every whisper, every carving, every flickering lighthouse beam—they weren't fragments anymore. They were a body.

Marley blew out the lantern, clutching the ledger tight. The cellar exhaled as if relieved, and she climbed the steps with the knowledge that she was carrying not just paper, but the spine of Brookwood's forgotten history.

DAMIEN ARRIVED at the bookshop late, after the rain had stopped, his collar turned up against the lingering mist. Marley had left the door unlatched for him, the bell above the frame muffled with cloth to keep its sound from carrying into the night. He stepped in, his boots quiet on the wood floor, and found her already at the desk.

The ledger lay open between them like a heart split down the middle. Marley's eyes gleamed with equal parts exhaustion and exhilaration. "I found it," she said without preamble. "The ledger. Aurelia's ledger."

Damien slid into the chair opposite her and tugged off his gloves. His gaze caught on the brown ink across the front page, and for once he didn't bother to contain his reaction. "Her full name," he whispered. "Aurelia Ward."

Marley nodded, her throat tight. "It's not initials this time. Not rumor. She wrote herself into the book."

He reached for the loupe he always carried, bending close, his breath fogging faintly in the lamplight. He traced the name without touching it, his lips moving silently as though memorizing the script. "The hand is consistent with the mid-nineteenth century," he murmured, "but steady, practiced. She was trained—whether by formal schooling or apprenticeship. This wasn't guesswork."

Marley flipped to a later page, one she had marked with a ribbon. "Look at this. She recorded patients. Townspeople. Dozens of them." Her finger traced the column. "E. Sanborn. J. Nolan. C. Pritchard. All paired with treatments. Tinctures. Poultices. Balms. It's a physician's record, Damien. But she wasn't allowed to be one."

He leaned in further, the scholar in him warring with the human. "If this ledger is real—and it is—it reframes everything we've been told about Brookwood's founding generation. Aurelia wasn't a shadow. She was integral. A healer whose records prove she treated half the town."

Marley swallowed, her voice low. "And yet she was erased."

Damien turned another page and froze. Between neat lines of tinctures and prescriptions was a passage in the same hand, but the words bent sideways from medicine.

When the bell forgets to ring, remember the Grove.

He read it aloud. The syllables seemed to thicken the air. "This isn't treatment," he said. "It's code."

Marley nodded. "I thought so too. There are others. *Seven names to bind the circle, but the spiral must remain open.* And here—" She flipped to another page where the ink had faded almost to sepia. "*If fire takes the bridge, seek the river's second bend.*"

Damien sat back, his expression hardening into concentration. "Warnings. Instructions. Embedded inside the ledger so that anyone trying to dismiss her as a herbalist would miss the deeper record."

"And the Grove?" Marley asked. "Do you think it's the forest I saw in the vision—the spiral of stones?"

He rubbed his temple, thinking. "It could be. Early maps mark a common woodlot beyond the town's edge, referred to once or twice as 'the Grove.' It was parceled off by the turn of the century, but if the circle met there..." He shook his head, half in awe. "Marley, this ledger isn't just proof of Aurelia's existence. It's proof of an organized network."

She leaned closer, her voice tightening. "A circle. The same circle Eleanor wrote about. The one Clara wanted me to find."

Damien closed his eyes briefly, then reopened them, sharper. "If this becomes public, the entire founding narrative of Brookwood shifts. The town wasn't built solely by the Whitcombs and Sanborns. It was held together by women working under cover, weaving healing and warning into the margins. The men wrote laws and built ships, but the women bound the fractures."

Marley let the truth settle in her. It felt both exhilarating and terrifying, like standing at the lip of a cliff. "The Historical Society won't accept this easily," she said.

"They'll resist," Damien agreed. He flipped carefully through the ledger, his eyes catching every strange line of ink. "But this—this isn't folklore. It's artifact. And if we can cross-reference these names with church records, census rolls, burial registers..." He looked up, his voice certain. "We can prove Aurelia's hand kept this town alive."

Marley touched the page where Aurelia's name appeared, steady and unflinching. "She wrote herself into history. And now we've read her voice out loud again."

Damien closed the ledger gently, reverently, as though tucking a child to sleep. "This ledger reframes Brookwood," he said. "It's not the story of a settlement tamed by industry. It's the story of a circle of women who carried what men feared to name. That's the truth Clara left for you to carry."

And Marley, with the ledger warm beneath her palm, felt the circle's gaze pressing closer.

• • •

When Damien finally left—ledger photographs carefully stored, his promise to begin cross-referencing Aurelia's patient list with the town records written on his lips like a vow—Marley remained alone in the shop. The silence settled like heavy cloth, broken only by the groan of wood as the old beams shifted against the night. The lantern burned low, its light pressing shadows into the corners where books leaned and dust breathed.

She placed the ledger back on the desk and laid her hand across its cover. The leather was cool, rough with age, but beneath her palm it seemed to vibrate faintly, almost imperceptibly, like the low hum of a struck bell. The words Clara had written—*memory lives in matter*—rushed back, echoing in the marrow of her bones.

It was no longer a metaphor.

The longer she sat, the stronger it became: the ledger was not just a record. It was alive with intention. The ink carried not only Aurelia's hand but her insistence. The ledger did not simply want to be found—it wanted to be read, spoken, acted upon.

Marley opened it again to the coded lines. She whispered them aloud, her voice trembling but steadying with each word.

"When the bell forgets to ring, remember the Grove."

"Seven names to bind the circle, but the spiral must remain open."

"If fire takes the bridge, seek the river's second bend."

The phrases reverberated in her chest. They did not feel like riddles anymore. They felt like commands, written with the knowledge that one day another set of eyes would find them and feel the same pulse. The ledger was not a diary— it was a manual.

Marley pressed her fingers to the ink, tracing the shapes.

A chill climbed her wrist, spread up her arm, and settled over her shoulders like a shawl. For a breath, she swore the lantern dimmed, the edges of the room falling away until only the desk and the book remained lit.

Then, faint as breath on glass, a voice slid into the hush.

Do not forget us.

Her throat clenched. She jerked her head up, but the shop was empty, the front door bolted, the curtains drawn. Only her. Only the book.

But the presence did not recede. It pressed closer, filling the air, heavier than silence, heavier than shadow. Aurelia— or the circle, or both—was here.

Marley squeezed her eyes shut and steadied herself. She thought of Clara's calm voice, of Damien's patient certainty, of Eleanor Whitcomb's plea written in a hand that still lived across a century. She let the fear move through her, then named what she felt: not malice, not danger, but demand.

The ledger wanted more.

Marley's breath came shallow, but she leaned forward, refusing to shrink. "I hear you," she whispered. "I found you. And I won't turn away."

The presence thickened, not easing but acknowledging. She opened her eyes and found the ledger's page sharper, the ink darker, as though freshly written. She traced the final warning again: *The circle cannot hold if one is broken.*

Her hand trembled. She realized, with a certainty that cut deep, that it was not history calling her. It was present. The circle did not just want to be remembered. It wanted to be whole.

And she, somehow, was part of that reckoning.

The lantern guttered, throwing sparks against the glass. Marley exhaled and shut the ledger gently, laying both hands over the cover as though to seal her vow into it. Her aunt had known. Eleanor had known. Aurelia had written not for her own time but for someone else's, someone who would refuse to bury what was inconvenient.

Marley's chest ached with the weight of it, with the knowledge that she could not un-know what the book demanded. She had stepped too far into Aurelia's current. It would not release her.

The whispers seemed to retreat then, not gone but folded back, like the tide slipping beneath rocks. The shop returned to itself—the creak of timbers, the faint drip of rain outside, the smell of paper and dust. But the demand remained, imprinted on her skin like ink.

Marley blew out the lantern. Darkness filled the shop, but it did not feel empty. It felt watchful, waiting. She tightened her grip on the ledger, whispered once more—more prayer than promise—

"I won't let the circle break."

And with those words, the night seemed to settle into her bones, carrying both the burden and inevitability of what lay ahead.

25

MEMORY SHARED, VISION REVEALED

The Saturday morning sun filtered through gauzy clouds, softening Brookwood's edges into watercolor. The bookshop carried its usual perfume of paper, cedar polish, and faint lavender from Clara's long-emptied sachets. Marley had left the door propped open to the street, a quiet invitation, though she didn't expect many visitors this early.

She was re-shelving a stack of local histories when the bell above the door chimed. Damien stepped in, shaking mist from his shoulders. But he wasn't alone. At his side was a girl of about ten with chestnut-brown hair braided neatly over one shoulder, her expression a mix of shyness and curiosity.

Marley blinked. "You didn't tell me you were bringing company."

Damien's smile held an edge of apology. "This is Sophie. My daughter. She wanted to see the shop for herself after hearing me go on about it."

Sophie's eyes widened as she took in the shelves

climbing toward the ceiling, the ladders, the clusters of antique lamps. "It smells like stories," she said softly, almost to herself.

Marley's heart pinched. Clara used to say the same thing —that books carried not only words but scents, each one steeped in the memory of hands that turned its pages. Marley crouched a little, meeting Sophie at eye level. "That's a good nose you've got. Your father has excellent taste in assistants."

Sophie's shyness cracked into a small grin. "Do you have anything about sea captains? Papa said there were a lot here once."

Marley led her toward a shelf in the corner, where old maritime volumes leaned like exhausted sailors. She pulled one down—*The Voyages of Captain Morton, 1861–1872*—and handed it over. Sophie's fingers curled reverently around the cracked spine.

While Sophie settled into a chair, flipping through engravings of tall ships and stormy seas, Damien drew closer to Marley at the counter. "I hope this isn't... too much," he said, voice pitched low. "She's been asking questions. About why I spend so much time here. About what we've been finding. I didn't want to lie, but I didn't want to overwhelm her, either."

Marley glanced at Sophie, then back at Damien. "It's all right. The shop was meant for more than silence." She hesitated before adding, "But are you sure you want her near... all of this? The necklace. The ledger. The things that don't behave like ordinary history?"

Damien's gaze darkened, but he didn't look away. "I trust her. And maybe... maybe she should see. If any of this is real —if it's not just dreams and symbols and grief—then what better test than innocence?"

Marley's throat tightened at the word. She had been wrestling for weeks with whether she was chasing specters of her own making. But Clara had left trails too precise, and Aurelia's voice too insistent, for it to be nothing. Still, the thought of letting Sophie touch that weight made Marley's palms damp.

Sophie wandered back toward the counter, carrying the book open to a plate of a storm-tossed vessel. "Was this the ship that sank?" she asked.

Damien leaned over. "One of them. The healer left the ship just before it wrecked."

Sophie's brow furrowed. "A healer?"

Marley reached into the desk drawer before she could second-guess herself. The necklace lay coiled inside, the green stone catching the morning light. She placed it on the counter gently. "Some say her name was Aurelia Ward," she said softly. "She helped people when others turned them away."

Sophie's eyes locked on the pendant. "It looks like it's breathing."

Before Marley could stop her, Sophie reached out and pressed her small hand over the stone.

The air in the shop shifted.

It was subtle at first—the way the sunlight dimmed, the way the dust motes seemed to hang suspended rather than fall. Marley's pulse jumped. She saw Sophie's face go slack for a moment, her pupils dilating wide, her lips parting.

Then Sophie inhaled sharply, as though startled by something only she could see. Her free hand gripped the counter, knuckles white.

"Sophie?" Damien's voice cracked. He half-reached toward her, then froze, waiting.

Marley moved around quickly, kneeling beside the girl.

Sophie's eyes weren't vacant—they were tracking something far away, something behind the veil of the shop. Marley spoke softly, the way Clara once had when Marley woke shaking from a dream. "It's all right. You're safe. Tell me what you see."

Sophie's lips trembled. "A woman... by the river. She has green eyes. She's... she's putting stones in a circle."

Marley's heart slammed. Damien's face drained of color.

Sophie's voice grew steadier, as if speaking pulled the vision closer. "There are other women, too. They're singing, but it's not in words I know. The green-eyed one is smiling at me. She's..." Sophie faltered, tears welling. "She says, *don't let them forget.*"

Marley gathered the girl gently against her, one hand at her back, whispering, "You're all right, Sophie. You're all right. You saw her, that's all. And she saw you."

The necklace slipped from Sophie's fingers back onto the counter with a muted clink. The air eased; the dust began its fall again. The sunlight warmed.

Sophie clung to Marley's arm, breathing hard. Damien's hand trembled where it hovered above his daughter's shoulder, finally settling there with a father's fierce protectiveness.

Marley rocked slightly, as Clara used to do for her, and felt the truth settle like a stone in her chest: Aurelia's legacy wasn't confined to Marley alone. The current ran through certain bloodlines, carried in marrow and memory, passed down like a secret inheritance.

When Sophie finally lifted her head, her face was pale but her eyes bright, awed. "She was real," the girl whispered. "Papa... she was real."

Damien's expression fractured—fear, grief, disbelief all colliding. But for the first time, Marley saw something else in him too: surrender.

. . .

FOR A LONG MOMENT, the shop held its silence, thick and pulsing, broken only by Sophie's shallow breaths. Damien hadn't moved, his hand still resting on his daughter's shoulder, as though anchoring her to the floor. Marley could feel the tremor in his stance—the rigid line of a man who had been trained all his life to trust ink and stone, now staring into something far less tangible yet undeniably real.

When Sophie steadied, Marley guided her toward the armchair near the front window. The child curled up, pale but alert, her eyes darting between them with the dazed look of someone who had glimpsed too much light at once.

Damien finally spoke, his voice tight. "That wasn't suggestion. That wasn't you feeding her words. She saw—" His jaw worked, the muscle tightening, as though the rest of the sentence refused to form.

Marley sat opposite him, her hands clasped in her lap. "She saw what I've seen," she finished softly.

Damien's eyes cut to hers. "And you didn't tell me."

The accusation was quiet, but it landed with weight. Marley lifted her chin. "I did. Not everything, but enough. The visions, the whispers. I told you about the necklace. About the ledger. About Clara's phrase—memory lives in matter. You thought I was romanticizing grief."

"I thought—" He broke off, running both hands over his face. He looked at Sophie, who was now tracing the embroidered arm of the chair, lost in thought. Then back at Marley. "I thought you were exhausted, raw. I thought Clara's death left you vulnerable, searching for patterns in shadows. I didn't want to dismiss you, but... I didn't believe."

"And now?" Marley asked.

Damien's exhale was long, weighted. "Now I watched my

daughter touch that stone and see a woman neither of us described to her. A woman she called green-eyed." His gaze sharpened, haunted. "That's what you've seen, isn't it?"

Marley nodded. "By the water. In the dreams. At the edge of the crowd during the festival. I thought at first it was grief's trick—Clara in another form, my mind conjuring her. But then the details multiplied. The spiral, the warnings, the light in the lighthouse. And now Sophie saw her too."

The admission pulled something taut between them, like a line strung from her chest to his. Damien leaned back, staring at the ceiling as though searching for a language he hadn't spoken in years.

"You realize what this means," he said finally. "If memory lives in matter... if Aurelia's presence clings to these objects—ledger, necklace, music box—then it isn't just you carrying this. It's anyone who touches them. Anyone connected."

Marley's hands tightened together. "Bloodlines," she whispered.

Damien's head dropped forward, his eyes heavy. "God help me, but I think you may be right. And if Sophie carries this too..." His hand drifted unconsciously back to his daughter, protective. "Then what we're doing isn't just uncovering the past. We're involving the future."

Marley wanted to reach across the desk, but she let the distance remain. "I didn't ask for this," she said gently. "Clara left it. Aurelia left it. The circle left it. And it isn't only my burden anymore. Sophie's vision proves it."

Damien's expression softened into something rawer—fear, awe, reluctant belief. "Tell me," he said. His voice dropped, almost pleading. "Tell me what you've seen. All of it. Every vision, every whisper. Don't spare me because you think I'll retreat."

The demand startled her, not because of its force but because of the vulnerability beneath it. She inhaled and began.

She told him of the first time she opened Clara's writing desk and found the spiral etched into the wood. Of the hidden room with its bricked-up window, the boxes labeled with women's names. Of the recipe book, the strange salve, the vivid childhood memory that had never been her own. She told him of Hazel at the tea shop, of the whisper that had risen like breath when she set the recipe on Clara's desk.

She spoke of the bridge, the locket with Aurelia's initials, the child's voice calling her name through the fog. Of the map in the lighthouse, the flickering signal of three short, two long. Of the visions: Aurelia's hands placing stones in a spiral, Aurelia calming storm-tossed sailors with herbs and prayer.

Damien listened without interruption. His face moved through disbelief, grief, and wonder, but he never looked away.

When Marley finally fell silent, her throat raw, the shop seemed to lean into the hush. Sophie was asleep in the armchair, her head against the cushions, the sea captain's book fallen to her lap.

Damien folded his hands together, pressing his knuckles to his mouth. When he spoke, his voice was hoarse. "You've been carrying this alone. And I doubted you."

"You were protecting yourself," Marley said quietly. "You lost enough. Believing meant risking more."

"But Sophie..." His eyes dropped to his daughter. "She doesn't lie. She doesn't invent visions. And now..." He trailed off, shaking his head. "Now I can't dismiss it. I can't call it folklore or suggestion anymore. This is happening. To her. To you. To us."

For the first time, he said the word without hesitation. *Us.*

Marley let the word rest between them. She felt no triumph, only the gravity of it settling in her bones.

"Then we press forward," she said. "Not because it's safe. Not because it's easy. But because it's already chosen us."

Damien closed his eyes, his lips parting as if in prayer. When he opened them again, his gaze was steady. "Then we press forward."

THE RAIN HAD RETURNED OUTSIDE, a soft patter against the shop's windows, as if the town itself exhaled after what had just happened. Marley moved toward the armchair where Sophie had dozed off. The girl's breathing had evened, her small body slack against the cushions, but Marley could see the traces of the vision still clinging to her: the faint tension in her brow, the way her fingers twitched as if holding onto something unseen.

Marley brushed a loose strand of hair from Sophie's forehead, a motion more instinctive than deliberate. Clara had done the same for her once, years ago, when Marley had come running up from the cellar in tears after hearing whispers she thought were mice. Clara had told her that some sounds weren't pests at all but memory—places that remembered what people tried to forget.

Now Sophie was caught in that same current, and Marley realized with a shiver that the circle wasn't limited to her bloodline alone. It was wider, deeper, and more intricate than she had imagined.

Damien stood a step away, his frame tense, arms crossed

as though holding himself together. But his eyes never left his daughter. The scholar's detachment had cracked entirely. He wasn't watching for evidence anymore—he was watching for her safety, her peace.

"She shouldn't carry this," he murmured.

Marley looked up at him. "Neither should I. But we do. And maybe... maybe that's the point."

Damien's gaze snapped to her, full of both grief and dawning comprehension. "Are you saying this is inheritance? That the circle chose her the way it's chosen you?"

Marley shook her head slowly. "Not chosen. Connected. Bloodlines, memory, objects—they're all threads in the same weave. Sophie touched the necklace and Aurelia reached for her, just as she reached for me through the ledger, the recipes, the music box. These aren't random encounters, Damien. They're invitations."

The word hung heavy between them: *invitations*.

Marley returned her attention to Sophie. She took the child's hand gently, feeling the warmth of life pulsing steady through it. Sophie stirred, eyes fluttering open briefly. "She was kind," she whispered, voice drowsy. "She wanted me to know she's still here." Then her eyes closed again, sleep reclaiming her.

Marley smoothed the girl's braid against her shoulder, her own throat tightening. "She isn't frightened," she said softly, more to herself than Damien. "She saw, and she isn't afraid. That matters."

Damien stepped closer, his voice low. "And you think I can keep pretending this is imagination? After hearing her repeat the very words you told me only days ago?" His tone carried no anger now, only resignation.

Marley rose to face him fully. He looked older in that moment, worn not by years but by the sudden recognition of weight he could no longer set down. His hand flexed at his side before he finally reached out, resting it briefly on the back of the chair where Sophie slept.

"I don't know what I believe anymore," he admitted. "But I believe her. And... I believe you."

The admission struck Marley with more force than she expected. Weeks of carrying her discoveries alone, of second-guessing her sanity, of doubting whether Clara had sent her on a fool's errand—all of it cracked under the simple weight of those words.

"I needed to hear that," she whispered.

Damien's eyes softened. "I know."

The rain pressed harder against the windows now, as though punctuating their fragile truce. Marley looked at Sophie again and then back at Damien. "This isn't just about uncovering history anymore. It's alive, Damien. It's demanding. And now it's touched your family too. The circle..." Her voice faltered, the truth too vast to name. "The circle has widened."

Damien glanced at the ledger still lying open on the desk, its pages marked with Aurelia's coded phrases. He rubbed his temple. "If the circle is widening, then Brookwood itself is about to change. The town won't let go of its myths quietly. There will be resistance—more than whispers this time."

Marley drew herself taller, her hand still resting lightly on Sophie's. "Then we stand in it. Together."

The word seemed to surprise both of them, but neither retracted it.

The clock on the wall ticked past midnight. The air in the shop grew heavy with the scent of wax and rain-dampened wood. Marley realized that whatever path they were on now, there was no stepping back. Sophie's vision had sealed it. This wasn't only Marley's burden or Clara's legacy. It wasn't only Aurelia's memory pressing through matter. It was a binding that had leapt generations, threads weaving them together into something larger than choice.

She tightened her grip on the child's hand and whispered, barely audible: "We won't let them forget."

The lamp flickered once, as if in answer.

26

TRUTH AT THE COVERED BRIDGE

The sky was bruised with late evening, streaked violet and gray, when Marley and Damien walked toward the covered bridge. The air smelled of river water and damp cedar, the kind of scent that clung to fabric and skin as though it wanted to mark you. The planks of the path groaned under their weight, the old timbers swollen by decades of storms.

It had been Marley's suggestion to return here, though the idea had pressed at her more than formed in words. Ever since Sophie's vision, the circle felt less like something she was uncovering and more like something tugging at her, pulling her steps toward places already chosen. The bridge was one of those places.

Damien carried a lantern, its flame muted against the heavy dusk. He moved with his usual carefulness, though Marley could see the tension in his jaw, the way his free hand clenched and unclenched as if rehearsing the act of pulling someone back from the edge.

They stepped inside the bridge's belly, the world narrowing to wooden beams and echoing footsteps. The air here was cooler, tinged with river spray. The sound of water below roared louder than usual, swollen by the rains of the past week.

"Here," Marley said, stopping near the central support. Her palm pressed to the weathered plank where she had once heard the child's voice. The memory sent a shiver down her arms.

Damien crouched, lantern held low. "The wood here looks different," he said after a moment. "See? This panel doesn't quite match the grain around it. Could be replaced at some point—or hiding something."

Marley knelt beside him, running her fingertips over the seam. The wood was splintered, edges rough, but the faintest hollow sound rang when she tapped it. A hidden cavity.

"Clara left you everything else," Damien said softly. "Why not this?"

"Because this wasn't Clara's to give," Marley whispered.

They worked carefully, prying at the seam with a small iron tool Damien had brought from the shop. The wood resisted at first, but then gave with a groan, as though reluctant to surrender what it held. When the panel shifted loose, Damien reached inside. His hand emerged with a small iron box, blackened with rust and age.

It was no larger than a loaf of bread, its surface mottled with the marks of time. Marley's breath caught. The box looked impossibly old, older than the bridge itself.

"Wow," Damien murmured, setting it down between them. "This could have been here for more than a century."

The box had no lock, only a simple latch, corroded but intact. Marley's fingers hovered before she dared to press it open. The hinge creaked, stiff with disuse, and then gave.

Inside lay a folded parchment, its edges browned, its

surface embossed with strange inked sigils that had bled into the fibers over decades. Across the top, in faded but legible script, were the words: *The Circle of Seven.*

Marley's heart jolted. She traced the title with trembling fingers. The ink seemed to hum faintly beneath her touch.

They spread the parchment open with care, weighting the corners with stones. The writing inside was formal, a script of oaths and pledges, each marked by symbols rather than full names. The sigils curved in spirals and lines, strange and intricate, unlike anything Marley had seen in Clara's journals.

She read aloud, her voice steady despite her pulse hammering. "*We bind ourselves to the keeping of memory, to the tending of body and spirit, to the guarding of truths men fear to name. We vow to remain whole, seven woven into one, until time itself releases us.*"

Damien leaned close, his eyes narrowed in awe. "It's not just notes or recipes. It's covenant. This is their founding charter."

Marley nodded, her chest aching. Each line spoke of duty, of secrecy, of sacrifice. The language was careful—never naming, always circling—but the intent was clear. These women had sworn themselves into something larger, something that had no place in Brookwood's official record yet was more foundational than anything the Historical Society celebrated.

Her eyes caught on a phrase inked near the bottom: *To forget is to break. To break is to lose. The circle must remain whole.*

The words reverberated in her ribs. She whispered them again, softer. "The circle must remain whole."

Damien touched one of the sigils. "If we can match these symbols to the ledger, to the initials—we could identify them. The Seven." His voice was hushed, reverent. "Marley, do you realize what this means? This isn't folklore anymore. This is record. Proof."

But before Marley could answer, the air shifted.

A wind rose suddenly through the slats of the bridge, fierce and cold, as though the river itself exhaled. The parchment trembled, its corners lifting despite the stones. Marley pressed her palm flat to it instinctively, and as she did, the water below seemed to shimmer unnaturally—its surface glinting with light though the sky above was dark.

Damien steadied the lantern, his eyes wide. "Do you see that?"

Marley nodded, unable to speak. The water rippled in patterns, concentric circles that formed then dissolved, formed then dissolved, as though echoing the parchment's spiral sigils.

The wind whipped harder, rattling the beams of the bridge. Marley clutched the parchment as though it might be torn away. The shimmering grew brighter, spreading across the river's surface like a second sky.

And for the first time, Marley understood: this was not only history. This was covenant still alive, still binding. The Circle of Seven had sworn themselves into memory, and memory itself had teeth.

She gripped Damien's wrist, their eyes locking across the flickering lantern light. Neither of them spoke, but both knew: the bridge was no longer just a relic. It was a threshold.

THE LANTERN FLAME flickered violently as the wind tore through the bridge. Marley pressed her hand down harder on the parchment, anchoring it against the wood. The shimmer on the river below refused to fade—it pulsed like a heartbeat, each concentric ring rolling outward as though summoned by the very words written before them.

Damien crouched beside her, his eyes darting between the text and the water. "We need to read it—really read it," he said, voice raised above the gusts. "If this is oath, not record, then it's meant to respond when invoked. That's what we're seeing."

Marley nodded, though her throat had gone dry. She shifted her weight, drawing the lantern closer so its light fell directly across the parchment. The sigils seemed to move under the glow, as if the ink were alive, curling and uncurling like vines. She forced herself to focus on the words written between them.

The first line repeated: *We bind ourselves to the keeping of memory, to the tending of body and spirit, to the guarding of truths men fear to name.*

She whispered it again, and the shimmer below brightened, a silver pulse racing across the current.

Damien steadied the page with his hand, his scholar's focus cutting through the storm. "These are vows. Not symbolic. Actual binding vows." He traced a spiral etched in the corner. "This—look at this—matches the spiral carved beneath Clara's desk. And here—" He shifted to another sigil, a crescent enclosed by seven lines. "This is on the apothecary ledger. Aurelia used this as a marker for her own hand."

Marley leaned in, her pulse hammering. "So each sigil marks a member."

"Exactly. Seven women. Each symbol unique, like a seal. And they signed not with names but with oaths."

Her gaze swept across the page. The spirals, crescents, leaves, and stars—each one distinct, woven between the lines of text. They were signatures disguised as images, and each one hummed with the same strange energy.

Marley's fingers hovered over a sigil shaped like an open flame. She remembered the line from the ledger: *If fire takes the bridge, seek the river's second bend.* Her chest tightened. "This one... it's tied to warnings. To fire."

Damien nodded, his own finger resting on a sigil shaped like a teardrop enclosed by two hands. "And this—healing. Protection. It matches the salves you tested from the recipe book."

The words on the page blurred as the wind pressed harder, but Marley forced herself to keep reading.

We vow to remain whole, seven woven into one, until time itself releases us.

Her mouth formed the words silently, but the air seemed to catch them anyway. The shimmer on the river surged, silver bright against the dark current, and she gasped.

Damien turned sharply to her. "You feel it too?"

"Yes." Her voice trembled. "It's not just light. It's... recognition. Like it hears us."

Damien exhaled through his teeth. "Memory lives in matter. Clara wrote it, but Aurelia lived it. These oaths weren't left here as record—they were left to be renewed. Each time someone speaks them, the circle stirs."

The thought chilled her. "Then what happens if we finish it? If we read them all?"

His silence was answer enough. He wasn't ready to guess.

Marley turned back to the parchment. Near the bottom, after the oaths, another line caught her attention. *When the bell forgets to ring, remember the Grove. When the water shines without moon, the circle is near.*

She whispered it aloud, and as if in answer, the shimmer

beneath the bridge flared once more, brighter than before. The river itself seemed to carry a glow, silver waves cresting where none should.

Damien's hand gripped her wrist, not harshly but firmly. "You see it too. It's not imagination."

Her eyes met his. "It's real. All of it."

They both bent over the parchment again. The final section bore the seven sigils arranged in a circle, each interlocking with the next. At its center, a spiral—the same one carved into wood, etched into recipes, pulsing in visions.

Damien brushed his hand across it carefully. "This was their mark. Their covenant. And if we can map these symbols to the ledger, to Aurelia's initials, to the other clues—"

"We can name them," Marley finished, her voice hushed. "We can give them back their place."

But as she spoke, another sensation washed over her, heavier than awe. It was weight. The weight of being watched—not by unseen townspeople, not by hidden protectors, but by the circle itself. The parchment pulsed faintly under her palm, warm as skin.

She drew in a sharp breath. "Damien... it wants something."

His brow furrowed. "What do you mean?"

"It's not just a record. It's a demand. A call to action." Her voice shook. "The circle isn't asking to be remembered. It's asking to be continued."

For a long moment, neither of them spoke. The wind howled, the shimmer rolled across the river, and the oaths burned quietly between them, alive on the page.

Finally Damien whispered, almost reverently: "Then we're not just historians anymore."

Marley met his eyes, her heart hammering. "We're successors."

The shimmer surged once more, as though sealing their recognition. And the river below, for one terrifyingly beautiful moment, looked like liquid silver burning in the dark.

THE STORM that had begun as a restless wind grew teeth. Rain pelted the roof of the covered bridge with a fury that drowned the sound of their breathing. The lantern flame guttered in protest, throwing shadows across the parchment, the sigils appearing to ripple like things alive. Beneath their knees, the bridge seemed to shudder, the great beams straining as though they too felt the tension of what had been unearthed.

Marley gripped the parchment tighter. The words—*The circle must remain whole*—blazed in her mind as though branded there. She could feel the storm pressing against her chest, each gust of wind whispering the same truth she had been running from since Clara's death: she was no longer just an observer. She was implicated.

Damien steadied the lantern, his face lit in fragments by its weak glow. "It's as if the storm knows," he muttered, half to himself. His voice carried awe, but also a tremor. "As though it's waiting on us."

Marley's throat tightened. "Because it is." She gestured to the parchment. "This wasn't meant to be a relic tucked away. It was meant to be... renewed. Repeated. Kept alive through those willing to bear it."

The words tasted like iron in her mouth, heavy with responsibility.

Lightning split the sky, and for an instant the bridge was illuminated in stark white. The shimmer on the river flared so bright that Marley had to shield her eyes. When she lowered her hand, she thought she saw shapes forming in the water's glow—seven figures, indistinct yet undeniable, standing in a spiral that mirrored the sigils inked before them. Then the thunder cracked and they vanished, leaving only the pulse of the current below.

She swayed, dizzy. Damien's hand closed around her arm, steadying her. "Marley?"

"I saw them," she whispered. "The Seven."

His expression was caught between disbelief and reverence, but he didn't question. He only tightened his grip, as though grounding her in the present.

The storm raged louder, rain hammering the boards, water dripping through cracks to spatter the parchment. Marley brushed the drops away urgently, terrified of losing the words, though some part of her knew no storm could truly erase them. They were etched deeper than paper, woven into the marrow of Brookwood itself.

She pressed her palm flat against the parchment, her pulse wild. "If we speak these oaths aloud," she said, "what happens? Do we take their place? Do we bind ourselves into what they began?"

Damien shook his head. "I don't know. But isn't that what they wanted? Not to be remembered as ghosts, but to be continued as flesh?"

His words hit her like another crack of thunder. For weeks she had thought of Aurelia, of Clara, of all the women tied to the ledger, as voices pressing against her, demanding she tell their story. But perhaps that had never been enough. Perhaps the circle was not satisfied with remembrance. It wanted incarnation.

The lantern hissed as a spray of rain nearly extinguished it. In the dim flicker, the parchment seemed to glow faintly of its own accord. The sigils pulsed, and Marley felt the thrum in her bones, the same rhythm as the shimmer below.

She realized suddenly that her breath matched the rhythm, her heartbeat too. The circle was not only outside of her—it was inside.

Her knees gave slightly. She gripped the desk of wood and iron, whispering, "It's too much. Clara, why didn't you tell me it would be this heavy?"

The bridge groaned as another gust ripped through, beams rattling. For a moment, Marley thought it might collapse beneath them. The storm was no longer simply weather; it was demand given shape.

Damien crouched lower, close enough that she could feel the warmth of his shoulder against hers. "You don't have to answer it tonight," he said, though his voice carried the same urgency she felt. "Not now. Not like this."

But even as he spoke, they both knew the choice wasn't theirs to postpone. The air itself was thick with expectation, as though the bridge were holding its breath, waiting.

Marley's eyes returned to the final line on the parchment. *The circle must remain whole.*

Her lips formed the words, though she did not speak them aloud. She felt their shape anyway, reverberating in her chest, echoing back from the water, from the storm, from the very wood around them.

And she knew, with a clarity that stole the breath from her lungs, that she could not walk away. The bridge would not let her. The circle would not let her. Clara's absence was no longer absence at all—it was a mantle laid across her shoulders, a mantle she could neither deny nor remove.

Damien's hand pressed gently at her back, grounding

her again. His face was pale but his eyes steady, as though he too had recognized the shift.

They did not speak. They only knelt together in the storm, over the parchment that pulsed like a living heart, while the river shimmered and the bridge trembled and the night itself seemed to pause.

Waiting.

Holding its breath.

For their decision.

27

A LIGHT LEFT BURNING

The storm had followed Marley home, though it had lost its teeth by the time she reached the bookshop. The thunder had retreated into the distance, low and tired, and the rain had dwindled to a mist that clung to her hair and coat. She let herself inside, her shoulders aching from the night at the bridge, her mind still thundering with the words of the parchment: *The circle must remain whole.*

The shop was dark, the windows rattling faintly with the wind off the water. Marley shut the door behind her, breathing in the familiar scent of paper and dust, mixed now with the lingering dampness of her clothes. She moved slowly across the room, careful of the creaking boards, until she noticed it—the glow.

On the desk, where Clara's old writing implements still sat, a candle burned. Its flame flickered steadily, not new, not wavering as if just lit. It had been burning long enough for wax to pool around its base.

Marley froze, every hair on her arms rising. She hadn't

lit a candle before leaving for the bridge. She hadn't lit one in days.

The flame leaned toward her as though acknowledging her arrival, and for a long, shivering moment, Marley felt she wasn't alone in the shop. Clara's presence—or Aurelia's, or the circle's—hung in the air as thick as the scent of beeswax.

She walked toward the desk, her breath shallow. The flame bent again, as if following her motion. She whispered, half in awe, half in fear: "Did you light this?"

The room offered no answer but the silence of old wood. Still, she could not shake the certainty that the candle had been waiting.

Her fingers brushed the desk's surface, warm beneath her hand, as though the wood itself remembered the touch of whoever had placed the match to the wick. Clara's phrase echoed in her mind—*memory lives in matter*. Was this proof again, another reminder that the boundary between object and spirit was thinner than she wanted to believe?

She sat, pulling the candle closer. Its flame illuminated the ledger still resting nearby, the necklace wrapped in its oilcloth, the fragments of history she had unearthed one by one. They looked almost arranged—artifacts in a ritual she hadn't yet learned to perform.

A knock startled her. Sharp, quick, hesitant.

Marley jerked toward the door, her heart lurching. At this hour? With the storm only just passed?

She crossed the shop, hesitated, and then unlatched the door.

Damien stood on the stoop, damp from the mist, his hair darkened by rain. In his hands he carried a small paper sack and a thermos.

"Forgive the intrusion," he said, his voice low, almost sheepish. "I thought... after tonight, you shouldn't be alone."

Relief and surprise collided in Marley's chest. She stepped back, allowing him in. "You didn't have to—"

"I know." He managed a small, strained smile. "But I wanted to."

She closed the door behind him, and he followed her to the desk. His eyes fell immediately on the candle. He paused. "You lit this?"

"No," Marley said quietly. "I found it burning when I came back."

He stared for a long moment, his expression unreadable. Then he set down the sack and thermos, pulling out two mugs and a wrapped loaf of bread. "Tea and something warm. From the bakery—they were closing when I passed."

The gesture undid her more than she expected. After the weight of the bridge, the storm, the parchment's demands, this simple kindness cracked her guard.

"Thank you," she said, and the words carried more than gratitude.

They sat across from each other, the candle between them. He poured the tea—strong, herbal—and the steam curled upward into the flickering light. Marley wrapped her hands around the mug, letting the warmth seep into her palms.

For a while they ate and drank in silence. The storm whispered outside, the candle burned steadily, and the shop seemed to hold them in its own suspended breath.

When Damien finally spoke, his voice was rough, as though dragged from deep within. "I owe you an apology."

Marley looked up, startled.

"For doubting you," he said. His eyes were fixed on the candle, but his words were meant for her. "For insisting this was grief, or imagination, or folklore. I wanted so badly to keep the world ordered, to keep Sophie safe inside reason, that I refused to see what was right in front of me. What's been in front of me for weeks."

Marley's throat tightened. She thought of all the nights she had questioned her sanity, the days she had carried visions like stones in her chest. She thought of Clara, and how lonely Clara must have felt, carrying this legacy without anyone who would listen.

"Damien," she said softly. "You don't need to—"

"Yes, I do." His voice cut gently but firmly. His eyes met hers now, steady, unflinching. "You've been brave enough to name what others would rather bury. And I dismissed you. Tonight, watching Sophie... watching her see what you've seen..." His breath hitched. "I can't ignore it anymore. And I can't let you carry it alone."

The words settled between them like an offering.

Marley felt something shift inside her—not release, not entirely, but a loosening. A recognition that she was no longer standing at the edge of the circle by herself.

The candle flame leaned again, as though in agreement.

Damien leaned back, his hand brushing the edge of the desk. His eyes lingered on hers a moment longer than before, and in the fragile silence that followed, Marley felt the beginnings of something more than alliance. Trust, yes. But also something softer, more dangerous: closeness.

The kind of closeness that made the air between them hum, the kind that carried its own vow.

THE TEA HAD COOLED, but Marley still cradled the mug between her palms. The warmth had seeped into her hands, steadied her breath, though her chest still carried the weight of the bridge, the parchment, and now Damien's apology. She studied him across the table, the lantern glow catching the planes of his face, the exhaustion beneath his eyes. He looked not unlike herself—someone who had been carrying more than he could admit.

Damien broke the silence first. His gaze remained fixed on the flame between them. "When I first came here," he said slowly, "I told myself I was looking for quiet. A place to raise Sophie without reminders of what we'd lost. But the truth..." He hesitated, his throat working. "The truth is, I was running. I thought if I could shut the door on everything I couldn't explain, everything that hurt too much, then maybe I could control what was left."

Marley's heart pinched at the admission. She remembered the way he had dismissed her visions early on, the impatience in his voice when she tried to describe Aurelia's presence. That wasn't only skepticism—it was fear disguised as reason.

"You lost her," Marley said gently. "Your wife."

His eyes flicked to hers, startled by the directness, but then softened. He nodded. "Jackie. She... she believed in things I didn't. Dreams, intuition, signs. She used to say storms carried messages if we were brave enough to listen. I called it nonsense." His hand flexed on the table, the memory tight in his muscles. "And when she tried to tell me she saw what was coming, I told her to stop. I told her it was imagination. Denial. But she was right. And I silenced her anyway."

The words fell heavy between them, heavier even than the storm outside. Marley felt them settle into her chest like stones. She set her mug down, reaching across the table without thinking. Her hand covered his briefly, a gesture of witness, not absolution. "You didn't know," she said softly.

His hand didn't move from beneath hers. "But I should have listened. If I had—if I had believed her even once—maybe she would have felt less alone." His voice broke slightly, the scholar's control unraveling. "That's what I can't forgive myself for."

Marley's throat tightened. She thought of Clara, of her aunt's quiet solitude, the journals filled with truths no one else was willing to acknowledge. How many nights had Clara sat here, candle lit, waiting for someone to listen? How many times had Marley herself brushed off Clara's oddities as eccentricities, never realizing the weight she bore?

"I wasn't there for Clara either," Marley confessed. The words surprised her, pulled up from a place she hadn't let herself touch. "I loved her, but I didn't see. Not until she was gone. I thought she was collecting old books and recipes because she couldn't let go of the past. I didn't see that she was preserving something that mattered, something alive. And when she died, she left it all to me, as if I was supposed to understand. But I didn't. I still don't."

Her voice caught. She looked down at the candle, the flame steady despite the draft. "I keep asking why me. Why Clara thought I was the one who could carry this. And some days I think maybe she was wrong."

Damien leaned forward, the intensity in his eyes pulling her gaze back to him. "She wasn't wrong."

The certainty in his tone startled her.

"You've uncovered more in weeks than the Historical Society has in a century. You've followed whispers no one else dared to hear. Clara knew you would listen, Marley. That's the difference. You listen, even when it terrifies you."

The words sank into her like warmth, though they

unsettled her too. To be seen that clearly by someone who had once doubted her—it was both comfort and danger.

Their hands were still touching, his beneath hers, the candlelight etching their shadows together on the desk. For a long moment, neither moved. The air between them thickened, not only with history and grief, but with something fragile and new. Something unspoken that hummed beneath the surface like the current of the river under the bridge.

Marley broke the silence with a whisper. "Do you ever wonder if we're being pulled into something too big for us?"

Damien's eyes lingered on hers, dark and steady. "Every hour. But I also wonder if maybe we're exactly where we're meant to be."

The words left them suspended. The shop felt suddenly smaller, the walls leaning closer, the air charged not just by ghosts but by the possibility of something else—something alive and dangerous and human.

Neither reached further, but neither pulled away. The moment stretched, unbroken, and Marley felt the weight of it settle deep inside her.

The candle flame flared briefly, as though acknowledging what passed between them, before steadying again.

THE SILENCE in the shop grew dense, not empty but full—alive with words that neither Marley nor Damien could quite release. The candle's flame trembled in the draft, throwing their faces into shifting relief, but it never faltered. Its steady glow painted the room with an intimacy Marley had never associated with this space before. Clara's bookshop, long a keeper of dust and secrets, had become suddenly warm, human, shared.

Marley realized her hand still rested lightly against Damien's. Not a grip, not a declaration, only the simple contact of skin against skin. It was enough to hold the room together, to keep the ghosts at bay for a few precious moments. She wondered if Clara, or Aurelia, or any of the circle, had ever known what it was to be joined in silence this way, where history and heart collided so powerfully that words felt like an intrusion.

Damien shifted slightly, not pulling back but angling closer, the lantern's glow catching in his eyes. They were searching her face, and for once she didn't look away. The pain of his confession, the weight of his guilt, had left him raw. But beneath it she could see something steadier forming—a willingness to stand beside her, even in the storm of truths neither of them fully understood.

"You should sleep," he said finally, voice quiet, almost hoarse.

"So should you," she replied. Her lips curved in the faintest trace of a smile, but it held no levity. Both of them knew rest would not come easily, not tonight.

He nodded, as though acknowledging the futility of his own advice. His hand slipped from beneath hers, leaving a ghost of warmth on her skin. The absence startled her more than the contact had, leaving her fingers tingling, restless.

They sat back in their chairs, not retreating so much as creating space for the moment to breathe. Outside, the rain had dwindled further, the rhythm of it soft now, like a lullaby whispered through the streets of Brookwood. Somewhere in the distance, the sea answered with its eternal hush.

Marley glanced toward the shelves, shadows bending across the spines of forgotten books. How many secrets had this place kept for Clara? For the women before her? The desk, the ledger, the necklace, even the candle—it all seemed arranged now in a pattern she hadn't yet learned to read. And Damien had stepped into it with her, uninvited yet necessary, his presence altering the rhythm without breaking it.

Her voice felt fragile when she finally spoke. "I keep waiting for the moment when all of this will stop. When I'll wake and it will be just me again, just the shop, no visions, no circle."

Damien leaned forward slightly, his elbows braced on the table. "Do you want that?"

The question caught her. She opened her mouth, then closed it again. Want. The word was too simple for the knot of emotions in her chest. She thought of Clara's candle burning unattended, of Aurelia's whispers in storms, of Sophie's sudden vision when she touched the necklace. She thought of Damien, sitting here now, his presence as unexpected as the light still flickering between them.

"No," she said finally, the honesty pulling at something deep in her ribs. "I don't want it to stop. I just want to know I won't be carrying it alone."

He didn't speak immediately. But his gaze lingered, steady and unflinching, the answer in his silence more powerful than words.

The moment stretched, their eyes locked, the candle flame between them bending and straightening with the draft, never once extinguishing. Something fragile had taken root, something neither of them dared to name yet. Trust, perhaps. Or the beginnings of it.

Damien reached for his coat, the movement slow, reluctant. "I should let you rest."

Marley nodded, though part of her wanted to ask him to

stay. She didn't. Not yet. The balance of the moment was too precarious, too new.

He stood, pausing with one hand on the chair back. "I'll come by tomorrow. We can go over the ledger again. Piece more of it together."

"Tomorrow," Marley echoed.

At the door he hesitated, as though weighing whether to say something more. Then, with a small nod, he slipped out into the night, the mist swallowing him.

Marley remained seated, her hands curled around the cooling mug. The candle still burned, its wax pooling at the base, its flame unwavering. She leaned closer, whispering, "You lit yourself, didn't you? You wanted me to see."

The flame leaned toward her again, as if in answer.

For the first time since Clara's death, Marley felt not only burden but also steadiness, the faint, fragile foundation of something new. The circle pressed at her still, but now it was not only their weight she carried. Damien's presence, Sophie's vision, even the silent flame—each had joined her in the widening ring.

She sat in the quiet shop until the candle had burned low, its light still steady, a symbol that trust—like memory— had begun to live here.

And it would not be extinguished easily.

28

TOWN HALL CONFRONTATION

The town hall smelled of polish and dust, the kind of scent that belonged to old institutions and older grudges. Marley's boots echoed against the hardwood floor as she entered the chamber, her satchel heavy with the weight of the ledger, the parchment from the bridge, and her carefully written notes. She'd rehearsed her presentation half a dozen times, but now—faced with the sight of the Brookwood Historical Society seated in stiff-backed chairs like judges—the words fluttered inside her chest, half-tamed birds threatening to take flight.

Damien had insisted on coming, though he now sat a few rows behind her, keeping to the edges of the crowd. His presence was both anchor and warning. She could lean on him, yes, but this was her moment. And if she faltered, no one else could bear the blame.

The board was composed of nine members, most of them elderly, their faces carved with years of guardianship over the town's official narratives. Marley recognized Professor Edmund Ashcroft and two others from her aunt Clara's funeral, their condolences as stiff as their posture now. At the center sat Chairwoman Edith Tuller, tall, sharp-eyed, her gray hair twisted into a severe bun. She tapped a gavel once, silencing the low murmur of the room.

"Miss Taylor," Chairwoman Tuller said, her voice clipped, formal. "You've requested this special session to share... findings. The floor is yours."

Marley nodded, adjusting her satchel strap across her shoulder before stepping to the front. She spread her notes across the podium, her hands trembling only slightly.

"Thank you, Madam Chair," she began, her voice steadying as she spoke. "My name is Marley Taylor, and many of you know I've recently inherited Clara's bookshop. In the weeks since, I've come across records, journals, and artifacts that shed new light on Brookwood's early years—particularly on the women whose names were erased from our history."

A ripple moved through the room at that. Marley pressed forward.

"Among these discoveries is an apothecary ledger signed by Aurelia Ward, a healer active in the mid-1800s. The ledger contains not only medicinal recipes but coded warnings, references to the Grove, and symbols that match carvings found across town sites. These are not folklore embellishments—they are records of a living tradition maintained by women we've ignored."

One of the board members, a ruddy-faced man named Carlton Price, let out a low, dismissive laugh. "Herbal recipes and scribbles in margins? That's what you're calling new history?"

Marley gripped the podium tighter, but she kept her tone calm. "Yes, recipes—and more. Rituals. Oral traditions encoded in kitchens, in candles, in songs. I've found the same spiral sigil carved beneath a desk panel, embossed in a bakery tin, even echoed in the town's founding letters. These women weren't eccentric footnotes. They were a collective—seven of them—bound by oaths we've deliberately forgotten."

The murmurs rose now, some curious, some openly hostile. Chairwoman Tuller raised her hand for silence, but her eyes narrowed. "Miss Taylor, Brookwood has always valued its traditions. But to suggest a—what did you call it? —a circle of women conspiring in secret?"

Marley straightened. "Not conspiring. Preserving. They healed what men feared to name. They carried memory in matter, in recipes, in symbols. And they left a record, not in the places we were told to look, but in the places we dismissed as ordinary. My aunt knew this. She preserved it, waiting for the time it could be spoken aloud."

Her voice rang against the chamber's rafters, sharper than she'd intended. She saw some of the board shift uncomfortably, others folding their arms like barricades.

Price shook his head again. "Ghost stories. Local color. Every town has them. To drag them out as fact—it's dangerous, Miss Taylor. Dangerous and misleading."

Marley's pulse quickened, but she refused to retreat. "Dangerous is pretending the truth doesn't matter. Dangerous is erasing the women who built this town alongside the men. Dangerous is calling history folklore because it doesn't fit the narrative you prefer."

The words hung heavy. She could feel the room tilt against her. Eyes sharpened, lips pursed. Yet beneath the resistance, she thought she caught something else in a few faces—hesitation.

Chairwoman Tuller leaned forward, her voice colder now. "You speak with conviction, Miss Taylor. But conviction is not proof. Do you have anything that cannot be explained away as imagination or coincidence?"

Marley lifted the ledger from her satchel, laying it flat on the podium. She opened to the page with Aurelia's full name. The ink, though faded, still carried a dignity, a weight. She let the silence linger before she spoke again.

"This is proof. Aurelia Ward was real. She lived here. She healed here. And she was protected by others—women whose names have been erased, but whose marks remain. The Circle of Seven existed. And Brookwood owes its survival to them as much as to the men in your ledgers."

The storm she'd carried from the bridge seemed to surge again inside the room. Murmurs rose, sharp and heated. One board member muttered "nonsense," another "blasphemy."

But Marley stood tall, her hand resting on the ledger, the candlelight from the windows pooling across its pages as if the women themselves bore witness.

This was no longer about convincing them. It was about speaking aloud what had been buried. About refusing to silence the voices pressing at her from every artifact, every vision, every storm.

And for the first time, she did not flinch beneath their scrutiny.

THE MURMURS SWELLED into a tide of dissent. Marley felt it break against her where she stood, a wave of disapproval rolling off the rows of stiff-backed board members and townspeople who had drifted in for the session. Some shook their heads with open disdain, others whispered behind their hands. Carlton Price leaned forward, his ruddy face growing redder by the second.

"This is reckless," he barked, his voice carrying over the chamber. "A healer's ledger, a few scratched symbols—this is not scholarship, Miss Taylor. This is fantasy. And to parade it in front of the Society is to cheapen the serious work we do here."

Several members nodded vigorously, their eyes narrowed. Marley's throat tightened, but she kept her palm pressed to Aurelia's ledger as though it could root her to the floor.

"I'm not here to cheapen your work," she said evenly. "I'm here to add to it. To correct what's been left out."

Tuller rapped the gavel once, the crack echoing off the rafters. "Enough. Miss Taylor, we appreciate your... enthusiasm, but this Society is dedicated to preserving verified history, not to indulging speculation. We will take your materials under advisement, but your presentation is concluded."

The finality in her voice stung more than any outright insult. Marley could feel the ledger trembling slightly under her hand, though she wasn't sure if it was her nerves or something deeper—a thrum that reminded her of the bridge's shimmer, of the voices pressing to be heard.

"No," Marley said, surprising even herself. The single syllable rang out louder than she intended. Heads turned. "You can't dismiss this. Aurelia Ward's name is here. Her recipes align with traditions still alive in this town. The sigils match carvings across Brookwood's oldest sites. You can't call that coincidence."

"Coincidence is precisely what it is," Price snapped. "And if you insist otherwise, then you are dabbling in superstition. Dangerous ground for someone bearing your family name."

The words landed sharp, meant to wound. Marley stiffened. She could almost hear Clara's voice beneath the insult, urging her not to back down.

Before she could respond, a voice from the back rose, dry and reedy. "Miss Taylor."

It belonged to Harold Fenwick, the oldest board member, his frame bent with age, his eyes pale but alert. He rarely spoke in meetings, known mostly for his silence and the occasional nod of agreement with Tuller. Now, however, he leaned forward, his gnarled hand resting on a cane.

Marley turned toward him, uncertain.

"May I see the ledger?" he asked softly.

The room grew still. Tuller's eyes narrowed, but she did not object outright. Marley lifted the book and carried it to him. His hands, though trembling, were careful as he traced Aurelia's name with one finger. His lips moved as though sounding it silently.

Then, so faintly she almost missed it, he whispered, "I remember hearing of her."

Marley's breath caught. "You do?"

But Fenwick only shook his head slightly, his face folding back into neutrality. He closed the ledger and handed it back. "I thank you," he said aloud, his voice formal now, returning to the guarded silence expected of him.

Confused, Marley returned to the podium. Tuller had already seized the pause. "We will adjourn. Miss Taylor, you've had your say."

The board began to shuffle papers, the murmur of dismissal swelling again. Marley felt the sting of failure rising in her chest, heat climbing her throat. She wanted to shout, to demand they look closer, but her words lodged heavy.

As she gathered her notes, a hand brushed hers—so

light she almost mistook it for accident. She glanced down. Fenwick, shuffling past with the aid of his cane, slipped a folded scrap of paper into her palm. His face gave nothing away.

Marley tucked it into her satchel quickly, unnoticed by the others. Her pulse thundered as the session dissolved into clamor.

She wanted to leave, to read the note in solitude, but the eyes of the Society still pinned her. Some glared openly, others with pity, as though she were a misguided girl trespassing in serious men's work.

But she knew better. The ledger in her satchel, the candle burning of its own accord, the shimmer under the bridge—these were not fantasies. They were proof of memory pressing against the town's walls, demanding to be seen.

And now she carried something more: a hidden message, a lifeline slipped from one who had sat silent too long.

Her hand closed around the satchel strap, her jaw tightening. Let them dismiss her. The truth had already begun to stir in the cracks of their silence.

The flame could not be smothered forever.

THE CHAMBER BUZZED with the sound of shuffling papers, murmurs, and dismissive coughs. Marley held herself still at the podium, her satchel heavy at her side, the folded note from Fenwick like a coal pressed into her palm. She wanted to shout into the noise, to break their smug dismissal, but her throat constricted. Clara's candle flame, so steady the night before, wavered in her mind's eye.

And then, a voice cut across the din.

"I believe her."

The words hung in the air, sharp and shocking. Silence rippled through the chamber like a sudden gust of wind. All eyes swung toward the back, where Damien Hawthorne rose from his seat. His tall frame cast a shadow across the rows as he stepped forward, his face unflinching under the weight of every stare.

Marley's breath hitched. She had not asked for this, not expected it. Damien had always hovered at the edges, cautious, measured. For him to speak now, here, was no small thing.

Tuller's brows arched in disdain. "Mr. Hawthorne, this is a session of the Historical Society. Visitors may observe but are not—"

"I've observed long enough," Damien interrupted, his voice firm but controlled. "And I've listened. Miss Taylor's findings may unsettle you, but I have seen too much alongside her to dismiss them as fancy."

A low rumble of disapproval moved through the board. Carlton Price's ruddy face darkened further. "And what exactly have you seen, sir? Phantoms? Dreams? You would lend your reputation to superstition?"

Damien did not flinch. He stepped closer, until he stood near the podium beside Marley. "I've seen records—letters, carvings, ledgers—that match across sources. I've seen a symbol repeat itself in too many places to ignore. And I've seen things I can't explain, things that defy every rational framework I once clung to. Call it superstition if you want. But I call it history, hidden and waiting to be acknowledged."

Marley's pulse quickened. His words weren't rehearsed; she could feel the raw honesty in them. He was staking his place beside her in the circle, publicly, without hesitation.

Tuller rapped her gavel sharply. "This is highly irregular. The Society will not be swayed by emotional outbursts."

Damien's voice rose, quiet steel lacing every word. "This isn't an outburst. It's a reckoning. You've spent decades curating a version of Brookwood's past that flatters certain names and erases others. Miss Taylor is asking you to face what's been buried. If you refuse, that doesn't make her wrong—it only proves how much you fear the truth."

Gasps rippled through the room. Several members exchanged uneasy glances, shifting in their chairs. The authority of the board had rarely been challenged in public, least of all by someone of Damien's standing in town.

Marley stood straighter at the podium, her heart hammering. The heat of humiliation and resistance that had pressed against her moments ago now loosened, replaced by a current of strength flowing through her. Damien's words had cracked the veneer of authority in the room.

Tuller's eyes narrowed, her tone glacial. "Mr. Hawthorne, you risk undermining the very fabric of our Society with such talk."

Damien leaned forward slightly, his gaze sweeping the room. "Maybe it's time the fabric was mended. Maybe it's time we admitted it was torn from the beginning."

The silence that followed was heavy, fraught. Marley glanced at the board members—saw suspicion hardening in some faces, but hesitation flickering in others. Seeds had been planted, even if the soil was rocky.

Fenwick's pale eyes met hers briefly from the far side of the chamber. For a fleeting second, his lips pressed together in the faintest shadow of a smile. The note in her satchel seemed to burn hotter. *There are still those who remember.*

Tuller finally set the gavel down with a sharp crack.

"This session is concluded. Miss Taylor, Mr. Hawthorne—you may do as you wish outside these chambers, but the Society will not be co-opted by unverified legend."

Chairs scraped against the floor as the board rose. Some members moved quickly, eager to escape the tension. Others lingered, their glances less certain, their steps slower. The chamber fractured into small knots of whispering voices, the air thick with unease.

Marley stepped back from the podium, her knees trembling. For a moment she feared her strength would give way—but Damien's hand brushed hers, steadying her as they moved toward the door.

"You didn't have to do that," she murmured, still reeling.

"I did," he said simply. His eyes held hers, unwavering. "You weren't wrong to speak. And you won't stand alone in this again."

Something in her chest unknotted at his words. She tightened her grip on the satchel, the note within it, the ledger, the fragments of Aurelia's memory. The Society might deny her, might cast her out—but she had allies now. Damien. Fenwick. And the unseen circle pressing from beyond.

As they stepped out into the cool night, the town hall looming behind them, Marley realized something had shifted irrevocably. The resistance was open now, yes. But so was the fight. And with Damien at her side, with the candle still burning in her shop, she felt the weight of history settle more firmly into her hands—not as burden, but as purpose.

Brookwood's past would not be silenced again.

29

THE BOOK OF BROOKWOOD

The rain had settled into a soft mist by the time Marley returned to the shop, her satchel bumping against her hip with each step. Inside, the silence was a balm after the firestorm of the town hall. The bookshelves stood like quiet sentinels, the scent of dust and paper filling the air. The candle she had left on the desk earlier had long burned down, its wick a thin curl of ash.

She set the satchel on the table, withdrew the ledger, the folded parchment from the bridge, the necklace still wrapped in its protective cloth. She laid them out carefully, like relics on an altar. Then, reaching into the drawer, she drew out a fresh bound journal—a gift Clara had once tucked away, its leather cover unmarked, its pages pristine.

Her hands lingered on its smooth surface. The blankness of it felt daunting, yet necessary. If Brookwood's truth had been buried in ledgers, scraps of parchment, coded recipes, and whispered dreams, then it needed a vessel now that could carry it whole.

Marley uncapped her pen and began to write.

The Book of Brookwood.

She let the title sit at the top of the page, the ink seeping into the paper, anchoring it. A shiver moved through her. For months she had been pulled along by fragments, guided by visions and whispers, half-afraid she was losing herself to imagination. But here, now, the pieces could come together in one place. She was not only uncovering memory; she was preserving it.

She began with an introduction. Not about herself—not yet. About Aurelia.

Aurelia Ward, once dismissed as a myth, was real. She lived in Brookwood in the mid-1800s. She was a healer, a keeper of remedies and warnings, a woman who bore the weight of fear and hope in equal measure. She was not alone. She was part of a circle—seven women—who carried memory in matter, who preserved their knowledge in symbols and recipes, in carvings and candles. Their names were hidden, their voices silenced, but their work has endured.

Her pen scratched steadily across the paper, her words flowing faster than she expected. She described the spiral sigil, the recipes coded in food and drink, the ledger's warnings, the shimmering water under the bridge. She wove in her dreams, her visions, not as fancy but as testimony. They were part of the record now, as real as the parchment or the locket.

Hours passed. The shop dimmed as dusk pressed against the windows, but Marley wrote on, pausing only to stretch her stiff fingers. She felt Clara's presence, steady and approving, as though her aunt were standing over her shoulder.

By the time the clock struck ten, she had filled dozens of pages. The introductory chapter about Aurelia was complete, framed not as legend but as history reclaimed. The ledger entries had been transcribed, the Circle of Seven named as best she could from initials and symbols. She leaned back, her shoulders aching, her eyes burning, but her spirit alight.

The bookshop seemed different now—less a place of ghosts, more a place of guardianship. Clara had left her a sanctuary, and Marley was finally stepping into its purpose.

A knock startled her. She turned, heart racing, and saw Damien standing in the doorway, his coat damp from the mist, his expression unreadable.

"Still at it?" he asked softly.

Marley nodded, brushing a stray strand of hair from her face. "I couldn't stop. It has to be written, Damien. Not just scraps. Not just whispers. A book. Their book."

He stepped inside, his eyes moving across the desk, the piles of paper, the new journal open like a heartbeat on the wood. Slowly, he reached for it, running a finger along the fresh ink of the title. *The Book of Brookwood.*

"You've given it a spine already," he said.

Marley's lips curved faintly. "It's only a start."

He met her eyes then, something steady, almost reverent in his gaze. "Then let's make sure it holds."

And for the first time in weeks, Marley felt not only the weight of the past pressing on her shoulders but the strength of the present beside her, carrying it with her.

DAMIEN SET his coat on the back of a chair and drew nearer to the desk. The lamplight cast his face in warm relief, catching the silver threads at his temples, the sharp line of his jaw. Marley pushed her chair back a little, allowing him space to sit, though she kept one hand on the open journal as if to guard it. This was her labor, her voice finally taking form on the page. Letting someone else read it felt like handing over a piece of herself.

He sat down, careful with the papers. His long fingers traced the edge of the new pages before lifting one, then another, scanning the dense handwriting. The silence stretched between them, broken only by the faint tick of the wall clock and the whisper of his turning pages.

Marley's nerves rose sharply. She leaned against the back of her chair, arms crossed, forcing herself not to fidget. "Well?" she asked at last, her voice thinner than she intended.

Damien looked up, his brow furrowed, but not with disapproval. "You've written this like a scholar and a witness both. It's thorough, detailed... but it breathes."

She blinked. "Breathes?"

He nodded, setting the book down and resting his hand on its cover. "This isn't just transcription. You're not only recording what you've found—you're carrying their voices forward. That matters more than you realize."

The compliment disarmed her. Clara had been the one with the patience for documentation, not her. Marley had always lived more in her senses than her pages. But this, she realized, was different. The Circle had asked for memory to live in matter, and she was giving it ink and paper, something no council could bury again.

Damien leaned back, exhaling slowly. "But if you want others to believe this, it has to be more than beautiful. It has to be structured. Cross-referenced. A body of work that no one can dismiss as rambling."

Marley frowned slightly. "You're saying it's too loose."

He shook his head. "Not too loose. Just... raw. Which is

natural. You've lived these discoveries, one vision, one relic at a time. But if this is to be *The Book of Brookwood*, it has to be more than a record of your journey. It has to stand as history itself."

She considered that, her hand drifting toward the ledger again. The thought of reshaping her pages—of letting someone else guide their form—stirred resistance in her chest. Yet beneath that, she recognized truth in his words. Her account needed a spine stronger than her memory alone.

Damien's voice softened. "Let me help."

She looked up, startled.

"I've edited manuscripts before," he said. "Compiled town records, cleaned up archives for publication. I know how to make things legible not only to believers, but to skeptics. Let me read through this with you. We'll keep your voice intact, but we'll also give it weight the Society can't ignore."

Marley hesitated. She remembered the sting of the town hall—their sneers, their dismissal. Even when she'd held Aurelia's name in ink, they'd brushed it aside as fancy. To shape this book into something unassailable, something undeniable—that mattered.

But more than that, she realized, he was offering more than skill. He was offering solidarity. After months of keeping distance, of half-believing and half-doubting, Damien was stepping into this with her, word by word.

She slid the journal toward him, her hand lingering only a moment longer before releasing it. "All right," she said softly. "But only if you promise not to cut Aurelia's voice out in the process."

He gave a faint smile. "I wouldn't dare. She'd haunt me, I think."

That earned the smallest laugh from Marley, one that loosened something tight in her chest.

They leaned over the desk together. Damien pointed to passages where she might clarify a date, or cross-reference an artifact with a known event. He suggested organizing chapters not only by discovery but by theme: recipes, visions, sigils, testimonies. Marley bristled at first, but the more they spoke, the more she saw how his structure didn't erase her work—it strengthened it.

When he spoke of the introduction, he said, "Aurelia has to come first. Not as a myth, but as the spine around which everything else aligns. You've already written her into the beginning. We'll keep her there."

Marley watched him as he worked, the way his brows furrowed in concentration, the gentleness with which he handled the fragile papers Clara had preserved. He wasn't only invested in the text—he was invested in her.

Hours passed, the lamplight deepening into midnight shadows. Their conversation wound between practical edits and quiet confessions. Marley admitted how much the visions unsettled her, how some nights she feared she was drowning in echoes. Damien confessed he still carried guilt from dismissing Clara's eccentricities when she was alive. Together, they wove those threads into the pages before them, shaping not only a book but a bond.

At last Damien set his pen down, stretching his stiff shoulders. He looked at the title page again, *The Book of Brookwood*, the ink slightly smudged where Marley's hand had brushed it earlier.

"It's time the truth had a spine," he murmured.

Marley felt the words settle deep inside her, heavier and steadier than any oath the board had ever spoken. For the first time since stepping foot back in Brookwood, she believed not only that the truth could survive—but that she wouldn't be the only one carrying it.

The candle flickered gently beside them, its flame holding steady.

THE SHOP HAD FALLEN into its midnight hush, the windows black mirrors reflecting only the golden lamplight and the bent forms of two figures leaning close over the desk. Books surrounded them in heavy silence, as though they too were listening, their spines leaning in. Marley sat with her hands folded on the leather-bound journal, staring down at the title Damien had traced earlier. *The Book of Brookwood.*

She could still hear his words echoing in her mind: *It's time the truth had a spine.*

For weeks, she had carried the discoveries alone, hoarding them like contraband. The necklace's visions, the locked room, the recipes, the bridge's whispers—they had pressed against her chest with the force of a burden, heavy as stone. Now, with Damien's hand steadying hers across the pages, the weight felt different. Not lighter—never that—but shared. And in the sharing, transformed.

She watched him as he made one last note in the margin, his pen gliding with care, then setting it aside with finality. He leaned back, exhaling as though he'd crossed some unseen threshold. "This isn't just your work anymore," he said quietly. "It's ours."

The simplicity of the statement struck her harder than she expected. She swallowed, her throat tight. "I didn't think you'd ever say that."

Damien's gaze met hers, steady and unflinching. "I didn't either. But tonight, after everything—the ledger, the bridge, the town hall—I can't stand on the sidelines anymore. You were right. Clara was right. This isn't about whether I understand it all. It's about whether I choose to ignore it."

Marley's eyes burned, though she refused to let the tears fall. "They'll fight us harder now," she whispered. "Tuller, Price—the board won't sit quietly while we rewrite their version of history."

"Then let them fight," Damien said, his tone firm. "The more they resist, the clearer it becomes what they're afraid of." He rested his hand on the open journal, his palm broad and warm against the page. "This book isn't only evidence. It's endurance. Once it exists, it can't be unmade. And they know it."

The thought sent a tremor through her. Clara's voice returned again, as insistent as it had been in dreams: *Memory lives in matter.* This book would not just hold her notes—it would carry the Circle's voices forward, preserve what generations had buried. It would be, in every sense, the vessel they had been waiting for.

Marley drew a long breath and let it out slowly, trying to steady the thrum in her chest. "Do you think we'll finish it?" she asked. "Do you think we can put all of this together— the recipes, the visions, the fragments—and make something that holds?"

Damien's lips curved faintly, though his eyes were solemn. "We don't have to finish it. We just have to begin it well. The rest will follow."

The words settled deep into her. Beginning well—that was what Clara had done. Not completed, not solved, but prepared the ground so Marley could walk further. And now, perhaps, she and Damien were preparing ground for someone else after them.

She turned the journal's pages again, her handwriting filling the margins, spilling across the blank spaces. Aurelia's name glimmered on the opening line. *Aurelia Ward.* Marley traced the letters with her fingertip, feeling for a moment as though she could almost touch the woman herself.

"This isn't just a record anymore," she said softly. "It's a promise."

Damien's head tilted. "To whom?"

Her gaze stayed on the page, but her voice firmed. "To the Circle. To Clara. To Brookwood itself. If this town has lived too long under half-remembered truths and deliberate silences, then this book is the answer. Not just a story, not just memory. A vow to carry them forward. To keep the circle whole."

The words left her with a weight that was not crushing but grounding, as if she had finally set her feet on solid earth.

Damien studied her for a long moment, then nodded slowly. "Then let it be a promise."

The candle beside them burned low, its flame steady despite the drafts that sometimes whispered through the old shop. Marley glanced at it, struck by how long it had lasted, how it seemed to defy the night's reach. It reminded her of that first evening when she had found one lit without memory of striking the match. She no longer doubted. The circle was here. Watching. Urging.

And now, finally, she was ready to answer.

She reached for her pen again, drew a line beneath her last entry, and wrote the words: *This book belongs not to one, but to all. Let it be the beginning, not the end.*

Damien's hand brushed hers as he set his pen beside hers. No words passed between them, but their eyes lingered, steady, and the quiet stretched not as uncertainty but as recognition.

Outside, Brookwood slept under the weight of its ordinary night. But inside the bookshop, something had shifted. The ledger, the journals, the visions—all of it had coalesced into this moment. A blank volume was no longer blank. It carried a name, a purpose, a spine.

And with it, Marley felt, so did she.

The candle burned on.

30

———

A NEW CHAPTER

The decision settled into Marley not as a thunderclap, but as a slow dawn, one she could not deny once it had risen fully inside her. For weeks she had spoken as though her time in Brookwood were temporary, as though she were only here to tend to Clara's affairs before slipping back into her old life. But that life no longer felt like hers. Every shelf in the shop, every carved mark in the bridge, every flicker of the lighthouse had woven itself into her marrow. Brookwood was not just where she lived now—it was where she belonged.

She began in the bookshop. The floorboards still creaked in protest beneath her weight, the glass panes still fogged with condensation each morning, but there was a liveliness now in the air that had not existed when she first turned the key weeks ago. She moved through the rooms with new intent, not as a caretaker temporarily sweeping cobwebs, but as an architect shaping something enduring.

The front display, once cluttered and dim, she cleared entirely. In its place she set a long oak table, layered with cloth she had found in Clara's trunks, the deep green fabric embroidered faintly with spiral motifs. On the table she arranged books of history and healing, local lore, poetry— works that spoke not only to knowledge but to memory. A small placard stood in the center, hand-lettered in her careful script: *The Book of Brookwood is not alone. These are its companions.*

Behind the counter, she set up a wall for rotating displays: photographs of Clara, facsimiles of ledger pages, excerpts of recipes paired with jars of herbs Hazel had provided. The effect was not that of a conventional shop, but of a sanctuary—a place where stories could breathe, where memory was not static but alive.

Each step she took seemed to press her further into purpose. The act of cleaning shelves became ritual; the polishing of brass handles, reverence. The shop was no longer merely hers to manage. It was Brookwood's, and beyond Brookwood's, it was the Circle's.

She worked for days in a quiet fever, sometimes forgetting to eat until the sun had long dipped into the ocean's line. Damien came often, sometimes with Sophie, bringing baskets of bread or pots of tea, sometimes only himself, his presence steady as a counterweight. He never intruded, never dictated, but watched with a gaze that made her aware of the depth of what she was doing.

"You're turning it into something more than a bookshop," he said one evening as he leaned in the doorway, sleeves rolled, eyes following her movements.

Marley paused, her hands resting on the edge of the oak table. "Clara was, too. I think she always meant for it to be more."

"More what?"

Marley considered, glancing around at the shelves, the green fabric, the candle burning near the desk. "A sanctuary.

For memory. For stories. For voices that didn't get to survive in the town's official records."

Damien nodded, his expression unreadable but not dismissive. "And for you?"

She looked at him then, feeling the pull of the question. "For me, too," she admitted. "It's where I finally feel like I'm not just looking after Clara's work. I'm living mine."

The lighthouse confirmed her decision days later. For weeks its beam had faltered, sputtering as though echoing the town's unrest. That night, as Marley closed the shutters of the shop and stepped into the cool dusk, she looked out toward the coast. The beam cut through the mist in a clean, unwavering sweep, steady and bright. She stilled on the street, her breath catching.

For the first time since her arrival, the light held. It was as if Brookwood itself had taken note of her choice.

She turned back toward the shop, its windows glowing with lamplight behind her, and felt no hesitation. Clara's house was her house now. Clara's stories were hers to carry forward. The bookshop was not a relic to be sold or shut away. It was the beginning of something new.

And she would stay.

THE NEXT MORNING, the bell above the bookshop door jingled faintly, though Marley hadn't unlocked it for customers. She turned from the counter, half-expecting the sound to be some trick of memory, and saw Damien stepping inside, a folded newspaper tucked under his arm and two steaming cups of coffee in his hands.

"You're here early," he said, a wry smile at the corner of his mouth.

Marley glanced at the clock on the wall—barely past

seven. She had been up since before dawn, fussing with shelf arrangements, revising a section of the new manuscript she'd started, and sweeping the entryway twice over. The shop smelled faintly of lemon oil and beeswax.

"I couldn't sleep," she admitted. "It felt like today was... different."

Damien handed her a cup. "It is. You've chosen to stay. That changes everything."

She took the coffee, letting the warmth seep into her palms, and gestured toward the main room. Together, they moved among the shelves and tables, the morning light slanting in through the front windows in thin shafts. The air was quiet but alive with the possibility of voices, as though the shop itself approved of their partnership.

Damien set the newspaper down on a table but didn't open it. Instead, he let his eyes roam the space. "Clara built this place as more than a shop. You've been saying it. I can see it now. It's a kind of archive, but one that breathes."

Marley sipped her coffee, steadying her nerves before replying. "I think she meant it to be a sanctuary—for stories that couldn't survive elsewhere. For women like Aurelia. For people who were silenced."

He nodded, thoughtful. "Most towns have a museum or a society to keep history safe, but Brookwood—its history has always been curated to protect reputations, not truths. This..." He swept a hand toward the shelves. "...this could undo that. Or at least balance it."

Marley tilted her head at him, studying the way he said it: not as a scholar or historian, but as someone who had crossed a threshold of belief. "You think we can really do that?"

"I think we already have." He met her gaze. "The ledger, the bridge, the oaths—those weren't just discoveries. They were reclamations. And your book—it's the spine we were missing. You're not just telling stories, Marley. You're shaping what survives."

His words sank into her slowly, as though her heart needed to try them on before her mind could accept them. "But it can't just be me," she said. "If I'm the only one writing, then it's still too fragile. If this is going to last, it has to be shared."

"That's why I came." Damien moved closer, his presence filling the room with quiet steadiness. "Let me help. Not just carrying boxes or fixing shelves. Let me edit, organize, format. I've done more writing than I care to admit, even if most of it's buried in grant proposals and reports. Together, we can make sure this isn't just a private journal. We can make it a book. Something people can't ignore."

Marley felt her breath catch. She had expected his support in spirit, perhaps, but not this: not his willingness to sit in the trenches with her, to shoulder the shaping of every page. The thought of partnership—real partnership—both steadied and unnerved her.

"You'd really do that?" she asked softly.

Damien's expression held no hesitation. "Yes. Because this is bigger than either of us. And because..." His voice faltered, and for a moment his eyes flicked away. "...because I don't want you to carry it alone."

Marley looked down at the coffee in her hands, her heart thudding against her ribs. She thought of Clara's whispered lessons, of Aurelia's visions, of the Circle of Seven who had carried knowledge in secret, always together, never alone. She realized then that this was the echo of their work, resurfacing in her own life: memory demanding to be held in more than one pair of hands.

She set the cup aside, reached for the journal they had

begun, and slid it across the desk toward him. "Then let's do it together."

Damien opened it carefully, his fingers brushing the inked title page. He scanned her opening words about Aurelia, the Circle, and the coded recipes. For a long time, he didn't speak. Then he nodded, his voice low but certain. "This is strong. It's the kind of beginning that can hold. We'll need to refine it, expand it—but Marley, this is already history being made."

Her throat tightened, but this time she let the tears blur her vision. She blinked them away quickly, unwilling to let them fall, but she didn't hide the emotion either. "Then we'll give it the spine it deserves."

Together they bent over the desk, the lamp casting a warm halo around them. Page by page, word by word, they began to shape the raw fragments into something coherent, something that would endure. The morning light grew stronger, pouring through the windows, until the whole shop seemed to glow.

And for the first time since arriving in Brookwood, Marley felt that she was not chasing shadows. She was building something solid, something shared. Something that might finally answer the voices that had been whispering all along.

THEY CLOSED THE SHOP EARLY, not as retreat but as ritual. Marley flipped the sign to *Back at Dusk*, though dusk was already gathering in the alleys, turning windows into burnished mirrors. She tucked the journal—their journal—into the canvas satchel Clara once carried to the market, and Damien slid the strap over his shoulder as naturally as if it had always been his to bear. When they stepped outside, the air held the briny cool of evening, the kind that slipped beneath collars and woke you up from the inside out.

They walked the familiar path toward the covered bridge. Brookwood settled around them in quiet layers: a dog barking twice and then giving up, the echo of a piano scale from an upstairs apartment, the distant hush of tide working its patient math along the shore. Over the rooftops the lighthouse threw its clean, steady beam. It didn't falter. It didn't blink. The sweep crossed the street, touched the signage of the bookshop like a blessing, then moved on.

Damien noticed. "Still steady," he said, softer than conversation, as if he didn't want to jinx the thing that had finally chosen to hold.

Marley followed the light's arc. "Maybe it was never broken," she said. "Maybe it was waiting."

"For what?"

"For us to stop pretending this was just research."

They reached the bridge as the last orange bleached into violet. Inside, the world became wood and shadow and the river's unhurried voice. The planks answered their footfalls with the same tired complaint, which somehow felt welcoming now. At the center span, they paused, standing where the oaths had once hummed through the storm, where the water had shimmered like liquid silver. Tonight the river kept its surface ordinary, the kind of ordinary that still makes itself known—small tongues of current flicking at a support, an occasional bubble, a slow curl where the depth changes. It looked like rest, not absence.

Damien set the satchel on a crossbeam and drew out *The Book of Brookwood*. In the dimness the leather seemed to drink the last of the light. He handed it to Marley without ceremony and without reluctance: a simple gesture that said here, and also said ours. She traced the title, then pressed the book to the rail, feeling the vibration of the river through the wood travel up into paper and skin.

For a long time neither of them spoke. The hush didn't demand words; it made space for them if they came. A heron lifted from the reeds upstream and moved across their patch of sky like a careful thought. Far off, a bell clanged from a buoy—one reminder of the world beyond this span, another. The lighthouse threw its line of light again, serene.

"We could mark this," Damien said at last. "Not for the town, not yet. For us." He glanced at the open page. "A place where we say what it is we think we're doing."

Marley smiled because he'd given voice to what she'd brought the book for and because she didn't want to cry when she did it. "A foreword to the work," she said. "Or a vow."

"The Circle called it an oath."

"And we're not the Circle."

"No," he agreed, "but we're in its wake."

She uncapped the pen. On the blank leaf before Chapter One, in a hand that had steadied through weeks of transcription and nights of doubt, she wrote:

This book is offered to the living and to the remembered. To the hands that gathered leaves, to the mouths that spoke warnings, to the eyes that kept watch when no one else would. We name what can be named and hold gently what cannot. Memory lives in matter, and we will tend it.

She stopped, flexed her fingers. The river answered itself around a bend.

Damien stood so close she could feel the radiant warmth of him even in the cooling air. "One more line," he said, voice quiet. "Say what we owe."

She nodded, and below the last sentence she added:

We promise to keep the circle whole.

They watched the ink sink into the page. The words didn't glow; they didn't stir the water into light or bend the air. They simply settled, and in that settling Marley felt a gravity she trusted. The promise didn't belong to spectacle. It belonged to endurance—like the steady sweep of the beacon, like the way the bridge kept holding after so many storms.

"May I?" Damien asked.

She offered the pen. He didn't sign his name; he drew a small spiral in the margin—the same unadorned form carved beneath Clara's desk, the same shape inked and re-inked across recipes and margins and dreams. He set the pen down.

"Partnership," he said. He looked almost shy as he said it, which made the word feel earned. "Beyond the pages."

Marley let the word stand between them. "Beyond history," she answered, and it didn't frighten her the way it would have weeks ago. It felt not like a leap but a landing.

They sat with their backs against the beam, shoulders almost touching, the book closed now and warm against Marley's palm. The light slipped through the slats and striped the floor at their feet. A child's laugh drifted from upriver, then vanished as quickly as it came. The town lived its evening, unaware—but not hostile, not in this moment. The anger at Town Hall felt far and small under the vaulted quiet of wood and water.

Damien broke the silence again. "Sophie asked if we could shelve books tomorrow."

Marley turned, surprised into a grin. "We'll give her the front table. She can choose what stands beside Aurelia."

"A dangerous responsibility."

"She'll rise to it." Marley sobered. "She sees more than people give her credit for."

"So do you," he said, and the calm certainty of it threaded her with warmth.

They fell quiet, and in that quiet Marley inventoried her fears: that the board would harden into open opposition, that old stories would weaponize themselves against new ones, that in a town built on careful forgetting, remembering would come with a cost. All of it remained true. The cost would come.

But she took inventory of what stood with her too: a ledger with a name, a parchment with oaths, a necklace that carried a life's residue, a candle that lit itself, a child whose vision had widened the circle, a man who had stepped from skepticism into faith without asking for perfect explanations. And a book with a spine.

She could carry a cost in such company.

The lighthouse beam traced the mouth of the river again, as dependable as breath. A breeze lifted, bringing the salt of the bay and the green of the marsh. The bridge creaked not as complaint but as reminder: the wood held because people repaired it, because they refused to let it rot away. Memory required the same stubbornness.

"Say it," Damien murmured, and Marley recognized the request though he hadn't named it.

She looked out through the bridge's opening, where the sky's last color gathered like a secret kept for the right ears. She tucked the book against her ribs, felt the press of its promise there, then leaned forward just enough that her words would fall into the river and be taken where they needed to go.

"This is only the beginning," she whispered.

The phrase touched the water, and whether the river

accepted it or simply bore it, Marley couldn't say. She didn't need to. The acceptance lived in her, a resonance that answered down to the soles of her feet.

Damien's hand found the rail beside hers, his knuckles brushing her skin—no claim, no haste, only proximity and the reliability of it. That was enough for now. The slow-burn warmth had its own clock, and she trusted it the way she trusted the beam to return after each sweep.

They sat until the violet thinned to a deep, companionable blue. When they rose, the bridge gave one last settling sigh. Marley slid the journal back into the satchel, the leather soft from use already. On impulse she reached into her coat and pulled out the music box. She wound it once, twice, and the small melody—hers and not hers—threaded the ribs of the span. It sounded different here: less like a summons, more like thanks.

"Tomorrow," she said as they started back toward the town, the lantern unneeded in the clear dark. "We'll set the first display. Aurelia at the center. The recipes, the ledger pages. And the foreword."

"We'll print broadsides," Damien added, the practical smile pulling at his mouth. "Invite the town to read before they decide what to fear."

"You like poking bears," she teased.

"I like telling the truth where bears can hear it."

They walked through the lanes with the easy hush of people who did not need to fill space to keep it. The lighthouse kept its vigil. A curtain lifted in a second-story window, then fell—a domestic ghost, ordinary and kind. When they reached the shop, Marley paused on the threshold and looked back.

The beam swept the rooftops again, regular as a heartbeat. The town neither called to them nor turned away. It held its breath the way a body does right before it says yes.

Inside, the shop exhaled dust and lemon oil and the faintest thread of beeswax. Marley set the satchel on the desk and drew the book free. She didn't open it. She laid her palm on the cover, closed her eyes, and let the day pass through her—the vow written on the bridge, the steadiness of the light, the weight and lift of partnership that was finally more than spoken.

"This is not a record," she said into the quiet, not needing an answer. "It's a promise."

The candle by the ledgers flared as if it had caught a draft, then steadied. From somewhere in the walls, the old building gave a settling pop, the way houses do when they approve of the weather or the people inside them.

Marley smiled. Tomorrow they would argue over headings and footnotes. Tomorrow she would test Hazel's newest blend in the back room and listen for a whisper that might or might not come. Tomorrow the town might push back again.

Tonight the lighthouse was steady. The bridge held. The book had a spine.

And for the first time since the fog had rolled in at the beginning, she knew the shape of home.

She turned down the wick. The room dimmed to a soft ember. Outside, the beam swept and returned, swept and returned.

Only the beginning, she thought again, and the thought did not frighten her. It felt like a door she had finally learned to open.

She left it open.

EPILOGUE: THE CIRCLE HOLDS

She noticed it first in the mornings. When she opened the door to the shop, the bell overhead gave its ordinary jingle, but the air carried the faintest undertone, like a chord waiting for its resolution. The floorboards no longer groaned under her step as if they were reluctant hosts. The shelves themselves seemed to lean forward, patient but insistent, as though they too had been waiting for stories to return to their rightful place.

Clara's shop—her shop now—looked less like an inheritance and more like a vow fulfilled. The circle wasn't only something in journals or symbols; it was a living current, running beneath the town like the river under the covered bridge.

The first weeks after the Historical Society meeting were uneasy. Marley felt the stares when she walked to the market. Conversations tilted away when she stepped near. People whispered, "too deep" and "stirring trouble," the same phrases that had followed her aunt. But this time, the whispers had cracks. A few nodded. A few smiled. A few lingered longer at the shop's window than they used to.

And when the first customer came asking—not just for a novel or an atlas, but for *The Book of Brookwood*—Marley realized that silence had been broken.

She hadn't wanted to sell it at first. The manuscript felt too raw, too alive, a thing not meant to be bartered. Damien convinced her otherwise. "Truth doesn't belong on a shelf," he told her. "It belongs in circulation."

So she had printed a small run—bound in plain covers, no advertisement—and placed them in a basket by the counter. People picked them up as if touching contraband. They read quickly, then slowly. A farmer came back three times in one week, never saying a word, only setting coins on the counter and taking another copy, as though each had to be placed in a different pair of hands.

It was happening, Marley thought. The Circle was widening.

And yet, the bookshop still lit candles of its own accord. The necklace still warmed when she touched it. The lighthouse still burned steady, yes, but every so often its beam gave a faint, strange stutter—reminder or warning, she didn't know. The past wasn't done with her.

One night, she sat at Clara's old writing desk, running her hand over the indent where the spiral was carved. The memory of the voices pressed gently at her again—no longer a whisper, but not quite command.

Memory lives in matter, Clara had written.

Marley believed it now more than ever. But she also believed something larger: memory lives in people, and people must decide what to do with it.

When Damien stopped by, carrying Sophie's half-finished drawing of a lighthouse to tape on the wall, Marley showed him the newest journal entry.

"I keep thinking," she said, "that this isn't an ending. It's a handoff."

Damien leaned on the doorway, studying her, studying the shelves that now bore as much history as fiction. "Maybe that's what legacy is. Not weight. Not burden. Just... the circle making sure it doesn't break."

Marley didn't argue. She only turned back to the page, letting his words settle like stones in the spiral of her thoughts.

The circle held. And because it held, she knew her work had only begun.

The seasons in Brookwood had always marked time more with weather than calendars—the fog settling heavy in October, the ocean turning slate in February, the gulls nesting noisily come spring. But now, Marley began to notice something subtler than the turning of leaves or tides. She noticed conversations changing.

At the café, where gossip once hardened like salt on the tables, people now debated—sometimes awkwardly, sometimes heatedly—about the stories they had read in *The Book of Brookwood*. At the market, women carried herbs tucked into their baskets not only for cooking but "for remembrance," words whispered with the same cadence once reserved for prayers. And children—Sophie among them—began to treat the covered bridge not as a haunted place, but as a kind of living monument, daring each other to stand in silence and listen, as if the water itself might speak.

The book had not transformed Brookwood overnight. Many still resisted, still scowled when Marley passed, still dismissed the Circle as folklore dressed up in ink. But the resistance no longer held the town in its fist. Something else had begun to pulse beneath the cobblestones and clapboard homes—a current too steady to ignore.

Damien noticed it too. One evening, as they walked from the lighthouse back toward the shop, he said quietly, "They'll fight you less openly now, but more cleverly. When truth begins to shift roots, those invested in the old soil don't simply walk away."

Marley glanced sideways at him. The lantern he carried cast his face in amber light, deepening the lines of grief but also sharpening the resolve she had come to rely on. "And you? Will you keep standing with me when the cleverness sharpens?"

His pause was long, but not uncertain. "I've spent years apologizing to ghosts—my wife, my past, my daughter—for refusing to see what stood in front of me. I won't live like that again. If the Circle has called you, then by standing with you, I stand with something larger than either of us. So yes. I'll keep standing."

Those words, more than any candle or ledger, anchored her. They reminded her that stewardship was not solitary, that the Circle had always been a collective. She carried the memory of Aurelia and Clara, yes, but she was not alone.

Together, they began to shape the bookshop into more than a business. Shelves of fiction remained, of course, but side by side with them grew a section titled *The Circle's Memory*. In it went the reprinted ledgers, the transcribed letters, the careful interpretations Damien insisted be footnoted like a historian's archive. Local artists began leaving sketches of herbs. The baker donated a framed imprint of the old scone tin. Hazel, sent over jars of dried blends with names that felt more incantation than commerce: *Clarity, Threshold, Binding Light.*

Some evenings, Marley and Damien hosted gatherings

at long tables pulled from the cellar. At first, only three or four came—curious, cautious. Then a dozen. Then twenty. They read aloud from the Circle's writings, debated their meaning, shared personal memories that had been kept silent for generations.

One elderly man, his voice trembling, admitted his grandmother had once spoken of Aurelia in whispers, a healer unjustly cast out but never forgotten. "I thought it was just old wives' tales," he said. "But reading her name here, seeing it written, makes me realize she lived—and we failed her."

Marley touched his hand, her heart aching with the weight of his words. "You're helping us not fail her now."

The gatherings were not always solemn. Sometimes laughter bubbled, music hummed. Sophie read her poems aloud. A young girl asked if she could write her own story into the ledger. Marley encouraged her, realizing that this was the true measure of their stewardship: not only protecting the past, but making space for new voices to inscribe themselves into the Circle.

And yet, beneath the warmth of community, Marley still felt the old pulse of unease. Some resisted openly. Notes left under the door warned her to "stop conjuring." Anonymous letters arrived, accusing her of blasphemy, of trying to stir up division. At night, she sometimes heard footsteps outside the shop after hours—never confirmed, never explained.

Damien's warnings were not misplaced. But instead of silencing her, the resistance clarified her path. The Circle had not survived because it was safe; it had survived because it was necessary.

One evening, after the last guest left and Sophie had curled up in the reading nook, Damien and Marley lingered by the counter. A single candle burned, its flame steady but strong, as if drawing breath from some unseen source.

"This shop," Damien said, his voice low, "it feels like a lighthouse now. Not for ships—for people. A place that cuts through fog."

Marley's throat tightened. She thought of Clara, of Aurelia, of all the women whose names filled the ledger. "Then we'll keep it lit," she whispered. "No matter who tries to snuff it out."

Outside, the fog pressed against the windows. But inside, the circle held.

The days after the first Circle gatherings carried a rhythm Marley hadn't expected—part exhilaration, part exhaustion, part something heavier she could only call consequence. For every person who leaned into the story of Brookwood's forgotten women, another leaned away, wary or even hostile. She could feel it in the air: the town was shifting, yes, but shifts were never smooth.

And through it all, Damien stood beside her.

One late afternoon, they closed the shop together after Sophie had gone home to her grandmother's. The tables were still scattered with teacups, pages of notes, and a faint scent of beeswax from the candles. Damien lingered as Marley stacked chairs. He didn't need to; he had his own home to return to. But lately, he seemed less inclined to leave, as if he knew the weight of the silence pressed more fiercely when she was alone.

"You've taken on more than Clara ever did," he said suddenly, his voice thoughtful rather than critical. "She guarded the memory. You're... pushing it forward. That's different. Harder."

Marley looked up, a chair half-lifted. "Are you saying I'm reckless?"

He smiled faintly. "I'm saying you're brave. And brave people often mistake their scars for weakness, when really they're proof they've walked through fire."

The words hit her with an unexpected force. She set the chair down. "You talk as if you've seen those fires."

"I have." His gaze shifted to the shelves, to the candle still burning steady near the counter. "And I've spent years pretending I hadn't. My wife believed in things I brushed aside—signs, intuitions, the weight of the unseen. I thought I was being practical, rational. But when she died... I realized I'd robbed her of my listening. I carried that guilt into Brookwood, thinking silence was safer. Then you walked back into town with your aunt's key, and the silence broke."

For a long moment, the only sound was the low hum of the ocean through the walls. Marley felt her chest tighten, not from fear, but from the sheer recognition that the Circle hadn't just claimed her—it had claimed him too, in his own way.

"Damien," she whispered, "you don't have to carry that guilt anymore. Not here. Not with me."

His eyes met hers then, steady and unguarded, and for a heartbeat it seemed the room itself leaned closer, the walls and shelves listening to a truth finally spoken aloud.

He crossed the space slowly, as though testing whether the air would hold him, and rested his hand lightly on the back of hers where it lay against the counter. He didn't squeeze, didn't press—only anchored.

For Marley, it was enough. In that quiet gesture lived the fullness of his partnership—not just in research or meetings, but in presence. In steadiness. In the vow, unspoken yet undeniable, that he would not walk away when the town's tides turned rougher.

The circle wasn't hers alone to bear.

In the following weeks, the shop's dual identity deepened: part bookstore, part sanctuary. Farmers left herbs by the door "for the shelf." Fishermen carved small wooden spirals and tucked them between books. A seamstress offered embroidered cloths bearing Aurelia's initials. It wasn't organized, not formally, but it was unmistakable: the Circle's memory was seeding itself back into the town's fabric.

And with each offering, Marley felt both uplifted and weighted.

She lay awake some nights, staring at the ceiling beams, the necklace warm against her chest. She thought of Aurelia Ward, of Clara, of the women in the ledger whose initials still blurred into mystery. She thought of Sophie's wide-eyed vision, the girl's hand trembling as she described what she saw. It was no longer just about remembrance. The Circle wanted continuation. Action.

One night, she rose and went to the window, the fog pressed thick against the glass. Beyond it, the lighthouse beacon burned steady, unwavering for the first time in weeks. Its glow reached the shop, faint but unbroken, as if saluting her.

This is no longer about me, she thought. *It's about Brookwood. About what survives when silence is broken.*

The realization didn't scare her. It steadied her. For all the resistance, all the muttered warnings, all the unease that still threaded through town, she knew: the Circle's story had demanded her voice, and she had given it. Now it demanded Brookwood's voice, and slowly, surely, the town was beginning to answer.

The next evening, she and Damien walked together beneath the covered bridge. The sun set low, streaking the water with bronze. They sat side by side on the old beam, the air carrying both salt and the faint trace of wild mint from the banks.

Marley leaned forward, resting her elbows on her knees. "I keep thinking, Damien. What if this book, this shop, everything we've done—it's not just a record. What if it's a promise?"

He studied her profile, the sharp edge of her determination softened by dusk. "To the Circle?"

"Yes," she said, her voice quiet but certain. "To them. To Aurelia. To Clara. But also to this town. To Brookwood itself. We can't let the memory fade back into silence again. Not after this."

The words settled between them like stones in water, rippling outward.

For a long while, they sat in silence, listening to the steady rush beneath the bridge. Then Damien reached over, not hesitantly this time, and took her hand in his. Their fingers wove together, simple, certain, enduring.

Above them, the lighthouse beam swept across the horizon. The circle held.

And Marley knew, with the deepest clarity she had ever felt, that this was only the beginning.

THE BRIDGE OF ECHOES

By late afternoon the fog came in from the bay as if the sea had decided to walk the streets. It slid over rooftops and curled through alleyways, seaming the town with a soft thread. In the bookshop, the light went a gentle honey—lamps warm against the gray—and Marley welcomed the quiet like a friend who knew not to talk too much.

She had spent most of the morning and half the afternoon doing the work that no one clapped for and that she had discovered she loved: mending spines with linen tape, rubbing a little oil into the oak counter until it glowed again, labeling a new shelf *The Circle's Memory: Letters & Ledgers*. People came and went all day—Sophie had sorted children's books by color until the display looked like a tidepool—jade, sand, sea-glass green—then dashed off with a poem in her pocket to read to her grandmother.

When the bell above the door stilled, the shop breathed. Marley liked to think it exhaled. She stood a moment with her palms flat on the counter, feeling the grain of the wood under her skin. The lighthouse beam, when it reached this far, sometimes threw a thin pale stripe across the ceiling and was gone. Today the fog gentled it, but she felt the rhythm anyway, the sweep like a heartbeat the town had learned to trust again.

On the desk by the shop window, the first small print run of *The Book of Brookwood* sat in neat stacks, their plain covers picking up the lamplight. They had gone out faster than she expected. People were reading them in kitchens and on porches, under quilts and by workbenches. She had found one propped open by the till at the café, another tucked under a bench near the covered bridge as if whoever had brought it needed the river's voice to keep her company. The board at Town Hall had not endorsed it; of course they hadn't. But the town did not belong to the board. It belonged to the people who got up in the dark to bake or fish or listen. The book had found them anyway.

Damien had stopped by after lunch with a box of manila folders and that careful quiet he wore when he came bearing something the past might argue with. "Sea Captain's logs," he'd said, eyes glinting. "Fenwick handed them over himself. Said he was 'tired of his closet being haunted by paperwork.'" He'd stayed an hour to help her index before a tutoring appointment—student essays about lighthouse lore, he said—with a promise to be back before closing.

Now it was only Marley and the shop and the fog. She tied twine around a stack of books bound for Hazel's shelves and wrote a note to tuck under the bow—*For your corner: recipes, warnings, and the oath they still ask of us.* She liked the way the paper drank the ink. She liked the way the words anchored what kept wanting to float away into feeling.

When the clock ticked past four, she carried a tray of returned volumes to the back. The room behind the counter —the one Clara had made into an office and, later, into a sanctuary—held objects that refused to be ordinary no matter how gently you put them down. The necklace lay coiled in its oilcloth like something alive. The apothecary ledger, now sealed under mylar when the shop was closed, seemed calmer since the book had been printed, as if the act of giving its contents a spine eased some pressure in its paper. The music box waited on a shelf, patient and sure of its own small power.

Marley set the tray on the desk and paused. The spiral carved into the underside of the desktop—she had found herself touching it more often lately, like a worry stone. It didn't bring voices the way it once had. It brought steadiness, a sense that she could hear more when she wasn't straining so hard to listen.

She took down the ledger and set it beside a new notebook. There were still initials that refused to match the town's records, still blank seams in the story. She had accepted that some gaps might not close. The circle, she was learning, held both knowing and not-knowing with the same open hand.

A soft tap at the glass made her start. She looked up to see a boy of maybe nine standing outside, his cheeks flushed, his sweatshirt dark with fog. He held something wrapped in brown paper.

Marley opened the door and the boy thrust the parcel toward her, urgent and a little breathless. "From my Nana," he said. "She said to give it to the book lady who hears things."

Marley kept her face from breaking into too wide a smile. "I might know her," she said, taking the parcel. "Thank you. Tell your Nana I'm grateful."

The boy nodded, already backing away. "She said 'no charge, just care.'" Then he was gone, absorbed into the fog the way small messengers are.

Back at the desk, Marley untied the string. Brown paper gave way to a cloth wrapping, and inside that an object heavy for its size: a small iron triangle with a handle, the kind used to call men from the fields a lifetime ago. Its surface was pitted with age, and someone—long ago, no one alive to admit it now—had scratched a little spiral into one corner. The triangle's striker lay beside it, wrapped in the same cloth like a companion.

Underneath, a folded note in an old hand: *When the bell forgets to ring, remember the Grove.*

Marley traced the phrase with a fingertip. It had been in the ledger, a warning and a direction both. She had never seen the bell itself. Here it was—not a bell, precisely, but something that made a sound you could follow.

She set the triangle on the desk. The urge to strike it pulled at her, simple and clean. She lifted the striker, held it poised, then lowered it again without making a sound. Not yet. Not alone, and not without knowing what it would call.

She wrapped it back in the cloth and left it where the light could find it if the lighthouse beam reached this far.

When the bell above the door rang for real, she didn't jump this time. Damien stepped in, the fog trying to follow him before the door swung shut. His hair was damp at the temples and he had the look of someone who had been walking fast enough to turn thinking into heat.

"I brought you something," he said, holding up a paper bag.

"If it's scones, I call that an act of devotion."

"It's something better." He set the bag on the counter and drew out two folded broadsides, the ink a crisp black against thick paper. Across the top in an old serif: *The Brookwood Echo.* Beneath it, a date from 1891 and a headline: **FOUNDERS'**

GROVE PETITION WITHDRAWN. The rest of the page was blank. No column text. No story. Just the architecture of an article and the void where words should have lived.

Marley reached out before she could stop herself. The ink was raised the way old printing does, a tiny ridge of black you could almost feel with your eyes. She looked up, and Damien was already watching her.

"Fenwick again," he said. "He says when the Society resorted the basement, these were in a drawer mislabeled 'School Notices.' He doesn't remember the article ever running. Thinks someone set type, pulled proofs, then—" Damien lifted his hands in a gesture that said the rest.

"Then decided not to speak," Marley finished for him.

"Or was told not to."

She smoothed the paper gently on the counter. *The Brookwood Echo.* The title struck her in a place that was not quite language. Echoes belonged to bridges and caves and the mouths of bells; they belonged to children calling their own names into hollows and waiting to be better acquainted with the sound that came back. Someone had named a paper after that. Someone had believed that a town could be that kind of place.

"What was the petition?" she asked.

"Fenwick doesn't know. Or says he doesn't know." Damien's mouth tilted. "He wants us to look, which either means he truly doesn't remember, or he remembers all too well and needs a pair of hands that aren't bound by the Society's oath to find it."

Marley lifted one of the broadsides to the lamplight. The blank columns glowed a little, more suggestion than shine. "Do we think this is the Grove from the ledger? The same grove the warnings point to?"

"If it is, someone tried to put it in print. And someone else made sure they didn't."

They stood a while in that small weather the two of them made—ink and paper and breath and fog—feeling how a blank page can be louder than a printed one. Then Damien rolled the proof carefully, slid it back into the bag, and leaned his elbows on the counter.

"Close early?" he asked.

"To go where?"

"I thought the bridge," he said. "If we're going to be haunted by echoes, we might as well stand where echoes like to live."

Marley glanced at the clock and was surprised to see how the afternoon had slipped. She turned the sign on the door to *Back at Dusk* and took her coat from the hook. The iron triangle she wrapped on instinct and added to the canvas satchel, almost embarrassed by how natural it felt to bring it along. She slid the music box in, too, and the notebook with the Grove entries. If tonight was only a walk, let it be one she took with what mattered.

They stepped out into a town that had let itself be softened by fog. The lamps along Harbor Street had come on early, small moons lodged in glass. A fishing boat hooted twice in the outer harbor, a sound that always startled and then soothed her. They walked without talking. The quiet between them had learned to hold shape.

At the mouth of the lane that emptied toward the covered bridge, Marley saw something she had never noticed though she must have passed it a hundred times: an old wooden placard, weathered to the color of driftwood and mostly stripped of paint, tacked to a post gone soft with moss. There had once been letters there. Now there were only traces: a capital E, stubborn and clear; a curve that might be an O; and, if you looked with the sort of attention the Circle had taught her, the ghost of a word you could almost assemble.

ECHO.

"Odd," Damien said, as if he, too, felt the way certain words can graft themselves onto a place. "This path had some other name."

Marley touched the wood with two fingers, the way you touch a sleeping creature you don't want to wake too fast. "Or it has the same name, and we forgot how to read it."

They crossed onto the bridge and the world became old wood and the river's patient articulations. It sounded like something thinking. They stood at the center where the span widened a little, the boards giving under their weight as all honest things give. In her satchel the iron triangle seemed heavier than it had in the shop. The music box, lighter.

"You want to try it?" Damien asked, nodding toward the bag.

Marley shook her head. "Not yet."

They watched the water do its slow arithmetic around the pilings. The last of the day's light, such as the fog allowed it, made a pale stripe down the middle of the current like a spine. She thought of the blank newspaper columns. She thought of the Grove. She thought of the times she had heard her name here—soft, a child's voice— but tonight there was only the ordinary kind of sound that persisting makes.

"Listen," Damien said.

At first she heard nothing new. Then, under the river and the fog-hushed street beyond, a smaller sound reached them: a faint, arrhythmic ticking, like someone far away setting type. It came and went, shy of identification. She turned her head toward the old mill across the water, the one that now housed a hardware store and a storage room that belonged, somehow, to the Historical Society. The sound might have been nothing. The sound might have been anything.

"You hear it?" he asked.

"I do."

They kept hearing it until they didn't, which is how it is with shy things. Damien slid a hand into his coat pocket, drew out the folded proof again, and held it where the bridge's ribs could keep it from the fog. *The Brookwood Echo.* A story that had tried to be told and then hadn't. A word that belonged to this place written into the top of a page and then erased below.

"Tomorrow," he said. "We go ask the mill what it remembers."

Marley nodded, feeling the yes down in the place where, lately, answers liked to lodge. "Tomorrow."

They turned back toward the shop when the cold made their hands insistent. At the end of the bridge she looked once over her shoulder. For a breath the mist at the far entrance shaped itself into something that might have been a figure—a narrowness at the waist, a fall of fabric—and then it smoothed into air. She didn't call out. If it had been a greeting, she had already answered.

Back at the door, she unlocked the shop and let them in out of the wet. The bell over the lintel did its small, faithful ring. She set the satchel on the counter and, before she could change her mind, unwrapped the iron triangle. The fog had left a thin moisture on the metal that made it cooler than the room. She steadied it with one hand and, with the other, lifted the striker.

"Just once," she said, though she hadn't planned to say anything, as if speaking built a harbor for sound to find.

The note struck bright and ran up into the ceiling beams and along the shelves like a thread someone tugged. It wasn't loud. It was exactly as big as the shop. The tone seemed to linger a second longer than it should have, as if the wood wanted to keep it. When it faded, the quiet left behind was softer than the quiet before.

Marley wrapped the triangle again and set it down. She felt as if she had rung a doorbell without being sure which door it belonged to.

Damien didn't say anything. He was smiling in the way you do when something gentle has confirmed itself. He held the proof as if it might decide to be less blank if he gave it patience.

"Tomorrow," he said again, and the word was a promise that did not overreach.

Marley reached up and turned down the lamp a notch. The fog pressed its cheek to the window like a curious child. The lighthouse beam, invisible but present, did its clean work. In the desk, the spiral under her fingertips was the cool of stone. Down in the river, the pilings held. Somewhere in the mill, something waited to be asked.

A book with a spine sat ready on the counter. Beside it lay a proof with no story where a story should have gone.

The town had learned to live with its echoes. The next thing—Marley felt it without needing to name it—was to follow them to where they began.

The morning after their walk to the bridge, the fog lingered like a guest reluctant to leave. It clung low across the harbor and seemed to seep into the bones of the town. Marley had grown accustomed to its moods—the way Brookwood breathed with the tides—but this particular fog carried weight. It was as though the town itself held its breath, waiting for someone to dare exhale.

Damien met her at the bookshop as promised, the rolled proof of *The Brookwood Echo* tucked beneath his arm. His jacket bore the damp of salt mist, and his expression had the intentness of a man both weary and unwilling to turn away. He nodded at Marley, not with surprise or ceremony, but with the quiet affirmation of partnership already formed.

"Ready?" he asked.

She gestured to the satchel on the counter—the triangle wrapped in cloth, the ledger, the notebook of her own half-formed notes. "I've been ready longer than I realized."

They walked together through narrow lanes toward the old mill that loomed above the river. Once it had housed machinery loud enough to rattle windows across town; now only its bones remained, repurposed into a hardware store and a cluster of rooms the Historical Society claimed but rarely opened. Marley had always thought the building too large for the town that clung to it, as if Brookwood had been built to fit the mill rather than the other way around.

Inside, the store smelled of sawdust and machine oil. Damien led her through a side door marked *Society Records —Authorized Only.* His key turned the lock with a reluctant groan. The room beyond was dim, the air heavy with paper and neglect.

Rows of cabinets and shelves leaned under the weight of unfiled history: boxes labeled in uncertain hands, folders yellowed at the edges, ledgers stacked like bricks against the wall. Marley felt both overwhelmed and summoned. Memory lived here, as Clara had written, and it waited for hands willing to touch it awake.

Damien unrolled the proof and set it on the central

table. "If the missing story ever existed," he said, "its shadow will be here."

They split the work in silence, each tugging at drawers and boxes with the reverence due to fragile things. Marley sorted through stacks of pamphlets and church newsletters, their ink faded to brown. Damien sifted through brittle town ledgers, his fingers careful despite the urgency in his eyes.

It was Marley who found it.

At the bottom of a box mislabeled *Festival Posters—1910s*, beneath curling broadsides of fiddlers and pie contests, she uncovered a small wooden frame wrapped in wax paper. The wood was scarred but intact, and within it gleamed a faint trace of metal: an unfinished printing plate. Its surface bore the etched outline of letters never inked, words frozen in preparation.

Marley held it to the lamplight. The letters were incomplete, some lines broken where the etching had stopped, but enough remained to read a title: **Petition Regarding the Grove.**

Her breath hitched. "Damien," she said, her voice thinner than she meant.

He crossed the room in two strides and bent over the plate. His jaw tightened. "So they began to set it. They meant to print it."

"But never did," Marley finished. Her thumb traced the half-formed letters, careful not to press too hard. The plate felt colder than the room, as though it carried the chill of a story silenced before its telling.

Damien's hand rested briefly against hers on the edge of the frame. "Proofs blank, type pulled, plate unfinished. Someone stopped this deliberately."

Marley swallowed. "What petition could be so

dangerous that even its printing had to vanish?"

He met her eyes. "The Grove."

They returned to the table, setting the plate beside the proof. Together they made an incomplete pair: one with blank columns, the other with words arrested mid-formation. Between them lay a silence louder than any proclamation.

For a while they didn't speak, only studied the fragments as if willing them to reveal what lay hidden. Marley felt again the subtle pressure of the Circle, the way names and places pressed themselves upon her until she could hardly tell where her own memory ended and theirs began. She thought of Aurelia. She thought of the seven. And she thought of the children who ran through town today, unaware of the oaths laid down long before their steps.

"Here," Damien murmured, pointing to the margin of the plate. Almost invisible, etched small as a signature might be, was a symbol: a spiral of seven stones, unmistakable to anyone who had stood at the bridge with eyes open.

Marley exhaled as though struck. "They were going to show the Circle publicly."

"Or at least hint at it," Damien said. His brow furrowed. "No wonder the story was smothered. It wasn't just about land or trees—it was about memory. About the power of women whose names the town preferred to file under folklore."

He leaned back, rubbing his temple. "And now it's here, waiting. As though someone knew the day would come when silence could no longer hold."

Marley studied the plate, the unfinished etching like a wound that had never scarred. She felt it pulse faintly beneath her fingertips—not literally, but in that way the Circle's relics often seemed to hum when noticed. The words *Petition Regarding the Grove* rang louder in her mind than the quiet of the room should allow.

The Grove.

The ledger had whispered of it. The triangle had carried its echo. And now, here, in iron and absence, was another thread pulling them toward it.

She wrapped the plate gently in the wax paper and placed it in her satchel beside the triangle. The weight shifted, heavier than either object should account for, as if the satchel itself understood it carried more than matter.

Damien closed the box and leaned against the table, watching her with that mixture of worry and respect he never quite voiced. "You realize what this means."

Marley nodded. "It means the Circle left us enough pieces to find the rest. It means Brookwood's story was interrupted, not erased."

"And it means," he said softly, "that someone—maybe more than someone—will want it to stay interrupted."

She met his gaze, the lamplight catching in the gray at his temples. "Then we'll give it a spine," she said, the phrase echoing his own words about her book. "Not just this story, but the one still waiting."

He smiled faintly. "A spine strong enough to carry echoes."

The clock in the corner ticked, ordinary against the weight of what they held. Outside, the river moved beneath the fog, tireless, whispering to the bridge. Marley felt the town pressing close, not hostile exactly, but watchful, as if to measure whether they could bear what they had uncovered.

She straightened, sliding the satchel strap over her shoulder. "We follow it. To the Grove."

Damien hesitated, then nodded, the decision settling like a shared oath. "To the Grove."

As they left the archives, Marley glanced back once. The shelves and cabinets stood patient, their dust unmoved, their silence intact. But she felt the weight of unfinished words lingering, as though the room itself remembered what had been denied it.

Outside, the fog was breaking. Threads of late sunlight slanted through, setting the harbor to a dull gleam. Marley paused on the steps, the satchel heavy at her side, and for a moment thought she heard it again—the faint arrhythmic ticking, like type being set in some room beyond sight.

She closed her eyes. The sound faded, but the certainty it left did not.

The story had begun to echo. And echoes, she knew, always find their way home.

By dusk the fog had thinned into veils, as if the town were allowing a little color back into its evening. The harbor lights pulled long paths across the water. The lighthouse did its quiet, ordinary work—steady sweeps, unhurried as breathing. Marley stood in the bookshop with her hand on the satchel and knew what she was going to do before she admitted it aloud.

"I should come," Damien said. He'd returned for the last hour, sorting the broadsides that had begun to surface now that Fenwick had decided to remember. He had the look he wore when care met caution—shoulders squared, resolve clipped to practicality.

"You will," she said. "Tomorrow. When we ask the mill what it kept. Tonight...I think I need to go first."

His mouth tightened, then softened. He didn't ask her to explain, which was why she didn't waver. He only reached out and gently adjusted the strap on her shoulder, the ordinary intimacy of it steadier than any prayer. "Take the lantern. And if the mist does that trick where it looks like people—"

"—then I'll remember it sometimes is," she finished, and the half-smile he gave her said they had learned the same lesson at different speeds.

He walked her to the door. "You can call me," he added, "for any reason or for none."

"I will."

The bell over the lintel made its small vow as she stepped into the street. In the satchel, the iron triangle wrapped in cloth felt heavier than it should, the unfinished plate colder than the air. The notebook with the Grove entries pressed a square against her hip. She took the lane that sloped toward the covered bridge, where the river's voice was already lifting to meet the hour. Brookwood had outlived a thousand evenings just like this one—the kind that looked harmless from a distance—and yet the skin at the back of her neck lifted as if the night had reached out a fingertip.

She passed the wooden placard at the lane-mouth—the weathered board with its stubborn E and O and the ghost of a word whispering itself into being. ECHO. She touched it again, feeling the splintered grain under her fingers, and continued.

The bridge took her in the way a long breath takes in the body. Inside, the world became angles of timber and the patient syllables of water. She went to the broader center span where the oaths had once pressed their meaning into the storm and set the satchel down on the beam. The lantern burned steady. The river made its arithmetic around the pilings. Somewhere upriver a gull scolded the falling dark and was answered by nothing but falling dark.

Marley unwrapped the triangle and held it in two hands.

It wasn't a bell, but it was a bell the way a whisper is still a voice. The striker, warm from the cloth, lay on the wood beside the lantern. She didn't strike it. Not yet.

"Why here?" she asked the bridge in the quiet way she'd learned from Clara's desk, a voice pitched for wood and water rather than for people. "Why now?"

The bridge answered the way honest things do—by continuing to hold.

She set the triangle down and pulled out the unfinished plate, folding the wax paper back. *Petition Regarding the Grove.* Even silent, the letters threw a faint insistence into the air, as if the metal remembered the pressure of the tool that had begun to write and then been stayed. Down the rail, someone had carved initials decades ago—a small, ordinary transgression that felt tender now: proof that a person once needed to tell the wood they had been here.

Marley took up her notebook and copied the plate's title onto a waiting page. Under it, she wrote the line that kept returning to her whether she invited it or not: *When the bell forgets to ring, remember the Grove.* She studied the words until they lost their edges and blurred into meaning: the bell, the forgetting, the act of remembering—a way through silence, not just around it.

When she looked up, the mist at the northern mouth of the bridge had thickened into a pale braid. It hung exactly at the place where, months ago, a child's voice had said her name and then dissolved. The braid lengthened, thinned, then puckered into a shape that was not a shape at all, and still her breath hitched—because it stood where a person might stand if they were leaning in to listen.

"Marley," the bridge said, or the river did, or the air—no louder than the scrape of a leaf along the plank. It wasn't her aunt's voice and it wasn't the low cadence of the women who had come in dreams. It was a small voice, a girl's, striped with distance the way sound is when it travels from one world to another.

Marley's fingers found the triangle's handle. "I hear you."

The mist didn't advance. It re-gathered itself, the way a careful thought does when you've said you're ready to listen. The lantern's flame did not quiver. The river did not say anything different than it had been saying all day, but the pitch of it felt changed—as if an overtone had surfaced.

"Say it back," the voice said, barely there.

She could have asked *what*. She didn't. The Circle had taught her: some questions turn the shyest truths away. Instead she lifted the striker and gave the triangle one clean tap.

The sound went out and touched every rib of the span, then returned not as a repetition but as recognition, like a name spoken by someone who loves you. It ran along the underside of the beam and slipped down the pilings into the water, where it kept traveling, because that is what honest sounds do.

Three short pulses of light swept the river's skin—no, not light: imagined memory of the lighthouse's old pattern, three short, two long. Her body felt the echo of it even as her eyes saw nothing but fog. She gave the triangle two longer taps, spaced like breath. Metal answered wood, wood answered water. The sequence—hers, the lighthouse's, the town's, the Circle's—nested together like shells.

The mist at the far end of the bridge drew tighter, like a figure bracing against a wind that wasn't there. The voice came again, not louder, just nearer.

"Bring the bell," it said. "To the Grove."

Marley lowered the striker. The phrase slid under the

first line in her notebook and settled there as if it had been waiting all along.

"What grove?" she asked, though she suspected the answer.

"The one they almost printed," the voice said, and a surprising humor threaded it, as if the child found adults' reluctance to name things a little silly. "The one that remembers what the town forgot."

"And where is it?"

The mist shifted—a small arm lifting to point, or the suggestion of an arm—toward the east bank beyond the mill, where birches made their pale declarations in spring and their patient white in winter. Marley pictured the path she had not taken in years because it led nowhere anyone called important: a skirt of pines, a shallow dip where water gathered after storms, a stand of old stones that might have been boundary markers or might have been a circle once. The map in Clara's desk had an empty patch there, left blank not because there was nothing but because someone had not been invited to draw it.

"What do I do when I get there?" she asked, the practicality in her voice making her almost smile at herself.

"Listen," the voice said. "Say it back. Bring the bell."

A heron lifted out of the reeds upstream, its slow wings carving the dusk into pronounceable syllables. The mist's shape loosened. The girl's voice thinned with it.

"Wait," Marley said, and the word carried more than the question. It carried all the moments in which she had run too fast through a story and left meaning in her wake.

The voice paused one heartbeat, obliging, as if the child understood that grown people need time to catch up to their own decisions.

"Your name?" Marley asked softly, not because she

needed it for proof, but because names are bridges and she wanted one to cross.

The mist's braid loosened entirely, became only air. Yet as it went, a syllable skimmed the length of the span and left itself on the railing like sea-salt does when an evening dries out: "Lena."

Marley repeated it, so the bridge would know, so the river could carry it downstream and hand it to the bay. "Lena."

The lantern flame steadied, which meant nothing and meant everything. She closed the notebook over the fresh words and slid it into the satchel with the triangle and the plate. The weight felt right now—less burden than ballast. She stood a long while without moving, because staying is also a form of listening, and then she gathered her things and stepped back into the town.

Harbor Street had put on its lights. The café window showed a few late sitters cupping warmth. Down by the docks, someone laughed the kind of laugh that turns into a cough and then a laugh again, because work and relief are neighbors. The lighthouse gave its clean arc and folded it back.

At the shop door she paused, key poised and not turning. Through the glass, the shelves looked like trees readying themselves for winter—upright, patient, asking nothing they could not ask for a long time. Damien's shadow moved inside; he'd stoked the stove and set out two cups, either because he knew she'd come back or because he liked the way a room looked when it invited.

He opened the door before she could fit the key. "Well?"

Marley stepped in and the bell wrote its faithful word in the air. She set the satchel on the counter and unwrapped the triangle. "The bridge spoke."

His brows lifted. He did not ask *how*, which is another reason she could tell him anything. "And?"

"A name," she said. "Lena." The sound of it surprised her by fitting. "And an instruction."

He waited, the attention in his face a form of gentleness.

"Bring the bell to the Grove." She set the triangle on the desk beside the unfinished plate and the proof with its blank columns. "Tomorrow we ask the mill what it remembers. Tomorrow night, we go east."

He exhaled, the kind of breath that makes enough room in a chest for what is coming. Then he nodded once, as if putting his signature in a margin. "We'll take Sophie to her grandmother's for the evening," he said. "Hazel will insist on sending tea named to make us brave. And I will pretend I don't need it."

"You'll drink it anyway," Marley said, and the almost-smile that bent his mouth felt like consent to all of it—the plan, the risk, the partnership.

He poured tea they already had—common leaves, common heat—and set a cup by her hand. For a moment they stood as they had stood too many times to count, in the soft center of beings who have stopped pretending they live separate lives. On the counter the iron triangle waited. The printing plate held its unprinted headline like a breath. The blank newspaper proof lay there like a challenge. The shop's ordinary night gathered around extraordinary things and made a home of them.

Marley touched the cover of *The Book of Brookwood* and felt the page with the promise—they promise to keep the circle whole—warmed now by ordinary hands. She understood with a steadiness that surprised her: this was how beginnings arrived in towns like theirs, not with trumpets, but with a small bell waiting to be lifted and a path everyone had learned to overlook.

She raised her cup. Damien did the same. They drank, and the tea was only tea and also something else, because that is what happens when you name a thing and hand it to another person to hold with you.

Through the front window, the fog drew back half a step as if giving them room. The lighthouse kept time. Somewhere in the mill, metal remembered to tick.

Marley set down her cup and laid her hand on the satchel. She didn't say *only the beginning* because the room already knew. The book on the counter had a spine. The town had an echo. The Grove had been waiting.

One chapter had come to rest. Another—she felt it as surely as she felt the wood under her palm—had already started walking toward them.

AFTERWORD

A Reflective Legacy

The Brookwood Mysteries begins, as so many stories do, with silence.

It was the silence of a bookshop whose shelves held more than novels—the silence of Clara's vow, of words written in margins, of echoes that could only be heard when someone dared to listen. Marley stepped into that silence not as an intruder but as an inheritor, though she did not yet know it. *The Bookshop Secret* showed her—and us—that history breathes through the most ordinary doors, waiting for hands brave enough to turn the lock.

From there, the path winds into resonance. *The Bridge of Echoes* carries voices across time, testing whether past promises could be trusted in the present. Each echo reminds Brookwood that memory is never idle—it insists, it demands, it shapes. Marley and Damien began to realize that listening was not passive but covenant: if they carried the echoes, they must also answer them.

The Lighthouse Prophecy shifts the gaze outward, to signals cast against darkness. It asked: what do we guard, and what do we guide? In that season, the town learned that prophecy is less prediction than mirror. The light did not foretell what must be—it illuminated what already was: a community standing on the threshold of its own forgotten story.

The Winter Bell gives voice to stillness. A bell that should have rung but didn't, a vow that had been broken, a bride whose absence echoed for decades. Silence again—but this time charged, asking whether absence could be as loud as sound. Marley and Damien discover that love and loss, entwined, toll not as ending but as call.

And finally, *The Hidden Grove* reveals itself as culmination, not simply continuation. The stones, the spirals, the ledger, the seed—all mysteries unfolded into memory, and memory unfolded into inheritance. What began as secrecy becomes community. What began as whispers becomes vows. What began as one woman's step into a bookshop becomes an entire town's covenant with its own roots.

Brookwood's Legacy

The mysteries are not puzzles to solve, nor riddles to conquer. They are invitations—to listen, to remember, to rise. At every turn, Brookwood asked its people a single question: *Will you keep what was entrusted to you, not as possession, but as promise?*

Marley answered yes. Damien answered yes. The townsfolk, hesitant, divided, afraid—they too answered yes.

And so the series does not close on a solved case or a quiet conclusion. It closes on a circle, still widening. Children's hands pressing seeds into soil. Elders whispering names into bark. A grove alive with bloom and resonance.

The mysteries of Brookwood will always remain, not

locked in secrecy but alive in inheritance. And so, the circle holds:

We remember. We root. We rise.

Brookwood Mysteries
    Book 1 - The Bookshop Secret
    Book 2 - The Bridge of Echoes
    Book 3 - The Lighthouse Prophecy
    Book 4 - The Winter Bell
    Book 5 - The Hidden Grove

ABOUT THE AUTHOR

Jordan Jace is a Pacific Northwest author whose mysteries and heartwarming tales are set against stunning landscapes. With a deep connection to the PNW region's natural beauty, Jace infuses each story with the magic of misty mountains, lush forests, and tranquil coastlines. Jace believes that joy can be found in the smallest moments and the most unexpected places. When not writing, Jace is exploring the world, seeking inspiration in every corner for the next unforgettable story. Discover more at visionsinprint.com